LURED BY HER

THE REFLECTION SERIES
BOOK 2

BY BRIANA MICHAELS

COPYRIGHT

All names, characters and events in this publication are fictitious and any resemblance to actual places, events, or real persons, living or dead, is entirely coincidental.

All rights reserved. No part of this publication may be reproduced, stored, or transmitted, in any form or by any means, without the prior permission, in writing, of the author.

www.BrianaMichaels.com

COPYRIGHT © 2021 Briana Michaels

OTHER BOOKS BY THIS AUTHOR

THE REFLECTION SERIES:
Burn for Her
Lured by Her
Struck by Her

HELL HOUNDS HAREM SERIES:
Restless Spirit
The Dark Truth
The Devil's Darling
Hard To Find
Hard To Love
Hard To Kill
Raise Hell
Raise the Dead
Ruler of the Righteous

SINS OF THE SIDHE SERIES:
Shatter
Shine
Passion
Bargains
Ignite
Awaken
Rise
Exile
Discord

DEDICATION

For the ones who broke their chains and those still trying.

CHAPTER 1

There were two sides to Lucian's coin: fucked and fucked up. Lately, it was becoming increasingly difficult to detect the difference between those two lifestyles. He needed to get out of town for a while. Get some space between him and his duties and blow off a little steam. Have someone to hose his sorry ass down and scrub away the filth in his soul—like the five am crew who scrubbed Bourbon Street clean every morning.

Instead of the cleansing he yearned for, he was about to get filthier. It couldn't be helped. Earlier today, he texted Tessa—a Sub with dirt on her own soul—and now he was enjoying a magnificent show. The theatre's dim lighting cast everyone in shadow. The rich, red carpet between the aisles matched the heavy velvet curtains on stage, giving the ambiance of both sophistication and seduction. The orchestra playing was drenched in black, many wearing masks over their faces.

Not that Lucian paid attention to any of it.

No, his eyes were glued to the masterpiece seated three rows ahead, center-left. Tessa faced the stage, enraptured by the music. Her dove gray satin gown poured over her thin body like silver water, and her pale skin glowed like moonlight. She looked like a swan floating in a sea of eels.

Lucian ran a finger across his bottom lip. Sitting still as a statue, he barely breathed while he watched Tessa become more and more enraptured by the music. She finally leaned forward, exposing the plunging back of her gown. He wanted to mark her skin, brand her with his touch, so the world knew who she belonged to.

As if sensing she was being watched, Tessa turned and looked over her shoulder. Her eyes scanned the theatre. She bit her lip.

Lucian didn't move to gain her attention. He remained perfectly still and hidden from her. She might be suspicious that he was here tonight, but then again, they never sat in the same row or even the same section at these things.

He kept her at a distance for her safety and ultimately for his pleasure. He loved watching her like this. Seeing her come undone by music. Eating her up with his hungry gaze whenever she wore something he bought her. Lucian enjoyed dressing her up almost as much as he enjoyed stripping her down.

In the depths of his dark mind, he could hear the melodies on stage. But it played like background music in his ears. Too focused on Tessa, he barely noticed the melodic notes seducing the audience. His heart beat strong and fierce in his ears, pumping blood to his cock. His gaze couldn't tear away from Tessa even if the theatre caught fire. He was as enthralled by her as she was by the music.

Masquerade Theatre was secretly owned by vampires and was one of the few places Lucian could meet Tessa without worry. It was a safe, controlled environment. Security here was top-notch, the perimeter dusted often, and the cameras were constantly rolling. The hotel they'd head to after the show was just as safe, just as controlled, and vampire-owned as well.

Playing with humans was a dangerous game. It left too many opportunities for the enemy—the *Savag-Ri*—to interfere. Lucian always took every precaution when he brought an innocent human into his life to play with because of the dangerous nature of his world.

Tessa ran her slender fingers along the back of her neck. He wanted to sink his teeth into that flesh and leave his mark on her. Flip her dress up and ruin it by fucking her hard and coming all over the satin. He sent her that dress two days ago, no longer able to keep away from another meeting with her. It had been months since their last meeting. Felt like years. With all the shit that's been going down lately, Lucian craved a little control and Tessa was always willing to surrender hers to him.

Tonight, he was going to crack open a little. For now, he was going to watch her crack open.

Lucian smiled when she gripped the armrests of her seat. The orchestra was playing a dark symphony, notes to seduce the mind and devastate the soul. The string section lamented. The ivory piano keys wept. The percussion bellowed. Not a single note played without pain and pleasure. Hearing such things made Lucian's heart bleed out, and those notes screamed at Tessa's broken soul.

Every time a new song began, and the violin sang its first string of notes, Tessa's knuckles whitened from her tight grip on the armrests. He noticed how her breath caught and delicate shoulders tensed. The entire audience made a collective sigh as the melodies caressed their darker natures. Both vampire and humans were enjoying the show tonight.

Lucian's chest ached as he watched the violin strings pull at Tessa's soul. As if each note were another finger to wrap around her heart and pluck it free from her ribcage, she suffered as much as she savored it. Lucian had never met a woman so taken by music before. It was one of the reasons he found her so addicting.

Other instruments joined in, one at a time, until the audience swayed with the spell of their melody. Vampires were not without their own arsenal of seductive tricks and magic. To compel, enthrall, seduce, and bewitch were basic skills many had. Using such devices on humans, however, needed to be done with a great deal of caution. Even the musicians were taking calculated risks on the stage tonight.

Not all of them were vampires. But everyone was getting turned on.

Tessa's toes curled, her body going rigid with intense emotions. Lucian's cock hardened to the point of pain. Rubbing a thumb along his bottom lip again, his gaze remained fixed on Tessa while she writhed in her seat. She came undone to music like this. It bled into her body and spread through her soul like black fire igniting the darkest parts of her. By the end of the night, it would drip down her inner thighs and soak the bedsheets.

This was why he chose Tessa. Why he *always* chose Tessa.

She got him on a level no other did. And she rocked him as no other could.

This was a dangerous game to play with a human. He knew that. But right now, Lucian couldn't give two shits about how badly this would end for them both. All he cared about was getting her riled up and setting her loose to destroy his mind, one orgasm at a time.

Tessa unraveled in her chair. Lucian leaned in and ate up the sight of it. Her body, mind, and soul were one-hundred and ten percent engaged in the music tearing through the small theatre. He loved the sheen of sweat on her temples. He bet she was wet between her legs already.

Lucian never sat with her when they met like this. He didn't trust himself to be that close to temptation. She trusted him implicitly, so if he told her to do something, she obeyed. When he sent her outfits, like the dress she was in tonight, Tessa wore them without being told. When he told her to get into position later, she would not hesitate. This woman was dangerous. Too unhinged for her own good. Too perfect for a vampire like Lucian.

It made her both a treat and a threat.

When the final act ended, Lucian pulled out his cell and texted her.

Rise from your seat.

He smashed the *send* button and waited. Tessa pulled her phone from her clutch and read his order. When she stood up, he groaned. There was a wet spot saturating her satin dress. Members of the audience began exiting their aisles to leave. Lucian never lost sight of her and texted again.

Walk through the lobby.

Keeping himself hidden in the crowd, he watched her read his message. She bit her lip and smiled. Tessa knew better than to look around for him or to even respond back. That was part of their contract—he contacted her. Not the other way around. In public spaces, they were never together, but he remained close. In private settings, it was only ever the two of them. Lucian called the shots and named the destinations. He set their scenes and anything else he wished. This one-way contact rule extended to outings like this one.

It was for her own good, and for Lucian to practice self-control.

Rolling her shoulders back, Tessa followed his orders and walked through the lobby. Lucian always marveled at her perfect posture and willowy physique. She looked so frail and delicate, yet he tested her limits time and time again and knew she was absolutely unbreakable.

Tessa was his enigma.

Tessa was his forbidden fruit.

Tessa was going to have to be replaced soon.

That last bit always made Lucian recoil. Four centuries of living a tormented life, and he'd yet to find someone who compared to the woman now walking out of the theatre with her arousal staining her gown. She wore her hair loose tonight as he preferred. Her nails were bare of paint. Only the lightest brush of eyeshadow graced her eyelids. His Tessa was a rare and raw level of beauty that made his mouth water.

As he stayed out of her sight, Lucian watched Tessa leave the theatre and enter the lobby. Damn, the plunging back of her dress nearly kissed her ass crack. The cut flaunted the graceful structure of her shoulders, back, and slight flare of her hips. With another groan, he sent a third text.

Crimson Hotel, Suite 17. Key at front desk. Be in second position.

Still clutching her phone, Tessa looked down and read it, then shoved it back in her clutch and headed right through the front door, past the doormen, and into the night.

Sticking close, he made sure she got to the car he reserved for her this evening. Only when she was safely in the back seat had he finally unleashed the breath he'd been holding. Heading to his Mercedes S-class, Lucian strangled the steering wheel the entire drive to the hotel. Even knowing Tessa was safe with the vampire driver, he couldn't help but feel possessive of her. Her lust would be everywhere in that car. The idea of another male smelling it set Lucian's fangs on edge. But that was the price of keeping her safe.

It was excruciating.

He followed her car at a respectable distance the entire way to the hotel. Even with metal and asphalt between them, his body roared to bury itself between her thighs and thrust them both into oblivion. He was dying to take her in every way possible. Make her scream and break and fray until she was a whimpering and spent puddle of lust on the hotel floor.

Jesus, he needed to get a grip. His need for her was beyond healthy. It was borderline insane.

This had to be the last time he saw her. It *must* be. He was getting too comfortable, too addicted to her. And that wasn't allowed.

His cell buzzed. He glanced down at it. Shit, it was from his mother.

Memorial service is tomorrow evening, our home, 7pm. If you even care.

Lucian tossed his cell into the backseat on that note.

If you even care. Wow. All Lucian did was care. For her to throw this at him — last minute, by the way — showed how little she knew him anymore. Or how little he mattered to her. *If you even care.* How dare she say that.

Lucian shook off the anger, refusing to let family drama or his guilt ruin tonight.

Pulling up to the front of the hotel, he parked in a reserved spot. Being a vampire owned establishment meant they took every precaution necessary to keep guests safe. *Savag-Ri* prowled everywhere, and vampires couldn't be too cautious.

He'd love to take Tessa away for a long weekend. Hell, even going to a nice restaurant would be heaven. But no way would he risk her. That meant their rendezvous were carefully planned in controlled environments, and he only ever paid cash to keep paper trails to a minimum if they stepped outside vampire territory for any reason. Call him paranoid, but his life wasn't the only one in jeopardy. As far as *Savag-Ri* were concerned, any human caught entertaining a vampire was fair game. Tessa's life could easily be at risk just because she was seen with him.

And she had no clue what he was.

One more reason he needed to end this relationship. Maybe he'd break it off tomorrow. Or next week. Tonight, he needed her more than he needed air.

Keeping his head down, Lucian beelined to the elevators, swiped his key card, and stabbed the button to the third floor. By the time he reached his destination, Lucian's heart was pounding in his ears. It was always like this when he met Tessa. The insufferable ecstasy of suspense and buildup of tension in his body grew more intense every time.

He entered their suite and bit back a groan. She was a vision.

Tessa's dress had been replaced with the flesh-colored leotard he'd laid out for her earlier, along with the usual set of pointe shoes.

Her blonde hair was pinned in a tight bun so he could see every inch of her slender, fragile neck. Poised in second position—like he told her to be—Tessa's body was in perfect alignment.

For now.

"Up," he commanded from the doorway.

Tessa rose on her tippy toes and held her position. Posture perfect, ass tight, thighs flexed as she remained balanced for his inspection; she was a goddamn wet dream.

It had been five months since they last saw each other. Was it possible she'd grown more beautiful during that time? Yes. Yes, it was.

Pulling off his tux jacket, Lucian tossed it to the floor and ripped the bow tie from his neck. Marching right over to his waiting violin, he ran a hand through his hair and stepped into the scene, ready. "*Grand plié.*" He dragged his bow across the strings with the first of many tortured notes to follow.

Tessa held each position he commanded her into. Her face remained gracefully impassive, though sweat beaded across her brow five minutes into holding a *demi plié en pointe*. Her toes must ache by now, her muscles screaming. But she wouldn't move until she was told to, or she used her safe word. *Such a good prima.*

"What color are you?"

"Green," she panted.

They had a color system she preferred, and he checked in with her often, always keeping his focus on her body language. If Lucian fell into his own personal dark space watching her self-inflicting machinations go to too far, he'd have to pull them both out. He wasn't about to let it that happen, so check ins were key.

Lucian stalked in a circle around her while he played his song. Music did incredible things to them both. For Tessa, it brought control. For Lucian, it set him free. He allowed the melody to chew on his heart. Let the position Tessa held crush her resolve. Moving seamlessly into another song, he picked up tempo and continued his intense stroll around her and said, "*Arabesque.*"

She shifted with such fluidity that Lucian locked his jaw to contain his lust. Tessa transitioned until she was balanced on one foot with her other leg kicked out at a perfect ninety-degree angle. One arm reached back, perfectly parallel to her extended leg, the other arm stretched out forward, as if reaching for his soul.

He nearly dropped to his knees at the sight. If Lucian asked her to do this pose on the tip of a champagne bottle, she could. She had. This woman's talent was un-fucking-paralleled.

Keeping his gaze locked on hers, Lucian played whatever notes flitted into his mind next. The song began morphing, growing, twisting to a crescendo. His mind was fraught with pain and torment. Guilt and agony. Hollow except for the screams he never cut loose. Those noises came out through his violin.

Could she feel his pain? Could he seep into her like she had him? Should he push her limits tonight like she was already pushing his?

This relationship was dangerous. *Destructive.*

Tessa wrecked him without knowing it. And she made damn sure Lucian gave her what she wanted by the end of each night they spent together.

"*Arabesque penché.*"

Just look at his perfectly broken ballerina. Her lips parted — the only sign of struggle she ever allowed him to see. He wanted to play his violin for her until his fingers bled. He wanted to set her loose and watch her dance, however she felt moved by his music. He wanted her to weep with his melody and clutch his heart. Tear it out and hand it over.

But he couldn't have any of that. She was human. He was vampire. This was a temporary fascination that must end after tonight.

He just needed one more evening of her body writhing beneath his. Tomorrow, it would be over, and he could go back to his constant torment. And his brother's memorial service.

CHAPTER 2

"*Arabesque penché.*" Lucian's commanding voice cut through Tessa's mind as she dropped to a flat foot and tipped forward. Her gaze broke away from his, her outstretched hand no longer reaching for him. She pivoted until her one hand pointed towards the floor and her back leg swung up towards the ceiling. Her heartbeat faltered as his music cut her to the core.

It had been five months since their last meeting. One hundred forty-seven days, to be exact. Each one was sheer torture without him. Tessa's guilt rode her harder than her paranoia over it. Had he somehow discovered her secret? Was that why he'd stayed away?

So many questions ratcheted her insecurities up and her guilt weighed her down to the point where Tessa sometimes couldn't get out of bed.

Tell him, her instinct scolded her for the bazillionth time. But she couldn't do that. If she told him her secret, this illusion would shatter. It wouldn't only break the scene, it would destroy *everything*. Tessa wasn't willing to sacrifice this arrangement yet.

"Say my name."

Tessa almost smiled at his next command. She couldn't say his name with her voice. He wanted it said with her body. Straightening her stance, she sucked in a few breaths and ignored how her limbs burned already. He hadn't pushed her to her limits yet, but he would. That was the thing about Lucian. He read her body like a well-worn book of poetry. He somehow sensed when she was pleased, distressed, and close to her breaking point.

That was why he checked in with her often.

"What color are you?"

See?

Tessa wasn't near Red. Wouldn't be for a while. They'd only just begun, and she was built for this.

"What color are you?" he repeated.

"Green." Close to Yellow. She'd worked her body once already today for five solid hours.

Rolling her shoulders back, Tessa allowed his music to pluck her down to bare bones, and she twisted around in a fluid motion, spelling out L-U-C-I-A-N with her body. As she dropped into the final N — one foot pointed down with her toes digging into the floor, her other foot was pointed up with her knee digging into the floor. *Nailed it.* Position firm, calves straight, thighs in perfect alignment for the middle part of the N, Tessa contorted her lower half into a perfect uppercase N. She leaned forward, resting her forearms on the floor and held the position. Triumphant, her gaze locked dead ahead. She bit back her satisfied smirk. This was, after all, a serious scene no matter how much fun she was having.

Tell him. This would be a good time to do it. Just tell him. She bit her lip and sucked back her desires. If she could still think, Lucian wasn't giving her what she needed right now. She needed something harder. Harsher. More impossible to do.

Or a punishment.

Cocking her eyebrow at him, Tessa unfolded her body and dropped into a deep grand plié. Her toes dug into the floor, her thighs screaming with the burn as she planted her hands firmly on the hardwood with her fingers splayed. Defiant, she stared at Lucian, daring him to correct her. To punish her for the position he'd not told her to get into yet.

But he was lost to his music and staring at her half-enthralled.

God. Damnit.

She wouldn't last a minute with that look on his face. Immediately, Tessa looked away and kept her body locked.

Lucian squatted down in front of her, his violin's lament hanging on an agonizing note as he dragged the bow across the strings for the last time. Her breath caught. His gaze was dark, hungry. The music stopped playing, and she nearly lost her balance as they plunged into an eerie silence.

Her thighs no longer quivered. They were all out shaking. The rest of her body began to follow suit. It got a thousand times worse when Lucian gently placed the violin down and lifted her chin with the tip of his bow. He forced her to meet his gaze again, then he dragged the tip of his bow down her chest and across her right inner thigh.

Thwack! He cracked her with it.

Tessa flinched. The pain was searing. Wanted. Needed.

"What color are you?"

"Green." Bright, fluorescent, glorious Green.

"On the wall." Lucian's tone was seductive and deadly.

Inwardly, Tessa squealed with delight. As her body lit up at his dark tone, her mind scrambled to get a grip because this was going to hurt.

Good. She deserved to hurt.

She deserved way worse.

Tell him. If she told him, it would be over. Her guilt. Her torment. *Tell him.* "Lucian, I—"

One sharp flick of his wrist and he whipped her ass with the carbon fiber bow, cutting her confession in half. "No speaking," he growled against her ear. Her pussy swelled from how hot his breath was on her flushed skin. Her body erupted in goosebumps; her nipples hardened.

"Hands," he growled behind her.

She placed her palms against the wall and her eyes fluttered shut when he trailed the tip of his bow down her spine. She wanted to arch into it. Beg him to use it on her ass again. She kept her mouth shut and swallowed the urge to mewl. When he tossed it to the side like it was trash, her brow pinched. She wanted him to use the bow to correct her. She wanted that sting. Needed those red lines whipped across her ass and thighs.

"You want the bow? Earn it, Tessa." He spanked her with his palm and didn't soothe the burn with a rub afterwards. Instead, he spanked her five more times, alternating between ass cheeks.

She was glowing inside and out. Under the heat of his hands, Tessa's body set on fire. Her lungs squeezed and eyes fluttered. She nearly unraveled right along with her hair as Lucian pulled it from the tight bun. Her blonde tresses fell down her back, and she relished his fingers combing through it. Then he wrapped a good amount around his fist and pulled it hard enough to make her hiss.

Tell him.

Nope. Never. Not a chance. Why would she jeopardize this?

"Where's your head at, Tessa?"

Where's yours? She wanted to ask back. She remained silent.

His grip tightened. "Tell me what's going on so I can help you."

She was perilously close to blurting out the one thing threatening to be her undoing.

"Come on, Tessa," he urged in her ear. "Don't you trust me?"

Lucian was the only one she trusted. And that made him dangerous.

There was a difference between love and lust and love and sex. Lucian was the kind of guy one could easily fall in love with. He was strong and bold, yet vulnerable and attentive. He made her feel breakable and invincible in the same touch. It was why she was so taken by him. It was why no other lover would ever compare.

Tell him.

If she told him, this fantasy would be ruined. Was she ready to destroy it?

He placed his hands over hers, pinning her against the wall and, nope, she wasn't ready to give any of this up yet. Pressing his chest flush against her back and ass, Lucian reminded her of his size and strength. Of her safety with him.

Like love and lust, there was also a difference between protection and possession. Well, there was *supposed* to be. Lucian never distinguished the difference for her. Somehow, he took the acts of protection and possession and coated them in pleasure. It was as inconceivable as it was undeniable.

It made him addictive. Like a sugar-coated drug.

She had no idea what this guy did outside the four walls they occasionally met in. She wasn't even sure if he lived in the same state as her. Had no clue if Lucian was a kindergarten teacher, a lawyer, head of the mafia, or a lumberjack. He wasn't married. Being unattached was a prerequisite for them both when writing up their contract.

Her knowledge was, otherwise, limited outside the fact that he was a musical savant with a body of a god, the appetite of a warlord, and patience of a clam. But she knew nothing personal about him besides his name. And lately, she was starting to wonder if Lucian was even his name or just some made up one to fool her with.

"Talk to me, Tessa." The way he said *Tessa* made her crumble a little. The T shot out of his mouth, hard and sharp. "Where's your mind right now?"

"On you."

He was silent for a heartbeat. "Why me?"

Tell him. "Because you're smothering me."

He reached around and massaged her tiny breasts, rolling her pebbled nipples between his fingers with a hard pinch. She wished he'd use his teeth.

"You're seeking more punishment than usual tonight. Why?"

Tessa tossed it right back. "You're being more lenient than usual tonight. Why?"

What's changed? Why was he holding back? Why was he—

Holy shit. Tessa ripped her hands out of his and spun around so her back pressed against the wall. When she saw the look in his eyes, her fears were confirmed. It was in the coldness of his gaze. The silence of the room. The tossed bow on the floor.

Lucian was detaching himself. He was going to leave.

This was the last time she'd ever see him.

The realization nearly made her knees buckle. *Please, no.* Tessa struggled for breath. Lucian must have somehow found out about their breach in contract. How? She hadn't told a soul! Biting her lip, she figured he must have read it in her eyes and posture. He was too observant. Too attentive. Read her way too well. She loved that about him before and hated it about him now.

He knows.

So, what was this then? If he was leaving her, why come at all tonight? Why give her one last evening of pure bliss just to walk away in the end? Furious with him and herself, Tessa slapped him so hard her hand went numb. Lucian's head snapped to the side, his jaw locked, then he turned slowly to meet her gaze again. His movements, so slow, controlled and deliberate, made her heart stutter. His cold eyes deadlocked on hers.

She slapped him a second time. He took it. Accepted it. Embraced it.

No! No! No! This entire thing was ruined, and it was all her fault! So what if she breached the contract? How could she not! He set her up for failure and knew it. Was this all on purpose? Everything perfectly calculated to fall on her shoulders and crush her heart?

Tell him. Tell him and find out.

But even as her instincts roared, her self-preservation shot it down. She wasn't telling him *any* of her secrets. Whether he knew the truth or not, no longer mattered. Lucian was done with her. This was over.

Oh God, it was over...

Tessa shoved him, but he didn't back off. He held steady and turned into a goddamn concrete wall. Cold. Unfeeling. Unmovable.

"Tell me why you're punishing yourself this time," he said.

Did he really need to hear it? Well, she wasn't going to give it to him. He didn't deserve to hear it. It was his fault this was happening in the first place! If he hadn't been so easy to be with, so hard to get a hold of, so impossibly perfect in every way for her, maybe Tessa wouldn't have—

This was bullshit.

Tessa slid out from under his looming body and marched, still in her pointe shoes, towards the door. She needed to get out of here before she started crying. Lucian hadn't earned the right to see her tears. And she didn't deserve to have them to begin with. This whole thing was just as much her fault as it was his.

A distant echo of coldness crept into her bones. She was turning everything off. It wasn't deliberate. It was automatic.

Time to leave.

Tessa made it all the way to the door before he stopped her. How he got there so fast made no sense, but her mind wasn't right tonight—too drunk on lust, music, pain, and things she couldn't have—Tessa's focus was off big time.

Blocking the door, he said in a calm tone, "You're not leaving until you tell me what's wrong with you, Tessa."

"Everything is wrong with me. That's why we have this arrangement."

His jaw clenched. His gaze roamed her features, as if trying to read the unspoken words she always kept hidden so well. "You have too many secrets," he snarled.

"Like you don't?"

That must have stuck a nerve because his eyes flinched a tiny bit. "Don't leave."

"The scene is broken, Lucian. It's over."

She bent down and started unlacing her pointe shoes. God, her body hurt. And she hadn't found the relief she needed. Nor a release.

"Don't go." Lucian caged her in, but she knew he wouldn't hold her captive for real. "The error is mine. I'm not in my right mind tonight. Forgive me."

Tessa paused, one shoe on, the other off. "Why?" her voice was nothing more than a whisper. A prayer that maybe, *just maybe*, Lucian would share a piece of himself with her this time. *Please say he hasn't found out about what I've done.*

His silence rang loud in the air between them, and she took that as a bad sign. Tessa gave up and started unbinding her other foot, shaking her head in disappointment.

"I've lost someone recently," he said quietly.

The pain in his tone cut her to the quick. It was obvious whoever this someone was, Lucian loved them. God, she hated how that hurt. "A woman?"

"No."

Tessa slipped her other shoe off and stood back. The pain in his tone was nothing compared to the agony in his brilliant blue eyes. She'd never seen him so vulnerable. So raw.

She wanted more of it. If this was their last night together, then Tessa didn't want to crack Lucian open. She wanted to *shatter* him. That way, they'd be even when they walked away from each other in the morning.

Tessa backed off and made it all the way to where his precious violin lay. She picked it up, then retrieved the bow from where he'd tossed it earlier. Such expensive things discarded without care. It made her wonder if he held anything dear. He loved music yet was quick to toss the instrument. He'd likely tear this leotard off her body and ruin that too. Even her lust-stained dress was of no consequence earlier. All delicate, expensive, lovely items... all discarded without a care tonight.

Lucian didn't care about expensive things. He probably didn't care about her outside this room, either. Did he care about *anything*? Yes, the someone he lost. Tessa wanted to see more of that Lucian.

The one who had things taken from him. The raw and torn open man who hid so well under tailored tuxedos and devilish grins while he plucked the strings of his instruments.

And there was only one way to coax that side out of him.

Tessa held out the bow and instrument as she closed the gap between them. "Play."

"I already played for you."

"You're not going to play for *me*. You're going to play for yourself and the *someone* you lost." She shoved the bow and violin at him and let go of both at the same time. He caught them with lightning speed before either hit the floor.

How could he move so fast? The question barely registered before Tessa's mind focused on the way Lucian's body went rigid. In two years, she'd studied every bit of his body language when they were together, as he did hers. They could read each other almost too well at this point. So, him sensing something was wrong made anything she said as an excuse really nothing more than a lie. Lies were unacceptable between them. And his behavior screamed volumes about his pain and displeasure tonight.

Also, unacceptable.

He wanted to help her. She wanted to keep him. Neither was going to get what they wanted.

Lucian balanced the bow perfectly on the back of his middle finger, then twirled it lazily. She braced for the first of another heart-wrenching round of notes to rip through the room. Tessa almost felt triumphant when he stopped twirling the bow and stole her breath with a steely gaze.

"This isn't about me, Tessa." Lucian snapped his bow in half like it was no more than a dead, brittle twig. "Tell me what's wrong with you."

"Nothing."

He jerked as if she'd slapped him. "I'm going to ask you one more time," he warned, closing the distance between them. "What's wrong?"

"My answer remains the same." Her heart hammered in her chest. Tessa wasn't afraid of Lucian. He'd never hurt her. But this wasn't the Lucian she knew. This man was infuriated and hurt, which was all her fault. "We're supposed to trust each other," she whispered. "Has that changed?"

"Not on my end." He stalked towards her, making her choose between standing her ground or backing away.

Tessa held her ground. "Then trust me when I say nothing is wrong."

They'd worked too hard on their Dom/Sub relationship for it to fall to pieces on their last night. No matter how angry he sounded, or how lost he looked, or how fast he broke a scene and ruined her night, Tessa trusted Lucian and felt safe with him.

He gripped her chin. "When was the last time you were with another man?"

"A while ago."

His jaw set as he clenched his teeth. "Define 'a while ago'."

She smacked his hand, knocking it away. "You know when it was."

Lucian's shoulders relaxed a little. He was possessive, which both tickled and infuriated her. They had an agreement—no other lovers until their arrangement was over. That was her doing. She couldn't stand the idea of another woman touching Lucian and then for him to come crawling to her in bed. He agreed to it, on the condition that he was the only one who initiated their meetings. This had gone on for two years now, and she was starting to hate herself for ever climbing into Lucian's arms.

Tell him. The words were on the tip of her tongue. Her biggest and worst confession of her goddamned miserable life hung from her lips, ready for flight. But she bit back those syllables and swallowed them whole, nearly choking on them. "I'm not the one who's off tonight, Lucian. You broke scene. You're not here," she tapped her temple, "with me at all. And you've never destroyed your bow before."

His chuckle sent ice through her veins. "You don't know what I've broken or how many times I've destroyed precious things, Tessa. Don't speak as if you know me."

But I do know you, she wanted to say. Yet, those words jammed in her throat as if they were a fat lie that couldn't fit through her clenched teeth. *He's right*, Tessa realized. She only knew the Lucian in these four walls. She had no clue what he was like outside of a bedroom.

"You're trying too hard to punish yourself, Tessa. Why?"

She was, but all because Lucian was right with his accusation didn't mean she owed him an explanation other than, "It's been a long time and I'm wound up tighter than a snare."

He wasn't buying it. Lucian stared at her for so long, she nearly confessed. Then his shoulders drooped, he backed away, and grabbed his violin from the floor. "Goodbye, Tessa."

Her heart shattered when he left her with the broken bow still at her feet.

CHAPTER 3

It was a dick move to leave, but Lucian had no choice. His hypocritical ass couldn't stand another second of Tessa's glower or that hidden confession in her eyes. He'd gone back to the mansion and jacked off until his dick almost snapped. There was no amount of pleasure to be found. His body and mind were in opposite directions. Restless, he stalked the halls of the House of Death's mansion like a wraith. At this hour, most everyone was asleep and the few still awake were caught up in their own mind fucks.

Maybe he should call Dorian and see if he's out hunting? Lucian squashed the idea immediately. Dorian would be with his mate—either searching for *Savag-Ri* or destroying their bedding in epic ways—no way would Lucian be the third wheel there. He was happy as hell for Dorian, but lately, the Reaper's gain felt like Lucian's loss. Shitty, right? Everyone deserved love. Everyone including Lucian.

And Luke.

Help me, brother! HELLLP MEEEEE! Lucian swayed at the haunting screams of his brother's last words on this earth. Bracing against a side table, Lucian squeezed his eyes shut. He wanted to both burn that voice away and cling to it with all his might.

He hadn't been able to save Luke. The curse took him before Lucian even had a chance to help him find his fated mate.

Vampires lived forever in longing. It was a blood curse set by a scorned woman, which had passed through every vampire, and Lycan, for thousands of years. The only way to break the curse was to find, bond, and turn their *alakhai*—their fated mate. And the only way to find them was to first see their reflection.

That's why the House of Death's mansion was decked out in a million mirrors. It made one dizzy in some rooms, but Lucian was used to it now. The possibility of seeing his mate's reflection didn't freak Lucian out like it might others. But what happened when that day came meant something worse too—his blood curse would kick into the next phase. That meant he had to find, bond, and turn his *alakhai* before incinerating first. Lucian could literally burn to ash while looking for the love of his life.

Help me, brother! HELLLP MEEEEE! That's what happened to his brother Luke. He'd searched for his *alakhai* and ran out of time. He came to Lucian too late for help.

Would Lucian have been able to find Luke's mate had they not been separated by family hate and jealousy all these years? Hard to say. But Lucian would have stopped at nothing to help his little brother. Instead, he stood, frozen and helpless, while Luke burned from the inside out and crumbled to a heap of ashes before Lucian's boots right at the mansion's front door.

Lucian was never going to get that vision scrubbed off his soul. He saw it whenever he closed his eyes. He heard Luke's desperate screams whenever it was too quiet. He still felt the coating of ash on his hands from when he had to gather Luke's remains and pour them into an urn to send home to his family.

These past few months turned Lucian into a goddamn wreck. He didn't trust himself to get close to Tessa until he knew for sure he wouldn't do something stupid or careless around her.

She had no idea he was a vampire. Seeking comfort for a creature like Lucian meant fucking and feeding. Sometimes both, at the same time. It took him a little while to gather the control he needed so he could behave around her.

Could he have gone to The Wicked Garden to get his rocks off and drain some vein? Yes. The vampire kink club was part of his territory, and Lucian was one of the managers. But he didn't indulge there anymore. Not since he met Tessa.

Exhaling, he looked at his watch. It was four am. Damn, what a waste this day had been. First, he'd gone hunting and hadn't found a single *Savag-Ri* to kill, then he found out some hacker cracked their security systems at several businesses and couldn't do anything about it. Then he botched everything with Tessa. To round things off, Lucian wandered the halls with a raging hard-on, and would have to pack for his trip to his parent's estate in a few hours.

The front door opened and a bunch of snarling, hissing vampires stormed inside. Lucian was all too happy to put his energy into household matters instead of his personal woes. Looking over the balcony, he watched Reys and Victoria stumble in, supporting one another. Blood stained their clothes and dripped on the floor as they crossed the foyer.

Lucian rushed down the steps and grabbed Victoria before she collapsed. "What the hell happened to you?"

"*Savag-Ri* ambush," she panted. Lifting her hand away from her belly, Lucian saw a gruesome stab wound with the weapon still buried. "It's... a piece of... iron gate. Just the tip," she half-joked as she coughed up blood.

Crazy bitch.

"They used explosives and took out a warehouse we'd been casing. Thought it was a headquarter of theirs."

It most likely was, Lucian thought. *Savag-Ri* were notorious for destroying all evidence of their whereabouts if they suspected their enemies were too close. Those assholes used hidey-holes to trap vampires and Lycan to torture them for information. They also used undisclosed places to hold potential fated mates from being found, effectively killing the vampire looking for them without ever having to lay a hand on said vampire. It was rare, but it happened.

"Any deaths?" Lucian scooped Victoria into his arms and carried her to the kitchen.

"None that we know of," Reys answered, hobbling alongside Lucian.

"I'll fix you both, hang on a sec." Lucian carried Victoria into the kitchen and laid her on the massive island, kept clear just for this reason. If it wasn't too fatal of a wound, they could heal each other. If it was too gruesome, their healer would have to be called in. Lucian inspected Victoria's injury. The gash was puffed out, angry and bloody. But she was lucky.

"Just the tip," Lucian growled. "That's a massive tip, Vic."

"Well, size matters," she laugh-winced.

Reys dropped into a chair, panting. Blood saturated his pants, pooling on the floor. His femur protruded from his leathers. "I think my leg is broken."

Gee, ya think? Lucian shook his head at how nonchalant these two always were about serious shit. No wonder they were in the Mad House. The House of Death was home for all the crazy motherfuckers—including Lucian.

"On the count of three, Vic." Lucian bit into his arm and held it over Victoria's mouth for her to drink while he worked to get a good grip on the end of the iron spearhead piercing her gut. "Ready? One," *yank*! He wrenched the thing out of her. Blood spurted, and she screamed and bit down harder on his arm.

Fuuuuck this crazy girl had some jaw strength. What was she, part crocodile?

While he tossed the spearhead onto the counter, Dorian and Lena flew into the kitchen, also both covered in blood. "Is she going to be okay?" the Reaper, and House executioner, asked.

"Get me some towels," Lucian gritted out while Victoria continued to take hard pulls from his vein.

"Here," Lena said. She held out her wrist to Reys, who was still nursing a broken leg. "Take from me."

Reys held his hand up to stop her from getting closer. "And have the Reaper rip off my head and eat my heart out? No thanks."

Lena frowned. "You guys are idiots."

"Possessive mates are honorable mates." Reys tipped his head back and clutched his thigh. "I'm assuming, at least."

Dorian returned with a dozen towels stacked in his arms and helped Lucian get Victoria's wound closed.

"Dorian, tell Reys to feed from me," Lena ordered.

Her mate's response? A growl that rumbled through the entire kitchen and shook the glass canisters of flour and sugar on the far counter.

"Told you," Reys half-chuckled. "I like my head where it is."

Lena cocked her brow. "Up your ass?"

"On my shoulders."

"Damnit," Dorian went over to Reys and cut his arm with the karambit he always hunted with. "Drink." Reys latched onto him immediately and Dorian then turned to his mate. "Lena, set his leg before the skin closes with his bone still out."

Never squeamish, Lena dropped down and got to work. The wet sounds of bone cracking, tendons snapping, and skin tearing were nauseating.

"Good girl," Dorian winked.

"I hope I did that right." Lena leaned back on her haunches. "Tonight was messy, guys." She exhaled loudly. "And to come home to double standards pisses me off."

"Double standards are how vampires survive," Victoria sighed from the kitchen island. "Just let them have their macho-man, no-one-tastes-my-woman's-blood-but-me bullshit and relish in the fact that someone cherishes you so much they'd kill anyone who laid a hand on you, Lena. Violent or otherwise."

Lena rolled her eyes, unimpressed.

Double standards are how vampires survive. Damn, Lucian didn't need the reminder of that tonight. It was why he and Tessa's evening got wrecked earlier.

He needed to call her later and apologize. Maybe even grovel.

"Besides," Victoria carried on as she sat up and poked her freshly healed wound. "How would you feel if Dorian fed me?"

Lena's response? A nasty hiss. It must have come out so impulsively it surprised her because she slapped her hands over her mouth.

Victoria laughed. "Not so double standard, is it?"

Reys pulled off Dorian's vein and licked the wound closed. "Thanks, Reaper. I appreciate it."

The fact that Dorian offered his vein at all was a goddamn miracle. The vampire had gone almost his entire existence thinking he wasn't worthy of this House, and feared his blood was tainted, cursed, or worse. Never once did he offer his vein to someone before he met his mate. Now, it was common practice. If someone needed to heal, Dorian offered his blood.

Same for Lucian, but Lucian's came without the baggage. He bled out for people in his life at least ten times by now — and he had a lot of vampires in his life.

"Are we done here?" Lucian needed to shower, pack, and head out if he was going to make his brother's memorial service in time.

"Yeah." Reys stood and gingerly tested putting weight on his leg. "We're good. I'll go report what happened to King Malachi."

Lucian shoved past everyone and headed to his room. "Good. I'll be back in a couple of days. Dorian, takeover in my stead."

"Whatever you need."

Whatever you need. Oh, how loaded that phrase was. Same as *double standards are how vampires survive* and the ever overused, *I trust you.* The one that weighed heaviest, however, was what his mother had texted him: *If you even care.*

Sometimes weapons don't cut a male wide open. For Lucian, all it took was a loaded phrase, and he bled out all over the goddamn place.

Here's hoping he survived what was coming...

CHAPTER 4

Tessa took advantage of the gorgeous luxury suite, even if Lucian wasn't with her to share its amenities. No woman in her right mind would turn down a car-sized tub with jets. She also helped herself to the minibar and ordered room service. If Lucian had a problem with it, he could suck it up. It served him right for walking out on her.

Her fun ended at the eleven am check out. Now she was back home, stuck in reality. Boy, her ass was dragging like someone strapped fifty-pound weights to her legs. If only she drank coffee, maybe that supposed magical bean elixir could put a little pep in her step. Sadly, she wasn't even a tea drinker. Caffeine did terrible things to her system.

Instead, she chugged some water and cranked up a little Two Feet to put her head back on straight. She cleaned her apartment, one room at a time, and enjoyed the scrub down. She didn't have class until four today, which meant she had some serious downtime. Tessa didn't do well without staying occupied.

Halfway through her kitchen counter wipe down, someone knocked on her door.

"*Shit.*" Tessa knew who it was. Blowing out a big breath, she slapped on a fake ass smile and opened her door. "Hi Dominic."

"Tessa." Her greasy landlord tongued his toothpick. She always envisioned plucking it out of his mouth and stabbing him in the eye with it. "Rent's due."

"I have until midnight." As well he knew. She got paid today, so rent wouldn't be an issue this month. "I'll have it to you by then." Sooner, since she was paid in cash and wouldn't have to go to the bank with a check later.

Dominic leaned against her doorjamb and crossed his arms over his massive chest. Flashing a toothy grin, he flicked that damned toothpick with his tongue in rapid succession before saying, "I'll let you have a discount this month, if that'll help."

"Bye." She slammed the door in his face.

Dominic never made direct eye contact with her. The sonofabitch always stared at her tits when he made pointless proposals like sucking him off for a rent-free month. She had a feeling his persistence might be paying off with the woman downstairs. Hey, if that's what worked for her, great. Tessa would rather eat glass than put anything of that man inside of her.

The only man worth swallowing her morals for was Lucian. Aaaaannd that ship sailed at midnight last night. Damnit.

Tessa went back to cleaning her kitchen when her cell phone started ringing. *Speak of the devil*. Tessa's heart pounded when she heard his ringtone. It was hard to not be excited. Double hard to clamp down on restraint and not throw her cell out the window.

Pick it up, hurry! Before he hangs up!

She was all but trained to come when called. Yeah right. Tessa stalked over to her phone and hit the ignore button. Lucian was either calling to apologize for last night, which she didn't want to hear. Or he was going to chew her out for racking up his hotel bill without him — also something she didn't want to hear.

He called again. She let it ring. Again.

Then he texted. Boy, he must be desperate, huh? Sadly, so was she. Her hard exterior was more like eggshell than concrete. Leaning over, she saw his text pop up on her screen.

Sorry about last night. Do over next week?

Do over next week? Fuck him, if he thought that was okay. She replied with, *Busy*.

It sat on *read*, and he didn't respond. *Shit*. No, wait. *Good*. This was good, right? Nope... *shit, shit, shit*. Tessa's thumbs hit a bunch of sorry ass letters and then she deleted every single one of them because what she had to say needed to be done in person. Lucian deserved that much, and she owed it to herself to speak her truth to him face-to-face.

Her phone rang again. "Shit!" Startled, Tessa dropped the damned phone, cracking the screen. Great. Just perfect. Giving up on pretending to be stronger than she was, Tessa accepted the call.

Keep aloof. Be chill. "Yes?"

"Did you enjoy yourself last night?"

Holy Hell, Lucian's phone voice should be criminal. It made all the blood drain from her brain and pool between her thighs. Tessa sat down on her sofa and put her feet up. "That's a loaded question."

"And did you drink the entire bottle of Dom Perignon?"

"Down to the last drop." Tessa chuckled and hated how throaty and sultry she sounded. Jesus, she'd fallen right into line with him again. "You're lucky I went with the Dom. It could have been the Ruinart Blanc de Blancs."

"It *should* have been," he simply stated.

Only Lucian would tell her she should have gone with the two-thousand-dollar bottle of champagne. Tessa tipped her head back and sighed. She was going to miss this guy.

"You still sound tense," he said. She could tell he was driving somewhere—the purr of his engine a lulling background noise.

"I'm still wound up too tight," she confessed. "No ease."

Lucian was quiet for a minute. She almost spoke up when he finally asked, "How many times did you come without me last night?"

She should have said a dozen, but that would have been a lie. "None."

She heard his breath catch. Or maybe that was her overactive imagination kicking in.

"When was the last time you came, Tessa?"

The last time you touched me. "A while ago."

His chuckle wasn't humorous, it was edgy. "Define 'a while ago'."

His growly voice made her toes curl. Biting her lip, she finally admitted, "Longer than a week, less than a year."

He didn't appreciate her smartassery. "I'll make it up to you," he promised. "But for now, touch yourself while I listen." Before she could argue, he added, "I know I don't deserve it. Not after the way I acted last night, but... I can't bear the thought of you needy because I fucked up. Touch yourself and let me guide you through it."

She wanted to tell him no. She *should* tell him no. But she needed a release badly and hadn't found one since the last time they'd been together. It sure as shit wasn't for lack of trying. But nothing worked. No matter how close she got to a climax, she would lose it before it happened. It was a real problem.

"Okay," she held back all hope of this working. But if anyone could drive her over the edge with lust, it was this man on the other end of the phone line. His voice alone made her wet.

"Get your earbuds."

Tessa smiled. He bought them for her about a year ago so she could dance to whatever she wanted without disturbing her neighbors with loud music. They were noise cancelling too, which was lovely when Dominic was throwing large parties down the hall. "Okay. They're in."

"Get on the floor," he ordered. With his voice filling in both her ears at once, this discussion suddenly felt very… intimate.

She slid off the couch and squatted. "Done."

"Get on your hands and knees for me, Tessa."

She stifled her groan, her cheeks heating already. This felt awkward and hot at the same time.

"Suck on your middle finger." His tone dropped. "That's it, just like that."

Tessa's body tensed with anticipation. Holy shit, this man had a voice that could make paint drip off the walls, and ocean swells get wetter.

"Get it nice and wet for me, Tessa. That's it. Suck it. Swirl that pretty pink tongue of yours. Fuck yeah, Tessa. Just like that."

There he went, saying her name in a way no other ever could. It was like a spell wrapping around her body and twisting her mind with red ribbons.

"Rise to your knees and spread your thighs nice and wide."

She could do a split, but that wouldn't have helped. Tessa balanced on her knees, enjoying the carpet burn as she obeyed.

"Rub that sweet little clit of yours," he said in her ears. "Slow circles. Coax and tease it."

Her heart rate quickened. Thank God she had her earbuds in. She needed both hands for this.

"Good girl," Lucian purred in her ear. It made her pulse

stutter. "Use your other hand and fuck yourself with your finger, Tessa. Ride your palm and grind those hips for me."

She closed her eyes and whimpered as she obeyed. This wasn't the first time she'd masturbated, but it was the first time he instructed her over the phone like this. Keeping her eyes closed, she imagined him sitting across the room, watching with his dick out, stroking in time with the hand on her clit.

Something needy and hot coiled in her abdomen. Her thighs began to shake.

He groaned in her ears. "I can almost smell your lust. I want it on my tongue. I want it on all over my cock."

His engine purred faintly in the background. Lucian's breathing picked up. She fingered herself harder on the other end of the phone.

"Pull out and put your finger in your mouth, tell me how you taste."

Tessa laughed at that. "This isn't for your pleasure," she reminded him.

"The hell it isn't. Your pleasure is my pleasure. You know that. Had to pull over so I could give you my undivided attention. Now suck it for me."

She bit her lip. Defying him.

"Suck it, Tessa, and tell me what you taste like," he demanded again.

Submitting, Tessa did as she was told. "Tart," she whispered. "A little sweet."

"Mmm. Bet you're more than a little sweet," Lucian cursed under his breath, and she loved that he sounded so committed to this moment with her. "Get a vibrator. You got one, right?"

She had tons. "Why?"

"Just get it."

"What kind?" Damn, she was breathless now.

Lucian made a grunting noise. "You're killing me, Tessa. How many do you have?"

"You don't want me to answer that," she laughed.

He made a louder groaning noise. "I wish I was there with you."

"If you were, I wouldn't need a toy."

"Touché," he said. "Now get your favorite one and tell me

what it is."

She went for a small clit stimulator, which she told him.

"Good girl. Now get in your bed," he demanded. "Back against the headboard, legs spread wide."

Tessa scrambled onto her bed. Her cheeks were hot and belly warm. "Done."

"You're so obedient, it annihilates my good intentions."

"Then give me your bad intentions, Lucian."

"Fuuuck," he groaned. "Turn it on medium speed and press it to your clit."

She did.

"Finger yourself and stare straight ahead. Don't you dare close your eyes."

She obeyed. So needy and worked up, Tessa was at the edge of her climax too fast to be considered anything but shameless. Watching herself unravel in the mirror across the room, she found her reflection terrifying and sad, glorious and pathetic, empowering and humiliating all at once.

"Look at you," he said in her ears. "Goddamn, you're stunning. Tight little tits, those narrow hips of yours. Fuck yourself harder. That's it. Just like that. Let me hear those wet noises."

She whimpered. Obeyed. Rose one thrust closer to a climax.

"Mmm, your nipples are so hard. I want to bite them. The whole room smells like your sweet pussy, and I want to inhale it, Tessa. Smother myself in it. I want to take you from behind and fuck you like an animal."

Goosebumps rippled down her body. He talked like he was standing right there, and with her wild imagination, she almost believed it was true.

His breathing turned ragged. "You want me to take you? Make that wet pussy clench and stretch at the same time?"

"Yes," she whimpered. Tessa pumped two fingers inside herself as the vibrator attacked her clit with precision. She was so wet, there were plenty of sloppy, wet, messy sounds for him to hear. "God, yes, Lucian."

"And then I'll lick you clean. You want that? Want me to devour you with my tongue?"

Her eyes fluttered shut. "Yes."

"I want to come all over your ass before I bury my dick inside you there, too."

She tensed and stopped breathing. *Close... so close*. Her thighs tensed, body growing more rigid. She barely breathed.

"I *ache* for you, Tessa."

She bucked.

"I obsess over you to the point of madness, woman."

Her head tipped back as her pace quickened.

He groaned in her ears. "I need you, Tessa. And I want your come. Give it to me, prima. Give me your—"

She pitched forward. "I'm too empty," she cried out, already losing her momentum. "I need something bigger than my fingers."

"Like my cock?" he purred. "You want me inside you?"

"Yes," she squeaked, squeezing her eyes shut with desperation to chase her release at all costs now.

"Tell me. Tell me what's on the tip of your tongue. What's saturated in your lust for me?" Lucian's breaths grew shallower on the other end of the line. "Fucking say it. Say it and come with me, Tessa."

Tessa, Tessa, Tessa. How he said her name made it sound like a brutal whip cracking her skin and tearing into her soul.

"Don't stop," he growled in her ears. "Come for me."

"I can't," she wailed. "I can't!" For a second, she thought the call dropped. That maybe he'd hung up. Her heart thundered, making her feel sick. Collapsing in near tears, she gave up and threw her vibrator against the wall.

"Tessa?" Lucian's voice morphed from seductive to intense. "What do you mean *you can't*?"

"I can't without you," she said between ragged breaths.

"Yes, you can."

She wondered if he was trying to convince her or himself.

"I don't want to," she finally said. "I have to get ready for work. Goodbye, Lucian." She hung up and threw her earbuds in the trash. Lucian wasn't the only one who tossed nice things away.

Now she was so furious and twisted up, Tessa was ready to climb the walls and set the entire building on fire. Jumping in the shower, she attempted to wash her emotions away. Scrub them the off. Drown them in hot water.

All to no avail.

At least she had three classes to teach tonight. Nothing like a room full of children in ballet slippers to make one stomp out their personal problems for a couple of hours.

After losing her position in a renowned dance company in New York, Tessa moved to New Orleans and settled for teaching others who might one day have the chance she'd lost. Getting dressed for class, she chugged water and shoved a granola bar in her mouth.

Someone banged on her door.

Well, wasn't she little miss popular today? Washing down her granola bar with more water, she hated herself for having the slightest hope that it was Lucian coming to relieve her and start things over. And she got doubly pissed when whoever it was knocked louder the second time.

Swear-to-God, if this was Dominic with another discount offer, she was going to claw his eyes out.

Tessa stormed over and wrenched her door open.

Not Dominic.

She looked the stranger up and down. "Can I help you?"

"You better hope so, Tessa Banks." The man pulled out a gun and pointed it in her face. "Because your life depends on it."

CHAPTER 5

"I can't without you." Tessa's ragged words made Lucian see red. She *couldn't* come without him or *wouldn't*? Those were two different things. Two distinctively, important things.

Lucian pulled back onto the road, calling her repeatedly as he hopped back on the highway. She didn't pick up. *Damnit*. If he was going to his parent's estate for any other reason other than his brother's memorial service, he'd postpone the trip and bust a U-turn so he could break down her door and give her what she needed. But he couldn't and it sucked.

Everything about this sucked.

Biting his bottom lip, he practically strangled the steering wheel the rest of the way to the airport. If only he had the gift of flashing, he'd be so much better off. Then he could get to Tessa's in a blink, make her orgasm, then flash out to meet his family obligations. Alas, he wasn't made with the gift that allowed him to be here one second and somewhere else the next. He had to slow motion his way around with planes, trains, cars, and regular vampire speed. Which meant he didn't have time for Tessa right now.

He replayed their conversation:
"How many times did you come without me last night?"
"None."
"When was the last time you came, Tessa?"
"A while ago."
"Define 'a while ago'."
"Longer than a week, less than a year."

He was almost positive Tessa hadn't come since the last time they'd been together. That might explain why she was so hellbent on driving him nuts last night with her perfect form and graceful transitions. She wanted to be rewarded... after she was punished.

What was he thinking the day he made a contract with a woman like that? He'd underestimated Tessa's stamina and ability to get under his skin.

Lucian obsessed over her the entire way to New York. He barely paid attention when he drove to the airport, nor did he recall boarding the plane or getting off it. Thoughts of Tessa pleasuring herself on the phone, the way she looked in her gown last night, how she contorted her body to spell his name at the hotel... those delightful visions kept him too busy to notice real life.

He arranged for a rental car and took the long way to his parent's estate. Pulling up to the massive house, Lucian stared at the pretentious statues gracing the front garden. The early 20th-century Italianate castle sat on three acres of green lawn, overlooking the Hudson River. It wasn't where he grew up, but it had the same elegance as his childhood mansion in Paris.

Lucian snagged his bag from the trunk and sighed. This was going to hurt. Just as he climbed the steps to knock, the double doors swung open, and a maid welcomed him. "Sadie," he smiled, relieved to have one friend here. He hadn't realized how much he missed Sadie until this very moment.

"Let me look at you!" She smashed his cheeks with her hands and planted kisses all over his face. "You're as handsome as ever."

"I pale in comparison to your natural beauty, Sadie."

She blushed and smacked his shoulder playfully. "Let me take your things upstairs."

"I'll take them myself."

"Still stubborn as ever," she teased as they walked up the grand staircase together.

The house seemed empty. Quiet. Like it was hollow and vacant. "Where is everyone?"

Sadie took a moment to answer. "Your mother is in the garden."

"And my father?"

Sadie bit her lip. Shit, it must be bad if Sadie wasn't saying. His parents were inseparable. Had Luke's death cut so deep it rocked their marriage? He couldn't imagine that being the case. Basil and Esmerelda practically shared the same heartbeat. "Is everything okay between them?"

"I think you should speak to your mother first."

"Okay." He wasn't pushing her for more information. It felt weird to have been gone from his family's circle for so long, but in less than a minute under their roof, Lucian got swept back into their dynamic again. Dropping his bag in one of the spare rooms, he bit the bullet and went in search of his mother.

Making his way through the main part of the house, he noticed that the rooms and walls seemed... bare. Where were the family portraits? Where were the indoor plants his mother treated like babies? Not even the hint of his father's cigars lingered in the air.

The house felt dead.

Lucian swallowed around the lump in his throat and made it to the other end of the ballroom. Swinging open the French doors, he looked out at the impressive gardens. His mother was easy to spot—Esmerelda was draped in enough black silk and lace to clothe a small country in couture. Her black, curly hair was twisted in an elaborate braid that ended just below her waist. Esmerelda was a vision—a pureblooded vampire worthy of having statues carved in her image to grace the finest art museums. Lucian took after her in ethereal looks and grace; his stubbornness and blond hair came from his father.

"Mother," he made his way towards her, making sure to keep his posture perfect, like the good aristocrat she raised him to be.

Esmerelda turned at the sound of his voice, her eyes red-rimmed from crying. Jesus, her face looked gaunt. Dark circles enhanced the pain in her gaze. She reminded him of a haunted spirit left to wither in some macabre garden. Her lips peeled back with a low hiss as he approached her. It made Lucian's stomach twist and confidence shrivel. She, and everyone else in the family, blamed Lucian for Luke's death. As if he was to blame for the curse itself.

"Lucian," she said quietly, and dabbed her cheek with the back of her hand. "I didn't expect you to actually come."

He reached out to hug her, but she pulled back from his touch.

So that's how it's going to be? Fine.

One might think a woman would remember she had more than one son, and that she wasn't the only one in mourning, but everyone grieved differently. If she didn't want affection, he wasn't going to force the issue. Regardless of the fact that he'd not seen in her nearly two centuries, he would stay respectful.

"Where is Father?"

"He'll be arriving shortly." Her tone was sharp as a razor blade. "With his *alakhai*."

Lucian stilled. *Uhhhh, his whatakhai?* "Say that again."

"You heard me. How dare you be so heartless as to make me repeat it." She stormed off, plucking the urn—one much more elaborate than what Lucian chose to send Luke home in—off its pedestal and walked away cradling the damned thing.

Luke would have hated that stupid urn, he thought.

Lucian watched her go and tried to grasp what the hell was happening around here. What else had he missed? No one told him his father left his mother... or found his *alakhai*. Esmerelda not only lost a son, but also her beloved husband of over nine hundred years? No wonder she was bitter. When had all this happened? Luke's death was fresh, but when had his father—

"Lucian."

Aaaannd there it was: All the anger, hate, resentment, and disgust wrapped up in one word. *Lucian.*

He heard his father approach from behind. Felt the presence of a female with him. It took tremendous control to not spin around and clock his father in the mouth. He'd done that once already in his lifetime and got put in the House of Blood's hole for it for almost a year. Worth it, but Lucian didn't have that kind of time to waste anymore.

With every ounce of control he could muster, Lucian turned to face the vampire who sired him. He looked well. Far better than his mother, at any rate.

"Father," Lucian bent at his waist and bowed deeply, as was customary. "My condolences."

"Yes, well..." His father cleared his throat. "Same to you."

"And," he looked over at the woman tethered to his father's arm. "Congratulations."

His father stirred and ended up keeping his mouth shut and

bowing his head in thanks. He was feeling guilty too, Lucian wagered.

As well he should.

Not only had Basil abandoned Esmerelda, he'd not been able to save Luke, either. As mad as he wanted to be about his father not saving Luke from the curse's final blow, Lucian knew anger was futile. Not even Lucian had been able to help Luke find his mate, so expecting his father to have done it was being hypocritical. He'd had enough of that word for one lifetime already, fuck you very much.

As for the guilt his father must feel for spending lifetimes with a woman whom he loved and showered with affection, whom he bonded and had children with, whom he worshipped on the same level as Gomez and Morticia motherfucking Addams... Finding his *alakhai* must have been a special kind of hell for the old bastard.

"I'm Lucian," he bowed to his father's fated mate.

"Anna," she smiled sweetly. "Basil has told me so much about you, Lucian."

Yeah right. His father probably never mentioned he had an older son. The minute Lucian chose to serve the House of Death, Basil said he was dead to him. And he meant it. "Lies don't become you, Anna," Lucian smiled. "But I appreciate the attempt at civility. My father could learn from you." He flashed her a smile and showed his fangs. She returned with her own set of much daintier ones.

Basil rolled his shoulders back. "I'm civil enough not to whip you for being here. Have you no shame?"

Lucian sized his father up. Lucian had him by about thirty pounds, but that wasn't the biggest difference between them. No, his father would pay another to bloody their hands on his behalf. Lucian enjoyed getting dirty and bloody. That's one of the many reasons he broke tradition and refused to join the House of Blood. He was a death dealer all the way.

"I take it your mother told you about today." Basil stuffed his hands in his pockets. "Or was it Sadie?"

"Mother," Lucian answered. "She texted me last night."

"She's had this planned for almost a month." Basil threw Esmerelda under the bus with that one.

"She must have forgotten to send me the details until late last night. She's suffered tragedy, and I'm sure that's made time slip, as it would for anyone in her shoes." Lucian dragged his gaze down Anna, then Basil. "Her losses keep adding up it seems, and I'm sure it's put her under a lot of stress."

Basil glowered, knowing exactly what Lucian was referring to. "It couldn't be helped."

"Sure, it could have." Lucian's smile was tight and unfeeling. "You could have never married her to begin with."

"And not share close to a thousand years of loving Esmerelda and having our children?"

Anna tensed, and jealousy rolled off her in waves. It would have been adorable if it wasn't so infuriating. Though Anna couldn't help herself, Basil sure as shit could have. And when Basil put his arm around his alakhai, Lucian wanted to snap his father's arm off and beat both of them with it.

The aggression was uncalled for. Deep down, he knew that. It wasn't Anna's fault that she felt a stab of possessive jealousy—it was part of their bond. Just like it wasn't her fault that she was a vampire's *alakhai*. He felt a little sorry for the woman now. But he didn't feel sorry for his father. "Perhaps if you'd have held out for Anna, none of us would have been born. Thus, Esmerelda would be free of her heartache, and Luke wouldn't have suffered at all."

"Lucian!" shouted another family member.

Great. Just perfect. Now he felt like the world's biggest asshole. Turning around to greet his sister, Lucian's gut twisted for saying what he'd just said. "Lizzy, holy shit!" He hugged her as hard as he could without hurting her baby bump.

His sister had taken a cue from their parents and married a vampire. They now had three children and one on the way. None of whom Lucian had met before, including the father of her children.

"I'm glad she called you," Lizzy said, rubbing her belly. "It's been so long, brother."

"Why didn't you tell me?" Was that sarcasm or hurt in his tone? Both. It was definitely both.

"I only found out about the service yesterday."

"That makes two of us."

Lizzy's shoulders slumped. "She's not been right since father left."

"How long ago was that?" He ground his teeth together.

"About a year now."

No one wanted to give him a heads up? What kind of bullshit was that?

Lizzy averted her gaze. "I tried a thousand times to find a way to tell you about them splitting up, but in the end, I wasn't sure you'd care given how, well, you know."

Why did everyone think Lucian cared so little about things? Was he that big of a dick and didn't know it?

"Children!" Lizzy called out. "Come meet your Uncle Lucian!"

Three children, all still too young to be anywhere near reaching their full power, dashed out from behind the well-manicured hedges. Lucian's heart thundered in his chest when they ran towards him, squealing and laughing. They all looked so fresh and beautiful—so young and naïve. He crouched down and smiled. "Hi."

"Do you really serve the Mad King?"

"Does he have six sets of fangs?"

"Is it true he eats one of his own vampires every full moon and that's why he hasn't died yet? Because he sucks their immortality out with curly straws?"

Okay, woah, yeah… inquisitive much?

"Children!" Lizzy's face reddened. "Remember yourselves!"

Lucian paid his sister no mind. "Yes, I serve as the head guard for King Malachi. He's the strongest of the vampires, and I assure you, is almost completely sane. As for curly straws?" He tapped his chin. "I think he uses the color changing ones, but not for soul sucking. Only fruit punch at brunch on Sundays."

They each started giggling. "What's it like?" the oldest asked. "I heard you have the Reaper!"

"He's my best friend." Lucian got pulled along by the children. He was happy to let them drag him away from the rest of his family. He needed some space from his father.

After a swift interrogation and proper introductions, he saw Lizzy watching from the rose bushes, a smile gracing her face while her children hung on Lucian like he was a tree to climb. Grunting, he marched up the patio steps, into the house, through the ballroom, past the sitting quarters, and into the kitchen with one child wrapped around his leg, one on his shoulders, and the youngest in his arms.

"When we were about your age," he said, pretending it was a struggle to carry all their weight and really made a show of it with grunts and strains. He stopped at the kitchen counter and panted heavily, as if out of breath. "Phew, you guys are heavy already! You must be quite strong to weigh so much."

"We eat real good," said the littlest. Then he popped his arm muscles and flexed. "See?"

"That's impressive," Lucian said with his eyebrows up in his hairline. "Nutrition's important."

"Nutrition's dumb. I'd rather eat sweets all day. Not carrots."

Who could argue with that logic? "We used to sneak into the kitchen at night and devour all of Sadie's cookies." Lucian leaned in as if he was about to tell a secret, dropping his voice to a whisper. "Did your mommy ever show you where the secret hiding spot is around here?"

"Yes, but Sadie only puts gummies in the jar now." The middle child pointed at the corner base cupboard.

"Gummies are good too." Lucian went over and opened things up. Grabbing the infamous cookie jar, he snagged all the packages of gummies. They had vitamins in them, he noticed. That small detail warmed his heart. These kids were still so small and would need all the nutrition they could get before they matured. Whether they liked it or not.

Lucian ripped open each of the packages as he handed them out. Then swung open another pantry and pulled out Oreos. "Does this make the gummies better?" He gave them each two.

"I prefer Sadie's chocolate chip cookies. Or her lemon ones."

"The lemon ones were your Uncle Luke's favorite." A knot formed in Lucian's throat thinking about it.

"Did you love Uncle Luke?" asked Lizzy's middle child.

"With all my heart."

"Then why'd you let him die?"

Fuck.

CHAPTER 6

"Sit." The man with the gun barked as he bulldozed into Tessa's apartment, forcing her to back up.

Dumbstruck, Tessa obeyed without protest. *My phone... where is my phone?* She backed away slowly as he came forward while tucking his gun away. A second man walked in and shut the door with a soft click.

"I said to sit down!" Standing around six feet tall with dark, short-cropped hair, fitted black t-shirt and jeans, Gun Guy looked straight out of the military. Or the mafia.

Tessa's heart thundered. She couldn't wrap her head around why this was happening. Why her? What did they want? What could she give?

While she remained frozen in terror, the second man—who was at least six-six if an inch and built like an MMA fighter—grabbed her by the arms and manhandled her towards the small dining table. He shoved her into a chair, his jaw set and eyes cold the entire time. Then he walked around the table with his hands clasped behind his back.

"Let's start over." Gun Guy sat across from her at the table, his shoulders semi-relaxed. "I'm Alex. This is my friend, Colton."

Alex and Colton. She didn't know anyone by those names. She didn't recognize them at all. "W-w-what do you want?" She didn't have a lot of money. Didn't have anything of great value, but whatever they were after, she'd give it to them. What choice did she have?

Colton pulled an envelope out and handed it to Alex. The rustling of paper was loud in the otherwise dead quiet apartment. Alex thumbed through whatever was in the envelope and plucked a photo out. "Do you know this man?" He held it up for Tessa to see before placing it on the table between them.

Her mouth dried up. The photo was of Lucian. He was dressed in a tight, black muscle shirt, dark pants—maybe leather—and wore a set of combat boots. He wasn't full-on facing the camera. Crouched on uneven concrete like a predator about to attack, he looked savage. Brutal. Vicious. *Beautiful.* His lips were peeled in a snarl as he stared at something the camera hadn't captured.

Tessa almost didn't recognize him. It both invigorated and confused her—neither of which helped now. The Lucian she spent time with was clean cut, well-dressed, well-mannered and calm at all times. This Lucian? He looked ready to rip someone's throat out with his teeth before slamming shots of whisky and setting the world on fire.

Heat bloomed through her body immediately. It was embarrassing and uncalled for and scared the shit out of her.

What kind of response was that? How deranged and broken was she that her lust would kick in at a time like this?

Damn Lucian. He wasn't just a sugar-coated drug. He was her goddamn kryptonite.

Alex's raspy chuckle let her know she'd been caught. "Now before you answer, let me remind you about something." He pulled out another photo from the envelope.

Tessa's blood ran cold. She stared at a photo of the dance studio she worked at. The picture was of a little girl going inside with her mother. *Oh God.* Staring back at Alex, tears welled in Tessa's eyes, making him blurry. Why did he have this photo? Was this a reminder of what's at stake should she lie? Was that little girl in the photo in danger if Tessa stepped out of line? Or was it just a bluff? It didn't feel like a bluff. No way was she risking someone else's safety just to save her own ass. Especially an innocent child. Tessa tore her gaze from the picture and swallowed around the tightness in her throat.

"I'll ask again." Alex tapped the first photo. "Do you know this man?"

"Yes. A little." She was too afraid to lie. He'd see right

through it if she tried. Even through the terror of her current situation, her body gave her away. His laugh proved so already. Even if that wasn't the case, Tessa didn't want his gun in her face again or for him to actually use the damned thing, so yeah, she told the truth.

"Good girl." With a victorious smile, Alex pulled out a third picture. Jesus, how many did he have tucked into that envelope? Her belly twisted when she saw this one. It was recent. Extremely recent. It was of the theatre last night. Tessa's blood drained from her face as she stared at the photo. Going by the angle, it had been taken from the corner of the balcony. There was a blue circle drawn around her. To the left, a few rows back, was Lucian with a red circle drawn around him.

The photo showed nothing that could have tied them together as lovers or even acquaintances. It made no sense that these men would draw conclusions about Tessa and Lucian having any relationship or knowledge of each other based on just this photo. Regardless, Tessa's mouth went dry because it felt like she'd been caught red-handed.

Looking back at the photo of the dance studio, she tried to piece this all together. Get a timeline. Figure out how long these men had been following her. The photo of her student at the studio had been taken before the new signage was mounted... soooo around five months ago. As in, right around the time she'd last seen Lucian.

Tessa remembered talking to him about starting her own dance company in New Orleans. He thought it was a great idea, but she was too hesitant to run with it. And too broke. Property wasn't cheap in NOLA and she rented her apartment, so she had no collateral. But that night, she'd opened up to Lucian about her dreams of getting a studio when she thought she was mentally and financially ready to make that leap. As always, Lucian encouraged her. Lifted her up. Told her he couldn't wait to see her do it. Then... he didn't call again for months.

Tessa gulped. Meeting Alex's icy glare, she struggled to understand what was happening here. "Who are you people? Are you Feds? Look, if Lucian's into something illegal, I don't know anything about it. I swear. I'm not sure what you want from me, but I don't know anything about his personal business."

"You *are* his personal business." Alex grinned. "We've been tailing that abomination for a long time now. We know you've been seeing him for at least a year, perhaps longer."

Double that, not that she was going to correct him. And how dare he call Lucian an abomination. She wasn't going to correct him for that either. Not now that he'd pulled the gun back out and placed it on the table between them.

"You've been watching me a long time." Tessa thought she was going to faint. She felt disgusted and violated and frightened. That's a bad combo for a person like her.

"Him, even longer."

Deep breaths. Stay calm. "Why?"

"He's extremely dangerous." Alex looked at her as if he suddenly cared for her safety. She didn't buy it.

Tessa tried to take in a breath, but her lungs felt sticky. "Again, I-I-I don't know what you want from me."

"We want you to help us lure him out."

Lure him out of what? *For* what? Tessa was a dancer, not a 0-0-7 agent, for crying out loud. "How do you expect me to do that?"

Alex's next chuckle made her cringe. "I think you know how." He pulled out a stack of pictures and started flicking them on the table, one by one. Tessa, in a gray gown, getting out of a car. Tessa entering the hotel lobby. Lucian walking in from the reserved parking area. Lucian, dressed in his tux, heading into the lobby after her.

The photos were all outside. Hmmm. They were keeping their distance from Lucian. Was it because he was as dangerous as they claim, or because he'd retaliate? If he retaliated, did that make him dangerous to only them or to anyone? "What's he done?"

"Lucian's a danger to society," Colton said from behind Alex. His voice was softer than she thought it would be for a guy his size. His eyes were a light brown, big and warm. He reminded her of a Teddy Bear, while Alex reminded her more of a badger. "We're only trying to protect innocent people, Tessa. We're hoping you can help us with that."

"Danger to society how?" She couldn't believe Lucian was a bad guy. No way. Then again, she didn't really know him outside the bedroom. Still, "You're the ones who came storming into my home, armed, and not only shoved a gun in my face, but you've stalked me for over a year."

"We'll do worse to you if you don't cooperate." Alex leaned back and took the gun with him, resting it in his lap. "We've used our manners, so far."

Dread coiled in her stomach. She wasn't sure how to get out of this.

"Like we said," Colton leaned across the table to get in her face. "Lucian's incredibly dangerous. You'll be doing our race a great service if you help us catch him. And you'd be rewarded."

She didn't want a reward. She didn't want any part of this. "I don't believe you." And that went for Lucian's reputation and their promised reward. These guys were trouble, not the other way around.

"I thought you might need a little convincing." Alex smiled over at Colton, who then moved in behind Tessa. She tried to stand up and run, but Colton's fingers dug into her shoulders, and he shoved her back down in her chair.

Were they going to kill her? Kidnap her? Beat her?

Alex tapped the photo of the dance studio again. "It would be a shame if your employer, and all your little dancers, found out what you did. You already lost your spot in the American Ballet Company, Tessa. How much more are you willing to lose to protect an animal like Lucian?"

She... she didn't have a response. Her ears began ringing. She felt faint. "I've done nothing to be ashamed of."

"These say otherwise." Alex tossed the rest of the stack of photos onto the table. It took Tessa a full minute for her brain to comprehend what she was looking at.

"No." She slid photo, after photo, after photo away from her. As if pushing them away meant they didn't exist. That she'd not been caught. *Oh God.* Pure terror seeped into her. "*No!*"

"Dear Miss Tessa Banks." Alex stood up and leaned into her, bracketing his arms on the back of her chair to cage her. "You have quite a temper, don't you?"

Her chin quivered. Tessa quickly looked away from him. She felt panicky. Trapped. How did they get those pictures?

"It's always the quiet ones," Colton tsked.

"So true." Alex pinched Tessa's chin hard, forcing her to look at him. "What will the children's parents think when they discover their precious ballet teacher is a murderer?"

"Those blackouts can be vicious," Colton added. "But it won't save you from prison."

Tessa went into fight or flight. She chose flight. Bolting up, Alex slammed her back down. "No!" she cried out.

His smile spread wider and showed off all his perfectly aligned white teeth. She glared at the pictures again. Vomit rose in her throat. This could not be happening. "This... you can't... I didn't... No!"

"*Yes*, Tessa. And these will be handed over to the police if you don't cooperate with us. We already know where the body is." He tossed her a shit-eating grin that made her shrivel. "And we have all the evidence needed to put you away for a long time." Alex tapped the photos of Tessa bent over a body. "Just in case these photos aren't incriminating enough."

She gawked at the photos. The victim lay face down on the ground, but she knew exactly who it was. Her hands trembled as she covered her mouth. She was going to vomit.

"I'd say you're looking at a minimum of twenty years, even if you try to claim self-defense instead of temporary insanity. What do you say, Colton?"

"Twenty-five to life by the sheer savagery of the attack. You certainly didn't stop even after the victim was dead. Did you really carve your name into his back, or am I not seeing things clearly? It's hard to really lock gazes on any one thing. You did a job on that poor bastard."

Alex feinted sympathy. "So brutal. You just never can tell what someone is capable of until you push them to their limits, can you?" He deadpanned her and waited for her to give a response.

Tessa's ears started ringing. Her face tingled. She felt like she was floating out of her chair. *This can't be real. This can't be happening.*

"I'll make it real simple, girl." Alex grabbed her chin again and forced her to look away from the incriminating pictures and back to him. "Help us or you lose *everything*."

She didn't have a choice. Defeated, Tessa dropped her hands into her lap. "Tell me what I have to do."

CHAPTER 7

The memorial service was a disaster. Esmerelda couldn't stop crying, and her heartache morphed into an anger so vicious, she'd torn apart her gardens with her bare hands. No mother should suffer the loss of a child. But this on top of having lost the love of her life, too? Lucian suspected it was a tipping point for her and she might never mentally or emotionally recover from it.

It made him feel guilty for not being there for her before now. The fact that his entire family, including Esmerelda, wanted nothing to do with him after he joined the House of Death didn't even matter. He should have pushed back instead of flipping them off. He should have fought to hold his place in the family instead of creating a new one made of friends. He never felt bad for walking away from his life—no matter how privileged it was. Until now.

Luke's death could have been avoided… maybe… if Lucian had been there with him from day one of seeing his mate's reflection and helped Luke hunt her down. He was resourceful and quick on his feet. Hell, he'd helped his best friend Dorian find his *alakhai* lickety split! This entire tragedy could have been avoided had he stuck around and followed tradition instead of his heart.

Same could be said for his parent's love life and ultimate marital destruction. That, too, made Lucian feel guilty. He felt bad for being born. Felt like shit that he hadn't been around to support his mother once his father abandoned her. And to know it happened only a year or so ago? Talk about a fresh wound. No wonder Esmerelda was falling apart. All she had left was a son she couldn't stand, a daughter who'd followed in her footsteps, and an ex-husband who had the balls to bring his mate to the funeral of her perfect baby boy.

Basil ended up pinning Esmeralda down before she did further damage to the gardens or herself. The thorns from the roses shredded her hands and arms. There were scratches all over her cheeks. Her eyes were puffy and red. She looked like a Shakespearian tragedy.

"Why?" Esmerelda screamed until her voice broke. *"WHYYYY?"*

What a loaded question. Lucian often asked the same thing himself. Why did this curse have to be so brutal and merciless? Why didn't they get more time to hunt for their fated mates? Why did some find them, and others didn't? Why Luke? *Why, why, why.* Why did his parents fall in love with each other and start a family all those centuries ago if they knew their *alakhai* would eventually show themselves in a reflection? Why spend a day in paradise when the separation would be hell?

"Shhh, darling," Basil swept the wisps of hair unfolding from her braid and sticking to her face. "Shhhh." He rocked his ex-wife on the stone patio like she was a baby in his lap.

It killed Lucian to see his mother clinging to the man she loved, who'd left her for his fated mate. How much heartache was one creature supposed to withstand before it became too much, and they snapped?

First Lucian broke tradition and refused to join the House of Blood. Then Basil found his mate. Then Luke incinerated. Guilt ransacked Lucian's soul, robbing him of composure and strength. He should have been here for his family.

If he'd stayed and joined the House of Blood, he'd have been here to support his family when his father took off to find his *alakhai*. Oh God... had Basil asked Esmerelda to help him locate her? Lucian couldn't imagine what that would have been like. Esmerelda would be forced to either turn the other way and let him die or break the curse on his own... or go hunt the *alakhai* down with him, knowing she was going to have to let the love of her life go into another woman's arms.

Did you doom the love of your life, or save them for someone else?

Never had Lucian hated the curse on their kind more than this moment.

Anna, his father's *alakhai*, sat off at a distance and kept Lizzy's kids busy while Esmerelda continued her meltdown in Basil's lap. If she was jealous, it didn't show. Her focus was on the children. Lizzy ran inside, unable to stand the sight of their mother falling to pieces. It pissed Lucian off, but there was nothing he could do about it. Lizzy was a reflection of her mother—had made the exact same choices and would one day suffer the exact same fate. Her husband was vampire and not her *alakhai*. Was she regretting her decisions right now?

Lucian watched the shitshow go from bad to worse.

Esmerelda tried to push away from Basil. He gripped her waist and whispered something in her ear. She slapped him so hard, they all felt the shock. Then she shoved herself up and set her dagger-gaze on Lucian next. Staggering, her heels clacked across the flagstones as she made her way towards him.

"*You*," she hissed, and her chin trembled. "If you'd been here, this wouldn't have happened!" She pounded into Lucian's chest, and he took her fury. Every point of contact between them hurt like hell. She was strong enough to bruise him and fast enough to slip past his defenses. Not that he bothered to put up a fight. He stood there and took her punishment. Welcomed her pain. Swallowed his agony and wished he could relieve some of hers. "You promised to protect him!" she screamed.

I tried, he wanted to say. But she didn't want his excuses. She didn't need to hear about what it was like to watch his brother go up in flames screaming at Lucian for help, either. To tell her any of that would put her on suicide watch.

"I hate you," she hissed at him. "You are no longer my son."

"Esmerelda!" Basil roared.

"I hate you too, Basil. I wish I'd never met you."

Lucian gritted his teeth. First, his father shunned him. And now his mother. It shouldn't hurt anymore, but it did. Her words cut him like a saw through bone.

"Mother," Lizzy came down the steps with a wad of tissues in her fist. She pulled Esmerelda into her. "Please, don't make this worse."

"Don't make it *worse*?" Esmerelda growled. "How much worse

can it get, Elizabeth?" She wiped her nose with the back of her hand and turned her furious gaze to Lizzy's belly. "You'll see soon enough, I suppose." Esmerelda backed away from her family and headed into her house. She swayed and clutched the doorframe, sobbing, before heading inside and slamming the door.

"Someone needs to stay with her." Lucian would happily do it, but she would never allow it. She hated him too much.

"I'll stay." Basil rubbed the back of his neck and stared at the ground.

"No," Lizzy said. "Anna's presence will likely send Mother over the edge. Sending Anna home will infuriate Anna and ignite her *alakhai* jealousy. You can't let that happen either. It's not fair to either of them."

"Anna will have to get over it," Basil snarled. "Esmerelda and I have too much history and love between us for it to not be me who stays the night."

Anna sucked in a breath from a distance, overhearing all of this. Basil's face reddened. The man was stuck between a rock and a hard place. No one felt sorry for him.

"I'll stay," Lizzy offered.

"And remind your mother of everything she's just lost? Not a good idea, sweetheart." Basil tipped his head back and stared up at the sun. "I can't stand this torture."

"I'll stay." Lucian sighed heavily. "Even if she hates me, hate's better than sorrow and hollowness. She can take her emotions out on me without regret. I'll handle it."

"Son."

"It's fine." Lucian really didn't want to have this conversation anymore. "I'll stay. You can go and I'll give you updates."

He'd not had contact with his family in a long time Honestly, Lucian hadn't really missed it, which made him feel like shit. But his spiteful anger over their reactions when he said he wanted to join the House of Death fueled him for centuries until it became part of his soul's energy. Their only mention of pride in him came after he climbed ranks faster than any other vampire had. But their joy in his success was short-lived because it was for another House, not theirs.

Lucian knew where he belonged, and it was never going to be with the House of Blood. For his family to ridicule and fight him over his choice of loyalty infuriated Lucian enough to cut them off entirely at one point. No amount of success pleased them. His family thought they were above Malachi's crew. They weren't. Luke was the first family member to contact him. And it was for help. Help he'd not gotten in time.

So much could have been prevented if they'd not been judgmental of each other. If they'd just been supportive and open-minded.

"She needs to feed." Basil stuffed his hands in his pockets and looked out at the destroyed gardens. "And she needs to rest."

"I'll have one of the blood courtesans brought in." Lizzy retrieved her cell and started dialing the House of Blood.

Lucian clenched his teeth and didn't say shit. The high-and-mighty went both ways—his family hated the House of Death for their brutality but needed them to hunt *Savag-Ri*. The House of Blood was not without their own viciousness. Lucian despised what the House of Blood did to get blood courtesans. Even if collecting blood donors was necessary, their methods were corrupt.

As if he had room to talk? The Wicked Garden in the House of Death's territory wasn't any better.

Vampires were such hypocrites. So many double standards, it was enough to make one's head spin.

Lizzy hung up and said, "Two will be here shortly."

"Good. I'll transfer a month's earnings into the king's coffers for them." Basil looked toward Anna and jerked his head, silently asking her to come to him.

She quietly came closer, and Basil reached out and took her hand. Kissing her knuckles, he tugged her into his embrace and kissed her lips. "I'm so sorry you had to be part of this," he whispered.

Lucian seethed. Sorry? He was *sorry* she had to be part of this? Fuck that. "As your mate, your baggage is hers now. She can put up with it for one goddamn day." Did Basil forget they were all gathered to mourn the death of his *son*?

"You have no idea what Anna's been through." Basil hissed at Lucian.

Lucian almost laughed. No idea what Anna's been through? As if she, in any way, took priority over Esmerelda here? Basil curled his arms around Anna. Seeing his father get protective over his mate set Lucian off. It didn't matter how aggressive instincts rode mated vampires. Lucian wanted to knock his father out for acting like a selfish bastard. Charging towards him, ready to lay his father out flat on the lawn, Lucian's fury burned white hot.

Basil growled low in his throat, putting his hand up to block him.

Laughable.

Was his snarl supposed to shake Lucian? Put him in his place? Stop him with a slam of energy to his chest? Lucian wasn't a kid anymore. Thanks to hunting *Savag-Ri* and fine-tuning his body, Lucian was built for combat now. And he was far beyond the fear of his father's fists. But if Basil wanted to test his power, hey, who was Lucian to deny such a thing? So long as Lucian didn't make the first swing, he should be in the clear of paying a penalty.

With a cold calmness, Lucian closed the gap between them. They stood eye-to-eye for several heartbeats. One of Lizzy's kids made a squeaky noise on the patio. Basil backed up and sighed, "Let's go, Anna."

Everyone left Lucian standing in the destroyed garden by himself. He had no idea how long he sat out there, but it must have been a while. It was dark by the time he could catch his breath without battling a severe ache and weight in his chest.

Sadie came outside and rubbed his arm. "The blood courtesans are here," she said softly. "Everyone else is gone."

Lucian stared at the urn perched on its pedestal. "Good," he cleared his throat. "Is she feeding?"

"She refuses." Sadie looked out at the ravaged rose beds. "I'll stay with her. I don't think it's a good idea for you to remain here."

Just twist the knife in deeper, why don't ya? "I promised to look after her," he said.

"And you are. Through me. You know I'd never let anything happen to her, Lucian."

He wanted to argue. No, he wanted to finish what his mother started and uproot every plant, bush, and tree within sight. Smash the fountain. Destroy the statues. Take a baseball bat to the greenhouse. He wanted to hug his mother and squeeze her tight like she used to with him when he got the belt from his father over something one of his siblings did. Even with a classical upbringing and privileges, no family was perfect. He learned to love his father even when he hated him. Basil wasn't without his own issues. No one was.

"I can stay." His throat felt like sandpaper. "My King will understand."

"You're not listening, Lucian." Sadie cupped his face and tilted it down towards hers. "It's not good for you to stay. You only remind her of everything she's lost."

"Jesus, Sadie." Her words nearly knocked him to his knees. "Way to kick a man when he's down."

"I'm not sugar coating this for you anymore," she continued. "You are the one who hurts her the most because you're the biggest source of grief she carries."

He didn't deserve that. He'd done nothing to warrant that level of cruelty.

"She and Basil..." Sadie's brow furrowed as she looked up at the house. "They only stayed together because of you."

"I'm sorry. What?"

"Esmerelda got pregnant with you," she whispered. "They were forced to get married."

"No. They've been married for nearly a thousand years." He was just a little over four hundred.

Sadie shook her head. "No. They were only courting. Both were holding out for their *alakhai*. But then she got with child, which changed things."

Lucian was going to puke. "So that's my fault?" Bullshit.

"It's not your fault." She wrapped her arms around him as if he was a kid and not a grown male twice her size. "But she sometimes confuses what's her doing and what isn't."

Yeah, Esmerelda was like that. She usually came around, though.

Except with Lucian.

His parents had always been tougher on him than on Luke or Lizzy. It inspired his desire to break away and join the House of Death as a hunter instead of sticking with the House of Blood as a recruiter.

"So, they were never married as long as they claimed?" He couldn't believe this. Was his entire childhood a lie?

"Their parents and the House of Blood's king forced their hand. Between your mother's bloodline and your father's family connections, it was a perfect match. You, growing in her womb, made it more necessary for their union to take place. Back then, it was frowned upon to be knocked up. It could have destroyed both family's perfect reputations. Marriage was the only way to make the pregnancy acceptable."

Only in the vampire's aristocratic circles, Lucian thought. Jesus, he felt like he was in a goddamn twilight zone.

"While she carried you," Sadie went on, "they fell deeply for each other. Then out you came, and it was as though fate joined them eternally by bringing you into their lives. They were so happy. So madly in love. They spoiled you rotten and had your sister and brother shortly after. Through unfortunate circumstances and social expectations, Basil and Esmerelda became our society's finest match."

"So why hate me for it?"

Her face fell and brows knit together. "I think her heart's wounds are too deep and fresh for her to understand the difference between circumstance and consequence. She'd have happily lived in an eternal tryst with your father until they each found their mates. Keeping him at arm's length if ever she felt their bond growing a little too tight around her. But after their forced marriage, and your birth, they *did* fall madly for one another, and had a life of luxury, love, lust, and loyalty with three perfectly happy children to top it off. Now? The rug's been pulled out from under her and she's struggling to stand on her own. She's never had to do that before."

"Not. My. Fault."

Sadie nodded. "I fear you are an example of everything she craves."

Lucian shook his head. That made no sense.

"Your strength, Lucian. Your freedom. You chose a new path for yourself instead of following tradition and doing what you were told. You've risen with great success. You're admired by every House. Don't think that goes unnoticed."

"I didn't think anyone here cared enough to acknowledge what I've accomplished."

"They care. They just care for the wrong reasons." She hugged him tight. "For that, I'm so sorry, Lucian."

"Don't apologize for things that aren't your fault."

"Then don't take blame for things that aren't yours."

Because it wasn't his fault that he lived his life, and his

mother hadn't. As a mother, she should be happy he was happy. Not jealous. And not pissed off and hateful.

He kissed the top of Sadie's head. "You're too good for this family. You know that, right?"

She chuckled in his chest. "I love you all so much."

He felt her shudder in his arms as she began crying. Lucian bit back everything else he wished to say and just held her while she wept. Sadie was like a second mother to Lucian, Lizzy, and Luke. She needed to mourn Luke's death just as much as the rest of them. Lucian doubted anyone had given her the chance to do so until now.

"Sadie," Esmerelda called from the doorway.

She broke away from Lucian to look up at her employer.

"I wish to have a bath drawn."

"Yes, of course." Sadie quickly climbed the steps and headed back inside.

Esmerelda let her slip by and kept her gaze locked on Lucian. "Why are you still here?" She cocked her perfectly waxed brow and glowered like he was a weed amidst her prized blooms.

"I wish to stay," he said quietly. "If only to protect you while you grieve."

"I need no protection," she gritted. "I need peace and you bring me none."

Lucian slowly walked up the steps, staring at his mother the entire time. He stuffed his hands in his pockets and stopped a foot away from her. "Do you really want me gone?"

Because if that was the case, fine. But he really wanted to stay with her. To help her heal. To do *something,* for crying out loud. He'd been so helpless with Luke. He couldn't stand being that way with his own mother when she needed help, too.

"Yes," she growled. "I want you gone immediately."

His heart dropped to his knees. Nodding, he dropped his dignity at the threshold. Without saying another word, he retrieved his bag from the spare bedroom and paused at the front door with his hand on the knob. Looking over his shoulder, he saw his mother glare at him from the ballroom's archway.

He barely recognized her anymore. Lucian was a stranger in his own family. A ghost in the mansion he'd grown up in.

"Why do you hate me so much?" God, how his voice cracked.

"I don't hate you," she replied coldly. "I envy you. And that, Lucian, I cannot survive right now."

He swallowed the lump in his throat and left after softly clicking the front door closed behind him.

CHAPTER 8

Returning to New Orleans, Lucian felt like he was floating. He needed some gravity to pull him back down or he might never recover from this trip. Of all things to contemplate, he fixated on Tessa. How shitty was that? He needed to leave her alone and not fall into the same trap as his parents apparently had. Walking around with a Tessa-sized hole in his heart would be survivable, right?

He doubted it.

What a nightmare. Was his entire upbringing a lie? No way. He refused to believe it. No one could fake a love like his parents had for each other. Even as Basil sat on the patio ground with Esmerelda in his lap, it was obvious they still loved each other deeply, even if they couldn't be together anymore.

This was so screwed up.

Pulling into the mansion's parking pad, he turned off his engine and just sat there. He didn't want to go inside. He didn't have anywhere else to go, though. Running his thumb across his phone screen, he contemplated texting Tessa.

Bad idea. He shouldn't drag her into his misery just because he needed a little something to take his edge off. Right? So why was he pulling up a text box? Why did his thumbs punch in the words *We need to talk*. And why was his heart beating so fast?

His thumb hovered above the *Send* button. Nope. Not doing it.

Deleting the damned message, Lucian tossed his phone onto

the passenger seat, no longer trusting himself to make a good decision.

He was so fucked.

Rubbing his temples, he tried to compartmentalize his life to make it more manageable. Luke was gone, his ashes in safe keeping at his family's estate. *It's over*. His father found his *alakhai* before the curse killed him too... that was good. *It's over*. His mother had Sadie to keep her company and to cry with... okay, that was good too. Esmerelda had someone she loved and trusted with her. She wasn't entirely alone to grieve. *It's. Over.* Lucian couldn't do shit for his sister, not that Lizzy needed help with anything, but at least she was with a decent vampire who would help her raise kids and love her until.... shit, until one of them saw their mate in a reflection and all went to hell for their family too.

Lucian gritted his teeth. He couldn't help Lizzy with that. It wasn't his place or his duty. Lizzy was a grown ass female who knew the consequences of her actions. Unlike Esmerelda, Lizzy got married without a push to do so. She married for love and companionship. Then had children on purpose.

But was that any better? Their ending would still be the same—an ultimate split up because either death, or a fated mate's reflection, would eventually sever them forever.

Which was worse? To be happy with a fated mate, only to live with the guilt of knowing you've left the love of your life behind.... Or leave both mate and love behind because the curse got you first.

Sweet Jesus, Lucian never wanted to be human so badly in all his life. Those creatures were clueless about how lucky they were. They might be fragile with short lifespans, but they could live life to the fullest. Vampires only found ways to entertain themselves until death knocked on their door and forced them to hustle. Time dragged. Slowed down. Sometimes it was as if it stopped completely.

Their curse made them live in constant longing. Nothing eased it enough to even take a full breath and find a spark of joy. Time moving slowly made it even more torturous.

He needed to get out of here. Run. Fight. Feed. *Something*.

Several armed vampires rushed out of the mansion at once and split off into groups to hop in their cars. Oh good, some action to keep him occupied. He rolled his window down. "What's happened?"

"We got a lead on a possible *Savag-Ri* nest. We're gonna check it out."

"I'll come too." He didn't have many weapons on him, but what he had was enough. He slammed on the gas pedal and took off with the rest of them. A hunt would help burn off some of his aggression and grief. He didn't have time for heartache or pity parties. Family business went on the back burner when House business needed his attention. He couldn't help his family, but he sure as shit could help his House.

And really, any *Savag-Ri* taken down was helping their entire race.

Those pieces of shit were the bane of a vampire's existence. They were the only predators a vampire and Lycan had. Those morally corrupt sons-of-bitches stopped at nothing to take out both species. They gave zero fucks about anyone except themselves and used anyone and any means necessary to take out vampires and Lycan. Body counts were all that mattered to them. Anyone caught in the middle was just collateral damage.

The amount of effort it took to keep *Savag-Ri* away was frustrating. All the bone dust, spells, guards, and video surveillance. To live among humans, vampires went to a lot of trouble to keep their kind, and humans, safe. Not that it was noticeable. Nope, humans lived as if threats weren't around the corner every minute of the day and night. You can thank a vampire for keeping things safe. Lycans were just as busy keeping the *Savag-Ri* count down in their territories, too.

You're welcome.

Lucian gripped his steering wheel as he followed his fellow House mates down the road. If there was a nest of them downtown, it needed to be destroyed, along with anyone in it.

The *Savag-Ri* have been relatively quiet lately, which was never a good sign. Lucian wasn't foolish enough to think they'd moved on to different hunting grounds. The hacked security videos came to mind. Maybe it wasn't some kid in his mommy's basement playing with them. Maybe it was someone more dangerous. Someone like a clever *Savag-Ri* with killer tech skills. As head guard, Lucian needed to stay on top of shit like this, because if it's someone other than an innocent human playing games, it could jeopardize everyone in the House of Death's territory. Speeding down the road, he took in a deep breath and blew it out between clenched teeth.

It was the duty of the House of Death to protect and bring retribution to those who threatened their kind. It was House of Bone's duty to grind the bones of their sworn enemies and lace it with magic that all vampires could use as protection to keep their properties safeguarded. The House of Blood was responsible for bringing in fresh veins—other vampires and occasionally humans to feed from when someone needed a vein tap.

Ultimately, vampires would do whatever it took to honor their obligations to their race. The House of Death was the most savage of the three Houses. Lucian loved his king and the vampires he shared his duty with. But lately there'd been contention brewing between the kings. The Houses were not getting along—not that they ever really did—but the power struggle was getting intense. With Malachi already seen as the Mad King, and his House considered filled with the most dangerous and depraved of all vampires, the other two Houses could certainly try to overthrow him and take the House of Death for their own. At the very least, they might try to derail the structure of the territories by using a breakdown of surveillance to find weak points in Malachi's territory.

Hmmm. Maybe it was one of them who hacked the surveillance cameras? Nah. Too juvenile and hands off. If a vampire from another House was fucking with them, it wouldn't be through a firewall. It would be far more sinister and damaging.

As the caravan of vampires navigated through the streets, Lucian felt the tension of his personal issues ease, and welcomed the aggression replacing it. By the time he pulled into the warehouse district, he was ready to slay.

Thankfully, this wasn't a commissioned kill—so any enemies they found here could die here instead of being hauled back to the Kill Box for questioning and torture.

Dorian, the Reaper, was already waiting for them. Like a wraith, he stalked out of the shadows to meet them with blood staining his shirt and a deep cut across his cheek. "Took three down, but the rest got away from me." His tone dripped with disappointment.

"You did well, man." Lucian yanked his blades out of their holsters. "Which way did they go?"

"They split in five directions."

"Where's Lena?"

"Home," Dorian's voice was deep and gravelly. "Thank fuck for that. This feels too dangerous for her to be in."

Lucian couldn't agree more. There was something in the air threatening even the oxygen they breathed. Or maybe that was just his paranoia. It seemed like everything was getting more intense lately. "You did well, Reaper."

"Not well enough."

No sense in arguing with him. Dorian was a savage animal who wouldn't stop slicing until he was the last one standing. Lucian's best friend was a killer, born and bred.

Wind kicked up. A storm was brewing.

"Magic or climate?" Dorian frowned as he, too, looked up at the darkening skies.

"Hard to tell." But this was bad news for New Orleans. Rain washed away bone dust. "Where's the nest?"

"I think in there," Dorian pointed at an old, abandoned building. "South entrance. It's spelled, but I didn't try to infiltrate without backup."

In silence, Lucian and the others split off and surrounded the building. No trace of a *Savag-Ri's* scent hit his nose. Just piss, stale food, and cold, wet metal. But the hair on Lucian's arms stood on end. A whiff of danger tickled his nose. Blades out and fangs bared, Lucian gave the signal and Dorian kicked the door open.

Someone inside screamed.

BOOM!

The building exploded, sending pieces of metal and glass everywhere.

Blasted back by the force of the explosion, Lucian and Dorian went airborne before slamming into the side of Lucian's car and leaving vampire-sized dents in the side. The impact stole his breath. Stars danced in his vision and a high-pitched ringing screamed in his ears. Crawling forward, he and Dorian both scrambled back onto their feet and looked for anyone else caught in the blast.

"Where are the others?" Lucian roared.

Dorian was screaming back at him, but he couldn't hear a

damned thing. His ears were ringing too loud. Swaying on his feet, he felt like he was going to puke. Dorian's mouth moved, but Lucian struggled to read his lips. Blinking hard, his brow pinched as Dorian went in for a repeat until Lucian understood the words coming out of his busted mouth.

Eastside. Someone screaming.

Lucian booked it while Dorian pointed in the opposite direction, indicating that's where he was headed. As he ran down the side alley, the other vampires met up with Lucian in various forms of injured. It seemed Lucian and Dorian took the worst of the hit, which was fine by Lucian.

Heading east around the fire and debris, Lucian's heart hammered. If any innocents were caught in this blast, so help him God, he'd personally find every last *Savag-Ri* in this territory and tear them apart with his fucking teeth.

Two more explosions went off in a distance. Even with his muffled hearing, he heard the boom. The ground shook beneath his boots.

What the—

Shit, he'd lost his daggers in the explosion. Good thing he kept a spare in his boot. Gripping his blade, Lucian sped past two vampires climbing a pile of rubble to get further into what was left of the building. "Look for casualties!" he barked.

Someone had screamed just before the explosion. Had they been in the building or out of it? He was too concussed to rub his brain cells together and figure it out. Lucian's hearing returned just in time to catch shouts down the street. Sirens wailed. The cacophony of chaos riled him up in a vicious way. His body hardened. He picked up speed.

Come on, come on. Just give me one. One motherfucker to tear apart. Where were they?

Lucian picked up the faint scent of blood. He followed it deeper into the disaster and gawked when he came upon someone's hand. Then… a leg. *Oh, no.* Lucian's nostrils flared. His head whipped around, his eyes slowly taking in the carnage. A torso. *Shit, shit, shit.*

He found more and more body pieces. His mind put them back together, but he didn't touch any of it.

Vests… straps… dynamite fragments. Swiping his mouth as

he took in the damage, Lucian felt ill. He needed to contact the others. Reaching for his—

Damnit! He didn't have his cell with him!

A war cry tore through the air, rattling him back into fight mode. That was Dorian. Shit! Lucian raced with him to meet up with the others two blocks down from the ruined warehouse. Blood permeated the air of the dimly lit street. Dead ahead, Dorian fought a *Savag-Ri* with his bare hands. More descended from a rooftop. Lucian's fangs ached as he jumped in to join the party.

His vision hazed red. Rage coursed through his veins and he didn't hold back. Lucian stabbed, kicked, bit, and punched whatever he touched. The other vampires jumped in. It was a goddamn riot on the streets—both sides hellbent on taking down the other.

Roars, shouts, sickening wet noises, and gurgles filled Lucian's ears and pumped fury into his heart. His mind dove further into dark territory. No matter how many dropped dead, it didn't put a dent in his need to kill more.

Someone hissed. A gun popped off several rounds. Shrieks, groans, laughter. It was enough to drive a male insane.

In the end, the vampires won.

Sort of.

Lucian's chest heaved as he sucked in air. "No survivors?"

"None." Reys confirmed.

"Anyone injured?"

"Not enough to piss and moan about," Xin said. "We're all good. You?"

"Fine." Lucian lied. That explosion really tore him up. Everything hurt but would heal with enough sleep and blood. Dorian must be feeling the same. "Reaper, you good?"

Dorian was too far gone to speak. The Reaper tore through the pile of *Savag-Ri* bodies, severing each head and pulling out their hearts. Yeah. He was good. Dorian tossed the organs into a pile. "Burn them."

Reys pulled out a lighter, squatted down, and set them ablaze. "Overkill much, Reaper?"

Dorian only hissed in response. The Reaper didn't know the meaning of the word "overkill". To him, nothing was too far when it came to taking out their sworn enemy. Lucian agreed wholeheartedly.

"They used innocents," Lucian's flat tone sounded detached even to his own ears. "They strapped explosives to humans and shoved them in their nest. Why?"

"What?" Reys rose to his feet. "You're certain?"

"As much as I can be with the pieces left. What I saw and smelled…" He swiped his mouth with the back of his hand. "Yeah. They were humans used as weapons."

"Or bait," Dorian snarled.

"Sweet mother of God," Xin rocked back on his heels. "What do we do now?"

"Figure out why they targeted this area for one." Dorian cracked his neck. His chest heaved from adrenaline and wrath. "I need to get home to Lena."

"Go," Lucian dismissed him. Dorian's instincts would demand he check on his mate and make sure she was safe. Sirens grew louder in the distance, reminding them it wasn't just vampire and *Savag-Ri* around here. "We need to get out of here."

"Agreed. We can't be here when the cops come." Reys spat at the burning hearts. "What about the bodies?"

"Leave them," Lucian ordered. It sucked to not take them for their bones, but there wasn't enough time. They were impulsive and sloppy tonight. The bones would have to be wasted. "Get out of here. Back to the mansion. *Now*."

Everyone flashed or ran out of sight.

Lucian took one last look at the destruction, his grief piling higher as he thought of the innocent human strangers who somehow got caught up in a war they didn't belong in.

As he gassed it all the way back to the mansion, his mind homed in one thing: Tessa.

Thankfully, he kept her at a safe distance so she would never be a part of his savage world.

CHAPTER 9

After a long meeting with King Malachi, and a lot of debate and planning, the House of Death's warriors broke up and headed out of the room, leaving Malachi to his mirror watching again.

Every bone Lucian possessed ached. His goddamn heart hurt. His eyes burned. He was exhausted, reeked, and also starving. He needed a hard fuck and a hot shower.

A vein too.

Knocking on Victoria's door, he slipped inside when she said, "Enter."

"How are you feeling?"

"Peachy," she snarled. Standing in front of a mirror, she took a blade to her hair, cutting it shorter for no real reason other than boredom, probably. "You were lucky tonight."

"We all were." Lucian leaned against her dresser and crossed his arms. Victoria's room was a wicked museum. She collected mementos that would make most men run home and cry to their mommies. Lucian looked over at a bear trap with blood still caked on the teeth. It hung on the wall by a chain like it was a dreamcatcher or some shit. Next to that hung a scalp with matted, disgusting hair the color of raven wings. Lucian never asked about half the shit in her collection. He didn't want to know.

Holding back a shiver, he rubbed the nape of his neck and focused on the sound of her slicing through her hair with the knife. It was oddly comforting and disturbing at the same time.

Grabbing another hunk of hair, she sliced and said, "You and

Dorian got hit the hardest from what I hear."

"The humans who exploded were hit the hardest." He scrubbed his face, feeling awful that innocents had been dragged into a war they didn't belong in.

"Don't," she warned, jabbing her blade in his direction. "Stop taking the world's woes as your own, Lucian. It's not your job to be responsible for everyone." She turned back and sliced more of her locks off. "That's the King's job."

She was right and wrong. "Innocents have been roped in."

"That's not new." She dropped her cut hair into a bowl on her dresser. Knowing Victoria, she would burn her hair, just like she did her nail clippings, because she didn't trust anyone to not use those things against her later. Magic was dangerous. Living in New Orleans and playing with Voodoo Priestesses had taught Victoria a thing or two about magic. She never let a piece of herself slip into another person's clutches because of it. "What do you need from me?"

Lucian's pulse quickened. "Blood."

"Here." Victoria sliced the underside of her wrist without a moment's pause and held it up to him.

Latching on, he squeezed his eyes shut and drank. There was nothing sexual about doing this with Victoria, but his body hardened regardless. Keeping his eyes closed, he held onto the vision of another woman. *Tessa.*

Lucian envisioned this was her blood he drank. Her arm pressed to his lips. Her body giving off that scent of lust and promises of pleasure. Victoria cleared her throat, and he popped his eyes open, immediately snapping out of his fantasy. Shit, this was awkward. "Sorry."

Pulling back from him, Vic licked the wound closed herself. "You need to get laid, Lucian. You're kicking off some serious pheromones."

Was he? Oh well. "No time."

"Make time."

"Too much to do."

Victoria's lips parted. Her gaze dropping to his mouth, then neck, then groin. "Holy Hell."

Okay, now he felt a little self-conscious. His massive hard cock punching out of his pants probably had something to do with that.

Victoria arched an eyebrow. "The Wicked Garden is always an option. For both blood and sex."

"I'm aware," he sighed. "Just not into it."

"Not since Tessa," she shot back with a grin. "If I didn't know you any better, I'd say you were catching feelings."

He flipped her off and headed to the door. "Thanks for the snack." He shut her door and headed towards his own bedroom—his dick getting harder with each step.

Don't do it. Don't fucking do it.

He was doing it. Yanking his cell out of his back pocket, Lucian pulled up Tessa's message thread and tapped the combo of letters necessary and hit *Send*.

Tessa ended up calling out of work last night and hadn't left her apartment at all since those men left. To not want to leave but also not feeling safe in her own home was a horrific feeling.

Alex and Colton left immediately after giving her specific instructions and programming their numbers in her phone. She didn't trust they hadn't also done something else to her cell. Maybe it was paranoia or having seen way too many movies, but she suspected they were tracking her now.

Neither of them touched her, yet she felt so slimy and gross. Showers hadn't helped. Neither had vomiting nor screaming into her pillow while crying her eyes out. Utterly exhausted, Tessa sat on her couch and stared at her coffee table. She couldn't process a damned thing. Simultaneously shivering and sweating, she felt like a balloon losing its helium, slowing surrendering to gravity's pull to bring her down, down, down.

Tessa's heart stumbled at the sudden sound of her cell dinging. Leaning over, because she wasn't willing to touch her phone, she whimpered when she saw it was a text message from Lucian. "Oh no. Shit." If she answered, Tessa was damning him. If she didn't, she was damning herself and possibly putting her dance students in danger too.

Squeezing her eyes shut, fresh fear and another wave of panic surged through her as she quickly tapped the screen and unlocked her phone. Oh God, she might puke. Clearly, Tessa wasn't built for this shit. How did spies and mafia bosses and all the other bad guys do this all the time? Did they take coping classes? Had they no morals? Was there a handbook for this level of fuckery?

She was a bad guy now. Time to learn how to be a villain.

Tessa stared at Lucian's text like it was in a foreign language: *We need to talk. Pinky's Diner. 10.*

A diner? She covered her mouth with a trembling hand while her brain glitched. A diner. *A diner?* This was out of character for Lucian. Her instincts went haywire about it. Did he know already? Could his spidey senses pick up on something being wrong already? Holy shit, her paranoia was hitting new benchmarks tonight.

What should she do? Part of her wanted to jump at this chance to meet up, so she could tell Lucian what happened. The other part of her wanted to toss her phone into the Mississippi River and pretend she hadn't received the message at all. Then pack her shit and run.

Then what? Running wasn't going to make this go away.

Her actions were finally catching up with her. With a small sob, Tessa hated herself for what she was about to do. Typing the reply, *Yes Sir,* took three tries. She hit send and threw her phone back on the coffee table like it electrocuted her.

She instantly felt like she'd done the wrong thing. Putting Lucian in danger was wrong. Bad.

It was also her only option.

He got himself mixed into some mess with those guys, she internally argued for the thousandth time. It was ultimately his fault that she got roped into this shitshow. Damn him. Okay, that felt wrong too.

Sweet baby Jesus, fix it.

Not bothering to wash her face and brush her hair, Tessa went to the diner dressed in jeans and a t-shirt with the neck cut loose. She couldn't stand anything tight around her neck, so most of her shirts were loose around the collar somehow. She left her phone at home and walked to the diner. It was a twenty-minute stroll in the dark, but she didn't give a rat's ass. She'd lived in New Orleans without a car for years and was used to it. Besides, part of her succumbed to the fact that she was dead already. Either by the men blackmailing her, the prison mates she'd meet if she didn't do this, or maybe the universe would take pity on her and have a bus put her out of her misery when she walked across the street.

Hugging herself, Tessa kept her head down and walked fast to the diner. Nothing like a crisis to get someone to power walk.

She chose a table in the back corner so she could see the entire restaurant—the entrance, as well as the kitchen.

"What can I get you?"

Tessa didn't look up at the waitress as she said, "Water, please."

When the waitress came back with the tall glass of iced H2O, Tessa panicked. Was it laced with something? Was this waitress being blackmailed to do Alex's dirty work, too? Maybe this was a trick. Maybe Lucian hadn't texted, and someone else was using his phone to lure her here under false pretenses? Maybe it was a test to see what Tessa would do when Lucian asked to meet.

Her palms grew sweaty. Her heart fluttered wildly in her throat. She felt sick and scared and frozen in place. In the booth across from her, a group of locals talked about an explosion in the warehouse district and how the streets were blocked off. Her heart clenched. Was that from these guys too?

Wait... was she giving them too much power? Too much credit?

Tessa scrubbed her face, her mouth filling with saliva as her stomach roiled. Tears stung her eyes. She never felt so trapped in her life. Terrified for a thousand reasons, she debated on leaving. Got so far as out of her booth and to the door before running smack into Lucian's hard chest. It was like slamming into a concrete wall. Tessa bounced off him and he caught her before she fell on her ass.

"Easy does it," he smiled.

Bad guys don't have a smile so warm, do they? Wait... *do they*? Alex's smile was nice, until it wasn't. Same for Colton. They had pretty eyes and hard bodies and good teeth. Same as Lucian.

Villains should come with greasy hair, bad breath, and a mouth full of shark teeth. That way they were easy to spot. Tessa stared up at Lucian, her gaze flittering all over his face as she tried desperately to find a sign that he was a good guy and not a monster—no, an *abomination*—like Alex said he was. Both those men insisted Lucian did awful things to people. She couldn't bring herself to believe it. In the end, though, her opinion didn't matter.

Her desire to stay out of jail did.

"Tessa. Are you okay?" Lucian's grip tightened, obviously seeing she was in distress. "What's happened?"

All she could do was shake her head. She wasn't cut out for this. No part of her could accept that Lucian *wasn't* a good person. Those men were the evil ones. They were blackmailing her. If they had those kinds of resources to catch her on murder charges with evidence *and* a body... then they had plenty of means to capture Lucian. They didn't need her to lure him anywhere. They should be resourceful enough to catch him on their own.

She swayed on her feet. *Oh God, what did they want with him? What would they do to him?* Her fingers dug into his arms, her nails biting into his skin.

"Jesus Christ, come on." Lucian escorted her outside. His aggression rolled off him in waves and it made her panic rise. Where was Lucian planning to drag her off to? What would he to do her?

"No!" Tessa ripped her arm out of his clutches. "I'd rather be inside."

Inside, there were people. Witnesses. Help and good lighting. Probably surveillance cameras.

Her composure fizzled away and left her terrified. She started sobbing uncontrollably and nearly spilled all her secrets onto the sidewalk between them.

"What's happened, Tessa?"

Lucian's eyes rounded as his gaze swept over her. It made her shrink back even more. She scrambled to come up with something other than the truth. "I... I'm...."

"Get in the car." He practically manhandled her into his vehicle. Stunned by his aggression, Tessa was in the car before she could break free of him and run off. *He's a threat to society.* Colton's warning shot through her like a bullet. She shouldn't have met Lucian tonight. Shit, she shouldn't have met him two years ago. If they'd never met, this wouldn't be happening right now.

Lucian slammed her door shut and stalked around to the driver's side. Tessa's hand hovered over the door handle, but she froze. That hesitation cost her the chance to run. Lucian dropped into the driver's seat, slammed his door shut, cranked the engine, and sped down the street.

Tessa's mouth went dry. She watched Lucian in her peripheral vision and tried to read him, to decode him. She got nothing. For all the times she was able to understand his body language, right now he was a mystery. A scary mystery.

Lucian's a danger to society, Colton's words kept echoing in her skull. *We're only trying to protect innocent people, Tessa.*

Alex's voice rolled in next. *You'll be doing our race a great service if you help us catch him.*

Race. Why did he use that term? As in the human race? What other way could he have meant by that? And if not the human race, did that imply there was another race out there? How many? What kind?

Her cheeks tingled with too much adrenaline. Overthinking was always her downfall. Tessa's gaze flicked to Lucian again as he sped down the road to take her who knew where. His jaw clenched. He was strangling the steering wheel to death.

Tessa stared at his knuckles. His hands were huge. Strong. Capable of snapping dainty necks. Her gaze sailed along his body. His arms were thick. Sinewy. Able to deliver killing blows and chokeholds. His body was solid. Heavy. Perfectly chiseled. Capable of pinning someone down and keeping them immobile until he wanted otherwise. His legs were long and muscular. He could run fast. His gait alone was most likely twice the length of hers.

There was a weapon strapped to his hip. She couldn't tell what it was, but there was *something* there. A gun? A knife? A taser?

No suit tonight, she noticed. Just jeans and a black shirt that stretched across his wide chest, which looked similar to what he'd worn in the picture those men showed her. Tessa flicked her gaze to his feet and gawked at his black combat boots.

Oh God.

Tessa couldn't catch her breath. Everything felt too tight. She yanked on the collar of her shirt, tearing it even more. "I can't breathe." She smacked the window, clawing at the buttons to make it go down. "I can't breathe! I can't breathe!"

The window opened, and she got hit in the face with hot, muggy air. It didn't help. Hyperventilating, she clawed at her shirt some more, gasping and crying.

Lucian stepped on the gas pedal, flying them faster to God

knows where.

He knows, she thought. *He knows I'm working with those guys, and he's come to take me somewhere to kill me.* She clawed at the door. Screams tore out of her lungs between her shallow breaths.

"Tessa!" he hit a side street, going so fast the buildings blurred.

Her cheeks grew numb. There was a ringing in her ears. Blackness ate away the edges of her vision.

Before she could escape, she passed out.

CHAPTER 10

Tessa woke groggy and confused. Cocooned in warmth that smelled divine, she sighed and let herself slowly fall into reality. What a fucked-up nightmare. Rubbing her eyes, the room came into focus as she rolled onto her back, expecting to see the ornate ceiling of the hotel suite with the gold chandelier dangling in the center of the room. Instead, she got a dark gray ceiling with a filigree pattern and a silver chandelier that had real candles burning in it.

What the—

Sitting up, everything came into focus, and she froze. Recent events flooded her system, accompanied by a fresh wave of nausea. *Oh God. It's real. I'm not safe.* Clutching the bedsheet to her chest, Tessa's gaze flickered around the candlelit bedroom until it found a landing pad. *Lucian.* He sat in a chair on the far side of the room—elbows resting on his knees, pitched forward, staring at her with a look that cut straight through her defenses.

She swallowed hard. Soft classical music played in the background. The room was filled with candlelight. It smelled like Lucian in here—the air, the sheets, the walls. It made her safe when she knew she wasn't.

"Where am I?" Dumb question.

"My home." Lucian's voice was deep and gravelly. His gaze remained so intense, she felt like she might catch on fire from it.

Licking her dry lips, she tried to regain her frayed thoughts. *Diner. Sidewalk. Car. Nothing.* She let out a shaky exhale. "I don't remember how I got here." That confession pierced a hole in her rotten heart. It had been a while since she had a blackout. The last time it happened ended in—

Her throat tightened as tears sprung from her eyes.

Lucian remained seated and silent. A foolish part of her wished he'd come soothe her. But he was dangerous, right? Wasn't that what Alex said? So why was her first instinct to want him close instead of gone?

Because she was a mental case.

Shit, that wasn't the only reason. If she was honest with herself, it was because Tessa *trusted* Lucian. They'd established an unwavering trust between them for two solid years. He never broke that bond. Never even fractured it. Lucian always fostered, nurtured, and strengthened what they shared together. Honestly, he was the only person Tessa trusted at all. She didn't have trust issues. Tessa just never allowed herself to get close to someone. Not after the accident. And hell, not before it either.

Lucian was the closest thing she ever had to a solid relationship. And it was with a contract and restrictions. Jesus, she was messed up. It made her feel worse about herself, and that's saying a lot.

"Tessa." His tone hit heavy with warning. She swung her gaze back to him, submissive as ever. His nostrils flared. Gaze darkened. "I'm going to need you to be honest with me."

She sat up straighter and rolled her shoulders back. Yanking the sheets off, she slipped out of bed and padded barefooted across the room. He watched her like a wolf tracking prey. Only his eyes moved with her. The rest of him stayed ungodly still.

"I'll try," she said quietly from the opposite corner of the room.

"What are you hiding from me?"

Lots of things. "Be more specific."

Lucian unfurled from his seat, and it was like he stood twenty feet tall while she was only an inch big. "Alright." He clasped his hands behind his back. "I'll go first. For every truth I give you, I expect one back."

She dropped her gaze to the floor. This was an exchange. A currency between them. It's how they came up with their dos and don'ts when they first started their relationship. "No."

"No?"

Tessa shook her head. "I want to ask you questions. Then I'll decide if I want to tell you anything."

Lucian stiffened. "Okay."

She couldn't hide her shock. Tessa hadn't expected him to be so compliant. Then again, what did she know about this guy? Nothing. Nothing past his skill with a bow and size of his dick. She was questioning everything now. "Are you dangerous?"

This was the dumbest idea under the sun. Deep down, she knew that. But even deeper down, like *way* deep down, in the marrow of her bones and the pit of her soul, Tessa honestly trusted Lucian to tell her the truth. Why? Had he somehow groomed her to be this stupid? Was this some kind of master-manipulative plan of his?

It didn't even matter. She trusted him, whether she should or not.

"Yes, I'm very dangerous," he said cautiously. "But not to you."

Why did that sound so believable? And why did her thighs clench? Stupid, stupid, stupid. Him making her feel special was not helpful. "Then to who?"

"Those who threaten me and mine."

Tessa swallowed the growing lump in her throat. "And... who are you and yours?"

"Those I'm in charge of taking care of." He slowly made his way across the room, closer to her. "Among others," he added quietly.

As he closed the gap between them ever so smoothly, Tessa lifted her chin to keep her gaze locked on his. He was about eight inches taller than her. "Others like who?"

"You," he said softly, cupping her cheek. The roughness of his palm contrasted with his gentle touch.

It confused her. Pulling away, she crossed the room again.

"*Tessa.*" His commanding voice almost made her pause. "What's happened that I don't know about?"

She shook her head. Bit her lip. Instincts warred within her. She needed to escape. Run and never look back. Get out! *Get out!* Turning, she raced to the door.

Lucian got there before she was halfway across the room and blocked her path. How... how the hell did he just do that?

"Let me go," she squeaked and slipped under him. Her hand clutched the doorknob just before he slammed his palm to the wooden panel, holding it shut. She wasn't strong enough to pull it open with him pushing it closed. Squeezing her eyes shut, she breathed through her terror. "Please, Lucian. Let me go."

"Not until you tell me exactly what's happened."

His hot breath against the shell of her ear sent shivers quaking down her body. She was drawn to him, as if his scent alone held the power to lure her into his arms. It took tremendous willpower to not spin around and bury her face in his chest.

This was so messed up. She needed therapy.

He pressed his body to her back and lowered his voice. "Tell me."

Tell him. "I can't." She wished she could.

Lucian's free hand ran down her arm soothingly. "I can help you. Whatever is going on that has you so rattled, we can deal with it." He turned her around slowly and she hated how his brow pinched and that he looked positively stricken. "You're so scared, it's killing me, Tessa."

Behind her back, Tessa's grasp tightened on the doorknob, her palm slick with sweat.

"Is it me?" The way he asked… That tone? It was vulnerable and unlike the Lucian she was used to.

"I… I don't know how to answer that." Why couldn't she lie to him? Just say, *No.* Or just say *Yes.* "I've realized I don't know you."

His fingers splayed across the heavy wooden door panel as he leaned in. "Then ask me anything and I'll tell you."

"Why?" *What's it matter?* "I thought we were no longer continuing our tryst?"

"Did you break our contract in some way?"

Tessa curled into herself a little. "Yes."

"*Yes?*" Lucian growled and pressed his body against hers.

Tessa cringed as she confirmed, "Yes." The honest answer would be her ticket out.

Wait, she didn't need an out. She needed to do what Alex and Colton demanded, or she'd face life in prison. How could she let that slip her mind? Had her fight or flight knocked the sense right out of her? Or had Lucian's scent? His presence? His voice?

Jesus, she needed help. Lots of it.

The hand at his side balled into a fist. His breathing turned ragged. Fury rolled off him in waves. Tessa spun around and clawed at the door, yanking on it, desperate to get away from him. "We're done. We're over. Just let me out and you'll never see me again."

Lucian spun her around to face him again. His eyes were nearly black. His jaw clenched, brow furrowing with deep lines. He didn't look pissed. He looked…

Crushed.

"Who?" His voice oozed darkness and cut like razor blades. "Who did you fuck, Tessa?"

"I… No… I…" She shook her head violently. That's not what she meant!

Lucian pressed his forehead to hers, his hands bracketing her head. His chest heaved as air punched out of him. "Who. Did you. Fuck. Tessa?"

Immobilized by his body pressed against hers, her stomach clenched. "No one," she whispered.

And of all things to feel, it wasn't fear. Tessa felt furious and insulted. *How dare he.* Lucian had so little faith in their bond that he'd assume the breach of contract was from her sleeping with someone else? "Damn you." Tessa shoved him. "I haven't slept with anyone, you asshole."

Lucian didn't budge an inch. His head canted to the side, eyes narrowing. Jesus, was it the lighting or were his eyes black? Was that physically possible?

You'll be doing our race a great service if you help us catch him. Her heart kicked into fifth gear.

"There," he jabbed a finger at her. "Right there, Tessa. What made your pulse race just now?"

Damnit, her chin wouldn't stop trembling. It made her feel stupid and weak. "Your eyes are black."

"Candlelight." Lucian closed his eyes and slowly reopened them. They were a little bluer. "You've seen that before. It's never shaken you."

He was right. In the throes of passion, she'd seen his eyes darken before. Tessa always blamed it on hotel lighting and her orgasms making her vision weird. Pressing against her again,

Lucian held her wrists with a firm grip. Bringing them up and over her head, he pressed his body flush against hers and deadlocked her again. "How did you break the contract?"

"W-what?" She couldn't think straight. Not with him so close. Not with his heat seeping into her.

"How," he growled, bumping her thigh with his knee and nudging her legs to spread for him, "did you break our contract, Tessa?"

"It doesn't matter," she said breathlessly. "It's broken. It's over."

"It matters to me." He held her wrists with one hand and collared her neck with the other. "And this is far from over, *prima*." He was binding her with his hands and body, securing her in a way that always made Tessa come undone. Why? Why would he do this?

"Say it," he growled. "Tell me."

"I…" Her eyes rolled when he nipped her neck. "I…"

She hated herself for having the physical reactions she did with him. He was exploiting her lust for his gain. And she was going to let him because it felt too good, and her mind was all fuzzy, and her panic made her foolish and reckless.

"Give me honesty." He licked the shell of her ear and the heat of his mouth shot fire straight to her pussy.

"I…" *Damnit, why couldn't she spit out a lie!* "I love you."

Lucian froze with his face still buried in her neck, one hand remaining gently wrapped around her throat and the other coiled around her wrists. "Repeat that."

"I love you." Tears fell down her cheeks and her knees wobbled.

Lucian peeled himself away from her, and she dropped to the floor, gasping for strength. The tears she'd kept in finally broke free. She wasn't even sure why she was crying over this. It wasn't wrong to love. And these tears weren't from fear. They were from guilt because she was going to betray the man she loved and had no choice about it.

Alex and Colton said he was a bad guy. They were liars. Had to be. She refused to believe otherwise. But that didn't mean she knew Lucian well enough to put her life on the line for him. She might trust him, but not enough to spill her guts and confess to murder. Regardless of what Lucian was into with those men, Tessa still had a prison cell with her name on it. She squeezed her eyes shut, furious that she was in this position. Liars. Everyone was a liar.

Including her.

Lucian squatted down in front of her and placed his finger under her chin. "Tessa."

She squeezed her eyes shut tighter, unable to respond.

"Tessa, look at me."

No. Nope. Go away. Go away. Go away.

He cupped her face with both hands. "You love me." He said it like he was testing the words out on his tongue. "If that's the case, why are you lying to me right now?"

Her eyes popped open. Lucian's gorgeous face invaded her vision, conquering every smidgeon of it. His high cheekbones, cut jaw, narrow nose, blue eyes, dirty blond hair, and arched brow drew her in until they were nearly brushing lips. Apollo and Adonis had nothing on a god like Lucian. And not even divine intervention could save her now.

"I'm not lying." She attempted to back away. Didn't work.

"You tried to throw yourself out of my car while I was going sixty miles an hour, Tessa."

She stiffened. Shit, she didn't remember doing that. She... *she didn't remember.*

"Did you black out?" He knew the answer, so why would he ask? *Because he's establishing a trust step again.* What a goddamn mess. "Answer me. Did you black out, Tessa?"

She nodded. More tears fell.

His tone was soft and agonizingly compassionate. "What's happened?"

She couldn't make words form—not on her tongue or in her mind. More tears spilled. "Lucian." That's all she could say. His goddamn name. "*Lucian.*"

She was a traitor. A horrible human being. A threat.

And damn her soul, but when Lucian wrapped his arms around her and whispered that he had her and everything would be okay, she clung to him and let herself believe it.

CHAPTER 11

I love you. Those three little words knocked Lucian's walls down. Demolished him. Sealed his motherfucking fate. Because she wasn't the only one to breach their contract. He'd fallen in love with her too, he realized. It just took him too long to recognize the emotion for what it was.

He hated himself for falling in love with her. It made him a traitor. A despicable piece of shit. A complete hypocrite. He was going to love Tessa until his mate showed themselves in a reflection. And then what? Leave Tessa in the dust to go after his *alakhai*? What kind of asshole did that?

His kind. His breed. His race. Treacherous, no good, evil, selfish vampires did despicable shit like that.

Curse his soul, but Lucian couldn't bring himself to care about how wrong it was. If he loved Tessa for a day or a century, he'd make it worth the heartache. Spoil her endlessly. Love her hard. Protect her fiercely. *If only for forever*, he wished silently. And perhaps he would love her forever. Hell, Basil still loved Esmerelda even though he had Anna now.

Lucian's stomach roiled. He hated hypocrisy. But that seemed to be all he lived and breathed lately. Kissing Tessa's head, Lucian felt her melt into him a little more even as she whispered, "I'm so sorry," into his chest.

"Nothing to be sorry for."

She shook her head as a fresh wave of despair rocked her because she didn't believe him.

Damnit, he needed to make this better. He couldn't stand her tears. Not when they were this crushing and painful. He loved the ones she wept when he had her flying apart in ecstasy. Screaming his name while her thighs shook.

Forcing her to look at him, Lucian swiped the stray hairs away from her face. She was so delicate, Tessa reminded him of jasmine. She was the kind of flower that bloomed on her terms, regardless of all the patience and constant caring it took to coax her to open up. Hell, even her scent was intoxicating. As was the taste of her pleasure.

Lucian's fangs ached with the sudden need to drink from her.

He always kept his canines hidden from her. Vampires could retract their fangs, though some never bothered. Like Dorian. That secret now felt like a huge deal. *I realized I don't know you*, she'd said. And she was right. That was his fault and for her own good. She didn't need to know he was a vampire.

Yet.

It was easy to be with Tessa in the darkness of a hotel room. Their meetings were all about her, so his attention, energy, focus, and pleasure all zeroed in on Tessa's needs and desires. As her Dom, Lucian was responsible for her. He built her up, gave her what she needed, and made sure she was safe.

That was their deal. Love and infidelity were deal breakers.

But the instant he suspected she'd gone to someone else's bed, he was ready to tear the world apart. Such raging possessiveness nearly cost him everything. It was unwarranted and unexplainable. He never felt so impacted in his fucking life.

I can't lose her.
I love her.
I need her.
I can't keep her.

Those truths needed to be unleashed a little at a time. He didn't want to scare her any more than she already was. And there was something more she was hiding from him. The stench of her fear was pungent. It rattled his nerves in a deadly way. Tessa didn't trust him enough to tell him the entire truth. He'd work on that. Rebuild their bond and hopefully she'd tell him the rest of the secrets affecting both of them, whether they were meant to or not.

Her happiness and safety rapidly became the most important

thing in the world to him.

The *Savag-Ri* war would carry on, his family could continue unraveling, the Mad House he lived in might very well crumble down around his ears in the next few days... and none of that would be as paramount as Tessa's well-being.

Holy Hell, what was wrong with him?

He didn't know, didn't care, didn't want to find out. All that mattered was Tessa and keeping her safe and happy at all costs. If the *Savag-Ri* ever found out he caught feelings for a human, they'd use her against him. Make her expendable, like those humans who'd been strapped with dynamite and blown to pieces in the warehouse.

Dread quaked through Lucian at the thought of Tessa in the hands of his enemy.

To be used as bait to kill his kind.

His arms tightened around her of their own accord. He wanted to keep her safe, always. Wanted to make sure the world he lived in never touched her life. How was that going to be possible? Lucian's mind reeled with game plans. Strategies. Outrageous options that made little sense. He had to keep her here at the mansion. It was the safest place for her. And he needed to get her to tell him exactly what was making her composure falter so drastically that she could barely hold herself up.

Her fight-or-flight response was a danger to her—especially considering she was willing to throw herself out of a moving car *and didn't remember it.*

If a human was threatening her, he'd take care of it. Lucian hadn't lied when he said he was dangerous to those who threatened what was his. Tessa was his. No one—human or otherwise—was exempt from his wrath if they threatened his woman.

"Look at me," he said quietly in the candlelit room. "Tessa, *please* look at me."

Her lovely hazel eyes, red-rimmed and glassy, drifted to his.

"I love you, too." His delivery should have been better than that. "I..." He brushed the tears from her cheeks. "Jesus, your tears are killing me, woman." He picked her up and carried her to his leather wingback chair. Sitting down, he placed her in his lap and cradled her. "I'm not going to let anything happen to you. Whatever else is going on, we'll handle it. Together."

He felt her heart pounding against his chest. She was terrified.

"I don't think that's possible," she whimpered.

She couldn't be more wrong. But Tessa didn't know him. Not really. Because if she did, she'd know exactly how possible it was. And how inevitable it would be.

"Trust me," he said, tightening his embrace. "That's all I'll ask of you, Tessa."

For now…

Tell him.

Those two words beat in her chest like a bass drum. *Tell him, tell him, tell him!* The instinct kicked her heart repeatedly until it was pulp.

Tell him.

So much could be solved with a simple conversation. So much uncertainty might be cleared away if people talked. But she couldn't tell him this. Not after Lucian just said he loved her. No one's ever said those words to her before. Call Tessa a selfish, too-stupid-to-live bitch, but she wanted one moment of bliss before her life combusted. She wasn't telling him about those guys. She'd handle it on her own. Insanity was the only explanation for this level of protectiveness she felt for Lucian. He wasn't bad. No bad man would feel this damn good.

With Lucian's unbelievable scent in her nostrils, his strong arms wrapped around her, his body heat sinking into her skin, his breaths matched hers and slowed to a calm pace. Something in the air between them lightened enough to breathe. Maybe that's what it felt like to surrender to fate. Whatever was going to happen, it could happen after she had one more slice of peace. One more kiss. One more touch.

One more dance.

With the melodies of Mozart's *Lacrimosa* filling her ears, Tessa buried her face in his neck and said, "This feels tragic on a thousand levels."

His chest rumbled with a chuckle. "Shall I play Vivaldi then?"

"Please?" She tipped her head up to look at him. "On your violin?"

His eyes softened. "You wish to dance?"

"I need to," she said before ducking her head back into the crook of his neck. "*Please.*"

Dancing was a release, a punishment, a reset, and a survival tactic for Tessa. Lucian understood that on a level no other did. Perhaps it was because he played the violin for a similar reason.

He lifted her off his lap and stood up, suddenly looking nervous. "I, uh… I actually was waiting to give these to you but never found a good time."

Her heart skittered around in her ribcage. *Huh?*

"One sec." Lucian headed into a massive walk-in closet. He came back out with a large black box tied with a red satin ribbon. "I've tried to work up the nerve to present this to you, but I…" His laugh was lighthearted, and he shook his head in amusement. "Holy Hell, I'm such an idiot."

"How so?" She'd never seen him act like this before. He was awkward and nervous and a little dazed. It was humbling, really. Lucian, for the first time ever, was showing he didn't always have control over himself or his emotions.

Lucian dropped to his knees and placed the box on floor between them, right at her feet. "I've loved you longer than I realized, Tessa." His fingers trembled as he untied the red ribbon. It slid with a whisper across the box. "I'm sorry I didn't breach our contract sooner. It might have saved us a—" he bit back his words, "I'm just gonna shut up now."

Yeah, she'd never seen him like this. Tessa found herself leaning in, more focused on Lucian's expression than whatever was in the box. This part of him was foreign to her. Mesmerizing. Decadent and vulnerable. It made her feel… quiet inside.

Did she like that? No. But she liked how he was willing to show her this side of himself.

I've loved you longer than I realized, Tessa.

He was going to break her. That confession, coming from his mouth while on his knees, would be her undoing. Tessa would go to prison with this memory being the only thing she carried behind bars with her.

Lucian raised the lid from the box and set it aside. Gently, carefully, he unfolded the black tissue paper to reveal a red slip of a dress and matching pointe shoes. "I had good intentions about it," he whispered. "Now I feel like they're not good enough for you at all."

Tessa's heart slammed to a stop. She bent down and placed her hand over his as he fingered the satin ribbons on the pointe shoes.

"This is too generous." And too good for her.

Lucian laughed. Tessa gawked when the points of his canines came into view for a split second. Had he always had those? She couldn't remember. Tessa never spent time looking at his teeth when he was railing her with his massive cock. Oh boy, what a fool she was for this guy.

But Lucian kept laughing, and she found herself almost doing the same. "What's so funny?"

"I take you to the finest hotels and buy you tickets to sold-out shows, but a simple pair of ballet shoes is too generous."

Some bit of her resolve melted because he knew those shoes, and what they represented, was worth more than any theatre ticket, hotel room, or bottle of champagne known to man. His shoulders shook as he kept laughing. The more he did it, the more contagious he got. Tessa ended up laughing right along with him.

"Damn girl, where'd you come from? Heaven or Hell?"

"Venus actually."

"Oh my God!" Lucian tipped his head back and laughed so loud, it startled her.

It felt good to do this with him. The playful back and forth. Maybe living in a fantasy for a day or two would help reality sink in later.

Candlelight danced around the room, and she couldn't drag her gaze away from him. His jaw cut sharp against the dim light. Shadows danced across his cheeks and hair. His teeth gleamed and his canines... his... wait—

"Can I help you get them on?" He canted forward, knees digging into the carpet as he wrapped his hot hand around her ankle. Pulling her foot forward to rest on his thigh, he looked up at her and smiled. "I've always wanted to do this."

"You've wanted to put shoes on my hideous feet?"

Tessa's toes were chewed up from the pressure and stress she put on herself while on the dance floor. Her pointe shoes destroyed her toes because they were too old and busted. She couldn't afford new ones yet because dance classes were slow and instead of getting a second job, she lost herself to melodies and mindlessness in her downtime. Especially over the past couple of years.

Whether Tessa wanted to admit it or not, she'd changed lately. Not in a good way. In a damned and self-destructive way. The good news? Her feet healed faster than they used to. Bad news? Her heart never did.

"There," Lucian said triumphantly. "Did I tie them too tight?"

She hadn't noticed he'd put them on her feet. It happened so fast, and she'd gotten too deep inside her head to notice. "Perfect," she grinned.

Wow, they fit like they were designed precisely for her feet. If she didn't know any better, she'd say they absolutely were. Lucian was clever enough to make that happen. And he always paid attention to every little detail about her. He knew her measurements exactly. How? She didn't have a clue. But every outfit he picked for her always fit with precision.

Tessa stood up to test them out. The box felt great as she hit the floor with a little force to soften them a bit. Keeping her weight balanced on the tips of her toes, she couldn't get over how the shank wasn't too wide either. And the length was perfect. Holy Hell. They were the ultimate dancing shoe.

"I had no idea you paid this close attention to my feet," she said as she continued testing them out. The shade of red was bold. The satin, feminine. The familiarity of the binds relaxed her.

"There's nothing about you I don't pay attention to, Tessa." Lucian rose and crossed his arms, staring at her legs. "Those jeans don't really work with them though."

He was right.

"Too late. These shoes aren't coming off." She'd sleep in them. That's how much this gift meant to her. "You'll have to deal with the jeans."

"Nope." He grabbed her waist and started unfastening them. "I want to see the whole package. Dress and shoes, Tessa."

Every time he said her name, a spark lit in her veins. "You'll have to cut me out of them then." She meant it as a joke.

"Don't tempt me." Lucian pulled out the weapon she'd noticed on him in the car. Had he been wearing that thing on his waist all this time? How had she not noticed?

Because she couldn't pull her gaze from his face. Damnit, she was an idiot.

A bold idiot.

An in-love idiot.

"Go ahead." She wiggled her ass. "But if you cut me, I leave."

Lucian's expression turned severe. "I'd never cut you. Not by accident." Her breath hitched as he pulled a wicked blade out and ran it along her thigh. "Now… if you ask me to cut you on purpose, that's a different game."

Her mouth dried instantly. The blood drained from her face. But even with the sudden fear she felt, something wild and hot pooled in her lower half. And when he grazed her inner thigh with the flat side of his knife, she found herself spreading her legs wider for him.

Still balanced on her tiptoes.

Talk about dancing on a razor's edge. One slip from his hand, or tip of her posture, and blood would run. Why did that thrill her? Why did she want to test it?

She was so messed up in the head right now.

Lucian's head dropped. "God, you're going to be the death of me." He tucked the knife away in the small of his back and unfastened her fly and zipper. With a playful push, he tipped her off balance. She bounced onto the bed, laughing.

A little tug, pull, twist and *swish*… Lucian had her jeans off in seconds without taking her shoes off or cutting the denim away.

He bent down and snatched the dress. Shaking it out, he held it up, inspecting it. Then dropped to his knees and held it open for her to step into. With a devilish grin, he pulled the dress up to her waist. Next, he grabbed the hem of her shirt, gracefully lifting it over her head. She wasn't wearing a bra and didn't hide her breasts from his gaze either. She loved the way he looked at her. His gaze always seemed hungry. As if he was starved for her body and wanted to eat her alive. Drink her up.

Tessa had a sinking feeling she'd let him too. Probably beg him to guzzle her down to the last drop.

Lucian groaned as he tied the straps around her neck before pressing a kiss on her bare shoulder. "I'd have you dance naked, but then I'd have to gouge my housemate's eyes out for seeing what's mine."

Tessa's heart skipped a beat. He sounded like he meant it. That shouldn't be romantic, right? Ohhh but it was.

"Then I'll dance for us in here." She didn't know he had roommates. Not that it mattered. She'd dance anywhere for his pleasure... and hers.

"No." He gathered her hair in his hands and tugged it a little, making her toes curl. "I don't think I'd behave myself with you in my room, naked, dancing to my music with nothing but red on. That's like waving a muleta in a bullfight."

He's dangerous. Her smile fell. Yet her blood fizzed with lust. "Then where am I dancing?"

"In the music room."

CHAPTER 12

Someone save my soul. Lucian swore he was on fire. Seeing Tessa in that dress and those blood red ballet shoes rocked his foundation. He allowed her to stretch and warm up before leading her out of his bedroom. His grip tightened on her hand while they walked down the hall. He wanted to carry her. Possess her. Own and keep her.

Drink her, mark her, take, and turn her.

It was a horrible feeling. Aaaannd that's why he chose to do this in a common room. Whistling loudly, he got the attention of every vampire in the Mad House. "Music room," he said to the first one who popped their head out of their private chambers. "Tell the others."

In another life, if Tessa had been his fated mate, he would have chosen this way as her debut into vampirism. Dressed in red. Dancing for the House of Death.

He knew it was wrong to indulge in such an impossible fantasy, but here he was doing it. Nothing like stacking up regrets, one by one, to bury yourself under later.

He asked permission from the king to bring Tessa to the House of Death when she'd passed out in his car. The request was granted, provided her stay was temporary. It was dangerous for her to be here, and Lucian wasn't ready to consider the consequences of pushing boundaries yet.

Hours ago, when he carried her, limp and unconscious, up to his room, every vampire had been warned that she was a human whose mind hadn't been tampered with. He didn't want to pluck her memories of him away. But now that she was this deep in his heart and life, he might not have a choice.

Was it foolish and selfish and shitty to wish his *alakhai* didn't show up until after Tessa died an old lady?

He stumbled at the notion.

Holy shit. He just thought about Tessa's life and ultimate death as if she were a library book with a return date. But that's what she was, right? A temporary escape? A moment's distraction from reality? She was on loan.

Not. His. To. Keep.

Lucian might puke. No longer able to keep his composure, he swept her into his arms and held her tight to him. Storming down the hall, he hit the steps and glided down those too. He felt like he was floating again. Pressing his mouth to Tessa's head, he inhaled the scent of her shampoo mixed with her natural fragrance, hoping for some grounding and strength here.

Once they entered the grand music room used for a myriad of therapies, he set her down, even though it killed him to let her go. Tessa looked around the room in shock and awe. It was a decently sized space, equipped with every instrument one could ask for. And plenty of space to dance in.

Vampires, or what she would think were normal humans, filed into the room with various degrees of curiosity and humor on their faces. Tessa gave a little gasp as she watched them enter and take their places around the room. Lucian cupped her face and pressed his mouth firmly against hers, kissing her back to his commanding voice. "No contract. No shame. Nothing owed or taken. Just us."

She blew out a nervous breath and nodded.

He tossed her a wink before heading towards the variety of string instruments lined against the south wall. Vampires relaxed against one another, curious and hungry. Giving them each a once over, Lucian silently reminded them that she wasn't theirs to play with. She belonged to Lucian and no other.

He plucked a bow from the wide selection and stabbed it at one of the younger male vampires. *Don't even think about it,* his eyes warned. Then he dragged the bow across his neck, quietly reminding the little bloodsucker that he'd be killed if he acted on his impulses. That guy was new in this House and Lucian didn't trust him yet. Now that all his Housemates were in a room with Tessa as the center of attention, Lucian regretted his decision to bring her here. Too late now. He needed to trust his House as much as he trusted Tessa. It shouldn't be as big of a deal as it felt. Shit, he trusted each of these vampires with his life on the daily, so why did it feel jarring to bring his woman into a room with them and hope they'd behave?

Possessiveness really ruled him some days.

Strolling around the room, circling Tessa and making sure everyone smelled his *keep-your-distance-from-my-woman* scent, Lucian got his mind set on music. Testing the strings, warming up. Once satisfied, he met Tessa's gaze and cocked his brow, playfully asking, *Ready?*

She tipped her chin and got into position. *Ready,* she winked back.

Damn, he loved this woman.

Lucian dragged the bow across his strings, the pitch perfect sound screaming from his instrument. Showing her no mercy, and knowing damned well she'd never want it anyway, Lucian fell right into Vivaldi's *Storm*. Tessa sprang to action, spinning, dipping, twirling and arching with his harsh, fast chords. His gaze remained locked on hers as she owned the dancefloor.

Immediately, she captivated the house and knew how to work them as well as Lucian played the violin, cello, and piano.

He transitioned into *You* by Two Feet and Tessa didn't skip a beat as her form slid from one step to the next. She made dancing look as effortless as breathing. On and on they went like this. He played till his fingers ached and she danced until she was breathless.

But the real showstopper was Sub Urban's *Freak*. Tessa playfully tiptoed around the room, a devious smile pulling at the corners of her mouth as she enthralled every monster watching her from the perimeter. For vampires to be so quickly enraptured by Tessa spoke volumes of her beguiling charm.

Her red dress clung to her body, wet from her sweat. Her eyes blazed, begging for more, though her limbs shook from exhaustion. She deliberately challenged herself with positions and poses. No. Not challenged. *Punished.*

They were perfect for anyone who didn't know her. But Lucian noticed her angles were perfect in some positions, and sloppy in others. She was doing it on purpose. He played Two Feet's *You,* and *Shape of Lies* by Eternal Eclipse no better than she danced. Perfect and flawless, yet he faltered each time she danced too close to their audience.

He could pretend he wasn't dying inside playing these songs, and she could act like this was all for fun. Maybe they both enjoyed his musical choices and would ignore the meaning behind them. Hell, maybe they could push each other until there were no limits left and the line between them faded completely.

No. The bottom line was: Neither of them were willing to cut loose. Not in front of an audience, at least. Perhaps not even in private.

How he longed to see her shake off her training and break her rules and give in to the music like he did on his darkest nights.

The bow strings frayed as Lucian ripped through song after song. His eyes ate her up while she danced like an entire room full of predators weren't salivating at the mouth to have a bite of her.

Watching Tessa dance with danger was hotter than he ever imagined.

It made him want things that would certainly send him straight to Hell.

Tessa was lost to the music. Became a slave to it. Lucian's song choices were odd. She thought they might be sporadic, but he morphed into them too effortlessly. And her body reacted without thought. This level of dancing was rare for her. To let go. To just... *move* without care of perfection.

Were her elbows up? Lines straight? Flex, pointe, plié, blah-blah-blah. She was surrounded by bodies in a room filled with mirrors, shadows, and secrets. It felt safe and dangerous all at once. Divine and unholy. Sacred and desecrated. Or maybe that was her soul projecting into the gazes of each member of her gorgeous audience.

Lucian had a lot of roommates if this many people lived with him. She'd barely seen any of the house when he carried her in this room, but the place was massive and old. Large mirrors were mounted around the music room, making her feel like she was in a twisted dance studio.

Keeping up with Lucian's notes, she smiled even though her legs burned and feet screamed. But so long as Lucian played, she'd dance. Tessa would likely go until her body gave out. And boy would she be thrilled for the relief from both the dancing and the exhaustion.

Spinning, leaning, twirling, leaping, Tessa playfully got close to some of the people watching her. Lucian was a gorgeous man, and his companions were a lot like him. Stunning. Hypnotic. She couldn't stare at any one of them because her movements never allowed her to stay still long enough to make solid eye contact. Except when she'd glance at Lucian. Somehow, she could use him as her focal point, and each time she did, his eyes were locked on her. They never wavered.

When the last note died, Tessa sank into a bow. Applause thundered around the room. She glanced upwards and her chest ached as Lucian handed the violin to someone on his left and swaggered towards her with fire in his eyes. Without saying a word, he picked her up and carried her out of the room with the applause still echoing in their wake.

She could have sworn half the room had fangs. She was also pretty sure Lucian was making super low animalistic growling noises right now—his chest rattled with a deep vibration as he held her close and carried her away.

What a headrush. Too high from dancing, Tessa remained quiet and let the songs Lucian played roll in her mind. Was there meaning behind him or just a set of challenges for her?

"You did well down there, Tessa," Lucian groaned against her ear.

Her thighs clenched at the sound of her name on his lips again. Why did she always have that reaction? It was stupid and lovely. "You played well. It was difficult to keep up with some of it."

"Hmmph."

"You have a lot of roommates."

"Big mansion. Lots of space."

Tessa wanted to know more. Wanted to know *everything*.

"You have a lot of mirrors around here. You must find yourselves very pretty."

"Aren't we?" He pulled back to meet her gaze. Then he showed off a wicked smile that made her heart faint.

"Too pretty," she rolled her eyes.

Lucian chuckled and nearly kicked his bedroom door open. He headed straight to the bathroom with her still in his arms. Propping Tessa on the counter, he started unlacing her shoes. Slipping them off, he placed them next to the sink, then playfully fingered the hem of her dress. Lucian's touch was fire on her collarbone. Swear-to-God, he licked his lips, and she felt it on her pussy. It made her breath catch.

"Pity," Lucian said, toying with her strap. "I love this dress on you."

Pity? Why pity?

Without another word, Lucian tore the dress clean down the middle.

"Well," Tessa half-laughed. "You loved it enough to destroy it, huh?"

"Mmm-hmm." He dipped his head down and kissed the crook of her neck. Her body erupted in goosebumps. "I do that with things I can't keep."

She pressed her palms on his chest while he continued kissing and licking her throat and chest. Her eyes rolled with how good he felt. But his words made it hard to enjoy what he was doing.

"You destroy things you can't keep?" Her breathlessness was unhelpful. "You going to destroy me too?"

"Does that mean I can't keep you?"

"Does that mean you want to keep me?" Damn her soul for this. Why was she torturing herself?

"Can I?"

Jesus, his expression was suddenly way too serious. Beautifully, intoxicatingly, everything-she-ever-wanted serious. "If I said yes?" *Which she couldn't.*

"Then I'll spoil and love you until you can't stand me anymore."

"And if I say no?"

Lucian ran his fingers up and down the sides of her thighs and didn't say anything for a few heartbeats. She almost took it back, but then he met her gaze and said, "Then I'll spoil and love you until you can't stand me anymore."

No matter her answer, his affection and attention would be the same.

She didn't deserve a man like him. "You're too perfect, Lucian. Even your answers are way too good to be true."

"I won't lie to you, Tessa. What I say, I mean."

It was foolish to believe him, but she did. Tessa trusted this man with everything—her heart, her body, and her safety. That shouldn't be. She needed to get this over with. Do what needed to be done, so she didn't end up in fucking prison on murder charges.

But something about this place and being here with Lucian, away from her world and deep into his, made Tessa want to forget for a little while longer. She wanted to pretend she wasn't the bad guy. Wanted to play into a fantasy where her life was here with Lucian, and they danced and laughed and worshipped each other day and night. Here, she felt safe. Here, she felt like someone else.

They can't get to Lucian in his house. The thought stuck to her skull like duct tape. *That's why they need me to lure him out in the open. They're going to hurt him. Maybe worse. Why?*

Tessa's hands coiled into fists. She wasn't going to let someone hurt Lucian. No way.

Tell him.

If she told him what happened, she'd lose him for sure. Tessa was a traitor to have agreed to help them at all. That level of betrayal was unforgivable. Had she acted on it? Sought him out? Nope. But she was here with him now, and she shouldn't be. To her, it felt like the second-worst thing she could have done. Now she wondered if Alex and Colton were tracking her somehow, even without her cell. She'd left it at her apartment, but what if they had scouts? What if they had drones or something?

Were they working for the Feds? The mafia? A gang? What kind of surveillance were they working with? What lengths would they go to in order to get to him? Certainly, blackmail wasn't the lowest they'd stoop. The possibilities made her shiver.

How far would Lucian go to get away from them? What was he, a secret agent working undercover? A robber? One of those hacker dudes that saved top secret info on weird USB sticks to use later for world domination?

Oh lord, she was losing her mind.

Tessa looked past Lucian at the rest of his bathroom. The place was kitted out with a giant shower, marble tile, fancy faucets. Everything high-end or old. Vintage clashed with modern. This mansion was huge. Lucian was wealthy. The little she saw of his roommates made her think they weren't hurting for much either.

So, what was Lucian? A drug lord?

As if reading her mind, he tipped her chin up into the light and scowled. "There it is." His tone made the hair on her arms stand on end.

She swallowed hard. "There what is?"

"That look on you is back." He stepped away, folding his arms across his chest. "Tell me what's going on, Tessa."

She shook her head. "Nothing." *Nothing you can help me with. If you get more involved, you'll get hurt, and I can't let that happen.*

"Nothing," he spat out. "*Nothing* looks like terror on you." With a disappointed huff, he turned around and started the shower.

Her heart sank like a lead balloon. His disappointment hurt. A lot. As her Dom, Lucian's reaction was insufferable to her. As her lover, it was no different. Tessa's need to please warred with her desire to keep him ignorant to her troubles. This kind of secret keeping could destroy what was left of their trust. Hell, it was already.

She was so fucked.

CHAPTER 13

Lucian bit down on his growl and refused to unleash his anger on Tessa. The high of their musical madness fizzled out the instant that look crept back onto her sweet face. She was terrified. Angry. Hurt.

Had he done that to her? Had someone else?

He needed to find out.

The only reason he didn't push things further yet was because, for an instant, she looked downright protective and possessive. The flare in her eyes lasted no longer than three seconds, but he caught it and that's what he intended to use to drag the truth out of her soon.

She didn't trust him. Not with her deepest, darkest secrets. Okay, fine. Lucian gave her no reason to trust him like that. Their relationship was based on sexual and emotional bonds that ended shortly after their scenes did. He planned to change that, starting now. This wasn't going to be easy, and he wasn't sure it would be possible. But he had to try, for both their sakes.

The idea of Tessa being with any other man killed him. The possibility that she was in danger tore him up. The fact that she looked ready to bolt from the bathroom made him furious, because he wasn't sure he'd stop her if she tried. It made him feel helpless and useless.

Fuck that noise. He'd sailed that worthless boat too often lately. Time to jump ship and swim into the unknown for a while.

Holding his hand under the spray to check the water temp, he waited for it to heat up. "Come here," he said, crooking his finger at Tessa.

Submissive as ever, she slid off the counter and sauntered over, all rosy-cheeked and wide eyed. God, her body was sinful. The way she moved made him want to drop to his knees and bow down to her. Eat her. Lick and devour her.

His shower was deep enough to not have a door, so Tessa walked right in and stood under the spray of water. Lucian took a minute to appreciate the killer view before he stripped out of his attire to join her.

Snagging the bottle of shampoo from the ledge, he put a dollop in his palm. "Face me," he said in the steam.

She turned around as the rain shower head wet her hair down. Her mouth parted a little as she tipped her head back to savor it. Lucian admired her flat, human-shaped teeth and fantasized what she'd look like with a pair of fangs. Mouthwatering. His Tessa would be *mouthwatering* with a set of sharp canines. His semi turned into a full-blown stiffy at the thought of those pointy teeth grazing his shaft while she sucked him off.

I could turn her, he thought. *I could make her mine. Keep her.*

Lucian squashed the idea instantly. He wasn't a selfish bastard. Turning her wouldn't solve their problems. It would create more of them. No, he needed to love her just as she was, for as long as she let him.

Or until he found his *alakhai*.

"You going to stand there all night, staring?" Tessa teased.

"Would it be wrong if I did?"

Her responding laugh was downright sultry. Lucian stood there like a dipshit with shampoo in his palm, absolutely enthralled by her.

"Use the shampoo on something... *Sir*."

His dick or her head? He groaned as he rubbed his hands together, debating which to massage first. Tessa was too exhilarating for her own good. One sip of her would likely be more intoxicating than an ocean of whisky.

He began washing her hair. The idea of her wearing his scent rocked him in lots of ways. Even his shampoo in her hair made him feel like he was possessing her in some way. He liked it way more than he had a right to. "I bet you command the entire audience's attention when you're on stage."

"Once upon a time, I did."

"Not now?" His brow pinched while he massaged her scalp.

"Not for a long time." She sighed with her head still tipped back and eyes closed. She was enjoying this and that made him feel ten kinds of lit up inside. He'd rather she be relaxed around him than on edge any day of the week.

"Why not get back into it?" He knew she'd lost her spot in a dance company a few years back. She never went into details, but all because she'd lost her position in one company didn't mean she couldn't go somewhere else. Right?

"That chapter of my life is over."

"Yet you dance like your soul's survival depends upon it."

"That's different."

They were quiet while he rinsed her hair out and started on the conditioner. With her long hair wet, it nearly hit her ass when her head tipped back like this. She looked like a goddess. Lucian's gaze locked onto her neck. The vein pulsed steady and strong, proof of how calm she was with him in here. He loved that as well. Loved that she trusted him.

She just didn't trust him *enough*.

"You've got to be one of the strongest women I've ever met, Tessa." He worked the conditioner into her ends. "I know you were in an accident. And I know you worked hard to get back to where you left off before that horrible night."

Tessa's breath hitched. She straightened up and looked at him. "How did you know about that?"

Time to fess up. "I did my homework on you before we made our contract."

He always did his research before getting involved with someone. Tessa became a principal ballerina at the age of twenty-eight. Less than a year later, she got into a fatal car accident that killed her friend who'd been driving. The other driver survived and was the cause of the accident. He'd been drunk. The accident made the local news. That was four years ago.

Tessa had been spared, though she had to regain the use of her right leg. Nerve damage and broken bones could make one's flexibility and agility difficult. As for the dance company? Well, they couldn't wait for her to finish rehab. The show must go on, after all. Her position was given to another dancer and Tessa had punished herself for who knows why ever since. She moved to New Orleans three years ago and danced only for herself and taught children on the side.

Tessa held his gaze for a long moment, then looked down. "It seems unfair that you know so much about me when I basically know nothing personal about you."

True. Time to remedy that. "Ask me anything."

She bit her lip.

"Tessa." Lucian ran his hand down her spine. She was so thin and yet, so strong. In this instance, she wasn't a fragile jasmine bloom anymore. She was a steel crowbar. Cold. Hard. Unyielding. He wasn't sure which he liked more, the flower or the weapon.

"What do you do for a living?"

Her question hung in the air between them as relief washed over him. She was asking him something. Good. That's a start. "I'm a guard."

"Like a security guard?"

"Something like that."

"Or a guard for the mafia?"

"Uhhh no. Not mafia." Lucian had to bite down on his laugh before she heard it. He hadn't expected that one. "Why would you think that?"

She turned around to rinse her back. "This house is huge, and you have a lot of roommates."

"So, your theories went to *mafia*?"

She shrugged.

No, no, no. There was something else that must have made her think that. "This place and my Housemates wouldn't give you that impression, Tessa. What else made you think that?"

He watched her throat work to swallow before she said, "Too much TV, maybe."

Yeah. Maybe. His gaze narrowed suspiciously, and he pulled her out of the spray to switch places with her. "Your turn." He slapped the loofa and soap into her hands and waited. Silently, she started to suds him up. And damned if she didn't go right between his legs and cup his balls with soapy, slick hands. His prima was playing dirty. "Ask me something else, Tessa."

"Like what?"

"Whatever you need to know so you can fully trust me."

Silence again.

Lucian cupped the side of her face while she washed his abs. "I've never broken trust with you in a scene, have I?"

"This isn't a scene, Lucian. This is real life."

"So were our scenes."

That truth was never spoken, even though they both knew it. Their music-enhanced scenes were never pretend. They were real. As were their feelings for each other.

Her jaw clenched as she scrubbed him harder. "Who do you guard?"

"My King."

The loofa in her hand scraped along his thigh. "Is that code for something?"

"Nope. He's a King."

"This is America."

"Don't see what that has to do with my King." Lucian turned and gave her his back. His vampire hearing picked up on her little groan. It was all he could do to not flex his ass for her just to hear that little sound again. "Malachi is old and not from America." He looked over his shoulder and grinned. "And he's not mafia."

"Where does he live?"

"Here." Lucian arched as she touched his back with her hands instead of the loofa. Fuck, her hands felt good on him. "I live here because he lives here."

"And he's rich, so you're rich."

"I'm comfortable. Not rich." He groaned when she swept her hands across his ass and slipped between his thighs. "Although the King pays me a good amount," *shit, that feels good*, "my money is family money. *Old* family money."

Tessa made a mocking groan. "Oh, you're one of *those*."

He laughed because he knew she was playing. Tessa squatted down to wash his calves. "What about you?" he turned around, giving her a face full of dick. And yeah, he smiled like a Cheshire cat about it.

"My family is all gone. Mom died of cancer. Father ran off before I was born. I've been on my own since I was seventeen. Had a full ride to three colleges and chose NYU over Juilliard."

He didn't miss the clip in her tone. "Why not Juilliard?"

She looked up at him, still washing his feet while she said, "My mother went there. I'll be damned if I was going to dance in her shadow or with her ghost."

Okay, wow. This Tessa? This was the one who played his style of music. This Tessa was defiant and confident. She stood up and snagged the second shower head from the wall and turned it on. Then she sprayed him down like he was a car.

Just as he was about to ask another question, she sprayed him in the face.

Lucian choked and sputtered and held his hands up to block the water from shooting into his mouth. He started laughing so hard that he forgot what a dangerous game this was.

The water cut off. "There it is," she shot back at him. "The look."

His brow cocked, and his smile took up his whole face. "What look?"

"The fun one," she said, waggling her finger at him. "The carefree one. Where's that Lucian been?"

Right here, waiting my whole life for you. "You didn't want fun Lucian. You wanted stern Lucian as your Dom. The perfectionist."

Tessa's gaze latched onto his mouth. He realized too late what had happened.

"Your teeth." She cleared her throat. "I... I don't think I've ever realized how large your canines are."

Fuuuuuck. He kept them retracted all the time around her, but tonight he'd been completely careless.

No. He'd been *carefree*. That's why he laughed. That's why he was in this shower. Maybe he was subconsciously trying to sabotage what they had or passively give her clues on what he was. Who the hell knows. Sometimes Lucian didn't understand himself.

Time to redirect things. He gripped his hard cock and stroked it, bringing her attention lower. "Yeah, well, it's never been about me when we meet. I serve you. Please you. Give you what you think you need. My dental records weren't really on the list of requirements from you. Just my musical talents, tongue, and cock."

She didn't back down from him, even after he pressed against her and toyed with her hard nipples.

"Well," she said in a shaky tone. "I'm realizing I may have

been a little selfish about that."

"No." He dipped his head and pulled one of her nipples into his mouth, careful not to graze her with his fangs. "You've not been selfish, Tessa. Knowing what you want, and asking for it, isn't being selfish. It's being true. And I knew exactly what my role was for you."

"Your role," she whispered as her hand dove into his wet hair and held him while he suckled. "Is that what you still are? A role to fill in my fantasy?" Before he could answer, she sighed, "I don't even care. I just want…"

He lifted his gaze and tugged her nipple hard with his teeth, making her cry out. Then he popped it free and arched his brow. "You want… what?"

"This. You. Whatever we… whatever this is."

Lucian lifted her up by the ass, and she wrapped her legs around his waist. Carrying her back out to his bedroom, they kissed the entire way, and it was as rapacious as it was intoxicating. He laid her on his bed, going down with her. "I've never met anyone like you."

"Good." She spread her legs wider to accommodate him. "Maybe I'll be unforgettable to you."

Her words hit him like a bullet to the heart.

CHAPTER 14

The air in Tessa's lungs turned to fire. She burned for Lucian in a dangerous, self-destructive, burn the world way. His hungry hands sailed down her body as he kissed her neck, sending sparks of unholy energy zipping along her skin. Her goddamn pussy throbbed.

With a wicked grin, Lucian flipped her onto her stomach and slapped her ass hard enough to make the breath she held fly out in a cry.

"That's for the sloppy elbow in the second set." He rubbed the sting away before slapping her other ass cheek twice. "Those are the for weak forms in the third song."

Tessa bit her lip as her eyes fluttered shut. Her pussy felt swollen and wetter now. *Holy shit.*

Lucian read her like a book. Was she a perfect dancer? Hell no. But this man's ability to distinguish deliberate mistakes from unconscious ones was astounding.

"Ass up, Tessa." He jerked her waist, making her rise on hands and knees. She tilted back, arching for his punishment. Silently begging for it. "Your pace slowed at the end of the first song."

Smack!

Her body coiled with desire. Heat lit her veins, making her blood turn to liquid fire.

"It was *Storm*," she gasped, half-lusty already. "That was an impossible song to jump into without a misstep."

"Impossible for others." He spanked her again. "Not you."

Two more cracks along her ass cheeks and she was undone. *More, more, more. Please!* "I didn't think you'd notice."

"You think I can't catch mistakes like that?"

Tessa clutched the bedding, unable to give him an answer. She knew Lucian studied her every time she danced. As if she was the only creature in the entire world, and made just for his enjoyment, Lucian watched her like a hawk. Always.

Out of every audience she ever danced in front of—from judge to artist to five-year-old—Lucian's was the only opinion she cared about when it came to her form and delivery.

I'd dance for you until I dropped, she thought, while he spanked her again for her trip up in the fifth song. *I'd dance for you until I died.* Tears sprung to her eyes that had nothing to do with his spankings. His corrections she loved. Needed. Lived for.

No, her tears were because there would be no dancing in prison.

Tessa buried her face in his bedding and refused to think about that shit right now. She let his scent fill her up and pull her back into the scene. Her body arched for more of his punishment, knowing the reward would hurt even more...

She screamed into the comforter when Lucian spread her cheeks and licked her from pussy to ass. Her toes curled when he did it three more times. Spreading her wide, Lucian destroyed her with the licks of his tongue, the heat of his body, the dig of his fingers, the brush of his wet hair, and graze of his teeth. She was too sensitive for this. And needed it badly. Unabashed, Tessa rocked back to grind against his face.

Lucian smacked her ass again. "Don't. Move."

Tessa melted into the bedding as he feasted on her. Sweat bloomed down her back. When he dipped his fingers into her, he worked both her holes at the same time.

"I'm fucking you in both places," he warned her. "Say yes."

"Yes," she squeaked. And dropped the *Sir*. They were beyond that now.

"I'm keeping you for tonight, Tessa. Say yes."

Only tonight? She squashed her outrage, knowing this was all they'd get. Even if they wanted otherwise. Lucian hooked his finger inside her pussy, dragging it down her inner walls. *Oh, hells yes. Yes,*

yes. "Yes."

"I want to mark you." He crawled up her backside and pressed light kisses on her back. "Say yes."

"Yes."

She hissed into the mattress when Lucian bit her shoulder. It hurt so damn good she nearly came on the spot. She loved him like this. Loved when he listed all the glorious things he wanted to do to her. She could say "No" to any of them, but never did. Who would?

Lucian worked her up with his music, primed her with his punishment, and now came the rewards for being his good little prima.

Nudging her thighs open wider, he slipped his hand under her pelvis. "Lift."

She was poised to possess. Face down. Ass up.

Lucian pressed the tip of his cock to her entrance. She braced herself as he rubbed her wetness along his head. Pushing into her pussy with slow strokes, going deeper and deeper, inch by thick, hot, glorious inch, felt like a special kind of torture.

Pressed to her back, Lucian laced their fingers together and drove her to madness with his slow, deliberate, diabolical movements. She was surrounded by him—his heat, his scent, his touch, his voice. Between the sheets he laid in every night, to the hard body looming behind her, thrusting harder and harder, and the sting from his bite still lingering on her shoulder, Tessa unraveled with lightning speed.

He swerved his hips, hitting a deep spot that made her breath hitch. Heat built in her belly. Her pussy was so wet and swollen, she was sure her lust could drip down her legs.

"Such a good girl," Lucian purred in her ear. "So tight and needy, aren't you?"

"Yes." Her fingers clutched the bedding harder.

Lucian reached around and rubbed her clit as he fucked her, adding just enough pressure and friction to make her fly apart.

The orgasm was an out-of-body experience. She screamed and bucked and clawed at everything within reach. He held her ass steady with one hand, his other still mercilessly rubbing her clit. She met his thrusts with a push of her hips. Her pussy clamped down on him while she came, pulsing and milking him.

"Fuck, Tessa. Yeah... that's it." Lucian quickened his pace.

"Come again for me. I love seeing your cream on my cock."

That filthy mouth of his was the perfect accompaniment to his massive cock inside her. "Come on, prima. Give me all you got." Leaving her clit, he pushed a finger into her ass and timed his thrusts beautifully. "Touch your body with me," he instructed.

She balanced and reached between her legs to rub herself while he filled her. Much like the songs he played, this pleasure mounted and transitioned into more and more. And just like he mastered the violin, he mastered her. Plucked, stroked, and played her until Tessa sang the notes he wanted from her throat.

It had been so long since she came, Tessa was overwhelmed with the sensations he forced upon her. It was head-spinning. Earth shattering. At some point, he flipped her over and took her every which way he could. Before long, she could barely hold herself up. Her pussy ached. She was dying of thirst. It was as if her body just made up for five months of lost orgasms in one session.

Lucian kissed every inch of her body. He left nothing unworshipped. Just when she thought she'd have to beg him to stop, he paused and looked up at her from between her thighs. "I want to bite you."

Hadn't he already? Tessa blinked slowly, completely blissed out. "Yes."

Yes, to everything. Yes, to anything. *Yes.*

He was giving her all the things she wanted and all that she fantasized about. They always had mind-blowing sex, but this time it was different. Instead of it being about her, he was asking for things himself. But they were still all about her.

Was this fair?

She didn't have the capacity to worry over it.

Lucian groaned against her inner thigh and kissed it. "Fuck, Tessa." He pushed up and sauntered into the bathroom, only to come out a blink later with a glass of water. "Drink."

She honestly couldn't even hold the glass. He pressed the cup to her lips and tipped it for her. "Keep going, that's it." She drank because she was thirsty and chugged because he was encouraging her to. It would make him happy. Lucian, she knew, loved taking care of her. Honestly, after they had a long session, she'd sometimes wonder if he tried to push her to the max just so he could spend longer on the aftercare.

Tessa drained the glass and fell back onto the pillows. Her bones were rubber.

"Better?"

"Yes." Her eyelids felt heavy, yet her lust was already cranking her body back up. God, he smelled incredible. No man's scent ever stirred her blood like Lucian's could. That cologne, soap, dryer sheet or whatever the hell it was he used smelled so divine she wanted to drown herself in it.

Lucian gently rolled her over onto her belly. She knew what was coming. Bit her lip and braced for it.

"Relax," he said in her ear. Then he trailed hot kisses down her spine and grabbed her narrow hips with both of his big hands. "Lift."

She was wet clay — pliable, moldable. Tessa groaned when she felt his finger slip back into her ass. It was slippery as he pumped it slowly in and out. It took no time at all for her to say, "More."

He chuckled deep in his chest. The sound vibrated to her core. "I love how eager you are, Tessa. How trusting you are with giving me your body." He nipped the back of her shoulder. "Thank you for that."

She started panting when he slipped a second digit in, working her open. A few more strokes later, her heart began hammering. He positioned himself behind her and pressed the head of his cock to her tightest hole. She let out a slow exhale as he pushed inside. "Relax," he said in a sinfully deep tone. "Let me in."

Let him in, her mind demanded. *Tell him. TELL. HIM.*

It took a few careful thrusts, but Lucian finally bottomed out and her thoughts scrambled from the mix of pain and pleasure. He rubbed her clit while he fucked her ass. It didn't take long before she started clawing the bed again, rocking into him, begging him to go harder.

"God, Tessa. I wish you could see this. Watch my cock thrust inside you. The way your body welcomes mine. My dick was built for your body." His pace quickened, his breath punching out of his lungs.

"Fill me up," she gasped from the onslaught of another orgasm building. "Fill me up and watch your cum drip out of me."

"Fuuuuck." Lucian's grip tightened.

The slap of skin-on-skin drove her wild. Rubbing her clit

faster, faster, faster, there was no stopping the orgasm from blasting her apart. They both detonated together. She felt his cock jerk and pulse as he came. When he pulled out slowly, she looked over her shoulder to see his expression while giving him the best view money couldn't buy.

He groaned once his gaze locked onto her ass. It was stretched from his cock and felt tingly. "Fuuuuck. You kill me, woman."

She giggled because if she didn't, she'd have cried. Tessa was going to miss him.

With swift, graceful movements, he lifted her into his arms and carried her back into the bathroom. She sighed into his chest, allowing him to take care of her, but first she wanted to check in, "You okay?"

"Yeah," his voice sounded gruff and strained. "You?"

"Mmm hmm."

"You were incredible, prima. Do you know how strong you are? How talented and hypnotic you are?"

She didn't respond, her eyes already drifting shut. Tessa vaguely heard the faucet running. Hardly felt the water on her skin when he submerged her in the tub. Barely noticed Lucian climb into the bath with her. The man peppered her with kisses and whispered a thousand sweet things against her skin.

Tessa was too gone to hear any of it. She was dropping. And with the crash, her tears, fears, and regrets ate her alive.

CHAPTER 15

Lucian was the luckiest son-of-a-bitch in the whole wide world. He also had the world's biggest hard-on. For the love of all things unholy, he was dying to bury himself in Tessa's wet heat until he exploded again. But that was going to have to wait. Her drop was a little too off-kilter, even for her. Lucian knew how to handle her aftercare. He was a master at it. But this time was different.

Wayyyy different.

His needs immediately went on the back burner, and guilt nipped his ass when he rehashed things in his head while tucking her into his bed. Tessa was completely passed out. She cried so hard in the tub, she'd exhausted herself to sleep.

Her tears weren't the normal ones. They were drenched in terror. And it wasn't from something he did. No, this was from something else. If only she'd just tell him, damnit.

"What's happened?" he whispered as he stroked her cheek. "Tell me so I can help you."

Tessa's brow pinched as she whimpered in her sleep. If he was a dream-walker, he could dive into her head and manipulate her dreams to decode her issues. But that was a violation he wasn't willing to make, even if he had that particular skill. No, he needed Tessa to trust him enough to tell him herself. He wouldn't rip it out of her subconscious or force her to tell him.

His ballerina was a complex creature. Tessa sabotaged and punished herself — took the blame for that accident which ultimately wrecked her career, too. That night had been her birthday. She probably carried the guilt of having gone out to celebrate and carried the weight of her friend's death on her shoulders, always. Tessa's heart was too big for her soul to keep safe. Lucian didn't mention knowing that little bit of information earlier. There was no reason to bring it up. That accident wasn't her fault, if only she'd accept it.

What other burdens did she carry that he didn't know about?

A soft knock on his door made him growl. Quietly, so he wouldn't disturb her, Lucian went over and cracked the door open. Peeking out—because he'd be damned if anyone was coming into his room with her lust permeating the air in here, and her lying naked in his bed—Lucian glowered at Reys. "What?"

"The King wishes to see you."

Damnit. "I'll be out in a minute."

"*Now.*"

Lucian swung the door open with a snarl. "Fine." He'd go naked then.

Reys cursed under his breath. "Get dressed, man."

Lucian's jaw clenched. He turned back and shut the door as quietly as possible with his temper raging for a fight now. He snagged a pair of jeans from his closet and stuffed his legs into them. Swinging open the door, he said, "Stand guard on *this* side of the hallway." He pointed right where Reys was already standing. "Don't let anyone or anything disturb her until I get back."

Vampires couldn't be trusted when a human like Tessa was in their territory—she was unclaimed, not turned, and unmated. That put her in a certain amount of danger here at the mansion. If Lucian wasn't with her at all times, another male might try to seduce her. Hell, so could a female.

Vampires were lusty creatures. As part of their constant longing, their cravings for touch and sexual conquests sometimes outweighed their morals. Most held it together, but not all. That's why they had The Wicked Garden—a kink club in the Garden District designed to give vampires something to cling to. Feed on. One orgasm was one more fix... one vein tap was one more thrill... one more moment of bliss in an otherwise dreadful, agonizing life sentence while they lived an eternity, a special kind of Hell.

So yeah, he needed to keep Tessa guarded. She was forbidden

fruit in the devil's playground.

Reys was a trustworthy vampire. If Lucian said, "No touching," Reys would keep his hands, mouth, and cock to himself. Victoria? Ehhh, she was iffy. Depended on her mood. Xin? Mmm, he'd rather not even ask.

The trek up to Malachi's quarters took forever. It felt miles and miles away, practically on another planet. In a different solar system.

Every step away from Tessa hurt more, felt heavier. Lucian's fangs ached. As bad as he wanted to bite her earlier, he couldn't do it. It wasn't right. Not without her knowing more about him first. But damn how he wanted to sink his teeth into her sweet skin, draw from her vein, suck her down and fill his body with—

Clenching his fists and drawing in slow, even breaths, he tried to snap out of his foolishness. No biting. Nope. None of that. Not unless she was his forever.

Holy Hell, Lucian couldn't shake the instinct to keep her. He knew damn well Malachi was going to tell him to get rid of her. Tessa's visit here was as temporary as an orgasm. Swift, earth-shattering, and addictive. But she couldn't stay, and Lucian knew it. Not without turning her, which wasn't on the table yet. Malachi had cut him a little break this time, because Lucian hadn't been in his right head lately.

Being a vampire sucked. No pun intended. How was anyone expected to live with this curse of longing and not cling to any smidgen of happiness that crossed their path?

Tessa was a corkscrew in his heart—digging down and winding her way deeper into him.

Fuck it, I'll break the rules. It wouldn't be the first time, or the last. Whatever punishment Malachi doled out when Lucian got caught was fine. Hell, it was worth it already. Tessa was worth any sacrifice.

I can do my job and love a human at the same time. No problem. Hadn't he been doing exactly that for nearly two years anyway? He just hadn't realized it until now. The possibility of losing her, the breach in contract, the suspicion that she was with someone else and the notion that Tessa might leave and never return was like a loaded gun blasting him in the heart until the chamber emptied and Lucian bled out.

He made a mental checklist: Bump up security at her apartment building. Set up a different communication system. Come up with a reason why she wasn't coming back to the House of Death ever again. He could meet her at... Where? More hotels? More theatres? The *diner*?

If they went back to her place, there was a chance he'd be tailed, eventually. If not by a *Savag-Ri*, then by one of his own House. Then they'd get caught and Malachi would force someone to erase all her memories instead of just those of the past forty-eight hours.

Break it off. Save her, spare her. Shut this down and let her go. Lucian braced himself against the wall in the hallway and sucked in a ragged breath. That was the best thing for her. The right thing to do. Lucian needed to break it off and set her loose.

But vampires had a lot of gray area in their morals.

Keep her. Love her. Spoil her.

Shit, he deserved love too, didn't he? Life was more than fighting, hunting, and plucking violin strings. His life was worth more than being a guard. He was a hot-blooded male with needs and a heart that beat only for Tessa.

How had he gone this long being so stupid? *Because in the end, the bottom line is, she's not the one for me. She's just the one for me, for now.*

Was he okay with that? More importantly, would Tessa be okay with that?

If Lucian was going to risk their lives to be with her for however long she let him, he needed to tell her the truth about everything. They had to decide their future with all cards showing on the table. No more secrets. No more hiding.

And that went for them both.

Running his fingers through his hair, Lucian stormed down the hall and entered the king's private quarters. As always, Malachi sat in his big chair, staring into an elaborate mirror. The Mad King rarely left this room except to take a piss or if a major emergency came up. He entrusted Lucian to handle matters of the House on his behalf, alongside Dorian and several others.

That saying, "It takes a village to raise a child"? Yeah, well try "It takes a House to keep a King." Malachi wasn't called the Mad King for nothing. The vampire was old, strong, and half off his rocker. He spent so much time fixating on the mirror before him, Lucian sometimes wondered if he was truly insane or just that dedicated to someone who didn't exist. Which, okay, could also mean he was insane.

Christ, his head hurt. "You wished to see me, your Majesty?"

"You're needed in the Kill Box."

What the hell? Was Dorian not working tonight? As the Reaper for the House of Death, Dorian handled all executions. Lucian was only back up for kill jobs in the chamber. "No problem." Whatever needed to be done, Lucian was on it. The sooner he finished House business, the sooner he could get back to Tessa. "I'll leave immediately."

Malachi leaned in. "You still have that little dancer with you?"

"Yeah." Lucian approached his king slowly. "Why?"

"She cannot stay."

"I'm aware."

"No, Lucian. I mean, she must be gone."

"I'll take her home soon." His heart plummeted. It was a special request for her to be allowed to stay the night. No humans, other than those discovered as someone's *alakhai*, were allowed in the House of Death. The king gave him permission to have one night with her in his space. But it came at a cost. Lucian was semi-hoping Malachi might have lost track of time. Talk about wishful thinking. The king never lost track of anything. *Ever.*

"I'm not ready to wipe her mind," Lucian blurted. "I don't want to."

"You know the rules," his king warned. "It's not negotiable."

"She's trustworthy." The instant he said it, Lucian knew he was in trouble.

Malachi was on him in a flash. A true flash. In his chair one second, across the room with Lucian's face smashed against the wall the next. "You jeopardize all of us for a piece of cunt."

"I know," he gritted out. To argue with him was futile. It didn't matter if Lucian thought Tessa was everything. To the rest of his kind, she was a human. A wet, warm hole. A meal.

"My leniency with you wears thin."

"I know."

"Be the vampire I need." Malachi gripped a handful of Lucian's hair and yanked it by the roots. "Understand me?"

"Yes, sire." Lucian stumbled when Malachi let him go. But he wasn't ready to give up so easily. "I want to keep her," he confessed.

"You're confused. She's not a pet. Nor is she a courtesan," Malachi flashed back to his seat and leaned forward, staring at Lucian through the mirror's reflection. "Unless you're saying she'll be the House's property?"

Lucian's blood boiled. "Absolutely not."

This wasn't the House of Blood where they kept humans and weaker vampires for food. He'd be damned if he allowed anyone to take one drop from her vein. Jesus, not even he had fed from her. No way was he going to let another creature touch her, let alone taste her. Lucian's body locked with a wild surge of aggression.

"There," Malachi growled, jabbing his finger at Lucian's reflection. "That's going to put you in an early grave."

Lucian's jaw clenched as he glared at his king. Malachi was right.

"She's a weakness to you, Lucian. If she's discovered by the *Savag-Ri...*"

"I know." He dropped into a chair and buried his head in his hands. "I know, Malachi."

"Then do something about it before it's too late."

"I've been careful," he argued. Lucian had gone to great lengths to keep Tessa at a distance. They only met in vampire owned places. They were never seen together in public. He had drivers pick her up and drop her off at her apartment. No paper trails. Little risk. Besides, Lucian had done his homework on Tessa before ever meeting up with her in person for their first session. She was clean—no *Savag-Ri* in her family. The woman didn't have friends. Her boss was clean. There was nothing to worry about on her end. "Please... just a little longer."

"No."

Lucian desperately wanted to push back about this but knew better. In the end, the king was right. He was always right.

"I've given you time to grieve your losses, Lucian, and I've made a horrendous exception to our House rules this one and only time for you, but you *must* stop this foolishness. Now."

"Is it foolish if it's love?"

Malachi leaned back with a vicious, rattling exhale. "It's

worse than foolish then. It's hopeless."

"I love her, Malachi."

"Then you must protect her at all costs," the king growled. "Even from you."

CHAPTER 16

Tessa rolled onto her back and sighed. Lucian's room was better than any hotel suite he'd ever taken her to. Inhaling, she filled her lungs with the scent off his pillows. Everything about this room screamed luxury. From the deep blue damask curtains closed over the tall windows, to the fine threaded black bedding and the four-poster carved antique bed, to the vintage dressers, tiffany lamps and leather wingback chair. Jeez, his room was nearly the size of her entire apartment. Why hadn't Lucian brought her here before? He was secretive about his life. Cautious about everything. Why?

Because he does bad things. He's a danger to society.

Tessa shook off those thoughts because they didn't feel right in her mind.

Where was he right now?

As if on cue, she heard a thud from inside the walk-in closet. Wrapping a sheet around herself, Tessa slid out of the bed and towards that sound. Why she felt the need to cover herself was silly, considering the amount of sex they had, but she felt exposed and too vulnerable to strut around in nothing but a smile.

Maybe it was the drop. Maybe it was guilt. Maybe it was the sudden chill in the air and the ache in her heart. Regardless, she wanted to be covered up.

"What's going on?" Her brow pinched together when she saw Lucian getting dressed in a hurry.

"I'll be back soon," his voice was clipped. Cold.

"Where are you going?"

"I have to take care of something."

Why was he being so short with her? Had she done something wrong? Dread threaded through her veins. Oh no, had she spoken in her sleep? Talked about Alex and Colton? Lucian once told her she chatted in her sleep. He said it was adorable. She called it embarrassing. Now she'd argue it was disastrous.

"Are you upset with me?" Tessa tugged the sheet around her shoulders and held it tighter.

Lucian shot her a confused look. "What? No!" He dropped his boots and stormed over to her, wrapping her in a big hug. "God no. Why would you think that?" He kissed the top of her head, then cupped her face, running his thumb along her jawline.

"I thought maybe..." She blew out a breath. "I thought I'd displeased you."

"I don't think that's even possible, Tessa."

She'd beg to differ.

"You amaze me. Always." He pressed a soft kiss to her lips. "I'm just in a weird headspace, okay? And I need to run out real quick." Lucian's gaze hardened. She had no idea what to call the expression on his face now. Worrisome? Apologetic? Frustrated?

It made guilt bubble up and fill her belly. *Tell him.*

Nope. She would figure a way out of this clusterfuck by herself. She was used to being on her own. Her survival instincts dictated she handle shit by herself. It was as much a trauma response as it was a way of life for her. So no, she wasn't telling Lucian anything. Yet.

"Do you trust me, Tessa?"

"Yes." *Mostly.*

Great. There was a darkness shadowing his gaze now. Lucian's expression morphed into something else. He was guarded.

Well, so was she.

He scrubbed his face hard with both hands and sighed heavily. He didn't look at her when he said, "I'll take you home once I return from this errand."

"I'll just go home now. I can take an Uber, it's not a big deal, Lucian." But yes, it was. She had a horrible feeling that once she left here, she'd never come back. Lucian's shortness with her, his hot/cold attitude in this closet, the way his expression kept changing, and the half-lies she was telling him all added up to one thing: Lucian and Tessa were over.

Maybe not right now, but soon. Very soon. As soon as Alex and Colton came back demanding Tessa give them what they wanted, it was definitely going to be over.

"There it is again." He got all in her face. "What? What is that?"

She pulled back and looked away. "Stop." If he quit reading her so well, she'd get through this with a little dignity.

"Get dressed," he ordered.

How could they go from bliss to blow up so fast? Because they were both hiding things from the other and their defenses were up. Tessa wasn't sure who she was madder at, herself or…

Tell him.

Not. On. Her. Life. Because that's what was on the line right now. Lucian could most likely handle himself in a fight against those guys, and since they haven't tried to come after him directly, Tessa figured Lucian wasn't on the execution block with Alex and Colton like *she* was. And Tessa didn't have a chance of survival if things went sideways.

So why not just tell Lucian everything?

Because she didn't want to be the ultimate disappointment. He made her feel good and special and perfect. He looked at her with adoration and lust and pride. Even with his cold-shoulder right now, he still couldn't meet her gaze without some level of warmth. If she told him, the only good thing she ever had — the only relationship that meant something to her — would be ruined forever.

Better to go to prison or her grave with this secret than ruin the best part of her life.

No way was she going to spill the beans and tell Lucian exactly what happened. At the very least, he'd kick her out of his life for even considering working with those guys — regardless of the blackmail — and at best he would try to keep her protected and might get killed doing it.

Fuck that noise. She might not be able to protect him, but she sure as shit could make him safer by keeping him in the dark about this and handling it by herself.

Wow, her moral dilemmas were giving her whiplash.

Tears stung her eyes, and she refused to let them fall. Time to get dressed and be done with this part of the scene. The fantasy was over. The sheet draped around her now felt like sandpaper. Dropping the cotton threads, she let it pool around her feet and turned to march over and grab her clothes.

Lucian jerked her back and crushed his mouth to hers. It was possessive. Demanding.

Confusing.

Tessa shoved him backwards. "I don't understand you, Lucian."

"That makes two of us," he huffed and snatched his boots from the floor next. It was like he was Dr. Jekyll and Mr. Hyde. One second, he couldn't keep his hands off her, the next, he was purposefully evading her.

"You act like you want me to stay one second, and in the next, you want me gone." Forget waiting for him to make up his mind. She was leaving with or without his approval.

"I just want you dressed because the thought of you naked in my room will fuck with my head and I won't be able to concentrate on my job."

Tessa paused mid-way across the room. Her hands balled into fists. "That's a little dramatic, even for you."

"Not everyone here is a gentleman, Tessa." She shivered and her nipples hardened when he was suddenly behind her, kissing the back of her neck. Holy Hell, she didn't hear him approach at all. How had he gotten to her so fast? Did it matter? His fingers grazed her exposed belly. His voice dropped to a lower register when he asked, "Do you trust me?"

"Yes," she whispered. Damnit it all the Hell, she shouldn't trust him at all.

"I'm going to lock you in here until I return, okay?"

Wait. What? "Why?"

Lucian smothered her with his body, robbing the oxygen from the room. "Because I want you safe."

"I'm not safe in your house?"

"This isn't my house. This is my *room*. There's a difference."

Fear crawled along her skin. Lucian was dangerous. His roommates were dangerous. Everything around her was fucking dangerous.

If she went home, she'd be a sitting duck. Were Alex and Colton already at her apartment waiting for her? Had they called her cell and were now furious because she hadn't answered? Did they know she left it at home because she was too scared to bring it just in case they tracked her on it?

Her loyalty, Tessa realized, wasn't even to herself. It was to Lucian. Even though she agreed to give those men what they wanted, she never intended to go through with it. It was a stall tactic. A last-ditch effort to self-sabotage. Now look. Even if... shit, she was in the worst spot imaginable. No more *even ifs*. She was trapped, no matter what. Staying in Lucian's room, locked up tight, suddenly seemed like the safest place to be. Better the devil she knew than blah, blah, blah.

The floor began to sway under her feet.

"Damnit." Lucian pressed his body into her, his forehead coming down on hers as his eyes blazed with concern. "You don't trust me enough to tell me what the hell is up with you." His tone wasn't pissed. It was torn. "It's killing me."

Tessa shivered under his scrutiny. It wasn't about trust anymore. Not telling him wasn't killing him. It was *sparing* him. She kept her mouth shut.

"When I return," he warned, "we're going to have a talk." Lucian marched over to his dresser and yanked the top drawer open. "Get. Dressed." He snagged something out of the drawer and slammed it shut. Keeping his back to her, he braced his arms on the dresser top and glared at her through the reflection in the mirror mounted above it. "Now, Tessa. I can't leave until you do."

Can't or won't? She almost wanted to challenge him but was afraid to. He looked furious. Murderous. Tessa's gaze drifted down his back, along the slope of his narrow waist, his fine ass, thick thighs, and heavy boots. He was built to kill.

"Prima," he groaned. "*Please.*"

She loved it when he called her prima. It was a reminder of how far she'd fallen. How high she once climbed. How temporary happiness truly was. It suddenly felt like the walls of his spacious bedroom were closing in on her, and for once, she welcomed the cage.

Steeling herself, Tessa stalked over to the pile of her clothes and got dressed. Sitting on the edge of his bed, reeling with self-disgust for allowing Lucian to push her around like this, Tessa grew furious for liking it so much.

He crouched down between her legs and rubbed his hot hands up and down her thighs. "Thank you," he whispered.

She clenched her teeth, refusing to respond. He pressed a kiss to her forehead one more time before heading towards the door. Without saying goodbye, he left, and her heart dropped when she heard the door lock. He actually did it. He locked her in his room like a hostage.

Or a pet.

Tessa let out a half-sob, half-sigh. This was her fault. She was in this position because she could never tell Lucian no. Tessa should have told him *No* about meeting at the diner. She should have said *No* when he asked her to stay. She should have said *No* about a lot of things. Not just to Lucian, but to Alex and Colton and….

Fuck.

Tessa stood and locked gazes on the wall to her left, surveying the structure as if she could bolt through the wall like the Kool Aid man and make a run for it. She padded barefoot across the room and paced at the foot of the bed like a caged tigress. Glancing at the door every now and then, her curiosity eventually outshined her restlessness. It was time she found out as much as she could about her lover. Tessa might be too afraid to play the tit-for-tat game with him—because that meant she would have to tell him things about herself he might not like and then he'd leave her—but she wasn't afraid to snoop.

Running her fingers over the top of his dresser, she opened every drawer starting from the bottom up. Rope was in the bottom drawer. Lots of it in a variety of colors. Her mouth watered from the ideas of what these ropes might be used for. Swallowing hard, she fingered the red one, imagining Lucian all knotted up and bound… or knotting her up and binding her. He never used Shibari techniques on her. Why?

Jealousy reared its ugly head. Had he used these on someone else? Now she wanted to set them all on fire. Slamming the drawer shut, she moved up to the next one. Candles. The entire drawer was nothing but taper candles. Tessa bit her lip. His room was filled with candelabras. These must be replacements.

Weird, right? A guy filling his room with candles instead of just using the lights. Unless… she growled with another shot of jealousy. Tessa slammed the drawer shut and clutched the handles to the third one. Yanking it open, she was almost disappointed to see it filled with undershirts and boxers. In fact, it seemed so normal that she re-opened the bottom drawer again. Yup, the rope was still there.

Shutting both drawers, she moved to the second from the top. Nothing but black folders. Strange. Why would he keep a filing system in a dresser drawer? Pulling one out, she almost opened it, but her heart slammed into her chest from guilt. She was prying too much. These were his private things. How would she feel if he went rooting through her stuff without permission or her knowledge? Consent was a big thing between them. Boy, was she a hypocrite, right?

Regardless, Tessa backed away. Whatever was in the top drawer, and those files, she had no business knowing what it was.

Turning around, she walked over to one of his windows and slid the curtain open to peer outside. The sun was bright today, not a cloud in the sky. It bathed the backyard, which looked like it had seen better days. Vines choked most of the garden and statues. There were three people drinking wine on the patio, laughing and chatting. Tessa wondered how many people lived here.

What kind of roommates did Lucian have? Clearly untrustworthy ones, if he didn't want her around any of them. Why would he live with people he didn't trust? Last night, when she danced for everyone, their gazes were hungry. There was no other word for the way they looked at her. If Lucian didn't want them around her, why did he flaunt her in front of them like that?

One of them on the patio looked up at her and waved. Tessa quickly backed away from the window with a gasp.

Damnit, this was stupid. Chewing on her bottom lip, she walked over and grabbed the red pointe shoes Lucian gave her. Toying with the ribbon, she itched to put them on and dance in Lucian's room. What else could she do while she waited? Her options were snooping, sleeping, pacing, or dancing. Overthinking everything went without question. She was already doing that, might as well put her racing thoughts to music.

Going over to the sound system in the corner of the room, she stopped and frowned. The Bluetooth speaker would only work if she had her cell to hook it up to. She didn't have hers. Damnit.

Lucian's room was Hell.

Pure. Fucking. Hell.

Blowing out a frustrated breath, Tessa meandered into his closet next. Suits, tuxedos, dress shirts, leather pants, sweaters, robes—it was a variety of luxury she never had in life. His shirts were arranged by color. Pants too. He had three tuxedos and a seersucker, which looked completely out of place considering everything else was dark colors. His shoes were lined on racks. From top to bottom, he had shiny dress shoes and boots, several pairs of running shoes, two pairs of flip-flops and on the very bottom were three pairs of leather boots that were all the same.

What was Lucian? A businessman by day, biker at night, and surfer on the weekends? This man was a clusterfuck. But he sure did smell good. The corners of Tessa's mouth lifted into a smile as she pulled out a hoodie and inhaled Lucian's scent. If someone could bottle this fragrance up, they would make bank. Tessa's ovaries exploded with one whiff.

On the floor in the back of the closet was a black chest. Debating on flipping it open, Tessa ran her hand along the old leather straps across the top and dropped to her knees. Should she peek inside? No.

But she did anyway.

The lid creaked and was heavier than she expected. Propping it against the back wall, Tessa had to move several of Lucian's dress shirts out of the way to ensure it didn't slam close on her. Peering inside, she frowned.

"Okay," she whispered slowly, with relief. Tessa had no clue what she expected to find hidden in this thing, but music sheets were not it. Pulling out a stack, she smiled. There was a lot of sheet music in here. Some of the paper was so old, it was brown and worn along the edges. She fingered through a stack of the older looking pieces.

Wait.

Tessa's breath caught. On the bottom of the first page of *Violin Concerto in A Minor* was a signature. "No way." This was signed by *Bach*? Tessa carefully put it back in the box, scared to death that her fingers were too dirty to touch it. Why the hell would Lucian have something so priceless shoved at the bottom of a box in his closet?

Her gaze darted along the other papers. Scribbles littered the margins. Some even had scroll marks across the notes themselves.

The language was different, but the penmanship was the same on each one. Dates ranged from the early 1500s to 2000s. *Huh?* She rummaged through some of the newer looking sheets of music and her heart jerked to a stop.

January 14, 1902
I hate it here. Malachi's mind is fraying, and the Houses are at war again. The streets stink of piss and rats ate through the Vivaldi collection my parents gave me. Gin is hard to find. I hate rum. Blood's too tainted around here and I'm hungry.

Tessa's brow pinched. She grabbed another piece of paper and read it.

May 3, 1911
Seven bodies found at the river. Dorian's on a roll. We celebrated at the Inn, but I'm sick of the women here. No one cares about anything but themselves. Malachi too. He sits and stares and the longer I watch him, the more I resent my choice to stay. I hate this place. I'm a prisoner. I'm starving. I'm an animal.

She exhaled and flipped it over to find more writing on the back.

I don't know what today is, but I fed. I gorged. I feel thick with life. Even as I write, my teeth ache for more. I want to fuck. Feed. Roll in sweat and lust and give, give, give all I have until I'm a shell. Am I shell yet? It feels like I am.

Tessa's hands shook as she set that note down and picked up another.

July 17, 1937
She felt good. Best I've had in a while. I drained her. She drained me. And yet my teeth still ache, and my cock is still hard. But she felt good. That's different. I think I like different. I'll try again.

Another piece of sheet music…

October 4, 1945

Savag-Ri 19
House of Death 3
I'll try better.

Tessa's breaths quickened. She couldn't wrap her head around anything in this box. Were these heirlooms? If so, how were they all written in the same hand? With the same tone? She picked up another and gawked at the date.

August 7
Tessa is the air I breathe.

No year was attached to it. She rummaged through several other pieces of paper and sheet music and found that, at some point between 1967 and now, he stopped adding the year to his entries.

He stopped putting… as if this could all be Lucian? That was impossible. And yet, her gaze drifted along the sprawled-out papers, and she scrambled to find more of the recent entries.

September 27
She wore the blue one tonight. Looked like the sky draped over her body. She's getting to me, and it pisses me off. She makes me bleed for things my heart hasn't known of before now. She tastes as sinful as she looks. Will she be as decadent in red? I'm getting tickets tonight. I'll find out.

Tessa covered her mouth with her hand. That was the night Lucian took her to the opera house, just after they'd been to the theatre the night before. She still had both dresses hanging in her closet at home.

November 4
I almost didn't go. She's under my skin and I hate it. I'm hungry.

Another…

November 5
I went anyway. She didn't disappoint. Tessa never disappoints me. How can that be possible? She's an animal. A wounded one. I want to gobble her up, hold her, protect her, and break her.

Tessa's heart hammered in her throat.

December 19
This is getting dangerous. I'm backing off. She's a drug to me. The torment in her eyes quakes in her thighs when she wraps them around me. I feel it everywhere. My bones. My soul. On the tip of my tongue and shaft of my dick. Tessa is raw and real. I'm raw and regrettable. I want her to keep fucking with me. I like how it feels when I have her obedience. If I give her a cue, she takes it. Arabesque, Fouetté, Plié, blah, blah, blah. She eats it like it's life. I feed it to her like it's poison. She's toxic. Seeps into me. Destroys me. I like it. I hate how I can't wait to see her again. I hate that I can't stay away.

Savag-Ri 7 today. All mine. Thank you, Tessa.

She let the paper flutter to the floor. *What. Is. This?* Tessa gawked at the mess of papers on the floor. All those dates. All those confessions.

What the ever-loving Hell was Lucian?

Tessa quickly shoved everything back into the box and scrambled out of the closet. Those dates. That handwriting. Those entries. She couldn't grasp any of it. Not a single goddamn bit of it. In her attempt to learn more about him, it felt like she knew even less. Lucian was a complete stranger to her.

Talk about a plan backfiring.

She squeezed her eyes shut and dissected his words and actions. Lucian always looked at her like she was the most gorgeous, enthralling creature on the planet. But what he wrote? *Arabesque, Fouetté, Plié, blah, blah, blah. She eats it like it's life. I feed it to her like it's poison. She's toxic.*

Tears sprung in her eyes, hot and furious. Toxic, huh? Never mind all the other shit he said, all that nonsense about how she was the air he breathes and blah, blah, blah.

She's toxic. That's the bottom line. That's how Lucian felt about Tessa.

And whatever the *Savag-Ri* thing was, she somehow was part of the scorekeeping. *Savag-Ri 7 today. All mine. Thank you, Tessa.* What was that? Some kind of tally mark? A weird ass slang term for a new notch in his belt?

Now she wanted to know everything. Tearing apart his closet, she searched for more secrets. Found nothing. She went over to his bed and looked under it. Nothing but violin cases.

She tore the sheets off the bed. Tossed the pillows across the room. Knocked over a candelabra and snapped the taper candles in half. Her rage was awful. Unstoppable.

Toxic.

Running her hands through her hair, she stormed over to the dresser and wrenched open the drawer with the files again. Grabbing the first one her fingers touched, she flipped it open.

Name: Katie Green *Blood Type:* A+ *Birthdate:* 10-20-1999

An address, copy of her license, and list of emergency contacts were below.

"What is this?" She thumbed through the papers and braced against the dresser, swallowing the bile rising in her throat.

Sex Name: Lady Jane

Kinks: bondage, role play, submissive brat.

Fears: abandonment and asphyxiation

Host: Pain

Erased: Yes

Behind that was more stuff about the kinks and what "Lady Jane" wanted for visits one, two, and three.

Tessa gawked. Her cheeks burned. Fury boiled in her veins. There was also a list of Lady Jane's carefully planned out fantasies—like it was a wish list or something. On the top of the paper was the name *The Wicked Garden.*

She'd heard of that place. It was an elite kink club somewhere in New Orleans. One Tessa never found her way into. But Lucian had, apparently. And by the looks of this drawer, he'd been going for a long time. As an employee. A *Host.*

Pain. Was that his sex name? God, she was such an idiot. No wonder he was so good in bed. And his role as Dom was certainly well-educated enough. Because he had tons of practice.

Tessa trembled from his betrayal. Their contract stated they were exclusive, yet the date on this file was last month. She couldn't stand the idea of counting how many files were in that drawer. It no longer mattered anyway because this thing between her and Lucian was now *over.*

As if to go for the icing on the cake, Tessa ripped open the top drawer.

Holyyyy shhiiiiitttt. The entire drawer was filled with knives, handcuffs, guns, ammo, razor wire...

She stumbled back to get away from all of it. Alex and Colton were right. Lucian was dangerous.

Tessa had to get out of here.

CHAPTER 17

Lucian made it to the House of Death's execution chamber—aka the Kill Box—before he started sweating. His instincts screamed to not leave Tessa alone. He couldn't shake the feeling that something bad was about to happen. Blaming it on nerves and grief, he shook that shit off and stormed into the ancient stone room with tight, theatre seating. He scowled at Dorian.

The Reaper was drenched in sweat and blood, his shirt sleeves neatly folded up his forearms, suit jacket hanging on a hook next to the assortment of tools used to torture their prisoners. Three *Savag-Ri* were lined up and chained to bolts on the floor. Each swayed in various stages of pain.

Relaxing slightly, Lucian approached the three fuckheads. "What do we have here?"

Dorian's chest heaved with restraint. In moments like this, where the dim light hid him in shadows, his hands wrapped around weapons that did more damage than a chainsaw, and blood spattered over his freshly starched and ironed clothing, Dorian looked exactly like the monster he always claimed to be.

Lucian loved that about him. In his opinion, the vampire community needed more savages like Dorian. He was here to protect, by any means necessary. It's why he and Lucian got along so well. Lucian trained him on how to deal with vampires. Dorian showed him how to skin a *Savage-Ri* alive with only a butter knife.

"These three were part of the explosions." Dorian wiped his hands off with a small towel.

Lucian's lips curled back with a hiss. "Where'd you find them?"

"Victoria caught them on camera lurking on the other side of the road by The Wicked Garden and called me." Lucian's expression must have read, *Why didn't she call me? I'm the one in charge of hunts like this*, but then Dorian added, "I was told you were busy."

Yeah, he was. But not so busy he couldn't have hunted. Tessa would have waited for him. Just like she was now.

Dorian and Lucian stared at the three *Savag-Ri* like two cats with a box of mice. Only these mice were half beaten and bleeding out already. "Why haven't you killed them?"

It wasn't like the Reaper to waste time and he didn't play with his victims. He killed them and moved on.

"They have something to share with you." Dorian grabbed the middle guy by his hair and tipped his head back. Lucian gawked when his best friend pulled a long, thin rod out of the guy's ear. "Tell him what you told me."

"Fuck you, Reaper." The *Savag-Ri* spat blood onto the floor in a spray that misted Dorian's shoes.

Oh boy. That was going to cost the dipshit in five-four-three-two—

Dorian stabbed him in the eye with the steel rod making the *Savag-Ri* howl in pain. "I can go all night, you piece of shit. Think I don't know how many holes I can poke in a sack of fuckage like you before your body gives out?"

Lucian squatted down. Narrowing his gaze, he inspected the damage done so far to each prisoner. Then he stood up and kicked the middle one in the face. The tip of his boot hit the bastard square in the nose and blood spurted everywhere. "That's just a taste of what I'm going to do to you for using humans for your dirty work."

Fury roared to life in Lucian. The last bit of euphoria he felt from spending time with Tessa now fizzled and scorched with a renewed sense of purpose. What if one of those poor humans had been Tessa? What if she was strapped with dynamite and blown up just to... what? Lure in vampires? Make some noise?

What the French toast fuck were they thinking, blowing up an abandoned warehouse like that? Usually, when their nests were at risk of discovery, they burned them down, which was bad enough.

But explosions were a different level of danger. A lot more innocents could be hurt or killed.

Not that *Savag-Ri* cared. They used humans as part of their battle plans all the time. But strapping them with explosives? They could have just as easily rigged the building's rafters. So why would they use humans? The only answer Lucian could conjure was too gruesome to think about. It made him sick.

The asshole on the right of him laughed, his throat gurgling with blood from whatever injuries Dorian gave him already. "Those humans were just practice. You have no clue what's coming to you." He smiled with his mouth full of busted teeth. "And your mother, your sister, your father… and everyone else you hold dear, Lucian."

Hold up. Pump the brakes.

Lucian collared the fucker with his hand and squeezed his throat. "You aren't in a position to make threats like that," he hissed. "You're done."

"As are Esmerelda and Lizzy," the guy coughed.

Lucian controlled his expression and gave nothing away. Not the panic. Not the fear. Not the belief that this piece of shit might not be slinging empty threats. It would be wrong to underestimate a *Savag-Ri*. They stopped at nothing to get what they wanted, which was every vampire and Lycan dead.

Keeping his gaze locked on the prisoner laughing without an ounce of regret for what he did to those humans, Lucian pulled out his preferred weapon — an antique blade from the Mughal empire, a birthday gift given to him by a Housemate, Xin. He put that sucker to good use by carving a jagged line down the *Savag-Ri's* right eyebrow, through his eye, and down his cheek. He stopped at the jaw. Hmmm, something was missing. Lucian decided to score the bastard's face from left to right, cutting across the bridge of his nose and deep into his left eye. There, that was better.

Blood poured and dripped over them both. The *Savag-Ri* didn't utter a word. Shit, he didn't even flinch. But he did stop laughing.

Stepping back, Lucian had to breathe through his rage. He wanted to rip the guy's face off with his goddamn teeth. Eat his tongue out for even saying the names of his family members. Chew his fingers off, one by one, so he'd never hold a weapon again.

Instead, he started with the *Savag-Ri's* eyes, carving into his face the symbol of his people.

All *Savag-Ri* had a cross in their eyes, right through the iris. It's how the legend of vampires being afraid and deterred by crosses came about. It wasn't a religious thing at all. It was a genetic alteration. An infliction that has been around since the dawn of time.

"It's too late," the blinded bastard growled. "Taking me out won't save them."

"Make him shut up, Reaper."

Dorian slid his short-handled scythe across the bastard's neck, taking it nearly clean off. The *Savag-Ri* dropped back with a crunch and thud as blood spilled like a leaky pipe out of his freshly opened throat.

"Who wants to go next?" Lucian practically purred.

Reaper smiled. "One for you, one for me?"

"That works."

The last two *Savag-Ri* tried to beg, plead, and barter, but it was no use. Vampires didn't work with liars. They sure as shit didn't work with the hunters, bred and born to kill their kind. When it was all said and done, Lucian grabbed the hose and sprayed things down while Dorian stuffed the bodies into coffins they used for transport.

Pro-Tip: Have a hearse ready and a crisp suit in the back. No one pulled over a meat-wagon.

"I'll call the House of Bone and let them know a delivery is being made." Dorian grabbed another towel to wipe his hands off with.

Lucian didn't say anything for a few minutes while Dorian made the call. These bodies wouldn't be wasted. Vampires used the bones of the *Savag-Ri* they killed and spelled them before turning each to dust. That dust was then sprinkled on the doorways and windows. Hell, sometimes the entire perimeter of a property to keep *Savag-Ri* away. Those spells were conducted by weavers—special vampires with witch magic.

Using the bone dust was an easy way to keep *Savag-Ri* from crossing certain lines. Effective, but a pain in the ass. A good wind or heavy rain meant the entire place needed to be re-dusted. That took time and resources. And there was more need for the dust than there were bodies to make it, which meant the precious commodity had to be used sparingly. It also meant it was getting harder and harder to keep everyone safe.

Hence the need for more hunters.

After spraying down the main area, Lucian cleaned off his blade. His mind buzzed with too many thoughts screaming at once. It made his head spin.

"They were telling the truth," Dorian finally said. "I wanted you to hear it from them though."

"I'm sure they think they can get to my family. They're not the first to try. Won't be the last." His parents swore by the House of Blood's ability to keep all their members safe. "I'll call and warn them this happened."

"I suspect these guys were the ones who hacked our surveillance cameras."

"Good possibility." Again, there wasn't much more they could do about any of it. Attacks happened. Raids, too. All Lucian could do was make sure everyone was aware, alert, and always armed. This was the life of a vampire. No rest for the wicked. No downtime from danger.

Together, they put the three bodies into cheap ass coffins and stacked them by the back door. Once done, Lucian looked around the empty room. "No vampires came for the show?" He hung some of Dorian's cleaned weapons back up on their hooks. "That's unusual."

"I kept this one closed." Dorian frowned. "I hate being watched while I work."

But many vampires loved it. They could watch the Reaper dole out torture all day, every day. Hell, one woman even asked if they could put in a bar and popcorn station once. Lucian rejected the idea, and that was the end of it. Like Dorian, Lucian hated being here any longer than necessary.

"I think you better put extra guards around your family until we understand what they're up to and why."

Lucian huffed a fake laugh. "They're up to no good because they think it's their place and duty to kill us. That's all the reason they need, Reaper, and you know it. No sense in wasting time questioning them about their purpose. We've known it for lifetimes."

Dorian ground his molars together. "This feels different," he said quietly. "Those men knew things about you, Lucian."

There was plenty to know. He'd been around the block a time or two and was a top pick for the *Savag-Ri*. They would no doubt put his fangs on a trophy wall if they could kill him. "You and I are both highly sought after, Reaper. You know that."

Dorian was the infamous executioner. The House of Death collected rare creatures like him and Lucian because, for some ungodly reason, Malachi favored them over the others. Not everyone who wanted to join the House of Death got in. No, no, no… you had to prove yourself. If one found favor with Malachi, it was because he saw something valuable in them.

Dorian was a beast—trained and raised by a serial killer. Used as the red hand of the king to kill, maim, torture and shred their enemies to ribbons. Lucian was a…

Well, shit, he had no clue what he'd done to gain the king's favor. He was just grateful to get accepted into the House of Death and rose rank so fast that it made some heads spin. Quite literally.

"The other explosion we heard in the warehouse district ended up being a church," Dorian tugged down his sleeves and grabbed his jacket from the hook. "No casualties there. The place had been vacant for a while. I suspect that was their nest. The warehouse might have been their temporary version of a Kill Box. Or a decoy. No clue."

"Jesus," Lucian scrubbed his face. "I wish they'd all die."

"One at a time, my friend. One at a time." Dorian squeezed his shoulder before they headed towards the exit. "What kept you? I called you in hours ago."

Oh shit. He hadn't realized Dorian had been torturing them for so long. "I was busy with someone." Lucian felt guilty not telling his best friend about Tessa. Keeping her a secret was for her own safety, not because he was ashamed of her. But now that he'd brought her to the mansion, the cat was out of the bag. "I met someone," he confessed. Christ, he sounded like an idiot saying that.

"Does she know what you are?"

"Not yet."

"You going to tell her?"

"Not yet." Maybe not ever. Lucian looked over his shoulder

as they left the Kill Box and he stared at the coffins waiting for transport. How could he possibly tell Tessa about this life? She was human. She wouldn't understand. And he kind of liked the fact that she didn't know about any of this. It kept her purer. Safer. More innocent.

He once called her toxic. Not to her face, but... in the bleak nights when his curse strangled him with a longing so deep, he could barely breathe through the agony, he'd called her toxic. And, God, how he craved it. Tessa was ambrosia. She was a song which clawed his soul to ribbons. A fire burning in his cold heart.

"I told her I love her," he said quietly as they made their way to the front door.

Dorian stopped dead. "You what?"

"Said, I loved her. Told Malachi too. I want to keep her."

Dorian made a half-choked noise about it. "That's not safe."

"I know, but I can't help it. I want her. Need her."

The Reaper's brow furrowed with concern. "And what happens when you see your *alakhai*?"

Lucian shook his head and sighed. "Maybe I'll take a page from your book."

Dorian had gone his entire existence without looking at a reflection. He kept away from all mirrors and shiny surfaces. Hell, he even ripped the rearview and side mirrors off his vehicles. Kept his curtains drawn so he didn't see anything in the windows either. That level of commitment to not finding a mate was commendable. And ludicrous.

"You know that won't stop fate, Lucian."

Boy didn't he know? Lucian saw firsthand how that worked out for Dorian. The poor son-of-a-bitch accidentally saw his mate's reflection in the mansion and his house of cards crumbled down around his ears within days.

Days.

Lucian had helped him find his *alakhai*, which was the easy part, ironically enough. The impossible task was getting Dorian to commit and accept his and his mate Lena's fate.

Would Lucian be in a similar situation? Would he be happy with Tessa until one day he found his mate in a goddamn mirror and all hell broke loose until he died or found his *alakhai*? Would he kick Tessa away and run towards his mate?

Having two women wasn't possible. Not that he'd want to go that route. But once a vampire found their fated mate, the desire to be with anyone else died immediately. If he found his *alakhai* while he was still with Tessa, she'd be the one to suffer.

And that was something Lucian wouldn't survive.

On the drive back to the Mad House, Lucian called his mother's cell and left a message. Then he called Sadie's private line because he realized he didn't have his sister's or his father's numbers. He left her a message explaining everything and asked for a callback.

He tried to not let the idea of neither of them answering be a red flag. Besides, their estate was big, and they'd likely not always have their cells on them anyway. If he didn't hear back from them in the next couple of hours, he'd try again. If he still got no answer, he'd handle it. Until then, Lucian needed to figure out what to do with Tessa.

Pushing open the doors to the mansion, he beelined it up the stairs and straight to his room. Waving his hand, he unlocked the door and stepped inside. "Sorry it took longer than I—"

His room had been ransacked.

"Tessa?" Heart hammering, Lucian couldn't grasp what he was seeing. At first, he thought someone might have come in and taken Tessa. But that wouldn't happen in this House. "Holy shit."

The rug pulled out from under him when it all clicked. She was gone. Left through the goddamn window. Lucian stumbled over to it and peered down onto the lawn, half-hoping she was still out there in the grass and hadn't gotten far. His prima had tied all his bedsheets together and shimmied down the side of the house like a damsel escaping a tyrant.

A hot breeze blew in, ruffling not only his hair, but the papers strewn about the floor.

Oh shit. He looked down and recognized the music sheets. Picking it up, he read what he once scribbled.

December 19
This is getting dangerous. I'm backing off. She's a drug to me. The

torment in her eyes quakes in her thighs when she wraps them around me. I feel it everywhere. My bones. My soul. On the tip of my tongue and shaft of my dick. Tessa is raw and real. I'm raw and regrettable. I want her to keep fucking with me. I like how it feels when I have her obedience. If I give her a cue, she takes it. Arabesque, Fouetté, Plié, blah, blah, blah. She eats it like it's life. I feed it to her like it's poison. She's toxic. Seeps into me. Destroys me. I like it. I hate how I can't wait to see her again. I hate that I can't stay away.

Savag-Ri 7 today. All mine. Thank you, Tessa.

Lucian crumbled the paper in his fist and marched to his closet. There, in the middle of the floor, was his chest of music. The lid had been pried open, the contents of his life and blood curse spilling out all over the place.

He was gutted. Exposed.

Discovered.

Staggering backwards, he gripped the sides of his head and slammed into the dresser next. The heavy piece of furniture rocked back, and he slipped on something laying on the floor. He nearly fell on his ass. His mouth dried up when he looked down. Several black files lay scattered around, all opened, their contents half-out of their pockets.

Closing his eyes, Lucian turned around and braced against the dresser, breathing deep.

So, this was what the breaking of trust felt like. He half-wondered if it was going to kill him. Snapping his eyes open, he came face-to-face with the reflection in his big dresser mirror. Then he looked down.

A blade was jammed into the wooden surface of his antique dresser. Next to it, Tessa had carved: *We're done.*

Lucian fought for breath. *This is for the best. This is for the best. This is for the best.*

And that was the truth. This *was* for the best—*Tessa's* best. Lucian was used to suffering, so he would learn to live with another layer of ache crusting over his shriveled heart. Tessa was a thousand times better off without him. They weren't from the same world. They didn't need the same things. To think he almost turned her vampire just to have a long-standing love affair.

Now he felt like he dodged a bullet.

Yeah, okay, this was going to be just fine. Right? *RIGHT*? So why couldn't he catch his breath? Why wasn't his heart pumping strongly? Why were his eyes blurry with tears?

She'd shimmied down the house like a mouse on a drainpipe. She was gone. Away from him, this place, this life and all the dangers that came with it. Good. That was… good.

He grunted, clutching his chest. Seriously, did hearts physically ache when they were broken? Why on earth did he feel like the victim here? Lucian kept who and what he was a complete secret from Tessa. Then locked her in his room with no ETA on when he'd return. Did he not expect her to snoop and find things that would freak her out?

Maybe he subconsciously self-sabotaged. Maybe he knew he'd never have the guts to leave her, so he put her in a position to run herself off. He'd asked for this, damnit. Put himself right on the train tracks and didn't budge when that sucker barreled down on him.

We're done.

Not only were those words carved into his wooden furniture. They were gouged into his soul. The Tessa-shaped corkscrew digging into his heart now wrenched free. His cork was popped. Bleeding him out.

Tessa was gone. Tessa was free.

Closing his eyes, Lucian bowed his head. "I'm so sorry," he whispered, knowing this could have been so much worse.

CHAPTER 18

Tessa made it all the way home in a massive brain fog. "I can't believe this is my life," she grumbled as she finally made it to her apartment door.

"Tessa," a man's voice rumbled behind her.

She clenched the gun she'd stolen from Lucian's top drawer, her finger on the trigger, and almost pointed the damned thing at the asshole behind her. But she didn't. "I'll have your rent, Dominic. Give me an extension."

"No exceptions, Tessa. You know the rules. You're officially late."

She kept the gun concealed and turned around slowly to look at her landlord. "I'll blow you if I don't get the money to you within forty-eight hours. How about that?"

His eyes brightened, as if he had an actual chance of getting that blowie. "Yeah. That works. See you soon."

She rolled her eyes, incapable of believing he bought the lie. And disappointed in herself for telling it to him. Tessa would rather eat horse shit than suck a man off to clear her debt. But she needed him out of her hair right now. With a gun in one hand, and her frayed confidence in the other, she was a hot mess who needed to get into her apartment and be left alone right now.

Besides, little did Dominic know, she had an emergency fund in her drop ceiling and would have the cash to him by tonight. First, she needed to rest. This had been, by far, the longest day of her miserable life.

She'd taken the gun because she was terrified of everything and everyone. The gun gave her security. And considering she'd lost her damned mind, and her only safe house, she needed a weapon for protection. Between looking over her shoulder every ten seconds and powerwalking for miles, she was exhausted.

Without her phone, Tessa hadn't been able to call an Uber. And since she was too scared to even talk to one of the other "roommates" of Lucian's, or kick down his door, she shimmied out of Lucian's second-story window like Ra-fucking-punzel once the patio cleared of witnesses and walked for what felt like forever until she got to the French Quarter. From there, she took a bus with money an old woman gave her after Tessa cracked and asked for help.

The entire journey home burned a new hole in her heart. And in the soles of her cheap shoes. The good news? She was exhausted, and Tessa hadn't shed a single goddamn tear over Lucian the entire way home. But oh, how she wanted to.

"I nearly risked everything," she whispered angrily to herself. Shoving her key in, Tessa unlocked things, stepped into her apartment, and slammed the door shut behind her. Sliding down onto her ass, with her back against the door, she finally let herself fall apart.

Her cell vibrated from the living room coffee table. With a sorrowful moan, she clapped her hands over her ears and closed her eyes. After a while, Tessa hauled herself back up, snagged a bottle of vodka from her freezer, and went into her bathroom and locked the door.

In some weird, screwy, angry part of her brain, Tessa almost hoped Alex and Colton came back to start some shit. She had enough hurt and fury in her right now to do something really stupid.

Like commit murder.

Turning on her faucet, she didn't bother waiting for her tub to fill before climbing inside. Her eyes itched. Her chest ached. Her legs and feet were killing her. Submerging herself, she let the water rise to her chin before shutting it off. Then? Tessa popped the top on her drink and took a long pull from the bottle.

More tears flowed. More vodka poured down her throat. It didn't take long before her belly burned and she had a decent buzz.

When was the last time she ate? Eww, the thought of food made her queasy.

Tessa needed to come up with a plan. But for the life of her, she couldn't snap out of her pity party. She continued to drink and feel like shit about herself and her life and her poor choices instead of packing her bags and getting the hell out of there.

Maybe if those guys came back, it would end everything. No more running. No hiding. No lying or fighting. No tricking or luring...

Maybe prison is a better option. Tessa stared at the bottle of vodka like it just came up with that ridiculous notion. Oh, hell no. Tessa wasn't going to prison for murder. And she wasn't going to work with those men to get Lucian, either. She was going to run and disappear. She'd done it before, she damn sure could do it again.

Her gaze sailed from the vodka in her hand to the gun on the edge of her tub, recalling how sometimes heartbroken women did crazy shit...

"What are you doing, mom?"
"Hmm?"
"What are you doing?"

Tessa closed her eyes, reliving the night she found her mother dancing on the rooftop of their old apartment.

"Get down before you fall!"
"A ballerina never falls if she has perfect balance."

Her mother's wry smile would haunt Tessa for life. As would the image of that woman pirouetting along the ledge of the roof.

Tessa remembered the jolt of fear she felt seeing her mother up there, dancing like the world was watching her every move. She was drunk on merlot, thin as a rail, and still pining over the man who'd left them both.

"You look like him," her mother said as she stared down at the street, seven stories below. *"Every time I look at you, I see him."*

That wasn't Tessa's fault. So why did she feel bad about it? "I want to dye my hair," she said. "Make mine like yours, Mom. I love your hair."

Her mother's back leg swooped up to the moon as she pitched forward and grazed the ledge with her fingertips. "Is that so?"

"Yes."

"You've gained weight."

"I'll diet."

"Diets don't work. You must change your entire lifestyle if you want to make it on stage. You don't own your body when you're a dancer, Tessa."

Then what or who did? Music? The choreographer? Fate? Tessa would say anything to get her mother off that ledge. "Teach me."

"I thought you preferred your instructor at the dance academy over me."

So that's what this was about? Her mother was jealous? Ugh. "I like Miss Gandy, but I know she can't get me into the best schools. Only you can."

"Because I was the top of my class." Her mother's grace faltered when she arched backwards. Tessa squeaked, scared her mother was going to fall over the ledge. Her mother corrected herself and went into a grand plié.

"You're the best of the best." Tessa cautiously moved closer. "Always."

"Until you were born." Her mother straightened, as if whatever song playing in her head had come to a stop. She hopped down from the ledge, drained her bottle of wine, and headed barefoot towards their fire escape to get back to their shithole apartment.

Tessa followed without saying a word. It wasn't her fault that she was born. It wasn't her fault that her mother fell in love. It wasn't her fault she had blue eyes and blonde hair instead of the fire engine red her mother had. It wasn't her fault that, at the age of eleven, Tessa outshined every other student in her dance studio and Miss Gandy had moved her into pointe to dance with girls twice her age, which still wasn't good enough to impress her mother.

But Tessa took the blame. She'd always take the blame if, just once, her mother looked at her with joy and pride.

Lately, her mother had become ill and wouldn't tell anyone what was wrong. If Tessa pried, she got slapped. But something wasn't right with her mother. Okay, there were lots of things not right about her mother, but that woman was all Tessa had, so she refused to let her slip away somehow.

"Come," her mother held her hand out and Tessa took it. "Get into second position."

Tessa learned quickly how to please. And how to hurt. And how to never ask a question beyond, "Was that perfect enough?"

The water turned cold. Tessa dunked her head under it and screamed until her lungs ran out of air. Resurfacing, she ran her hands down her face and repeated the process two more times. Then she grew dizzy and her belly clenched. She needed to eat.

Stumbling out of the bath, Tessa accidentally kicked her forgotten vodka over and it spilled across the floor. "Damnit." Reaching for a towel, she draped it over the mess and walked into the kitchen, a dripping, cold mess.

Her nipples hardened, even though it was balmy in her apartment. Wet, bare footprints left a trail from her bath to her fridge. She pulled out random foods and stuffed them into her face. She tasted none of it. Next, she got dressed and dug out cash from the envelope she kept hidden in her ceiling. Then she swaggered down to her landlord's door, knocked loudly, and slapped the cash against his stained, sweaty, tank top clad chest, and walked away. As she did, Tessa smiled and made a mental list of how she was going to pack up and leave as soon as she could figure out what to do about the dance studio. She didn't like leaving them in a lurch. And she hated the idea of abandoning her students.

But what choice did she have? Being a sitting duck, waiting to get arrested for murder, or worse — be murdered — wasn't an option. She had no one to run to. No one she could rely on but herself.

Lucian was the only person in her life she'd come close to trusting. They worked so hard on that aspect of their relationship, hadn't they? And for what? For him to turn out to be someone else? A complete lie? A dangerous man with weapons capable of murder, hostage material, and an obsession with sheet music.

Boy, did Tessa know how to pick 'em.

Kicking her door shut, she trudged over to the couch and flipped on the TV. She was too drained to put on music. Besides, dancing wasn't going to help her out of her headspace tonight. Her body still ached from everything she and Lucian had done in his bedroom, and the miles she'd walked home formed huge blisters on her feet.

"This is my fucking life."

How had it come to this? Was her mother watching her? It felt like it. A cold shiver ran down Tessa's spine and she almost laughed at how pathetic the feeling of longing was in her heart. She'd gone her entire life never being good enough. This shit with Lucian? Well...

Tessa is raw and real. I'm raw and regrettable. I want her to keep fucking with me. I like how it feels when I have her obedience. If I give her a cue, she takes it. Arabesque, Fouetté, Plié, blah, blah, blah. She eats it like it's life. I feed it to her like it's poison. She's toxic. Seeps into me. Destroys me. I like it. I hate how I can't wait to see her again. I hate that I can't stay away.

She's toxic. The truth hurt. Lucian hit the nail on too many heads with his journal entry. He's right. Tessa was toxic. To herself. She perpetuated what her mother had started, as if the world would tip over and all would be ruined if she didn't keep up the painful process of seeking perfection.

Arabesque, Fouetté, Plié, blah, blah, blah. She eats it like it's life. I feed it to her like it's poison.

At one point, dancing had been her life. All she breathed. She woke up with steps in her head. She went to school with steps in her head. She ate with steps in her head. She slept with steps in her head. Yet hours upon painstaking hours of practice never made her perfect.

It made her bitter.

When had she lost her love of dancing? When had it gone from fun to fever? Play to punishment? Life to addiction?

Did it matter? Tessa was her mother's daughter. She may have gotten to this point on her own pointe-shoed feet, but in the end, she was still dancing in her mother's shadow. Always almost perfect, but never enough.

Was this heartache what her mother felt when her father ran off? If so, she could almost forgive her mother's actions. Her neglect. Her hate.

Thank God Tessa was on birth control. There was little, if any, chance she was pregnant with Lucian's baby.

A baby. Tears suddenly stung her eyes as she thought about having that man's child. Kids weren't something she'd thought of. Not ones of her own, at least. But Tessa cared for the children in her dance classes... and now she'd have to give up the dance studio. No way was she willing to risk the safety of those children. Not with Lucian, Alex, and Colton lingering around. All it took was Alex showing her that picture of one of her students entering the dance studio, and it was over for her. Tessa was never going back there. No way would she risk any of those kids.

She had to leave town. Hopefully, those guys wouldn't find her or if they did, at least the danger was lured away from here. Away from Lucian ever knowing.

Completely drained, she closed her eyes and settled into the couch cushions. Sleep was going to have its way with her in about three seconds.

Tessa's cell buzzed again. God damnit. She popped her eyes open and kicked the phone away, so she didn't have to see it light up. It buzzed again. And again. And again.

She let it go to voicemail without seeing who it was. Some horrid bit of her hoped it was Lucian calling to grovel.

Fuck that.

CHAPTER 19

Lucian lasted what? All of six hours before he started calling her.

Yeah, he was a chump. A chump with a lot of explaining, apologizing, and groveling to do.

As he sat idle outside her apartment building, he wondered if she was looking out her window at him. That was dumb, right? So dumb and conceited and pointless.

Every atom he possessed screamed to go inside, kick down her door, and hold her tight. Bite her. Turn her. Love her and spend the rest of her life making up for his mistakes with her.

The trust they had was shattered.

The history they shared was on fire.

Against the king's orders, he wasn't leaving her alone. Malachi would either come to understand this, or he wouldn't. Either way, Lucian was all in with Tessa. The more he thought about it, the more it made sense to him.

He loved her, so why shouldn't he be with her?

As he sat in his car with the engine running, his palms sweating, his heart clenching, his teeth throbbing, Lucian realized he was no different from his father. Basil loved Esmerelda as hard as Lucian loved Tessa. All this time, Lucian kept Tessa at a safe arm's length away. He could have told her more about him. Could have shared some special memories. Could have earned a tighter bond with his little prima. But he hadn't because he'd been holding out for a mate. A fated mate who may not come for another five hundred years.

Was that any way to live? Waiting? Holding his breath? Keeping everyone out of his heart so he could lie to himself and say it's for the best? Yeah right.

He dialed her number again. The cell rang and rang until it went to voicemail. Again.

"It's me." Christ, he sounded like a douche. "I uhhh, I just... I need to explain some things. Like the music sheets? Yeah, and I... damnit, Tessa. I'm sorry. I'm..." *A vampire. I'm old as dirt and yet I still can't summon the brain cells to talk to you. I'm downstairs, let me in.* "I'm going to tell you a story."

The phone beeped and cut him off. He dialed again.

"Way back, like wayyyyy back, a woman had been seduced by two men. One came to see her by day. The other by night." A couple walked down the sidewalk, smoking cigarettes and laughing. Lucian kept his eyes on them until they passed her apartment building. "These two males," he went on to say, "both seduced her. She got pregnant with twins. Superfecundation twins, you know? Where it's two babies by two men? Anyways, neither father knew about the other and when the woman's condition was exposed, she was forced into confinement and went through the pregnancy alone."

Beep. He was cut off again. He dialed and waited for her voicemail to kick back in.

"As I was saying." He wished he could have done this in person. "She longed to see either of her lovers, though neither ever came to her. No matter how many letters she wrote, they didn't answer her. She spent her pregnancy longing for the men she loved and grew spiteful and hateful because they didn't return. When she delivered the babies, they both arrived for the birth of their sons. When they realized they'd both bedded the same woman for the same reason, they fought outside the birthing chambers."

Beep.

Mother. Fucker!

He dialed, waited, and continued after the beep. "Meanwhile, she hemorrhaged out and cursed both of their bloodlines in the process. The children, and all who came after them, would live forever longing for the love that would never come. Just like she'd longed for them to return to her all those months."

He was leaving out a significant detail here. He felt like a fool leaving this shit on her voicemail to begin with, adding that the two children, sired by two lovers, were vampire and Lycan seemed a little too much to leave in a voicemail.

Beep. Swear to God, he was going to strangle his phone. Blowing out a deep breath, he called again and waited. Again.

"But." Lucian said, and cleared his throat, "Because she still loved her children, her curse could *only* be lifted if they found their mates in time. Until then, they would remain cursed with constant longing. Any satisfaction they found would be painfully temporary, and their souls would be forever tortured and hollow without their true mate."

Because both the vampire and Lycan had been too late in coming back to her but *had* come at the bitter end instead of never.

Beep. He was cut off again. Dear. God. The universe was mocking him at this point. One last time, he dialed and continued.

"I'm part of this story, Tessa. I'm cursed." That's all he could say about it for now. "And I have no idea when my mate will ever come… or if they even exist." She should appreciate that because she wasn't into marriage or kids or anything long term. "I know what it looked like in my room, but I assure you it's not what you think. Aaaannd now that I've said that out loud, I realize it sounds stupid, but it's the truth. Please, give me a chance to explain everything. I've never broken our trust and yeah, I might not have told you everything about me, but you never asked either. That wasn't part of our contract. This relationship was about *you*. Only you."

Beep.

Lucian slammed his fist against the steering wheel and bent it. Sucking in a boatload of air, he blew it out. Fuck him sideways, he called again. *Jesus Christ, will this madness never end?*

"I never wanted to jeopardize what we built together. And my rules still stand—this is and will always be about you. That's my privilege as your…" *Dom? Lover?* "As the guy you came to when you needed no judgement and only a safe escape." His heart sagged in his chest like a deflated zeppelin. "I'll answer any questions you have. Explain it all, no matter how nuts you might think it is. Just… please… call me back?" Before he hung up, he rushed and added, "There are bad guys I go after. I'm not the worst thing out there,

Tessa. But I'm far from perfection too."

He hung up and refused to look up at her window to see if she was there. He knew she'd gotten home safely. Had seen her silhouette through the curtains as she went from living room to bathroom, flicking off and on all her lights. Right now, in the darkness, her window lit up from her TV.

At least she was home and safe. He needed to keep it that way.

Scrubbing his face one more time before pulling away, he gripped his busted-up steering wheel and drove back to the House of Death, hellbent on getting the king to approve Lucian's desire to dust her apartment as a precaution. Even if it was the outside perimeter of the building, bone dust would help keep the *Savag-Ri* from getting to her.

But... what about when she left her building to go grocery shopping? To the dance studio? Out to dinner?

Holy Hell. Lucian's chest tightened. There was no way to always keep her safe. Unless he took her hostage and kept her with him, explained everything, and made her believe his story?

Shit, was he capable of going to that level? Groaning, he hated himself for the truth corkscrewing back into his heart again.

CHAPTER 20

Three days passed since he left that pathetic string of voicemails on Tessa's phone. Lucian had been using his Shibari rope to self-tie for the past forty-eight hours. Even when he hunted last night, rope was knotted around his chest, waist, groin, and thighs. And yeah, he wore it on the outside of his leathers for the world to see.

Did he care that he was unraveling, in every way, in front of his entire House and a good portion of the French Quarter community? Hell no. They could all eat a dick.

These ropes kept him in check. Held his fragile, chaotic, no good, senseless, despicable ass together. No shame in that. Sometimes life required a serious bind to make one unravel. It's called a coping mechanism. Contained chaos. A form of falling to pieces on the inside while being held together on the outside.

At least that's how Lucian looked at it.

He only used these ropes when he felt out of control. He kept them in the bottom drawer of his dresser for emergency use. When his head got really rattled? Like, deplorably, messily, ruination-in-the-next breath freaked out? He'd call in Xin, who acted as Lucian's rigger, to tie him up in ways he couldn't get himself in and out of without assistance. His Housemates were a lifesaver on and off the battlefield.

Sadly, Lucian was getting close to making that call.

Pacing his room, he was supposed to be resting. Yeah right. As if he could sleep while his life was in ruins. He couldn't sit still for anything and was debating on calling Xin for a vigorous session that would leave him strung, suspended, and immobile in his safe space, thus allowing him to break apart for the night and finally get some goddamn rest.

But something held him back from making the call. The spark of hope still burning in his heart that Tessa would give him permission to come over and work this shit out.

Imagine his shock when his cell rang. Lucian fumbled to get it out of his pocket and answer. It wasn't Tessa calling. It was his sister. "About goddamn time, Lizzy."

"I'm going with Mom to France for a getaway."

Lucian's jaw clenched. He wouldn't argue with that—the escape was needed. Lucian hated the idea of his mother staying in that massive house alone, given all that's happened. France might be good for her.

He told Lizzy about how *Savag-Ri* captives had threatened Lucian, slinging their names around like knives to slice his composure.

"I assure you, we're fine. The House of Blood's main quarters are in France. That's where we're staying, so we're perfectly safe."

"Good." He rubbed his neck and took in a deep breath. That's real good. He started pacing again. The line went silent. "You still there?"

"Yes, fool. I'm still here."

He needed to talk his shit out with someone who wasn't one of his Housemates. Dorian was his first choice, but that vampire was up to his neck hunting and taking care of his mate. Lucian didn't want to burden him yet.

"I found someone," he confessed. Then his phone beeped with an incoming call. Checking it, he quickly said, "I gotta go." And hung up on his sister, to accept the call from, "*Tessa.*" Relief made him breathless. His ass dropped down in his chair.

"You said I was toxic."

He winced.

"You're right," she tacked on before he could say a word.

He heard her sniffle. Was she crying? Holy Hell, he couldn't handle Tessa's tears, especially not on the phone when he couldn't bring her into his chest and hold her tight. "Meet with me?"

"No," she exhaled in his ear.

"Tessa, I—"

I what? What could he possibly say at this point? Nothing would make a difference or fix what was now ruined between them. Because if a woman was willing to climb out of your window to get away from you, that relationship was over. If he were a smart, strong vampire, he'd have some dignity and bow out with grace and respect.

Lucian didn't have it in him to walk away though.

"Cursed, huh?" Her voice cracked. Then he heard liquid sloshing and her swallowing.

"Where are you?" Because he was on his way.

"Your story was... interesting."

Jesus, that sorrow in her tone was going to kill him. "It's the truth."

"I'm cursed too, I think." Her voice sounded muffled. He heard a zipper. More muffled noises. More swallowing. "Maybe we all are."

"Tessa, where are you? Are you home?"

"I'm sorry I dragged you into my rabbit hole." She sniffled again. "I'm sorry for lots of things."

"Don't be. I dragged you into mine too," he said softly. "But... I'm *not* sorry for it. I want you down here with me. I *need* you down here with me."

"You know what I wish?" She lightly chuckled. "I wish I'd met you before my accident. I wasn't as messed up in the head before then." Her next laugh was cold and turned into a choking sob. "Actually, I think I've been messed up for a lot longer than that accident. That crash was karma."

Lucian clutched the phone. Something was really wrong here. She wasn't acting or sounding like herself. He'd never heard her talk like this before.

"I wish I was stronger." She began crying harder.

Fuuuuuck. "You're the strongest woman I've ever met. Jesus, Tessa, how could you ever think yourself weak?"

"Because I know what I should have done, and I didn't do it."

"*Tessa,*" he used his more serious tone on her, "Tell me where you are. I'll come get you."

She ignored him. "Do you think there's a cure for people like us?"

"*Tessa—*"

"You said you're in constant longing." She sniffled again. "I'm sorry for that. I get it, and I'm sorry you're in this pain too."

This wasn't his Tessa. Nothing about this conversation sounded remotely like his girl. He'd caused this, hadn't he? Her tears were because of him. He needed to navigate this convo better. Make things right. "What if I told you there was a cure?" He facepalmed himself.

"Then I suggest you run to it. Immediately."

If she knew the depth of his curse and her advice on remedying it, would she think differently?

"I love you," he said with a voice full of glass shards and agony. "No matter what else happens, know that I love you, Tessa. We can work this out. Whatever you're thinking of doing? Don't do it."

"It's not that simple, Lucian."

"It's exactly that simple. Now tell me where you are so I can come to you."

More shuffling in the background. More sniffling. "I don't ever want to see you again."

His heart fell out of his ass. *"What?"*

"I'm leaving, Lucian. And I'm not coming back."

"Tessa, no!" Damnit, he couldn't lose her! Racing out of his room, he sped out the front door. "Tell me where you are. Let me come to you. Let me at least explain things better."

"I can't stay," she said, crying harder. "I don't even know why I called you back. I don't know why I stayed this long."

Lucian was already in his car, foot slamming down on the pedal, hellbent on keeping her on the phone until he found her. "Tessa don't do this."

"I don't have a choice!" she screamed. "But I didn't do it. No matter what you hear or find out, I *didn't* do it."

She hung up.

"Tessa! *TESSA!*" Lucian tossed his phone onto the passenger seat and weaved through traffic to get to her apartment.

I didn't do it. No matter what you hear or find out, I didn't do it.

What didn't she do?

CHAPTER 21

Tessa slammed her suitcase closed and drained her bottle of cabernet. Checking her window for the tenth time, the Uber should be arriving in about five more minutes. For the past three days, she got her affairs in order and prepared to blow her life up. Again.

She felt like a ticking time bomb. All she could think to do was run. Get out. Hide.

She shouldn't have called Lucian back. That was a stupid, weak, horrible thing to do. But Tessa needed to hear his voice one more time before she left town and never returned. His tone always soothed her. Made her feel confident and bold. She counted on it this time, planned to use it to boost her confidence since the cabernet wasn't doing shit. But instead, Lucian's voice cracked and ached. Just like hers.

She wanted to tell him everything. From the murder to the blackmail to the men, who were probably going to come after her because they couldn't get to him. She wanted to tell Lucian that he was the best thing to come into her life and that she was sorry she was too fucked up in the head for anything more to bloom between them. She wanted to thank him for his tolerance.

His. Tolerance.

Because that's what people did with Tessa. They tolerated her. Her dance instructors. Her dance company. Her mother…

She tipped the bottle of wine back, forgetting it was empty already. Staring at it like it just insulted her hairstyle, she threw the damned thing against the wall and it *thunked* to the floor.

Ugh. She should have gone for something stronger than wine.

Her phone buzzed in her hand again. It was Lucian. Squeezing the case, she wished she had the strength to crush it. Instead, she tossed her cell in the toilet.

There.

Done.

Shouldn't that have felt more freeing? More final?

God, she was a mess. Staring at herself in the bathroom mirror, she hated who looked back at her. Tessa was a hot mess—eyes swollen from crying, nose red, lips chapped. Her shirt hung over boney shoulders and lanky limbs. Chin trembling, her fingers wrapped around a pair of scissors as she debated on cutting her hair off. She could have dyed it but... well, she stopped dying her hair once her mother passed away. The thought of going back to that made Tessa feel queasy. Swaying with her hands still clutching the counter, she felt stuck in place. Bolted to the floor.

Why is this happening? Why me?

Tessa hated when she got to the lowest level of self-pity. But she hated her panic attacks and blackouts even more. There were worse things like blackmail and getting dragged to prison to deal with. She didn't have the coping skills for this amount of fuckage. Wine was useless, obviously. Running most likely was too. And it's not like she could go to the cops.

Tessa was on her own. Like always.

Go! Run! Now! Her instincts pushed her to pack her shit and get going, yet she couldn't do it. She'd stalled for three days. And for what? To give a miracle time to drop from the sky?

Or was this one more instance of self-sabotage? Yeah, that was most likely it. At least she could recognize her downfalls now for what they were. *Toxic.* Maybe she wanted to get caught. Maybe she wanted someone else to end her because she never had the guts to do it herself.

She was her mother's daughter, through and through.

Oh God. Tessa buried her head in her hands and cried. How was she this much of a train wreck?

What had Lucian ever seen in her to love at all?

Sucking in a deep breath, she got her shit together and rolled her shoulders back. Time to go. The Uber had to be downstairs by now. Alex and Colton were coming for her. She could feel it. The fact that they'd stayed away thus far wasn't a comfort. It was an anvil hanging over her head. Lucian might be a bad guy, but they were worse. At least Lucian didn't drag innocent people into things they didn't belong in. Lucian kept her safe. Lucian cared.

That's why she was leaving. There was no way on this green earth she could lure him out or give him up. Fuck those men and the pictures they had of her committing murder. Why?

Because she didn't do it.

Those photos were fake. Really well done, but fake. They had to be. Right? She squeezed her eyes shut and tried to remember. The harder she forced her brain cells to conjure up that night, the blacker her mind got. It was no use. It was never any use.

I wish I was stronger. Had she been something other than a weak, panicked rabbit the day Alex and Colton came into her home and shoved a gun in her face with this blackmail bullshit, she would have fought them off. Stood up to them somehow. Instead, she caved and played into their hands, if only to get them out of there and away from her.

Those pictures were her kryptonite. The unknown had sealed her fate. *Because what if they were right... what if I did blackout and do something unforgivable?*

If she went up on murder charges, could she plead temporary insanity? What would happen to her then? Tessa didn't want to wait around and find out.

Three days ago, she walked home from Lucian's house and got shitfaced. Two days ago, she quit her job at the dance studio, pawned her mother's ring, and burned all that "photographic evidence" in her kitchen sink, where the remnants and ash remained. Today, she teetered between running away, calling Lucian, and swan diving off the roof of her apartment building.

Seventy-two hours of doing fuck all and now what? Tessa glared in the mirror and hated who stared back at her. This broken, imperfect, selfish creature knew only one thing: suffering.

The ghost of her past stood behind her. Tessa wanted to wipe that smug smile off her mother's face. "You like this, don't you?" Her narcissistic mother would have loved seeing Tessa stumble and fall. *"You get what you deserve."* That's what her mother would have said. *"You pissed your life and talent away. You're a waste."*

Tessa huffed, still able to hear the echo of her mother's

condescending tone in the back of her head.

Sometimes Tessa wished she could blame her mother for how messed up she was now. Tessa shook her head. No, she only had herself to blame. Tessa could have worked on her issues years ago. Cut the cord tying her and her mother together should have been the first step. Instead, she'd boomerang back to her mother time and time again. Therapy was another option she never chose. And Tessa also could have found a way to rise above the noise in her head — the taunting memories, the insecurity and emotional abuse she allowed to drive her. But she did none of those things. Tessa *chose* to stay in that dark place. Maybe because, deep down, she loved her mom, and this toxic mentality was the only thing they really had in common. It was a link that wouldn't fucking break. Tessa remained haunted by a ghost who always reminded Tessa that she was the reason her mother's dreams burned to the ground.

Karma. That car accident was karma. Tessa braced her hands on the sink and squeezed her eyes shut. The wine-buzz faded away while heartache flooded her system with regrets. *That car accident was karma.* She always felt that way. Like the universe gave her a taste of what it must have been like for her mother. To have everything she ever wanted in her hands only for someone to come along and rob her of all of it.

For her mother, it was getting knocked up.

For Tessa, it was going out to celebrate her birthday.

They hadn't even gone out drinking because they'd had a long day at the studio and were due for dance practice at six am the next morning. Tessa had spent her birthday with her one and only friend shopping. It was one of best days of her life. They went out of New York and into New Jersey. Spent the morning at a café. Bounced from store to store. Had a light lunch. Went to the movies. The whole day Tessa tried to not overthink why this girl from the dance company would spend a whole day with her like this. They were friends, but only barely. Yet by the end of the day, Tessa felt like she'd gained something extraordinary. They laughed and joked and liked all the same things and it was spectacular. Tessa never felt so grateful in her life. She had a friend.

They headed back into the city late that night with music blasting and the windows down, joking about blowing off practice in the morning and getting pedicures. She'd never laughed so hard at the thought of doing such a thing.

That's when a drunk driver smashed into them. That's when everything changed. That's when Tessa realized what a curse she was. Had it not been Tessa's birthday, they never would have been at that spot, at that time. Her friend would still be alive.

Her friend. She couldn't even speak the girl's name for fear it would summon her ghost too. Sometimes it didn't seem real, like the whole memory was made up.

In both instances, Tessa's very existence had ruined two lives—her mother's and her friend's. She couldn't go to the funeral because she was in the hospital. Tessa was broken, inside and out. And she'd never fully healed. Guilt were ghosts who haunted her day and night with no rest given.

Swiping the tears under her eyes, Tessa rolled her shoulders and got her head back in the game. "Let's go," she said to the shadows of her past.

Turning to leave the bathroom, she grabbed her suitcase and shut off all the lights as she snaked through her tiny apartment. She was going to miss this place. She loved New Orleans. Loved the charm and excitement. The busy nights and quiet mornings. The food. The music.

Lucian.

She would miss him the most, and didn't that speak volumes for her level of fucked-up-ness? Part of her wished she hadn't climbed out his window and taken off. But she wasn't good at facing conflicts, so why start now?

Grabbing a duffel bag from the couch, she heaved it onto her shoulder and bent down to grab her suitcase next. Her entire life was packed into two bags. How poetic.

Bang! Bang! Bang! Her door nearly busted down with the force of someone pounding on it.

"Lucian?"

"Police! Open up!"

Tessa stumbled back and dropped her bags as her heart leapt into her throat. "*No.*" She backed up until her legs hit her sofa. She was trapped. The door kicked in.

"Tessa Banks, you're under arrest for the murder of Paxton Brown."

Lucian sped down the road, once again cursing his rotten luck for not having the gift of flashing. He could be at Tessa's apartment in a blink if he had that skill. But no. He was stuck driving like an ordinary chump, and it made him murderous.

He laid on the horn to make everyone move out of his way. The wheels to his car squealed with every sharp turn. His heart thundered. Palms slickened with sweat. Whatever Tessa was about to do, he hoped he got there in time to stop her.

Holy Hell, he never felt this way before. It was awful. Invigorating and stifling at the same time. Yeah, sure, he wanted to protect humans at all costs, and women were precious—no matter what species—but Tessa defied all laws for him. No rule applied to her.

Tearing through a red light, Lucian's heart went into panic mode. She was going to leave town; he could feel it. In the back of his mind, where good sense lived, he knew he should let her go. Cut ties and set her free. That phone call was her closure.

But he'd be damned if he was going to let her walk out of his life. He would tear apart the world if that's what it took to find her.

"Tessa, please wait," he growled through clenched teeth.

Lucian was prepared to grovel. Spill the tea and tell her everything. From the vampires to the Lycans to the weapons in his drawers and his obsession with music. Once he laid his truth out, plain as day for her, he would give her time to decide whether she wanted to be with him for life or not. And yeah, he was going to tell her about his fated *alakhai* and the curse that would eventually cure or kill him.

That shit couldn't be left on a voicemail.

If she saw his face while he told her, Tessa would understand he wasn't making this up. She had to believe him, damnit. He wasn't giving up until she was his.

The bottom line was this: Lucian wanted her. For now, for later, for however long he could keep her. But he wasn't going to pressure Tessa into anything. The choice was ultimately hers. Did she want to stay human? Would she want to be turned vampire? Did she want him to walk away and never come back? Whatever she wanted, Tessa was getting.

Glancing in his rearview mirror before changing lanes...

His life *shattered*.

Tessa stared back at him—her eyes red-rimmed, the tip of her nose pink.

Tessa.

TESSA!

Lucian's world blew wide open as he stared at her reflection. In that fatal second, his curse unlocked, and his body seized. It was like a steel door exploding deep in his bones. A tsunami wave crashing over his head. A hole blown into his chest big enough for all his instincts to roar out of him at once.

He gasped for air, his vision wavering as his car swerved. Lucian dragged his gaze away from the reflection just in time to see a delivery truck coming straight at him from the left.

SLAM!

A truck plowed into the side of his car. The impact was so sudden and violent, Lucian had no time to react. The airbags deployed but didn't do shit to block the blow. His face smashed into the driver's side window. His body crushed under the weight of the bent metal and the unleashing of his curse. He couldn't even scream as his car spun out and wrapped itself around a light post.

Trapped in twisted metal, Lucian couldn't breathe. The scent of gasoline tickled his nose. Something clicked under his foot. Heat swarmed him. Blood poured from a head wound. Shock wracked through him.

Tessa.

He needed to get to her.

Tessa.

His instincts kicked into fifth gear. *Go! Go! Go!*

"Tessa." Lucian's head lolled to the side. She was... she was his *alakhai*.

He tried to move. His body lay limp and useless. Shock made everything slow down. Screams erupted all around him. His vision darkened. The scent of chemicals, rubber, and hot metal stung his nose. Lucian clawed at the door, his legs trapped between the dashboard and his seat.

To add insult to severe injury, his blood curse drained his strength like water through a sieve.

Tessa.

He was going to mate her. Turn her. KEEP HER.
If he didn't burn to ashes before finding her first.

CHAPTER 22

Shock stole Tessa's breath as men stormed into her apartment and came straight at her. Her brain scrambled to the point where she couldn't understand what was going on.

"You're under arrest for the murder of Paxton Brown," barked a brown-haired man in military fatigues.

With a loud buzzing in her ears, she sucked in a breath and felt her lungs saw air to the point where she was wheezing, hyperventilating. Alex and Colton stood behind the man, claiming to have been the cops before breaking down her door.

"Where do you think you're going?" the big man snarled.

Tessa hadn't realized she'd run to the window, already trying to crawl out of it. He grabbed waist and ripped her backwards, away from the window, away from a chance to escape. Then he shoved her into someone else.

Alex.

"She's got spunk." The new guy laughed. "Good."

Her heart thundered. Eyes wide, Tessa shook her head, still unable to speak. She looked behind her at the man talking, then back at Alex, who said, "We told you what to do, Tessa. You didn't listen." He meandered around her apartment while the other guy restrained her. Then Alex got all in her personal space. She could smell his cigarette breath and the garlicy lunch he had earlier. "Now we're going to do things the hard way."

Tessa wasn't Tessa anymore. She was fury and fear and that combination had no filter or common sense. She hocked a wad of spit in Alex's face. "Fuck you."

"Trust me, sweetheart," the new guy grabbed a chunk of her hair and yanked it back. "If you hadn't been defiled by that bloodsucker, we'd take you up on the offer right now. But we don't dip cock in vamp cunt."

Okay. She was losing her mind. Or these men had lost theirs. Nothing made sense. Nothing about *any* of this made sense. She tugged and kicked, trying to fight her way out of the guy's hold. He probably wasn't even a cop.

Alex pulled a cigarette out and lit it. "Want the tranq, Simon?"

"Let her unravel a little more. She'll be easier that way."

Easier? Easier for what? To break? Frame? Rape? Tessa's eyes widened with all the scary options racing through her mind. She jerked herself to break free, but it was no use. The man holding her, Simon, was just over six-feet tall and about two hundred fifty pounds of muscle. "Colton," he said, "secure the area, make sure we're not attracting too much attention."

Tessa's eyes widened as Colton left the apartment. Was he going to hurt the other tenants in the building? She couldn't even allow herself to go there. Hopefully, Colton was only checking things over and wouldn't touch anyone else.

Alex took another drag of his cigarette and blew the smoke in her face. "I'll give you one last chance, Tessa. I'll make it extremely easy on you." He held the cigarette in the corner of his mouth, the smoke rising into his eyes, making him squint. Tilting his head while more smoke plumed out of his nose, he almost smirked. "Call Lucian and tell him to come here."

He would come. She knew he would. Lucian just spent their entire phone conversation asking where she was so he could get to her. It wouldn't take a rocket scientist to figure out she was probably at home. If not there, then her dance studio.

Part of her wished he would pull some magic John Wick inspired, Liam Neeson worthy rescue job and crash into her apartment with guns blazing and take these men down. Another part of her was darker than that. If she defied these guys, would they kill her? Put her out of her misery? Maybe that would be the better, safer option.

And yet, the part of Tessa in charge right now remained dead silent. She wasn't giving Lucian up. If she was going to do that, she'd have done so already. Or told Lucian about these men in the first place. She was protecting him, even at the cost of herself. Why? Because she meant it when she said she loved him.

Talk about complicating your life.

"I don't have his number." Tessa's voice sounded foreign and distant, even to herself.

Alex's eyebrow arched. He blew out another puff of smoke and glanced at Simon, who swung back and punched her in the gut.

Wheezing, she tried to catch her breath, but ended up dropping to her knees, gaping like a fish. Simon pulled her up by the hair again just as Colton came through the door. He looked over at her, his jaw clenching, and then he looked away again.

Tessa was sloppy on her legs when Simon jerked her against his chest. "Try again, little *prima*."

Tears made the room blurry, but she kept staring at Colton, hoping he'd take pity on her since it was obvious Simon and Alex weren't. Maybe she read him wrong, but Colton didn't look happy about any of this. "Colton," her voice cracked.

Whack!

Alex clubbed the side of her head with his fist. She lost her vision for a moment and stumbled.

"Call Lucian. Bring him to you!" Simon yelled in her face.

"I can't!" she screamed back. "I don't have his number!"

She looked over at Colton again. Whatever mercy she thought there might be had completely disintegrated. Staring at her with a cold, blank stare, Colton pulled his cell out and hit a few buttons. Tessa's voice played over the speaker as he held his phone out for everyone to get a good listen.

"Cursed, huh?" Her voice cracked. *"In a dark place,"* she said to his next question. *"I'm cursed too, I think. Maybe we all are."*

A pause.

"I'm sorry I dragged you into my rabbit hole." She sniffled again. *"I'm sorry for lots of things."*

Another pause, and Tessa remembered exactly what Lucian was asking her. He wanted to come to her. Be with her.

"You know what I wish?" Tessa's cold tone sent shivers down her body now as she listened to the replay. *"That I'd met you before my accident. I wasn't as messed up in the head before then."* Tessa's tears welled up again, hearing her recorded voice say, *"Actually, I think*

I've been messed up for a lot longer than that accident. That crash was karma."

Alex pulled the cigarette from his mouth and blew out another plume of smoke, his eyes burning as he glared at her. The recording ended just after Tessa said, "*I wish I was stronger.*"

They'd bugged her apartment. They'd been listening to her for three days. They knew she was leaving town. Knew she'd called Lucian. Knew she cared about him.

Rolling his cigarette between his fingers, Alex got inches from her face. "Call him."

I wish I was stronger.

Tessa relaxed in her captor's hold. "I. Don't. Have. His. Number."

"Lying *bitch*." Alex slapped her hard across the face.

The sting on her cheek didn't hurt nearly as bad as when he'd punched the side of her head, or Simon's gut punch. Either he showed mercy, or she was numbing out. Tessa figured she must be numbing out. It made her bold. "I threw my phone in the toilet and I don't have his number memorized. Sorry, not sorry."

Colton stormed past everyone and headed into her bathroom to verify if what she said was true. He came back out seconds later with her phone wrapped in a hand towel. "Soaked," he verified. "We can try and recover it."

Alex's jaw clenched as his gaze remained locked on her. Tessa steeled herself and straightened her spine until she had near perfect posture. Her breaths punched out of her, fast and hard. Her belly cramped and she might puke. But she wasn't cowering.

"You wish you were stronger," Simon said in a softer tone. "You're about to get trained on what it takes to reach that goal."

Alex raised his cigarette and put it out on her forehead. The burn from that lit end snuffing out on her skin made Tessa scream. She slammed her head back, cracking Simon in the face. He loosened his hold enough for her to twist like a rabid animal and get free of him. Without hesitation, she kicked Alex in the balls. He doubled over and she scrambled towards the kitchen.

She didn't make it that far. Colton smashed Tessa in the face with the back of his elbow. The breath knocked out of her when she landed on her ass, seeing stars.

"You bitch!" Alex barked.

Simon only laughed.

Tessa made a break for the kitchen again, but Colton stopped her before she took two steps. Her duffel bag lay discarded on the opposite side of the room, too close to Alex and Simon for her to attempt to get it. But that's where Lucian's gun was stashed and now, she wished she'd had more courage to have carried it instead of hidden it.

Locking her arms behind her back, Colton hauled her up to her feet as Simon came closer. She screamed and thrashed again until she felt a sharp pain pop in her shoulder and lost her ability to do anything but heave.

Simon laughed again. "Keep fighting, Tessa. Dislocate your other shoulder and see how useless you can really get."

She sagged in Colton's clutches, gasping for air.

"Do it," Colton growled, his grip tightening around her even more. Pain jolted through her dislocated shoulder. The edges of Tessa's vision blackened. Her body tingled. Her head screamed. Simon came even closer.

Something pinched her neck, making her breath hitch. Simon's hot breath tickled her ear as he said, "Nighty night."

Tessa dropped like a sack of bricks.

CHAPTER 23

Lucian was in a strange white space. Not a room. Not a field. Not anything... just white. He shielded his eyes against the burning brightness, squinting as he saw a figure come closer. He couldn't feel his body. Weightless, confused, and half-blinded, he practically floated towards the darkened silhouette. Then his breath caught. He knew that gait and stride. Knew it so well that his heart burst with elation.

"Luke!" He ran forward, tripping on nothing and pinwheeling his arms to catch his balance. "Luke!"

"Lucian!" His brother ran towards him and they almost collided.

Pure elation washed over Lucian. Love so big and strong and pure poured out of him in waves and tears. *Why am I crying? Why are emotions slamming me like this?*

Where am I?

"Help me, brother." Luke's face went from regal to ruined. His smooth skin crackled and split. His hair — long on top with a high fade — started to smoke and sizzle. Then it scorched and shriveled. His cheeks puffed up and charred like a set of marshmallows shoved into a campfire. "Help me!" Luke's eyes popped and blood oozed like tears. "You helped Dorian, but you won't help me?"

Paralyzed, Lucian watched his brother burn up like a box of tissues in a blaze. And there was nothing he could do to save him. Lucian couldn't budge. Hell, he couldn't even scream! He just stood there like a statue while his brother incinerated before his eyes.

You helped Dorian, but you won't help me. That was a cut he didn't deserve. Lucian helped his best friend Dorian find his mate, but that was *after* Luke's death. Plus, he'd known about Dorian's *alakhai* since day one of Dorian's glimpse in the mirror. Luke? Hell, Lucian hadn't talked to his brother in nearly two centuries. Luke came to him when all other options had run out. He came to Lucian already burning... already half-dead.

And still Lucian remained wracked with the guilt for not having the chance to try and help him. His family blamed him for Luke's death as if Lucian's failure was Luke's fatality.

While his brother's ashes fell into a heap before his feet, Lucian dropped down to his knees and screamed.

Blood rained down from the sky. Thick, soft, fat drops staining everything. Lucian scooped up handfuls of ashes and clutched them close, as if to mold and put his brother back together, force him to rise from the ashes like a phoenix.

"You should have come sooner!" he raged.

"You should have never left," his shadows whispered.

Could Lucian have helped Luke find his *alakhai* had he been part of the House of Blood like the rest of his family? Maybe. Maybe not. He would never know. It wasn't like Lucian carried super sleuthing skills and could find a needle in a haystack any better than some other vampire. But he couldn't shake the regret of not getting the chance to try. And now, look. His brother was gone. Forever.

Lucian wept hard and ugly over the pile of ashes before him. It had been so long since he'd seen Luke, they'd become near strangers to each other. But that didn't stop Lucian's blood from chilling in his veins the day Luke banged on the House of Death's door, screaming Lucian's name.

In his last moment, when he'd run out of options, he came to Lucian...

Part of him hated Luke for that. The other part wanted to turn back time to when they were kids and Luke was too little to reach Sadie's cookie jar on his own. As if by magic, the memory reformed right before his eyes:

Luke digging his toes around the cabinet knob for leverage. Hoisting his little body up onto the counter and almost falling.

"Whoa! Wait a minute," Lucian used his newly developed speed to catch up to Luke and pull him back down before he fell and cracked a bone. Luke was incredibly young. He was still too fragile in their mother's eyes. "What are you doing?"

"I wanted a cookie. I smell the lemon ones."

Lucian smiled. Luke's sense of smell must be blooming. "I'll get them." He climbed up on the counter, reached over the top of the cabinets, and snatched the hidden cookie jar from behind a decorative platter. His brow furrowed while he climbed back down with the goods. "You'd have never reached these on your own."

"I'd have figured out a way." Luke snagged the cookie jar from him. "Here," he said, handing two to Lucian after stuffing a few into his pockets and mouth.

"Save some for Lizzy," Lucian laughed.

"No, she didn't save us any last time. Fair's fair."

He was right. Lucian stuffed two cookies in his face at once and held three more in his hand. Once they emptied the jar of both lemon and chocolate chip cookies, Lucian placed it on the counter and steered Luke out of the kitchen to get back to his music lessons. That night, he asked Sadie to hide the cookie jar in a lower location, so Luke never climbed like that again. The last thing Lucian wanted was for him to get injured.

Sadie half-scolded him, saying she put the jar in an impossible-to-reach location because she was sick and tired of the jar being emptied the same day she filled it. It was hers to fetch, not theirs. Lucian just smiled and said, "Hide it better. Luke's scenting is getting stronger, the lemon ones are easiest to detect and are his favorite. Just bake one batch a week and when they're gone, they're gone. He'll get the point, eventually."

Sadie gawked like asking her to bake only one batch of cookies and allow them to run out — even one day — was blasphemy. She spoiled them rotten. Even more so than their parents did. No way would there not be endless cookies in the house.

"At least wrap them in towels or something to dull the scent. It'll be great practice for him." Lucian kissed her cheek before leaving Sadie in the kitchen and got back to his tutor...

The light brightened as the memory faded before his eyes. Lucian stared down at the pile of ash again. The taste of lemons was acidic in his mouth. More blood rained down on him.

No... not blood... petals.

Lucian slowly plucked a blood red rose petal from the pile of his brother's ashes. A shadow loomed over his head. He looked up.

An angel descended from the sky wearing...

A tutu?

He couldn't grasp any of this. Where the hell was he? What was going on?

The angel dangled from a red swath of fabric. Her blonde hair cascaded down her back in luscious waves and sunbeams. Her long-stem legs were taut with muscle. Her spine was ramrod straight as she clung to the red fabric and started swinging playfully. More red petals fell from the white sky.

The woman dipped her head back and rolled down the ribbon, pulling some serious Cirque Du Soleil shit. Their gazes locked. Her smile almost knocked him over.

I know you...

His bones hummed with familiarity. Lucian stood up and stalked towards her as if lured in by an invisible line.

I know you...

The angel flipped and spun, twirled and swayed, all while suspended in the air. Just out of his reach.

His body hardened. More red petals fluttered down from the endless white void above him.

Tessa.

"Tessa, come down from there." She was too high. Spinning too fast. She could get hurt. Or worse, fall and break her neck. "Tessa!"

She ignored his orders and continued taunting him in midair.

"Tessa! Stop!"

Fire blazed in his marrow. The blood in his veins coursed like hot lava, melting him from the inside out. White-hot agony burst through his body like an explosion of knives shredding him. He lurched forward. Stumbled. Lost his breath. Lost his balance.

Lost his mind.

Tessa. Blinding pain raced through him. Lucian fell back on his ass. He was burning alive. The pain was unimaginable. Back bowing, he clawed the air and screamed. Tears burned as if they were the temp of boiling water. His lungs stuck together, making it impossible to breathe. Clutching his chest, he bent forward and heaved.

Ashes poured out of his mouth. But the pain lessened. He could catch some air. "Help."

The bright white light faded. Tessa disappeared. Luke's ashes vanished. It stopped raining petals and blood. Lucian was all alone in a dark pit with nothing but pain and regret to comfort him...

"We're losing him!" someone shouted.

"Get him on his side!" said another person.

Agony blurred his vision. He tried so hard to see where he was, figure out what was happening, but his eyes were crusted shut. Or maybe they were stapled? Shit. Maybe he didn't have eyes anymore. He tried again. Okay, he definitely saw something this time.

Lights flashed. Shadows danced. There were so many different noises filtering in at once, it was a cacophony of chaos. His lips were fused together. Took him two tries to make words come out.

"I'm so sorry," he tried to say. He wasn't even sure who he was apologizing to. Luke, for not helping him in time? Tessa, for dragging her into his Hell even though he took every precaution to keep her safe and distant? Himself, for all his failures as a son, a brother, a lover, a friend, and a guard?

"Get the King!"

At the sound of men yelling, Lucian's body went slack, his own screams silenced.

Tessa came to. Her muscles ached with fatigue so fierce she might as well have had twenty-pound weights strapped to her eyelids. She tried to lift her head. Nope. "Mmmph." It took tremendous effort just to lick her cracked, dry lips. Nausea caused her stomach to flip and roil. It was like she was on a boat, rocking in tumultuous waves. She was floating, sailing, blowing away...

"Get her in the room."

"Tied?"

"Not yet. I don't think she'll give us any trouble now. She can't even walk."

Tessa tried to speak or crack open her eyes and figure out what was going on. The smell of cigarettes and aftershave made her mouth fill with saliva. "Sick," she mumbled. "I'm gonna be s—" she dry-heaved. Her abs contracted as her body tried to purge whatever rocked her system.

"You puke on me, I'll make you lick it all off," growled someone.

Alex.

The image of doing what he threatened only added to her nausea. She dry-heaved again. Tears poured down the sides of her face. Her cheeks tingled. Tessa's head throbbed so hard her teeth had a pulse.

"Give her to me."

They made a transfer. Cracking her eyes open to slits, all she got was a bunch of nothing. Black cloth. A chest, muscular and broad. Against her better impulses, she buried her face in this new chest like this asshole would shield her. Protect her.

Wow. How fucked up was that?

Grabbing what she could, Tessa's arms linked around his neck, and she grunted. Everything hurt. At least they'd popped her shoulder back in its socket. She'd bet Colton did it, not Alex. Or maybe it was Simon?

"Please help me."

The man didn't make a sound as he brought her into a room and kicked the door shut. Her eyes fluttered as something pinched her neck again. "Please... don't..."

Her world spun out of control.

Instead of succumbing to unconsciousness like last time, Tessa's heart raced, her eyes blew wide open, and her lungs inflated with stale air. It felt like fireworks exploded under her skin. The man carrying her—Simon, as it turned out—dropped her like a bag of trash in the center of the room. The air pushed out of her in a grunt. Her ass hurt from the landing.

"Grab the rope," Alex ordered from behind her.

Tessa gripped the sides of her head. The room made her dizzy. It was nothing but mirrors—the four walls and even the floor! She was locked in a room with several reflections of herself and her captors.

It made her feel outnumbered and surrounded by the dozens.

Tessa crawled towards the door and got kicked in the gut by someone. She didn't even get to see who. Sputtering, she clutched her belly and gasped for air.

"We tried to give you the easy way out of this," Alex tsked. He reached over and grabbed the rope Colton was holding. "We played nice. Gave you time and space. But you just had to fuck it all up."

She shook her head. Tessa locked gazes with Alex as he stalked towards her carrying a rope. It looked similar to what Lucian kept in his drawer. Red. Thin.

Her mouth dried up. "Why are you doing this?" Tears sprung from her eyes and she all but crumbled. "Please... I don't—"

Alex snagged her by the throat. Simon came out of a closet

with a metal folding chair and placed it in the center of the room, patting the seat like an invitation to her.

"All you have to do is be a good girl." Alex snarled in her face. "And do what you're told."

Between whatever they'd shot into her veins, the terror of her situation, and the fight-or-flight response she dove into, Tessa went ballistic.

After losing the last little strand of sanity she had left, Tessa vaguely registered the fact that she'd likely not remember any of this once her mind settled again. By the time that warning bell sounded off, however, she'd thrown six punches. Tessa would make damn sure these men understood she wasn't going down without one hell of a fight.

Did they think she was a weak little mouse? Did they think she wasn't willing to do whatever it took to get out of this Hell? They mistook her tears for weakness. Her stumbles for clumsiness. Her tremors and fear for submission.

But the joke was on them. They had no idea who they were dealing with.

CHAPTER 24

Okay, that hadn't gone according to plan, but Tessa still managed to bloody them up quite a bit before she was hit with something that knocked her out cold. When she came to, she was bound to a chair and unable to move much other than her head, which, by the way, had a marching band in it now.

Tessa heaved. Bile and spit pooled in her lap when she let it fly out of her mouth.

Someone chuckled from across the room. Alex. He leaned against the mirrored wall with his arms crossed and a smile smeared along his bloodied face. Well, at least she managed to get a few hits in. Too bad she couldn't remember it.

Tessa despised how she blacked out. It made her feel out of control on so many levels. The blank space it left in her memory sometimes made her question if certain events happened at all. Coping strategies sucked sometimes. If only temporary insanity could get her out of this mess instead of deeper into it, right? But nope. Here she was, tied up and helpless.

It's nothing like they depict in the movies. It hurt inside and out. Sweat stung the cuts she earned during her mindless attack. Her jaw ached. Tessa's stomach was an endless, horrible cramp. The ropes around her arms dug into her skin. How those women in movies were able to twist free or work their way towards something sharp to use and cut their bindings free must take way more strength and a big ass miracle to pull off.

And special effects. And convenience. Props strategically

placed in all the perfect places.

Tessa had none of that.

"Did he tell you about the curse?" Alex leaned against the wall on the far side of the room, smoking another cigarette.

What could she say? The truth wouldn't help. Lying wouldn't either. A sinking feeling oozed into her belly. *Lucian.* She should have told him everything. From these men coming to her, to the blackmail, to the suspicions she accused him of when she saw all that stuff in his room. Even the murder…

How was she going to get out of this now? Lucian wasn't coming for her. And these men definitely weren't letting her out. Maybe… maybe she could work a deal? Could Tessa build something like a bond with this asshole and use it to her advantage? Hell no.

"Did he tell you about the curse?" Alex repeated, anger lacing his tone.

Tessa bit her lip and stiffened when he walked over to her. Raising his hand, he shot off and slapped her across the face. Stars burst in her eyes. The sting of his strike shot straight down her spine.

I deserve it, she thought. *I deserve everything I'm getting now.* She tasted the coppery flavor of blood in her mouth. Tears welled in her eyes. Spit and blood filled her mouth. Alex leaned down, bracing his hands on either side of her thighs as he gripped the chair seat she was tied to. "Answer me."

Tessa spat in his face.

She wasn't going to get out of here alive. No way. And she wasn't going to drag Lucian into this tragedy if she could possibly help it. Regardless of everything, she loved him. No matter if he was the good guy, the bad guy, or actually cursed… she was in love with him.

You don't sacrifice the one you love. You save them.

Her protective instincts gave her a fresh wave of energy. "Go to Hell."

Alex didn't slap her a second time. He punched her.

Tessa sailed back and took the metal chair with her. The back of her head smacked the floor and pain exploded in her body from the impact.

She had very few fucks left to give. *I deserve it.*

Those toxic, and sometimes untrue, words seeped into her with resolve. She always said this to herself when things went badly. Just as her mother would say them to her when she failed to please the bitch. What became an assault to her confidence as a child, had morphed into a coping mechanism as an adult. It made things more survivable if she felt they were deserved.

Tessa always invited pain. Accepted her punishment. Sometimes asked for more of it just because it tasted familiar and familiar was nice.

Pain covered up pain, didn't it? Smear agony all over your imperfections and maybe they won't be so noticeable. There's always room for improvement. Always time for more practice-makes-perfect. Sometimes, Tessa couldn't tell if she was strong or just numb. Punishment was a blurry line for her. She hated how she needed it to survive herself.

She eats it like it's life. I feed it to her like it's poison. She's toxic. Seeps into me. Destroys me. I like it. I hate how I can't wait to see her again. I hate that I can't stay away.

Alex lifted her chair, setting her upright again. Tessa's left eye began swelling shut already.

The door swung open. Colton and Simon swaggered back in. Tessa tensed when Simon came closer only to cup her cheek. He tilted her head back. She cringed, braced for him to hit her. "She's close," he smiled.

Close to what? Her waiting grave? Losing her shit? Close to giving up and letting them kill her so she'd be put out of her misery? She was close to a lot of things. None of them helpful.

Lucian's voicemail from earlier replayed in her head. *There are bad guys I go after. I'm not the worst thing out there, Tessa. But I'm far from perfection too.*

Tessa almost smiled. These men were after Lucian. These men used and abused her. They were going to kill her. There was no question who the real bad guy was here. Even if Lucian wasn't perfect, he was perfect for her. To her. With her. For her.

But he wouldn't know about any of this. Not unless they tried to blackmail or lure him out themselves. If that was the case, they never needed her in the first place. No… there was something they needed from her in order to get Lucian.

It didn't make her feel special or hopeful. It pissed her off. The last thing she wanted was to die with Lucian's death on her hands. She should have told him about all of this instead of dancing in his mansion like a lunatic. She should have confessed her troubles to him instead of screaming his name to the roof as he fucked her.

Then, she was facing jail time for murder. Now, she was facing certain death.

Tessa's moral dilemma gave her whiplash again.

Maybe it was a good thing she hadn't said shit to Lucian. Knowing him, he might try to rescue her and then these assholes would get what they wanted. Nope. Not happening. Tessa rolled her head back and let out a long sigh. God, her face hurt. She focused on that pain and let it consume her. Pain was good. Pain was tolerable. Heartache and guilt weren't for her.

"You like this." Simon said, because he must have read the expression on her face. "Good." He tapped the tip of her nose with his finger. "That's really good."

Her belly cramped again. Tessa noticed Alex and Colton moving around in her peripheral vision. Simon squatted down and stared at her for a long minute. "Can you see it?"

Her brow pinched. *Huh?*

He tapped the corner of his eye. "Sometimes, when you're close enough, you can see it."

She shook her head, unable to follow him. See what?

"There's a cross here," he explained, tapping his left eye. "It's genetic."

Was she supposed to respond to that?

"It's where the legend started."

Tessa swallowed around the tightness of her throat. She didn't want to ask questions. She didn't want to put herself out there for them to take from in some way. But... she also had a stupid streak a mile long and a tiny part of her hoped if she played nice with Simon, he might be nice back and maybe untie her? She could work out an escape plan from there.

"What," her voice cracked, and she had to clear her throat. "What legend?"

"Get her water, Alex."

"But she—"

Simon jerked his head and glowered. "Water. Now." Alex immediately left the room to obey. Simon turned back and gave her his undivided attention. "The legend of vampires hating the sign of the cross. It was never a religious thing. It was this." He tapped his hazel eye again and shot her a grin. "We put the fear of God in them though, so I guess on that level, if you believe in having a maker, there's that."

"Vampire?" Her chest caved. This was hopeless. Simon was as crazy as the rest of them. Including her.

Alex came back in with a bottle of water and handed it over. Simon unscrewed the top and gently placed it against her lips. "Here, sip slowly. The drugs will have your stomach in knots for a while still."

She took a swig. The coolness flowed down her throat and chilled her belly. Holy Hell, she could feel the water like it was spreading through her limbs. It was refreshing. Alarming. Tessa was hyperaware in every sense of the word.

A far cry from the groggy aftereffects of the drugs they'd given her earlier.

Simon got their convo back on track. "Lucian didn't tell you he was vampire."

Tessa shook her head. He offered her another sip. She took it.

"Well, I'm sure he didn't want to scare you." Simon rubbed his thumb along her chin, swiping away a little of the water she'd dribbled. "Our kind have hunted vampire and Lycan since the dawn of time." He screwed the top back on the bottle and put it down. Clasping his hands behind his back, he sighed and started to pace. "At one point, we almost had both species extinct. Then, a vampire and shifter fell in love with the same woman and managed to get her pregnant at nearly the same time." He tossed her a cunning grin. "That was a game changer for all of us."

Tessa's chest tightened, making it hurt to breathe. He really thought this was real.

"The woman ended up cursing both the children she birthed and now vampire and Lycan are destined to suffer in constant longing. All satisfying methods of..." he paused and stared at the joining of her thighs, "*release*," he purred, his gaze flicking back to her face, "are short-lived and barely penetrate the deep-seated craving for something more."

Tessa's heart hammered in her throat. Lucian's voicemail story came back to her again...

"Because she still loved her children, her curse could only be lifted if they found their mates in time. Until then, they would remain cursed with constant longing. Any satisfaction they find would be painfully temporary, and their souls forever tortured and hollow without their true mate. I'm part of this story, Tessa. I'm cursed. And I have no idea when my mate will ever come... or if they even exist."

Okay, she'd play along. "What does this have to do with me?"

Simon clucked his tongue. "You are many things, Tessa. Stupid isn't on your list of flaws."

She cocked her eyebrow at him, wincing because her swollen eye still throbbed. "Are you saying I'm his mate?"

Tessa hated that her heart swelled with the prospect. But this wasn't real. They were delusional killers.

"We suspect you are." Simon licked his lips and began pacing again. "Lucian's incredibly careful. Especially with you." He laughed. "My men almost dismissed it completely, chalked it up to a lover's tryst, but then..." He stopped walking and looked over at her again. "Lucian's focus locked on just you. You don't keep his attention, you *own* it."

Tessa's lips peeled back in a snarl. The act was so automatic; she didn't have time to cover it up and keep her emotions in check.

Simon's expression turned to delight. "And there it is." He snapped his fingers at her. "That inexplicable possessiveness." He closed the space between them and held her face in his hands, tipping her head back again. "I can't believe you were right under his nose all this time."

Tessa jerked her face out of his hands. Or she tried to. But his fingers dug into her cheeks to keep her head tipped back. "What are the odds of it happening twice?" he chuckled with amusement.

What did that even mean? What happened twice? Simon ran his thumb along her swollen cheekbone, making her hiss in pain. He let go and took a step back.

"You were asked to lure him in." Simon pulled his cell out of his back pocket. Dressed in fatigues, he looked like he was about to go to boot camp, not orchestrate a murder. "I'm going to give you a second chance."

Tessa didn't want a second chance. Her whole existence was second chances, and she never failed to fuck them up. Biting her lip, she desperately siphoned through her options to scrape a plan together. Simon spoke in hushed tones to whoever was on the other end of the line. After hanging up, he signaled Alex and Colton to come over.

The room was big. About the size of the dance studio she worked at. With all the mirrors, it almost brought her a sense of comfortable familiarity, except for the hogtied-by-a-lunatic aspect. Also, the nausea from the drugs.

Salty sweat bloomed across her top lip, and along her skin, which made her wounds sting. The damn ropes on her wrists chaffed like a bitch. The men started moving under Simon's cryptic orders. Colton and Alex left and returned several minutes later with a bar, a duffel bag, and Tessa really didn't know what else. Her mind was shutting down again. Her fight-or-flight response glitched, and she was shrinking into herself now. Hiding. Darkening.

"Stand," Simon purred as he helped her rise from her chair.

She was free. She'd somehow just missed Simon cutting her ropes. Shit. Tessa needed to get a grip.

He positioned himself behind her and bumped her ass with his groin. "Get over to the mirror and place your hands on them."

Tessa's heart ran in panicked circles. "W-w-why?"

He yanked her by the hair, forcing her head to bow back, and he snarled, "Don't ask questions. *Obey.*"

Her body complied, even though her mind screamed in protest. Tessa walked over to the mirror and realized she was barefoot. She must have lost her shoes somewhere between her apartment and here. Face-to-face with her reflection, Tessa ignored her swollen eye, busted lip, bruised neck, and torn clothing. She placed her hands on the mirror and braced herself for an attack.

Was he going to rape her? Beat her? Kill her?

The insane part of her soul giggled at the idea that this was how she'd go. All her life, she sought out punishment. First from her mother, if only to have attention and praise. Then lovers… and finally, Lucian. No matter how perfect he claimed she was, Tessa would mess up her carefully constructed angles and poses so he'd be forced to find fault and spank her for it. Fuck her for it, too.

When had punishment become pleasure?

When had she turned into this creature?

Why did she assume Lucian would have only enjoyed her if

he found fault in her? She shook her head, unable to overthink anymore.

When Simon came up behind her and ran his hand along her hips and swept his palm across her ass, Tessa's cheeks clenched. Oh God, what was he going to do? A chill raced through her veins when he leaned into her ear and whispered, "Second position."

Her body, so conditioned to obey and go into this stance, automatically posed. Her hands, however, remained pressed against the glass. "Trained at Julliard, did you?"

His lips twisted in an amused scowl. "I studied you as much as I studied him, Tessa. I have some clue on how you fucking tick. Ballet? Really?"

She wondered what made *him* tick. What weakness did he have that she could expose and exploit? Tessa needed to come up with a plan to buy her time until she figured out how to escape this maniac.

Grabbing her by the back of the neck, he growled, "Dip lower."

Tessa bent her knees and descended gracefully. Simon pushed her head down, still not satisfied. "Lower. Lower. *Lower.*"

She went into a deep squat. If she'd not had her hands against the wall, she might have toppled over. Already her legs burned, her body having gone through so much recently.

"The blood curse makes it so once a vampire sees the reflection of their *alakhai*," he purred, running his finger down her back. Gathering her hair in his hands, Simon started to braid it. "They're on borrowed time unless they find, bond, turn, and mate with them. While vampires search for their fated mate, they begin to break down. Body temps rise. Their skin becomes sensitive, almost too fragile to stand the sun or extreme temperatures. Their impeccable speed slows down. They go color blind, lose their ability to taste food. Become deaf. Their sanity," he chuckled, "goes out the window."

Tessa's thighs quivered with the strain of keeping herself in position as Simon crouched down next to her. "Guess what happens after that?" he asked with a wicked smile.

More sweat tickled her upper lip. "W-what?"

"They burn." He tucked a wisp of hair behind her ear. "Like dead leaves in a wildfire."

Why did it sound so true? And if so... not only was he *not* crazy, Lucian may be in major trouble.

Simon rose to his full height and walked over to the duffel bag. The zipper giving way was loud in Tessa's ears. Panic revved her system again. She almost popped up and spun on him. Tracking him in the mirror, Tessa watched Simon pull out a whip. "Rise, Tessa."

She obeyed even as bile rose in her throat.

Simon licked his mouth. "I think you like this too much."

No, she really didn't. But her body would have looked otherwise. The blush of her cheeks, sweat, tremors, her fiery gaze — it could all look like lust to someone sick and twisted. And considering this was the exact thing she would beg Lucian to make her do, if only to feel his hard cock thrust inside her when it was over? Yeah, Simon wasn't the only twisted person here.

Tessa channeled her torment. Used it. Thrived on it.

"*Arabesque!*" Simon called out.

She didn't move a muscle except for her right hand. Staring at him in the mirror, Tessa smiled and flipped him the middle finger.

He chuckled behind her. "Oh Tessa, you're about to regret your stubborn streak."

With that, Simon raised his arm, and Tessa's cocky smile fell. He swung down. The whip lashed her back with a fierce strike.

Tessa wheezed from the agony. Stars burst in her vision as she slammed against the mirror.

"Second. Position." Simon ran the leather cord through his hand like he had her hair just moments ago. Affectionately. Calmly.

Tessa gasped for air. She'd never felt pain like that in all her life. *Oh God, this is going to get so much worse.*

"Tessa," he crooned. "Don't make this more drawn out than it has to be."

She closed her eyes, despair washing over her. "Why?" she whispered. *Why me? Why this? Why now?*

"We're giving you a second chance to lure him out," Simon repeated. "We can't get close to their headquarters, and they have the upper hand on us in most ways. This," he said, waving his hand around the room, "is the best option for us at this point. Now..." He leaned against the mirrored wall and grinned. "Are you going to be a good girl and help us, or do I have to use the whip to make you more obedient."

"Please," she cried. "I can't..." *I can't do this. I can't betray Lucian. I can't survive you...*

"Jesus, you're a headcase." Simon disappeared behind her again, and she flinched when their gazes met in the mirror. "I hope he's watching this," Simon purred. "If the curse doesn't kill him..." His arm reared back, whip in hand, "Watching you shred to pieces fucking will."

Tessa pissed herself just as the whip stuck her back again.

CHAPTER 25

Lucian gasped, his eyes popping open as a fresh wave of holy-what-the-hell-is-going-on cranked his ass up. Roaring, he arched his back and clawed the air.

"He's stable!" someone shouted.

Stable his ass. He could barely breathe. Lucian couldn't see a damned thing except blurry squiggles and blobs. The scent of fresh blood caught his attention. His fangs throbbed with the need of it. Reaching blindly, he snagged the first thing he touched — an arm — or at least he hoped it was an arm, and sank his fangs in.

Sweet mother of glory, this was some good stuff. Lucian took long pulls of the vein, letting the blood fill his mouth and coat his tongue and cheeks. He guzzled greedily.

What happened? Where was he?

Lucian pulled hard on the vein he'd latched onto. He sat up for better leverage to take more of that goddamn blood. It was thick and hot and almost sweet. Every gulp made him feel stronger. Every drop brought him a little closer back to earth, like it was made of gravity.

His vision sharpened. The buzz in his head faded. Some of his pain ebbed.

Then a new instinct gripped him — one that took a full minute of Lucian feeding for it to sink in.

Tessa.

His body was rock hard for her. Confusion hazed his impulses. Lucian pulled back, releasing Dorian's arm. He had to get her, mark her, turn her... keep her.

"Tessa!" He lurched from the bed and pain shot his ass right back to where he started, flat on his back, seeing stars. He noticed he was bandaged all over the place. Gone half-mummy or some shit, and most of the gauze was already turning red. His right leg was in some kind of splint. And don't you know his left arm was tied down along with his other limbs. "Let me go!"

The room began spinning. He was going to hurl.

"Easy," Dorian said to his left. "You've broken your leg in four places, ruptured your spleen, cracked every rib, punctured a lung, have a concussion, and fractured three vertebrae, plus your skull. Give yourself a fucking minute."

He didn't have a minute. Lucian tugged at his restraints, hissing in panic. Pain shot down his spine and he vomited. The fresh blood he'd just drank spout out of him like a geyser.

"God damnit," Dorian said. "You just wasted it."

"*Lucian.*" The powerful voice forced him to freeze. He literally couldn't move a muscle. Compelled by the king of the House of Death, Lucian was immobilized. "Give him more blood," Malachi ordered.

Reys stepped forward, a worried scowl on his otherwise handsome face. Biting down on his wrist, Reys held his freshly opened vein over Lucian's mouth.

Lucian shook his head, trying to fight back the need to feed and scream that there was something else wrong with him. But he couldn't. His body was in endurance mode—too many bones broken, too much blood lost. He needed all the strength he could muster to defend his mate when he got out of here.

His brows pinched together as he drank from the opened vein held out for him. Reys's blood was nothing like Dorian's. Reys was thicker, spicier, ten times more decadent. Inwardly, Lucian screamed. Outwardly, he was completely still. Malachi would likely keep him immobile until he was mostly healed. Lucian half-wondered if he was swallowing by himself or if Malachi was compelling his throat muscles for him.

Help me, he pleaded with his eyes on Reys. He continued drinking. *Help me out of here! I must find her. I have to—*

Lucian grunted as his leg cracked. Bolts of lightning shot down his limbs, his nerves firing off as they regenerated.

"Easy," Dorian said again. "Pull off before you drain him."

Lucian's mouth opened of its own accord, or rather, Malachi's compulsion. The king was controlling his every move. It was violating and humiliating for Lucian to be reduced to a busted puppet in front of his crew. Still, he knew better than to reject this gift. If Malachi was out of his rooms and by Lucian's side, then he must be damn close to death's door.

He licked his lips, relieved to have the use of his tongue at least. A numbness cascaded through him, starting at his cheeks and flowing down his throat, chest, arms, waist, legs, and reached his toes. He blinked. Everyone was in focus... but in black and white.

Shit. He'd gone color blind. It was just one more phase of his curse. His body was giving out on him.

"Tessa," he groaned, groggy as hell. Exhaustion slid over him with a heavy blanket. "Need... find... Tessa."

He crashed into a deep slumber.

———∞———

Tessa's head lolled to the side. She was so beat down, fear couldn't even phase her at this point. Her back hurt so bad, there wasn't a word for it. Raw. Bloody. Tender. She was all too thankful she couldn't see the damage done back there. Her torn shirt hung loose off her shaking shoulders, the cotton soaked in blood and sweat. Her pants were in worse shape since they were saturated in urine.

Rasping, Tessa pressed her face against the mirrored wall. The cold silver glass did little to ease her feverish terror.

"Tell us about him." Simon's tone was back to being soft and patient.

Tessa's lips tightened into a thin line. She'd told him already she didn't know much about Lucian. *But you're in love with him*, Simon scolded. Yes, she was. And now she didn't know why. When Simon drilled her with questions, none of which she had an answer for, he whipped her as punishment.

It wasn't sexual. It was agonizing. Demoralizing too, especially when he kept calling her a vampire whore and a cursed, defiled cunt.

Too beat down to fight back, Tessa submitted when he put his arms around her and escorted her into the chair she'd been tied to earlier. Silently, he picked up the bottled water and unscrewed the cap again. She didn't cringe when he pressed it to her lips. She sipped it, if only to soothe the burning in her throat from screaming.

"Good girl." He played with her braided hair and let it fall over her shoulder. Then he stared at her for a long while. She had no clue what he was thinking about. Didn't care because it didn't matter. She just wanted to be left alone to die.

"Have you been to their headquarters?" He gripped her chin and snarled, "Answer me."

Tessa blinked slowly, exhaustion making everything sluggish and difficult. Even moving her mouth took great effort. "I'm not sure. What's it look like?"

"It's a mansion. Old. Lots of property and tenants. Have you been there?"

"I think so," she whispered. She'd been to *a* mansion. Who knew if it was the place he meant or not. She'd never have called it a "headquarters" though. And she would never have called Lucian a vampire. Tessa really didn't know shit about shit.

Simon gave her another sip of water. Her back blazed like it was on fire. Her ears were filled with a weird whirring sound. Her busted eye was totally swollen shut now.

"Describe it to me."

Tessa slumped in the chair, unable to keep herself upright. The instant her back hit the chair, she cried out and pitched forward. Simon caught her and cradled her carefully against his broad chest. The switch of tone and behavior was jarring when he cooed, "You suffer for no reason, Tessa."

Wasn't that the truth? But suffering was what she knew. *Thanks, Mom.*

"Help us and we'll help you. We can relocate you, pay for everything, set you up in a new town with a new dancing job if you want that."

Lies. Simon said nothing but lies. And yet she desperately wanted to believe him. Why?

Because she was a stupid dipshit. Because for once, she wanted something to go okay in her life.

"I only saw a music room," she mumbled into his chest. Her face hurt from them hitting her. Her eyes burned from crying so hard. "It had instruments, a dancefloor, some furniture."

"Mirrors?"

"Yes."

"How many?"

"I don't know. I didn't count." Her eyes fluttered shut. Tessa felt like she just jumped off a cliff and was free falling. She jerked herself away from him.

"—his room?"

She missed what he asked. "What?" Her eyes fluttered shut again.

"Can you tell me about his bedroom?"

Tessa drooped against Simon once more, unable to do anything other than breathe.

"Alex, bring the witch in." Simon put his arms around Tessa carefully. "Hang on, Tessa." His voice was velvet and warm. "Hang on, baby."

Tessa couldn't even respond. Her arms hung at her sides. She felt like a wilted, dead flower. "Please," she rasped against his chest. "Please, stop this. I don't know anything."

Focusing on anything besides her pain, Tessa counted Simon's heartbeats as he held her pressed to his chest. Simon sighed into her hair. Too tired and confused to decipher whether that was a good sign or not, she felt herself fade out.

"Yes, Simon?" A woman approached behind him.

"Are you sure about this woman?"

"I wasn't wrong about his brother's *alakhai*, was I? What makes you think I'm wrong about Lucian's?"

Tessa felt Simon's chest vibrate as he argued, "How close is she?"

"Let me see her."

The room spun as Simon pushed her off him so the woman could get a glimpse. Tessa's vision blurred. She couldn't make out the details of the woman's face, beyond black hair, brown skin, and the scent of patchouli. Thin bangle bracelets tinkled on her wrist as she tipped Tessa's chin up. "She's almost there."

"Almost where?" she mumbled.

"Can we trigger it?"

The woman huffed. "You can certainly try." Then she let go and Tessa's head lolled forward again. "But without Lucian near, it's wasted effort. He might not have fed from her at all yet."

"Worth a shot."

"I hope you know what you're doing, Simon. Your obsession has not gone unnoticed."

"A vampire is a vampire. No one should care which I take out or why."

"You've depleted resources that weren't yours to spare for just this one," she argued. "The others are displeased."

"They can fuck off."

"I'll tell them you said so, *Savag-Ri*."

Savag-Ri. Tessa knew that term. *Savag-Ri 7 today. All mine. Thank you, Tessa*. The vision of Lucian's handwritten note was a jolt to her senses. She sat up and gasped.

Simon paused. His gaze narrowed. "You've thought of something."

She didn't know what to say that could get her out of this. "No," she lied. "My back is killing me."

"Weak little bitch," Alex snarled from the side of the room.

"Alex, take the witch out of here."

"I have a name."

Simon grimaced. "One I'll not speak lest it gives this one ammo on us."

"You plan to let her go then?" the witch asked.

Simon's gaze darkened. "*Leave*."

Tessa had no idea if this was a good or bad exchange. She also had no clue if Lucian's note was a good one or a bad one. If he went after bad people, which Simon, Alex, and Colton definitely were, then why was she dragged into this? What other phrases had they used again? Oh yeah...

"What's an *alakhai*?" she asked.

"It means All Key in a dead language."

How dead could it be if they still used the term? "What are you trying to trigger in me?" Tessa mustered enough strength to look him in the eyes. "What am I besides someone you tried to blackmail?"

"Bait." He pressed the water bottle to her lips again.

This time, she refused to drink. "I think you put too much weight in Lucian's opinion of me."

"What makes you say that?"

"He was nothing but good dick. I was nothing but a broken

ballet dancer he liked to fuck with. That's all we were to each other."

Simon played with her braid again. "I love that you're trying to convince yourself that's the truth. We both know otherwise."

"Because that lady says so?" She half-laughed. "Now who's trying to convince themselves of bullshit truths?"

He dropped her braid. "I like you." Taking several paces back, Simon crossed his arms.

"I can't help you." Tessa said. "I don't know anything more than what I've already said." More lies. "Whatever you think you're going to 'trigger' out of me, it's a waste of time and energy. I'm not about to sprout fangs or turn into a bat, no matter how hard you whip me. Vampires aren't real. You're delusional."

And she was as good as dead. *Just get it over with*, she wanted to growl. But if she said those words out loud, they might kill her. Tessa didn't want to die yet. She also didn't want to look weak in front of them. In a grand gesture fueled by stupidity and surrender, Tessa bent down and grabbed the bottle of water. Staring at Simon, she poured the water out onto the floor. The one bit of kindness he'd given her, now wasted.

Simon's eyes lit up. "God, you're going to be fun to play with."

She didn't respond.

"More fun than Luke's *alakhai* was. That bitch sobbed her eyes out until we finally shut her up by emptying a clip of bullets into her."

"Well, then..." Tessa cleared her suddenly dry throat. "At least you put her out of misery quickly."

Simon's smile spread wide, contorting his face and making him look ten kinds of cruel. "Oh baby, what makes you think we did anything to her quickly?" He sauntered over and grabbed Tessa's hair, yanking it by the roots. "Those bullets came *after* we tore her apart for a month." He kicked the chair out from under her and forced her to the ground. "And trust me," he snarled in her face, "she didn't appreciate where we shot her. No matter how many times we dug those bullets out and tried again." He dragged Tessa back to the wall. "Placement, as I'm sure you're well aware, really does make a difference in many things. Don't you agree, *prima*?"

CHAPTER 26

Simon commanded Tessa to hold fifth position. "If you budge, I'll shoot you," he warned. "And I'm a creature who appreciates perfect placement." He nudged her back foot, pointing out that she wasn't in perfect alignment. "Don't test me unless you're willing to take my degree of punishment."

Her heart slammed to a stop.

Simon pressed his body flush against hers. "I'll fuck your ass so hard my cum will spray out of your mouth. I don't have the same standards as the rest of my kind."

Scared, Tessa assumed fifth position, making sure her ankles aligned, and her feet pointed in opposite directions. This position was simple, but sometimes hard for her to hold because of scar tissue.

Simon raised her arms over her head, and he kissed her cheek. "Very nice," he whispered against her ear. She could feel his hard cock pressed against her backside. The burning lashes on her back overrode her fear of his dick though. "Perfect," he purred and stared at her through the mirror. "I hope he sees this. I hope he appreciates what you're willing to go through for him."

Tessa didn't know what to say to that. She just wanted all of it to stop. Simon backed away and finally left the room. While holding her position as perfect as possible, Tessa stared at her reflection and willed a miracle to form.

See me, she begged in her mind. *See me. Find me. Rescue me.*

Holy shit. How had she come to this? Held hostage, shoved

into a stupid dance position, Tessa was actually begging a man—who was accused of being a *vampire*, by the way—to magically see her in a mirror and come hunt her down to save her sorry ass.

Now who was the delusional one?

Her perfect posture lasted less than five minutes before her arms started sagging. There was no use in complying. They were going to kill her, no matter what. And honestly? She was stupid about some things, but not about this simple, terrifying fact: Simon was going to make sure he took his time with her. Tessa's death was going to be slow, agonizing, and awful.

God. Damnit.

"Fuck you," she growled at the mirror. Was it a two-way? Maybe he was watching from the other side. She almost hoped that was true. "Fuck. You."

Getting ballsy, she dropped her arms and touched the mirror to test her theory. Her finger and its reflection had a gap between them. So no, this wasn't a two-way. Damnit. Next, Tessa's gaze sailed upwards to check for cameras. Any indicator that someone was watching her.

She found nothing.

Her stomach clenched with hunger pains. Sinking down on her ass, Tessa stared at herself in the mirror and kept her focus on one thing: Lucian.

Part of her was furious to be in this mess because of him. Part of her was pissed with herself for not telling him about Alex and Colton from the beginning.

They spent two years building trust between them and when it mattered most, Tessa hadn't given him the benefit of the doubt. But really, come on. You can't just go up to a Dom, who you had a very restrictive contract with, and say something like, "Oh hey, I'm in love with you and uhhh, I'm also getting blackmailed for a murder I *miiiight* have committed, and the blackmailers are using me to lure you out because they hate you. Also, umm since we're being open and honest? What's up with the kidnapping station you got in your dresser? Those files? The rope? The weapons? Annnnd what exactly did you mean when you said I was toxic?"

See, no matter what level you're on with your Dom, none of that fit in a healthy, solid partnership. Communication was key, her ass.

Tessa should have gone to the police. That would have been the justified, reasonable solution to all this. So why hadn't she? Because Tessa didn't want to go to prison, that's why. Duh. Whether she deserved to go or not, she didn't want to do it.

Paxton Brown. That son-of-a-bitch was the one who smashed into their car and destroyed everything.

The night of that accident, Tessa was someone else. Someone who had a friend, a future, a career. Joy. After that night? Tessa was nothing. Her friend was dead. Her career given away. Her life's work gone in a flash of headlights and twisted metal. During recovery, she became a messy tornado of negative thoughts and cravings of revenge.

In a moment of nothing-to-lose, Tessa ended up on Paxton Brown's doorstep. To this day, she couldn't remember driving there. She only remembered hearing he was out of prison, having served only a third of his minimum sentence. That sonofabitch was in jail for less time than it took her to go through physical therapy to learn how to use her leg again. The whole thing was so unfair: He was out of prison. She was still in one. He was free. She never would be. And her friend? By then, Tessa had detached herself so effectively, her friend no longer had a goddamn name.

Tessa's breath hitched. Hadn't Simon mentioned something about not saying that "witch's" name in front of Tessa because it could be used against her like ammo? Tessa totally got it. Names held power. The power to destroy what little bit of sanity Tessa held onto.

But she said Paxton Brown's name often. Tessa never let go of the resentment she carried over what happened. Yes, it was an accident. But he shouldn't have been behind the wheel. He ended one life, and ruined another, all because—

Tessa stopped thinking and dropped back into her blank headspace. She wasn't getting out of here, and she had no idea how long they were going to keep her in this mirrored room. She'd be damned if she was going to waste a minute more thinking about Paxton Motherfucking Brown. What a bunch of bullshit.

Emotions slammed into her, like shoving grenades down her throat, piling up and prepping her for implosion. She was never getting out of here…

She wished she'd died the night of the accident. Tessa sucked back a curse, heartbroken to let that thought live rent-free in her mind. Because it was a lie. She didn't wish that. Not anymore. Tessa stared at herself in the mirror again. Tucking her knees to her chin, she started rocking back and forth. If by some miracle she got out of here, she wouldn't waste her life by living in resentment and dancing for her mother's ghost. She'd start fresh. Be someone else entirely. Maybe change her name too.

Closing her eyes, she imagined what a new life would look like. But those images kept getting smudged and overwritten with other visions. Instead of an apartment by the beach, it was a dark room in a mansion. Instead of ferns and flowers on the patio, it was a busted fountain. Instead of brightly colored bedding and white walls, it was a black four-poster bed and musical instruments in a richly decorated and decadent room.

Lucian. Even in her next life, she'd want him in it.

Have you been to the mansion? Simon's earlier question sent chills down her spine. He wanted to know what was in Lucian's house. Why? Was something hidden in there, like a priceless piece of art or flash drive or something? She shook her head and sighed. God, she watched way too many movies. But what else could it be? What was he looking for? Wait, he mentioned mirrors.

Vampires and mirrors. Reflections.

Tessa's heart tried to pick itself up but couldn't find the strength. She pressed her cheek and hand against the mirror. "Please," she whispered. "Please find me. You can keep me." Tears sprung from her eyes again, her throat tightening. "Please, Lucian. Find me and keep me. *Save me.*"

He'd saved her time and time again during their meetups. Did he know that? Did he ever realize those moments with him were what she lived for? He gave Tessa what she asked for, but instead of breaking her down, he built her up. Even if he pointed out her obvious and on purpose mistakes, he did it in a way that made her *want* to be imperfect. He called her stunning, strong, incredible with such confidence that she'd believe him. He brought out the best in her, no matter how hard she tried to do the opposite with herself. Lucian not only made her feel cherished, but he also lured her demons out and played well with them. She should have told him she was in love with him long ago. She should have done lots of things, truth be told. God, she was an idiot. *Stupid, stupid,*

stupid.

Time didn't exist in the room. Tessa ebbed between overthinking and numbing out. With her cheek pressed to the mirrored wall, her soiled pants sticking to her crotch and thighs, and her back mess of stripes and welts from that whip, pain ruled her from head to toes. Tessa sat there until the door opened again. Even then, someone coming in didn't register. Not until Simon snagged her arm and started dragging her across the floor again.

"No, no, no!" Tessa kicked and tried like hell to fight back. He let her go and walked over to a tray of food sitting on her chair. "Good to see you understand," Simon said.

Tessa tracked his movements. "Understand what?"

"That compliance won't gain you favors."

Yeah. She got that. "Old habits," she sighed, too tired to care now. He was going to hurt her over and over and she'd grin and bear it until her body gave up. The end.

"Get over here and eat."

Tessa wasn't sure she should. When was the last time she had any food in her stomach? Days, she realized. After she ran out of Lucian's house, she'd been too distraught to eat. There were no windows in this room, so she couldn't tell how much time had passed since they'd brought her here. But her stomach was well beyond cramping at this point. They'd given her water, but no food until now.

If she ate, she'd have energy to fight. If she starved, she might die faster.

Choices, choices.

"I can always force feed you." Simon reached over and cut off a piece of omelet with a fork. The tines scraped the plate as he pulled the egg off and held it out for her. "Crawl over here and eat this. Don't give me an excuse to shove this fork into something..." His gaze flicked to her chest, "not on this plate."

What was he saying? He'd stab her in the boob? *This guy...*

Tessa came over, but she'd be damned if she was going to crawl like an animal towards him. Simon sat in a chair at the back. The hair on the back of her neck stood on end. Holy shit, she'd really been unaware earlier when she tapped out against the wall. If she hadn't noticed he'd come in with a second chair, what else did she miss?

Grabbing the plate of food, Tessa eased down on the seat and winced. Every movement she made hurt. Simon wiggled the fork in front of her. She didn't eat the egg from it. Instead, she took the fork from him and fed herself. It tasted like shit.

Smirking, Simon tapped his finger on the glass of water next. It had ice in it. The little cubes clanked as she grabbed the glass and brought it to her lips. It sounded so loud. The sweat from the cold water chilled her fingertips. It pissed her off to take a sip, but she needed to. She was so thirsty. Gulping some of the water, the iciness flowed down her throat and spread through her veins. Her stomach cramped again.

"Why are you doing this?" she whispered.

"It's our duty." Simon leaned back in his chair, one leg stretched out and almost touching hers. "And our privilege."

"All because of a legend about two men knocking up the same woman who then got pissed and vengeful?"

His gaze sailed from her eyes to her nose, to her throat, then back to her eyes. "They're vile creatures, Tessa. We're not the bad ones. They are."

"*They*, the vampires."

"And Lycans."

Holy Hell, she was in the Twilight Zone.. Maybe she could navigate the conversation and learn something useful to get out of here. "What's so awful about them?" Tessa stabbed another forkful of the egg and shoved it in her mouth. "Do they blackmail, kidnap, and whip innocent people too?"

Simon's smirk fell. "They do worse."

"Oh, so they shoot their victims, then pull the bullets out and shoot them again with fresh ones? That kind of worse?"

Simon leaned forward, a different kind of smile playing on his face. "*Worse.*"

"What's worse than murder?"

"You tell me."

She drank more water and stared past Simon, over to her reflection.

"Eat," Simon urged. "You're going to need every ounce of energy you can get, Tessa." He dropped down to the floor and grabbed her foot. Her shoes were gone already. He studied her feet, pinching and wiggling her toes. Not playfully, it was more like an examination.

She dropped the fork onto the plate and nearly toppled the entire tray, including the water, onto the floor. "What are you doing?"

"Relax," he said.

Yeah, right.

Simon bent over and grabbed her left ankle. Setting it on his lap, he started massaging her foot. His hand was hot and strong as he worked on the tender parts first. She wanted to pull away from him. As if sensing it, his grip tightened. Then he glowered at the tray of untouched food balanced on her lap. "Eat."

"I'm not hungry." She felt sick. Woozy.

"Then at least drink." Simon's teetering from kind to cruel made everything more confusing. He massaged her heel next.

"Why are you doing this?" Her eyelids felt too heavy. Her shoulders drooped.

Simon's jaw clenched. He didn't answer. Instead, the bastard massaged her heel with one hand, and with his other, he pulled out a razor blade.

CHAPTER 27

Lucian jolted awake. Grappling in the dark, he recognized his surroundings on the feel of his mattress alone. The smell of sex and Tessa lingering in the fabric were pretty good indicators that he was in his safe space. Sweat soaked through his sheets. His hair stuck to his face. His heart galloped wildly in his chest.

What the ever-loving hell happened? Groaning, he swept a hand down his face. Or tried to. But there was a cuff on his wrist, attached to a strap. He was tied down.

"The fuck?"

The past few episodes of his shit-tastic life came barreling towards him like a train on full speed and he was tied to the railroad, unable to avoid the hit. Tessa. Dancing. Violin. Fucking. Fighting. Explosion. His string of voicemails. Tessa's call back. His need to get to her before she did something foolish. The reflection. The crash.

Wait. The reflection. Was that... had that really happened? Lucian cracked his eyes open and looked around his room. It was pitch black. Willing his lights on, his stomach dropped. His room was shades of gray, not silver, black, and blue.

He was colorblind.

Panic tore open the throat of his composure. With a roar, he yanked on his restraints and snapped them from his arms. Then he ripped them off his ankles. Getting tied down wasn't new. It was standard practice when a vampire was fatally injured. If they were strong enough to break free, they were healed enough to hunt

Savag-Ri again.

Lucian was more than strong enough. Dorian and Reys both offered their veins, which pumped with potent energy. Any injuries he suffered from the car crash were fading if they hadn't completely healed already.

Some days it was good to be a vampire.

Other days, it sucked. No pun intended.

Shit, his head was still groggy. He couldn't figure out if the colorblindness was his curse, or an after effect from cracking his noggin too hard in the accident. Lucian honestly didn't know if what he saw in that mirror was true or just his heart's last desperate attempt to conjure Tessa up in a delusional moment of panic.

He'd certainly imagined her enough times to be a goddamn pro at it. Lucian had every inch of her body, every slope, nuance and cut of taut muscle, memorized. From her manicured eyebrows to the slope in her nose, to the exact length of her throat column, all the way down to the bones of each little piggy. It's how he could always buy dresses that fit her like a second skin. It's how he was able to order her those perfectly fitted red pointe shoes.

So, had it been an illusion in that rearview mirror?

Lucian did an inventory of his body. Other than being colorblind, he seemed to be in decent shape. No burning blisters. No deafness or—

He bit his tongue and tasted the blood in his mouth. Nope, still had his sense of taste too.

So why didn't that make him feel better? Why was he disappointed his curse hadn't kicked in?

Because, deep down, he wanted Tessa to be his forever. Not his for now. Not his for later. His for-fucking-ever. And the only way that could happen was if she were his fated mate.

God, he loathed his curse.

Now she was gone. Most likely left town. He knew she wasn't going to stay, even after he tried to spill a little of his secrets to her on the phone. A voicemail with a sorry ass story wasn't going to be enough to keep her close. And why should it? He'd held back from spilling everything. Two years spent earning her trust and developing a bond with her, and he still hadn't been able to go all the way.

That restraint, however, was for her own good, not to save his precious pride. If he told her what he truly was, it might not end well. It would, at the very least, result in Tessa's memories being wiped, and Lucian didn't want her to forget about him.

He could have easily gotten his rocks off with someone at The Wicked Garden. The vampire kink club in town was the go-to place for creatures like Lucian. But nope, he just went there to refresh the rooms, restock supplies, and make sure the security cameras ran properly. The system of fucking and feeding they had there worked great for most, but Lucian found it empty. He craved connection. And with the three-visit limit rule at the club, Lucian couldn't get deep with anyone he played host to. So, he started seeking relationships elsewhere.

Tessa exceeded all expectations. If he could have made a wish list of his ideal partner, she'd check each box and then some. It took one night with her to get Lucian hooked. Since then, she was, by far, his most addictive drug of choice. So much so, no other woman or man — human or vampire — held a candle to her now. She was all he wanted. All he craved. When he wanted to blow off some steam, he took care of himself or called Tessa. He never looked elsewhere.

But really, how deep had he allowed himself to get with her? Not very. Lucian made their relationship all about her, which was fine, but now he regretted the distance.

Yanking open his bedroom door, he stumbled down the hall, naked and suddenly starved again. His fangs throbbed. The halls were shades of gray, black, and white. The mirrors glistened, taunting him, tempting him to take a peek. He gripped the banister and held it tight as he descended sloppily down the stairs.

He wasn't even sure where he was going. The kitchen? To see the king?

He found himself in the music room. Tessa's scent lingered in here as well. Lucian's nostrils flared, his lungs filling with a burning desire to suck her in.

Rubbing his chest, he felt off. Gee, could that have something to do with the mega car crash on top of the backlash from an explosion recently? His life was blowing up, in every sense of the word. But one thing kept him steady and focused: Tessa.

Jesus, why couldn't he shake her?

Lucian stared at his hands, turning them palm-side up, then back again. He didn't look any different. Aside from losing the ability to see in color and having a general achiness, he really didn't feel... *changed*. So why the weirdness in his chest? Why the urge to chase Tessa down?

If he was a decent man, he'd leave her alone. But he wasn't decent, and he wasn't a man. He was a hot-blooded vampire and Tessa was his, God damnit.

Fuck the rules. Fuck the House. Fuck his fate.

Lucian backed out of the music room and charged down to the king's quarters. Malachi sat in his big wingback chair, per the usual, with his gaze locked on the mirror. Lucian stopped at the threshold and gripped the doorjamb. "I'm going to find her. And I'm keeping her."

Malachi stayed eerily quiet. Lucian hoped to get his king's blessing, but if he didn't, that wasn't going to stop him from doing this. It was like two years of denial and dragging his feet was now downward spiraling into mayhem in his soul. He felt sick with it. The best way to get Lucian's claws and fangs out was to tell him he couldn't have something.

He'd take it out of spite.

But that's not what this was. Tessa wasn't a temptation he could walk away from. She was...

Fuck, he didn't know.

"I love her and I'm keeping her."

"You need to stand down."

"I can't." Lucian stormed into the room, naked and furious. "To Hell with the rules, Malachi. I can't walk away from her."

The king's gaze dragged away from his reflection and landed on Lucian with a thud. "You disobey your King?"

"Respectfully, this isn't about you, sire. I *need* her." He rubbed his chest to soothe the ache growing stronger there.

"You *need* to protect your House. You *need* to remember who and what you are."

Lucian's jaw clenched. He wasn't backing down from this. "I'll leave. Cut myself off from the House if I have to."

"You'd abandon your duties?"

"If I have to, y—" His final answer wedged in his throat. Was he really willing to walk away from the House of Death just to chase a human woman down? Was he really about to go Rogue just to have her for a little while?

What would life be like once she died, and he was left immortal and without a House? Making this move would toss his admirable reputation right out the window. No House would take him in because he'd be considered fickle and disloyal. Was he really willing to ruin everything he'd worked so hard for in order to chase down a human female and beg her to be with him?

She was skipping town. Leaving. If she hadn't left already.

"Think carefully, Lucian." Malachi's hot gaze remained on his. The king was a gracious vampire. He kept this home open to any who wanted to serve him, no matter how broken they were or what background they had. Of the three Houses, Death was the most honorable. Lucian didn't want to leave it. He loved it here. Loved his place at the king's side. Loved hunting *Savag-Ri* and sharing his days with his friends and nights with his lover.

"Please." He sank down on his knees, feeling so vulnerable he shook. "I can't explain this. I can't *not* have her."

"You cannot keep a human girl as a pet, either. That's not fair to either of you. There is a precedent in this House. If you want a pet, leave us and join your family. The House of Blood would welcome you. They like pets. She'd be well taken care of there."

Lucian's lips peeled back in a hiss. He didn't want to go to the House of Blood or anywhere else. It was Death or nothing. "Then I'll live on my own."

Malachi's dark brow arched, and his eyes moved away from him to settle back on his reflection. Lucian stood up and left the room without saying another word. To speak would be a waste of breath at this point. He'd made his choice, right?

Time to face the music.

CHAPTER 28

Lucian grabbed a bunch of whatever out of his closet. Pants, a shirt, or shit, that wasn't a shirt. Okay, now he had a shirt. He couldn't tell if his jeans were black or blue. Had no clue if his shirt was orange or purple. As if it even mattered.

Well, it sort of did.

If he was going to walk away from everything and propose starting over with the woman he loved—after chasing her down and explaining things—he kind of wanted to look presentable. It was the aristocrat in him. The trained parts of his youth demanding attention to showcase his good breeding. Dapper, polished and brimming with wealth and good genes, Lucian slicked his chin-length blond hair back, its waves settling and falling perfectly. When he bent down to put on his socks and shoes, his hair fell into his eyes again. It bugged the shit out of him. And he couldn't get a grip on his sock to put it on right. Christ, he was a mess. Tremors made it difficult to do even the simplest task. His stomach cramped. Ungodly heat rolled up his back causing him to break out in a sweat.

It made him panic a little. Lucian did a mental inventory of his body again. Aches came with the job. His accident certainly earned him a few breaks and bruises. But he couldn't shake a hyperawareness simmering under his skin. It was contradictory to the dullness of his senses. He reached behind him on the bed and grabbed a pillow. Bringing it to his nose, he inhaled deeply. *Tessa.* He could smell her, but not the scent of the fabric softener he used.

If… okay, hear him out, if his curse had kicked in, and he was in a ticking time bomb situation, he would be able to see only Tessa in color. Only smell her scent. His body would snap into survival mode and instinctively know the only thing that could save him was his mate. So, the only way to find out if he was dying or not, was to find her.

Slowly, he rose to his feet, dropped his socks to the ground, and prowled over to one of his mirrors. He had three in his bedroom—a floor length one standing in the corner by his instrument collection, a massive carved one over his dresser, and a small cheap one just inside the door. Plus, the big one over the sink in his bathroom.

Lucian took a good look at his reflection in the mirror. Holy hell, he looked like shit. Yeah, sure, he was just in an accident that had rearranged his bone structure and organ placement temporarily, but this was beyond that. He looked… primal. Like an animal left in the dark too long. Even his hunger raged like a beast, caged and aggressive, sensing its first meal in eons.

Leaning in, he pulled and squished his cheeks. Wow. He was really rocking the Walking Dead look. He needed sleep. And food. Blood healed him and made him stronger, but Lucian needed actual food too if he wanted to be at full-throttle-ready-for-anything level of strength. Especially if he was going to break off from the House of Death and support Tessa in a new life. He'd need to be at his very best to pull it off.

He tipped his head back and opened his mouth wide. His fangs were out. All the way. He hadn't noticed nor realized he'd cut his inner lip or tongue by accident. Yet there were fresh punctures on his bottom lip, welling with blood from his massive fangs.

Brow furrowed, he lifted his arm to his mouth and bit it. Didn't feel a damned thing.

Shit.

Maybe he had seen his *alakhai*? Maybe his blood curse was hitting his system. Lucian's gaze sailed along the mirror, and he silently begged Tessa to show herself. But there was no one except Lucian looking back at him. Just good old miserable, confused, rattled and wrecked Lucian.

He always said there were two sides to his coin—fucked and fucked up—but this was the first time in his life he felt like they were the exact same thing. He needed to get his shit together. Stop stalling and start his hunt for Tessa. Charging back to his discarded socks and shoes, he got a move on.

Someone knocked on his door. *Now what?*

"Enter." He hollered and Dorian slid in. Lucian shook his head, "Don't try and stop me." The king most likely summoned him here to talk sense into Lucian. The Reaper need not waste his breath.

His best friend came over and sat next to him on the bed without saying a word. Leaning forward, he rested his elbows on his knees and steepled his fingers. Keeping his eyes straight ahead, he said, "I'll support whatever decision you make."

Lucian grunted and shoved his foot in the first sock.

"But before we go all out and chase down a woman and scare the piss out of her with our impeccable stalking skills, answer me one question."

Lucian gritted his teeth and put on his other sock.

"Do you think you're self-sabotaging?"

"What the fuck, Dorian?" He shoved his boots on and started lacing them.

"I want you to think carefully before you answer me." He stayed silent as Lucian popped off the side of the bed and headed to his dresser to grab a couple of weapons as a precaution. "Think about it, Lucian. You haven't grieved your brother. You've kept Tessa so low key, not even I knew about her until recently. And now suddenly, you're willing to drop your entire existence and go after a human."

"Your point, Reaper?"

"I know you've felt guilty for breaking tradition and joining this House. I also know you blame yourself for not finding Luke's *alakhai* in time to save him."

He didn't want to talk about this anymore. He'd talked both subjects to death already.

"Now, you're going after the one thing you're not supposed to. And you know if you do, your reputation will be ruined." Dorian stood and made his way over to Lucian. "A reputation which has taken you centuries to build and maintain."

"So, the King loses a guard." Lucian shoved two small blades into his holster. "Boo fucking hoo."

"Not just a guard. His right-hand man."

"You can take my place. You're more suited for it."

"Aaaannd now you're lying to me." Dorian leaned back against the dresser and crossed his arms. "You look like Hell."

"I feel like Hell," he mumbled. "Since I woke up from the accident, I haven't felt right at all. And I thought—" he bit his lip and shook his head. Slamming his top drawer shut, he went back into his closet for a... shit, he didn't even know. What was he doing?

"You thought what?"

Lucian waved him off. "It doesn't matter." Whether Tessa was his fated mate or not, he loved and wanted her. It was time to get her.

He stormed out of his closet, beating feet to the door when Dorian stopped him in a flash. Glaring, the Reaper's gaze sailed over Lucian's face, down his neck and to his arms. Then his brow furrowed. Dorian leaned in with his nostrils flared. "You smell off."

Gee. Thanks.

"Your scent." Dorian took another whiff and his eyes widened. "Your pheromones are kicking out. So is your aggression."

"You can smell that?" Then he huffed and rolled his eyes. Of course, the Reaper could smell things like that. He was raised by Lycan, and they had fine-tuned his already acute sense of smell. Lucian scrambled to find a connection to Dorian's observation and his current situation. "I thought I saw her," he said cautiously. "In my rearview mirror as I was driving to her house. It made me freeze up, and that's when I crashed into the truck."

Dorian tensed and ground his molars so hard it sounded like boulders grinding against each other.

"It doesn't matter." Lucian tried to go around him. "Whether I saw her or not, I'm going to get her back and be with her."

The Reaper stepped out of his way. "I'll help you however I can."

"If we both hunt her down, she'll feel cornered. I just hope she hasn't left town."

"I heard she took off through the window."

"Yeah." Lucian rubbed the back of his neck as the spark of shame heated his cheeks. "She went snooping. Didn't give me a chance to explain anything she found."

"You going to tell her what you are?"

"What choice do I have? I can't expect her to be with me without her knowing exactly what I am and what it'll mean."

"If you go Rogue, you know that leads to bigger trouble."

Dorian knew about Rogues all too well, and now Lucian felt another twinge of guilt grind into his heart. "I won't lose my shit."

Vampires weren't meant to be on their own. Every necessity was controlled by the three Houses. Safety, blood, and strength all stemmed from the kings and the Houses they ruled. If Lucian broke off to be on his own, how would he feed? He couldn't expect Dorian to be his secret meal. That wasn't right. And although he figured Victoria, Xin, or Reys might contribute, they'd get in trouble for aiding a vampire who essentially abandoned his position and burned his bridges to be with a human.

Vampires couldn't live off human blood alone. If they tried, it made them go slowly mental. They also needed other things, like bone dust, for safety. That wasn't happening without a weaver to cast the spells on the dust. Lucian wasn't a weaver. He might get lucky enough to find some on a black market, but that was a major risk as well as an expensive one. His money was tied to his family and the House. Both accounts would be reclaimed, and Lucian would have nothing but what's in his pocket when he left here. There was so much more to being a vampire than food and safety. All of which he needed to figure out. Fast.

"I'll handle it," he said quietly. "I... I'll figure out something, okay? All I know is, I can't breathe without her. The thought of Tessa being out there without me has me ten kinds of fucked in the head. I feel like I'm going to claw out of my skin if I don't get to her."

Dorian stepped back and looked at him from head to boot. "Fuck."

Couldn't have said it better himself. Lucian scrubbed his face with both hands and exhaled a shaky breath. He couldn't stop trembling. "I feel like I'm about to rattle apart."

"We need to find her." Dorian started for the door. "I'll drive."

"I've got this, man. I don't want to drag you into my shitshow. Stay here with the King." *And take my place*, he thought.

"I'm going with you, Lucian. And I'm fucking driving."

He was half-relieved his best friend was going with him, but guilty about it too. "I can drive myself."

"The hell you can." Dorian ripped the small mirror off the wall by the door before stepping out into the hall and handed it to Lucian. "You're not taking your eyes off this mirror."

"Dude, I—"

"She's your *alakhai*!" Dorian gripped Lucian by the shoulders. "She's your fated mate, asshole."

The air whooshed out of his lungs. "How do you know?"

"Because your skin is already heating, and your eyes are bloodshot. Look at your arm."

Lucian glanced at his bicep and saw a patch of blisters. *Holy shit.*

Dorian stormed down the steps and made a beeline for the front door. "Come on, before you turn to ash and join your brother."

CHAPTER 29

Tessa moved at the speed of a sloth. She'd been drugged again. Simon gave her a foot massage long enough for the drugs to kick in, and then he sliced the bottoms of her feet with a razor blade. Such a twisted mercy this was. The drugs dulled the pain, but it also made her slow. She couldn't hold onto a thought for very long. All her movements were sloppy.

With Alex at the door watching as if taking notes, Simon turned on a small Bluetooth speaker and began playing music. Then he told her to dance.

Dance for her miserable life.

Dance for her merciful death.

"You're used to going until your feet bleed," he mused. "I only expedited the process. Now *dance*."

Any time she stopped to catch her breath, he whipped her. Stalking like a wolf with a rabbit, Simon never took his eyes off her. Songs ranging from Disturbed to Dubussy played in no order she understood.

Blood made the floor slick in no time. The bottoms of her feet looked like she'd taken a cheese grater to them. Sweat poured down her temples, chest, and back. Her palms were clammy. Every arch and bend made her back scream in protest. Each twirl and leap made her feet cry. And that was *with* the drugs pumping in her system, dulling all of it.

"I hope he's watching," Simon said with an appreciative tone.

"I hope he's already ash," Alex rebutted.

Tessa ignored them, desperately burrowing into a headspace that allowed her to handle this level of torture. She was going to tap out soon, and then what? Would he slice her somewhere else? Do something worse?

The unknown fueled her into a fresh dance. The drugs made her too sloppy to seek perfection, so if Simon was looking for her best work, he was going to be disappointed. She wished her hair had been pulled back in a tight bun. That severe tug on her scalp might put her in a better zone. Alas, it cascaded down her shoulders and her ruined, aching back because the braid had come undone. Between the sweat and her hair sticking to her skin, the wounds in her back felt like molten fire. She leapt into the air and landed hard on her cut toes. Collapsing with a gasp, stars burst in her vision. She breathed through the agony. Steeling her spine, Tessa forced herself back up to keep going.

Tessa was beyond crying now. Her eyes only burned. As did her pride, for whatever reason. Tessa never thought she'd die like this. Not that anyone expected to get kidnapped and held for someone's personal and dubious entertainment. As shitty as this was, it's not what had her so hurt.

It was that she would likely die dancing.

My mother would be so proud.

While the music blasted and the room spun, Tessa's thoughts lasered in on the simple fact that she was going to die in a plié. Or fifth position. Or in the middle of an ara-fucking-besque.

She'd spent her childhood making up for existing by pleasing her mother the only way she knew how. Doing what it took to get that bitter woman to pay attention to her—because even negative attention was still attention. Tessa always hated ballet. But as she got older and better at it, the lessons molded her into a carbon copy of her mother. She hated that too. Tessa hated everything about her sordid life.

If she could, she'd turn back time and tell Lucian she loved him, burn every pair of ballet slippers she owned, and be another woman entirely. Meeting Lucian and having him sign a Dom contract with her that perpetuated Tessa's toxic obsession with perfection, *en pointe,* was insane. She just hadn't realized it. Not until she read that journal entry of his...

The real ass kicker? She'd have kept going with it. Tessa

would have continued allowing their relationship to go down that dark road. Not because she desperately sought perfection in her stance, but because of how Lucian always looked at her while she danced. He gave her what she said she needed, plus so much more. He built her up when she tried to tear herself down. He even admired her mistakes. Tessa frequently caught his subtle smirks and little grunts. He loved watching her dance. And for him, she'd have danced until she died.

Too bad Lucian wasn't going to see her ever again.

Steeling herself, Tessa sucked in a breath and went into a series of steps that caused her bloody feet to paint the floor red. She was going to dance for him, even if he'd never see it. With her hair down and wild, her clothes stained in blood, piss, and sweat, Tessa was going to dance her soul out until she dropped for good.

———⊰∞⊱———

Lucian's stomach wouldn't uncoil. As Dorian sped down the road, following Lucian's directions to Tessa's apartment, Lucian kept a death grip on the mirror and wouldn't look up from it. No… he *couldn't* look up from it. His gaze deadlocked on his reflection, and he almost went into a trance. Thank God he had Dorian with him. The Reaper was right. He'd have never made it down the road on his own.

Three quarters of the way there, Lucian's muscles engaged, jaw locked, and fingers clutched the mirror. "Oh… God."

There she was. His *alakhai*. Her reflection took up the entire mirror as if it was a movie screen.

She was dancing. Twirling, limber and boneless, like she was water made woman.

Lucian leaned in and clutched the mirror harder. Tessa's hair was down instead of up in the bun she favored. Her movements were uncivilized instead of controlled. Almost aggressive. There was no other way to describe it. She wasn't a swan, moving with grace and poise. This Tessa reminded him more of a scorpion with refined, violent elegance.

His breath caught as she spun and leapt. The angles of her reflection changed again and again. No longer beguiled by her image, Lucian got a real good look at Tessa. His muscles tightened further.

Her reflection shifted again. What the hell? Now he was watching her from a position on the floor. At least, that's what he assumed. But how? And what's so red? Jesus, everything was smudged in red. Lucian's throat squeezed. That was blood. He could see it was red because it was *her* blood.

"Tessa," his voice was barely a cracking whisper. She was hurt. Badly.

Was she dancing until her feet bled? Holy Hell, if that was the case, then she'd done too much damage to herself already. Lucian couldn't breathe. He had to get to her. Stop her from hurting herself further.

His mind reeled. She was somewhere dancing with a lot of mirrors. Her studio? "Turn left," his voice dropped to a deadly tone. Lucian barely registered anything other than Tessa's reflection. *Stay with me*, he thought at her image. *Please stay with me*.

His wish was granted, by some ungodly miracle. But the angle of her reflection kept changing. "No." His fingers cut into the edges of the mirror. "*NO*." This couldn't be right. Her back. Was it—

Tessa bent and stretched, arched and reached. Lucian noticed her face was swollen. Blood stained her shirt.

What the flying fuck was happening?

"Go right!" He barked at Dorian. He could feel where they were on the route to her without looking up, he realized. He could have made this trip blindfolded. "Another right at the stop sign. Hurry up!"

The car lurched to a stop, wheels screeching as he and Dorian both pitched forward. Lucian slammed his hand on the dashboard to keep from flinging into the damn windshield. "Move!" he screamed. Dorian had slammed the brakes to avoid hitting a pedestrian. Once the narrow street was cleared, Dorian punched the gas pedal and took Lucian's orders the rest of the way, his hands strangling the wheel.

Lucian didn't wait for the car to halt. He jerked open the door and ran, full tilt, to Tessa's dance studio. It was morning and the doors were locked. DAMNIT! He banged hard enough on the door to dent it. Screamed her name until his throat shred. He knew she came to the studio during off hours to dance alone. She *must* hear him banging on the door. "God damnit Tessa!" he hollered. "Open the door!"

Nothing.

No lights. No sound. He shielded his eyes and peered in through every widow in the front of the studio. The classrooms didn't have windows, only mirrors, so he couldn't see which room she might be in.

"Do you smell her?" Dorian asked from behind him.

Lucian scented the air. Nothing… he got nothing.

Frustration rode his ass hard. He smashed his fist through the glass door, unlocking it with a reach-around. Shoving things open, he rushed inside and dashed into every room. All of which were empty.

"Tessa!" He glanced around, looking for signs that she'd been there at all. "Tessa!"

No music. No dancing. No scent of his mate or blood on the floor like he thought he saw in the reflection. Nothing. It was like she was a ghost, taunting and teasing him. Luring him to certain death.

His chest ached with a fierce burn. Shoving past Dorian, Lucian beelined it back to the car and hopped in the driver's seat. Dorian jumped into the car just as he pulled off. They headed to Tessa's apartment next. Lucian's protective instincts went haywire in a matter of heartbeats. Where else could she be dancing in a room full of mirrors if not her dance studio?

Maybe she rented another place? Maybe she'd already left town and was at a new studio in a new town. With her track record and reputation, it would be easy for her to find work, even on short notice.

Thank God her apartment was only a few blocks away from where she worked. Tessa didn't have a car, so she walked to most places or took the bus. They pulled up to her apartment complex and Dorian looked around for signs of threats while Lucian barreled into the building. Gripping the banister, he took the steps two at a time and reached the second floor with his heart thundering in his ears.

"Tessa!" he didn't bother knocking. Kicking her door open, he destroyed it with one smash of his boot. Lucian's eyes widened when he stepped inside.

"*Savag-Ri*," Dorian said behind him. "Their stench is every-fucking-where."

Oh God, no. "Are you sure?" Lucian couldn't smell a damned thing besides Tessa's unbelievably luscious scent. His lungs filled with it. His skin prickled from it. She always smelled like honeysuckles. But now that his survival instincts were running full force, her light, sweet scent was heady. Thick and sticky sweet. Lucian prowled through her apartment looking for signs of a struggle or anything that might give him a clue about what happened.

Tessa's bed was made. Her soft, dark purple towels hung on the hooks in the bathroom, shower curtain pulled shut. Hell, even the toilet roll was brand new on the dispenser. For a woman who was leaving, she'd made sure what she was walking away from looked pristine.

Such a Tessa move.

His woman thrived on perfection in all things. Especially in herself. Damn, how he longed to shake her of the habit and get her to cut loose. Be wild. Be… free.

That's what she was doing, though, right? Cutting loose? Setting free?

Fuck that noise. He stormed out of the bathroom and nearly tripped on the suitcase just outside her bedroom door. Where was she? Everything looked almost staged—cleaned up and perfect. Skirting past her suitcase, Lucian headed back into the living room and saw a duffel bag on the couch.

There were blood droplets on the floor.

Lucian slammed to his knees and shoved his face into the dried blood. Something awful and wicked tore out of him.

"Is it hers?"

"No." Lucian's voice didn't even sound like his own. He sounded like a demon. Fire lit his soul, sending lava coursing through his veins, burning with possessiveness. It might not be her blood, but someone was in her apartment and that someone dripped red droplets on her rug. Who? How? Why? When? "Can you smell anything else, Reaper?" Lucian felt murderous and useless at the same time. He was downward spiraling at an alarming rate.

"No," Dorian said cautiously. "Not yet, at least."

Lucian went into the kitchen and ran his hand along the countertop. Everything was wiped down. If his senses were on point, he'd bet a million dollars the air carried the scent of cleaning products and bleach. With his heart in his boots, Lucian traced a finger along the counter and walked towards the sink. *The fuck?* Lucian's brow pinched as he stared at pieces of burnt photos in the basin.

"No sign of a struggle anywhere." Dorian checked the windows and surveyed the bathroom and bedroom a second time. "But I swear I smell *Savag-Ri*."

Lucian knew what Dorian was hinting to. "She's not allied with them."

"You sure?"

No. He wasn't. But he refused to believe the worst of her.

"Does she smoke?"

"No."

"I smell cigarettes."

"Her landlord does, I think."

"Could he have come here and started something with her?" Dorian pointed at the blood droplets on the floor again.

"Doubt it." Lucian did his homework on him too. Dominic was just a greasy pig looking for a cheap thrill. He'd never resort to violence because it would cost him his kids and the guy only had partial custody as it was. But… if Dominic came here and tried some shady shit, Tessa might have hit him.

Hmmm.

The thought of Tessa cracking him in the nose made Lucian smile. She'd fight if she had to. He had every confidence in her ability to stick up for herself. But damnit, he hoped that wasn't the case. The idea of Tessa in a situation that forced her to violence didn't sit well with Lucian.

Looking in the sink, he picked up the pieces of burnt picture and tried to fill in the blanks. The scraps didn't offer much of a clue. But to him, it looked like a cathartic moment of closure where she'd burned her past…

Or destroyed incriminating evidence.

What had she gotten into? Who was in on it with her? The fact that Lucian didn't know Tessa as well as he thought struck him right in the soul at that moment. He was on the verge of losing his mind, and his fucking life, over a woman who kept too many secrets from him.

Pinching a random piece of burnt photo, Lucian ground his molars together. What had she done? And more importantly... was it going to jeopardize their future?

Lucian was a forgiving vampire. If she did something morally corrupt, he'd help her out of it. The only thing he couldn't stomach was infidelity. And he believed with his whole heart that she told the truth about staying faithful to him. So whatever trouble she might be in, they'd handle it. No problem.

But first he had to find her.

Glancing around the kitchen one last time before heading back into her bathroom, Lucian felt his stomach twist in knots. He kicked the door shut for a little privacy and braced himself against her tiny bathroom sink. He needed to piece this together. If she left, she'd have taken her suitcase. If she stayed, she wouldn't still be packed. If a *Savag-Ri* had her, surely there would be more signs of a struggle?

The answer was painfully obvious. If Dorian smelled *Savag-Ri*, Tessa wasn't here, and those were indeed droplets of someone else's blood on the floor...

Nope. Nuh-uh. Not possible.

He couldn't bear the thought of one of those bastards anywhere near his woman. How could they have found her? How would they have known about her at all?

Guilt wracked him. He should have been more careful. Should have taken more extreme precautions to keep her safe from them. He should have broken more rules and lined her apartment with spelled bone dust to make sure those fuckers never had a chance to get to her.

As if his heart couldn't handle the truth, Lucian's imagination took a wide left turn. Maybe the scents Dorian was picking up weren't *Savag-Ri* at all. Wasn't there a bowl of tangerines on the coffee table? *Savag-Ri* usually carried a faint scent of moldy citrus. Maybe it was just a bad piece of fruit?

He was really grasping at straws here. But how could he not? No part of this made sense. There was no way a *Savag-Ri* could connect the two of them together. Every place they met was vampire owned and protected. She didn't have a car. Lucian always sent a vampire chauffeur to pick her up.

"Oh, shit." *The hackers.* Did they have something to do with this? The theatre's security footage had been tapped into recently. They could have seen Lucian and Tessa at the theatre the other night. Okay, that was a stretch, but totally possible.

"Lucian!" Dorian called out from the main area. "You need to come see this."

He didn't want to leave that bathroom. Staring at his reflection, Lucian's temples throbbed, and teeth ground together with fury. His grip tightened on her sink so fiercely, he cracked the countertop.

"*Lucian!*" Dorian barked louder.

Flinging the door open so hard it smacked back and punched a hole in the wall, Lucian stormed straight to him. Too pissed to speak, too wrecked to think straight, he only stared at what Dorian held in his hand.

It was a piece of a picture from the kitchen, the black eaten edges standing out in the Reaper's palm as he held it out to him. "This is the theatre," he growled. "Look. You can see the rows of red velvet seats."

Lucian couldn't see red velvet seating. His vision was too whacked for colors. "Shit." His heart stopped. *The hackers.*

Dorian worked to piece together more of the photo fragments. "They're too destroyed," he mumbled. "I can't begin to think of what this one is." He held another damaged piece of evidence up.

Lucian felt sick. The scrap of photo was a close up of what looked like a body and a portion of someone's fingers stained dark. That was Tessa's hand. How he knew that went beyond reason, but he was certain of it.

"This looks like an act of violence," Dorian warned. "An incriminating one."

"Not possible." Tessa wasn't a violent person. She was a self-punisher.

Though, if she had no choice, would she—

Lucian's balls shriveled. Was this why she was a self-punisher? Did Tessa do things she then needed atonement for? He… he couldn't believe it. Refused to think this photo meant what they were leaning towards accusing her of.

If she killed or hurt someone, she must have had good reason.

Lucian's ears began ringing. A horrible burning scorched his lungs. He coughed and blood spurted out of his mouth. He wiped his lips and chin with the back of his hand. "She'd never hurt someone without good reason. Even then, I don't think she'd do it."

"We don't even know what this is, man. It could be nothing."

"If it was nothing, she, or whoever else was in here, wouldn't have burned it." Lucian needed to splash some water on his face and get his head back on straight. He was in the middle of one big, fat dead end and didn't know which way to go from here. Aaaannd his body was shutting down.

Fuck.

Storming into the bathroom again, he flicked the faucet and cupped his hands under the cold water. Splashing his face, he heard his cheeks sizzle. Holy Hell, he was burning. He was fucking burning! Anxiety, fear, worry, and rage consumed him. He splashed more and more water on himself, as if that was going to put out the fire his curse had lit.

It didn't.

Gritting his teeth, Lucian's fangs pierced his inner lip. *Ba-boom, ba-boom, ba-boom,* his heart jackhammered in his chest. *Eeeeeeeeeee,* went the high-pitched tone in his ears.

"Please... no." He braced himself against the sink, sucking in air. Rasping, wheezing, his lungs felt charred. How long would this continue before it worsened? How long could he hold out before it became too severe to survive?

Help me! Luke's screams roared in his ears, bouncing off his skull and pummeling into his heart. Lucian hadn't been able to help Luke, any more than he was able to help himself. This felt like an impossible task. Desperate, he looked up from the sink and glared into the mirror.

His world exploded. Rage bellowed out of him.

Tessa stared at him again, tears streaming down her cheeks. Her one eye was swollen shut and her face was badly bruised. Lucian stumbled back with his mouth open in a roar. Her mouth was moving, her brows pinched together as if she was scared and hurt.

"Where are you?" he yelled at her reflection, knowing damn well she couldn't hear him. "Tessa!"

Her head tipped back a second before her face slammed into

the mirror. Tessa's forehead splintered before his eyes. "NO!" he screamed as blood poured out from the split in her head. "Tessa!" Lucian slammed his fist into the vanity mirror as if he could break through and grab her. "TESSA!"

Her head smashed into the mirror a second and third time. More blood poured. More tears fell.

Shattered pieces of mirror fell around him and Lucian's instincts went apeshit. "Tessa!"

Her mouth moved, but he could barely see what she was saying. His vision was blurred with rage filled tears. Blinking hard, he shoved his face against the mirror and stared at her mouth.

Fuck you.

Fuck you. That's what she was saying. *Fuck. You.*

"No! *No!*" Lucian lost his shit. Smashing more of the mirror, he ripped the rest of the goddamn thing off the wall and shards scattered along the floor and counter, making a hundred Tessa's stare at him. All of them bloodied and screaming *Fuck You.*

"Tessa!" Lucian was about to incinerate from anger alone. "No!"

Her head slammed into the mirror a fourth time and she crumbled to the floor.

What he saw next made his hot blood turn glacial.

CHAPTER 30

Tessa stopped dancing. Numb. Tapped out. She was ready for the music to end.

"Kill me," she said. On wobbly legs, she made her way over to Simon. It felt like he stood miles away from her. Was the floor swaying? She listed back and forth as though she was on a boat. Tessa had no balance. No fear. And no hope. "Kill. Me."

Simon's unwavering stare was accompanied by a smug, shitty smirk plastered on his face. She was pretty sure he'd held that expression for the better part of the last seven songs. The drugs were wearing off and Tessa was acutely aware of each cut on the soles of her feet. The lashes on her back had torn and opened more. No surprise there, given how she'd gone all out with her dancing.

Talk about a subspace. There'd been no pleasure in her movements. No cathartic release. Nothing but detached floating and numbness. An opportunity to reflect without feeling any of the emotions she normally suffered when she got all in her head and couldn't escape.

When Tessa had found peace with herself and her fate, she'd stopped dancing. Stopped caring, praying, thinking, hoping. Determined to die, she planned to poke all of Simon's buttons until he shut her up permanently. "Keep smiling like that, I'll knock the smugness right off your face."

Simon laughed. "I'd love to see you try."

With a hefty inhale, she made her way over to the chair set to the side and tightened her grip on the back of it. Using it as a crutch, she tried catching her breath. Alex stood over at the door and hadn't moved since this whole musical mindfuck started, but now he pushed off and headed straight for her.

Simon put his hand up, stopping Alex from getting closer.

Tessa coughed and winced. "I need water."

"You just wanted to be killed. Now you want water. Pick one."

Death. "Water."

Simon chuckled as he pulled a bottle out from behind his back. "This one isn't tampered with," he assured her. Not that Tessa bought that for a second. Even after she heard the crack of the seal breaking on the cap, she remained convinced they'd poisoned it some other way.

She longed to drink every drop.

With one hand at the back of the folding chair to keep herself upright, she reached out with the other for the water. Simon came forward to hand it to her nicely. The instant he was within range, Tessa swung the chair out and smashed it against him, aiming for his head, but missed because her arms were too weak. She ended up hitting his side, which was protected by his arm.

Snarling, Simon snagged the chair by the leg and whipped it out of her hold. Tossing it across the room, it crashed loudly and skidded across the mirrored floor. *Oh shit, oh shit, oh shit.* Tessa put her hands in front of her—as if that was going to protect her? Simon roared in her face and wrapped his hands around her throat, choking her.

He didn't say a word as he continued to glare at her with his smug smirk still in place and dragged Tessa to the middle of the room with just one hand coiled tightly around her neck. Then he punched her in the gut, let go, and watched her crumble to the floor.

Wheezing, Tessa stumbled forward as she tried to stand back up. She couldn't suck in air. Dropping to her knees, her mind scrambled with options—each one looking more pointless than the last. The tiny bit of composure she had left just got punched out of her and Tessa was fresh out of ideas.

"Why..." she coughed and sputtered. Holy shit, she couldn't get in enough air. "Why are you doing this?"

"Because it's what we do," Simon snarled at her. "It's the only thing we do."

Tessa shook her head. Clutching her belly as she took in a small breath, she rasped, "What has Lucian done to make you be so evil?"

She wanted to know. Wanted to understand why this was happening. Sometimes bad things happen to good people, and guess what? That sucked. This situation wasn't the same. Tessa wanted to know why she was going to her grave on behalf of someone else. She wanted to understand why she was so willing to die for him. Why was she going through all this to protect him?

When Simon had asked her about the mansion, she hadn't given him anything helpful. When these pricks asked about others named Malachi, Dorian, and Victoria, she bit her lip and didn't utter a word. She didn't know those people, and even if she did, Tessa wouldn't say a word about them. Fuck Simon. Fuck Alex and Colton. Fuck everyone.

"Fuck you," she said when Simon wouldn't answer.

"That can be arranged."

Dread coiled in her empty, cramping belly. Fuck this. She wasn't going out with a whimper. Fear and optimism drained right out of her soul. Tessa looked over her shoulder at him. "I bet you'd love to get your dick wet with Lucian's cum and my pleasure all over that puny swizzle stick of yours."

She was insane. That's the only explanation she had for goading him.

"Stupid bitch." Simon stormed forward and fisted her hair. Dragging her to the mirror, he shoved his knee in her spine and yanked her head back by the hair. "Think I'd penetrate you with my dick? Oh no, baby. I've got much more interesting toys to shove into your holes."

Tessa put a tight leash on her panic and forced a smile onto her battered face. If he hated Lucian so much, maybe she could use him as the catalyst to get Simon to kill her and end this. "Afraid you can't compare? I don't blame you. Lucian's *huge*. I can see why you'd be intimidated. Is that why you can't even fight him face-to-face and had to have a woman do your job for you? Can't handle the inferiority, huh?"

Simon slammed her head into the mirrored wall. The impact caused her vision to flash black for an instant. When he pulled her head back from the fractured glass, Tessa rasped, "Fuck you."

He smashed her head again.

"Fuck you!" She said louder. A few more hits, she might just get a cracked skull and this would be over. "Fuck. You."

Simon smashed her head again, and this time she crashed to the floor when he let her go. Blood poured from her split skin. It got in her eyes, streamed down her face to soak her ripped shirt. That shit got in her eyelashes and inside her mouth. Tessa was so far past the hurt. Skull cracked, back a hot mess, shit, even her toes were broken from when she'd danced her soul out earlier. Tessa was nothing except broken pieces with a pulse.

Simon loomed over her, seething. Pulling her up by the throat, he slammed his hand on her back then and propped her up against the wall. Her spine ached against the glass. She didn't have the strength to move away, though. Using the mirror to prop her sorry ass up, she just sucked in air and groaned.

Oh God, this wasn't working out like she thought it would. She was digging her grave deeper and deeper with no guarantee she'd ever be put in it! She didn't move. Just leaned back, gasping for air as her head wounds painted the floor around her. Man, this shit really made a mess, didn't it?

Simon squatted in front of her. With a coldness similar to the way her mother used to look at her, Simon frowned. And in true Simon mind-fuck-fashion, he smeared her blood across her lips with his thumb in a gentle way that matched his now soft tone. "I see why he loves you."

The worst part about this moment wasn't the pain or the confusion or even the hopelessness. It was how her body sparked to life at the mere mention of Lucian loving her. And that, ladies and gentlemen, would be her ultimate curse. Because even at her lowest point, she wanted to do right by Lucian. Wanted to protect and love him and have him do the same to her in return.

Sucking in a ragged breath, Tessa struggled to hold her head up. "Why are you doing this to Lucian?"

At first, Simone didn't answer. He was too busy admiring his work. Or maybe he was enthralled with how grotesque she looked. Who knew?

"Answer me," she rasped. "Why Lucian? Why m—"

Simon bent down and screamed in her face, "*Because he*

exists!"

His fury and hate for Lucian blasted off like a grenade in her chest. Tessa scream-cried as he walked away and left her in a puddle of her own misery. The level of his obsessive hate went beyond irrational and straight into psychotic stalker, murder documentary territory. What had Lucian done to him that would make Simon and these men so... so...

Tessa slumped over as she slipped out of consciousness.

CHAPTER 31

"You're sure?" Dorian pressed the issue as he sped down the road.

Lucian gripped the sides of his head, his knuckles busted and bloody from destroying the bathroom in a fit of unparalleled rage. "*Yes*," he gritted out.

Just after seeing Tessa's head crack over and over against the mirror, she dropped, spun, and rested against whatever mirror she sat in front of. That's when Lucian got an up-close view of her mutilated back. And as bad as that was to witness, it got worse. Way worse.

Attached to her shredded, bloodied top was a note that said: *I hope you're faster than your brother.*

Lucian's bone marrow boiled with barely contained violence. The *Savag-Ri* constantly went after vampires and Lycans. As if their very existence insulted *Savag-Ri*, those creatures hunted their kind down and stopped at nothing to get them.

Now they had Tessa.

How did this happen?

I hope you're faster than your brother.

Lucian was going to tear apart whoever this motherfucker was. Rip him limb for goddamn limb. Rage ate away any grief he felt. Whatever this *Savag-Ri* was playing at, they invited the wrong vampire to the game.

Dorian swerved through traffic as they flew down the road. "We need to arm up," he said.

Hell yeah, they did. With all the fun toys like an Uzi and a flamethrower. Maybe a pair of tweezers and a cattle prod. Who was the last vampire to use the Pear of Anguish? Because Lucian could totally be up for a little orifice torture foreplay before he decapitated them. Okay, now he was starting to think more like his best friend. But how he could not fantasize about spectacular ways to destroy the bastards who'd taken his woman?

They would be lucky if Lucian had any patience at all while taking his revenge.

Rubbing his temples, Lucian squeezed his eyes shut and breathed deeply.

Christ! What were the odds that she was leaving the same time they'd come for her? Or had she known them beforehand? Lucian tensed. She'd been hiding something from him, right? Keeping a secret. Was this it? Had she known he was a vampire, and the enemy coerced her into seducing him? Was she sent to lure him in with temptation?

Had their entire relationship been a fucking lie?

No. Never.

Rubbing his thumb across his chapped lips, the world zipped past him as Dorian sped to his home to load up on weapons. Lucian squeezed his eyes shut, clutching the memory of Tessa's lips forming the words *Fuck you*. Was that aimed at him? Did she blame him for this? She should. It was entirely his fault. He should have never gotten involved with her in the first place. He sure as hell shouldn't have fallen in love with her.

Tessa being his *alakhai* had nothing to do with it because she'd been taken by the enemy *before* Lucian had his first vision of her.

Talk about timing. Jesus, the universe was laughing at him.

Was this entire situation karma? Was this cosmic payback for walking away from family and tradition and following his heart instead of the rules? Was this a cruel, twisted version of an eye-for-an-eye because he'd not been able to help Luke find his *alakhai* in time and now he'd suffer the same fate?

"Stop," Dorian growled, his voice deep and gravelly. "Your guilt is stinking my car up." He rolled the windows down.

Such audacity.

Lucian leaned back and squeezed his eyes shut. "Everything hurts."

"It'll get worse." Something Dorian knew all about since he'd nearly gone up in ashes himself recently. "Self-doubt has no room in your heart, Lucian. Neither does guilt or karma." The Reaper understood Lucian better than anyone.

"Hard to think otherwise, given my failures and shortcomings."

"You're saying this to a vampire raised by a psychotic serial killer."

"Yeah, well, you didn't grow up to be a disappointment."

Dorian snorted. "Nope, I became the House of Death's executioner. You learn to roll with your strengths." He turned onto his road slowly so he didn't endanger any of the kids playing in the street. "We're both weapons. Weapons don't have self-doubt or guilt. They are what they are. They do what they do."

"Hypocrite." Lucian remembered how Dorian fought—fang and claw—to not give into his curse and wanted to incinerate because he didn't think he was a worthy vampire for Lena to be tied to for all eternity. Even though that was far from reality. Dorian was a killer and his mate absolutely loved that about him. He kept her safe, loved, well-fed, and well-fucked. Couldn't ask for a better life than that, no matter who you were.

Lucian would offer the same to Tessa.

"Why's this happening now?" His throat felt raw and blistered. "Why couldn't this have started a month ago?" Had he seen her reflection sooner, this could have been so different.

"Fate must've had a reason to wait until now."

Bullshit. Karma was a bitch, and it was doing its very best to screw him over. *What a difference a day makes, my ass. What a goddamn shitshow.* "I can't breathe," Lucian tugged at his shirt collar. "I can't fucking breathe!"

The car slammed to a stop, and he fumbled with the door handle. Shoving it open, Lucian tumbled onto the sidewalk. His knuckles still bore the cuts from shattering Tessa's bathroom mirror. They'd not healed. *Thanks, blood curse. You're the gift that keeps on giving.*

"I need another mirror." He lost his vision completely for a second. "I can't see!" Was this blindness going to stick? How the hell was his body imploding so quickly? Gulping down air, he swayed on hands and knees.

"Breathe." Dorian squatted down and pressed his hand on Lucian's shoulder, massaging it like Lucian was a side of beef that needed tenderizing. "Breathe deep, Lucian."

In and out. In... aaannnnd out.

Took a hot minute, but his vision hopped back into semi-working order and the street came back, all in shades of gray.

Lena ran out of the house and helped Dorian pick Lucian's overwhelmed ass up off the cement and brought him inside. Holy Hell, he'd never felt this out of control and powerless in his life. Not even when his brother burned right before his eyes.

I hope you're faster than your brother.

He was going to puke.

"Get him water and ice," Dorian said to his mate.

Lucian barely made it to the couch before he tried to get up again. "I can't stay here. I gotta... I gotta go." He swallowed the bile rising in his throat. What were they doing to Tessa right now?

White. Hot. Fire. Consumed him.

Lucian screamed and arched his back as a searing spark of fire zipped down his spine. *Holy fucking mother of fucking fuckballs.* That. Hurt.

Dorian held him steady and shoved a glass in his face. "Drink."

"I can't," he pushed the water away. "How am I supposed to sit here and drink ice water while my girl is—" He couldn't even say any of it out loud. This was a nightmare. If his blood curse didn't burn him alive, his wrath would.

"You're going to do all you can to be strong enough to go after her." Dorian shoved the water in his face again. "Start with this."

Lucian grabbed the glass and water sloshed all over his lap and chest from how badly he shook. He barely got any into his mouth. "I can't even hold the glass. How am I supposed to hold a weapon?"

"You will." Dorian walked over and snagged a few blades laying on the dining table. "You'll be surprised what you're capable of once you see her in person."

Lucian's eyes rolled with a wave of nausea. "We need to google all the dance studios in the area."

Dorian paused. "What did you see?"

Earlier, it took Lucian the better part of a full minute to pull his gaze off Tessa's reflection and that letter, to look beyond her at any clues in the room she was trapped in. He needed something. A clue. Anything to give him a trail to follow and rescue her. And what did fate deliver?

"I saw barres. I think. Or the leftover pieces of them behind her. She's got to be in an old dance studio." Not even a *Savag-Ri* would go through the trouble of tearing down spaces to custom build an entire room tailored to their prey. They wouldn't consider the effort worth it for a vampire, Lycan, or their fated mates.

Unless this guy was a special breed of obsessive.

Dorian nodded and stormed off, returning seconds later with a laptop. "Start looking, Lena," he handed the machine over to his mate. Next, he went into Lena's purse and snatched a cosmetic mirror from it. "Here," he handed it to Lucian. "Keep an eye out for her."

Lucian cradled the small mirror as if it was precious treasure. Dorian moved around the room, plucking blades from his collection and handing some to Lena while she researched dance studios and Lucian stared at the mirror.

The Reaper didn't live in the mansion with Lucian and the other hunters. He preferred the privacy of his small house in Treme. It was close to the French Quarter and within the heart of the House of Death's main territory. As the executioner for their House, the Reaper owned more weapons than all other vampires put together. He preferred blades to guns. Regular bullets only slowed down or irritated *Savag-Ri*. They had a limited number of bullets designed to annihilate their enemy, but, just like bone dust, they weren't easy to make or keep in decent supply.

Nothing came easy for a vampire.

"I wish there was an easier way." Lena's fingers flew across the keyboard. "These assholes are like trying to catch an exhale in a hurricane."

"Don't give them that much credit," Dorian grumbled. "They're good, but we're better."

"I hope so," she whispered.

Lucian didn't say a damned thing. Waiting for her to reappear in the compact mirror, he barely breathed. Was she unconscious? FUCK. Lucian rocked back and forth with the need to fight, kill, and destroy his way to her. So help him God, he would raze New Orleans if that's what it took to get her back.

But Lena was right. Finding their enemy was never easy. Not unless they were out in the open, attempting to blend in with humans. And there was no going into *Savag-Ri* property either, even if it could be discovered, which was highly unlikely. Just like vampires had ways to prevent them trespassing, *Savag-Ri* had tricks up their own sleeves. They also never stayed in one place too long. At least not long enough to be discovered in time. Lucian knew they used witches to aid their mission, but they had to have something else beyond witchcraft in their spell-casting arsenal. Otherwise, they'd be extinct by now.

Bending over, Lucian ran his hand back and forth through his hair. He couldn't stand this. Shoving up, he headed for the door, but Dorian beat him to it. "No."

Asshole.

"Move, before I rip your throat out with my teeth."

"You go out there now, what do you think will happen? You're half-cocked, burning, and *slow*. You can barely hold a mirror, much less a weapon. Sit tight and wait for the others."

"Others?"

"I called Vic. She and some of the guys are coming over as we speak." Dorian put his hands on Lucian's shoulders and pressed his forehead to Lucian's. "We'll get her," he promised. "You just need to bite and turn her the second we do."

Sounded good to him. "I want the bastard in charge. I want him for myself," Lucian growled.

"No problem."

The small battle plan knocked his panic down a notch. "They've hurt her." Lucian wasn't sure who he was talking to—Dorian and Lena, or himself.

"She's a strong girl," Lena said to his left.

Lucian tried to fill his lungs with oxygen. He was suffocating again. "Yeah," he choked out. "She is." He ran his thumb across the mirror, sick with grief and fear for her. *I'm so sorry,* he thought. *I'll find and save you. I'll keep you forever, just hang on.*

Jesus, how many were there with her? One? Ten? Twenty?

Like vampires and Lycans, *Savag-Ri* also ran in groups. They didn't do the solo thing. There was power in numbers.

"I can't wait to meet her," Lena said, looking up from the laptop. In another room, a printer started whirring, so she must have made a list. Shit, how many studios could be on that list? How much time did he have left to find her? "What does she look like?" Lena asked, as if she really couldn't hear the screaming in Lucian's mind.

Beaten. Broken. Bloody. "Like an angel," he said quietly. "Blonde hair, violet-blue eyes. Tall and slim. She's a ballerina."

Lena grinned. "Then she's got endurance."

Leave it to her to see potential. Lucian appreciated her effort. "Yeah, she's..." he shook his head, uncertain where he was going with his thought process. "She's built for agility and stamina."

"All good things when facing the enemy." Dorian handed him another glass of water.

He didn't think he could drink any more. His stomach was in knots. But he sipped it anyway, scared at how icy it felt going down his throat. Lucian's gaze never wavered from the cosmetic mirror. "How long do you think I have to find her?"

"No clue." Dorian's tension grew.

"You're not going to burn," Lena argued. "No way would fate bring you all this way just to fuck you over."

"It did for my brother."

Lena's tone was heavy with sympathy. "Have faith, Lucian."

Easier said than done. First, he must find Tessa. Then survive the unholy wrath he planned to rain down on the bastards who did this to her. After all that, he needed to help Tessa heal... Turn her. Mate with her. Explain everything to her.

Not necessarily in that order.

Would she even want to be with him after this? He wouldn't blame her one bit if she ran for the hills and never spoke to him again. And if he died while she took off? So be it. Malachi's warning haunted him now. *"You must protect her at all costs, even from you."*

He'd failed spectacularly, hadn't he? Holy Hell.

Lucian hadn't protected her at all. She was hurt because of him. Kidnapped, held hostage, and attacked because of a war, she had nothing to do with and one he was at the forefront of. He fell back on his ass in the middle of the living room floor. The walls started closing in on him. His lungs compressed. A cluster of blisters formed on his left forearm. His sight faded, blackness eating the edges of his vision just like the charred edges of the photo fragments in Tessa's sink.

Everything in Lucian's life was falling apart. Burning down. Disintegrating and disappearing and fading away faster than he could save a single piece of it.

Give me time, he begged fate. *Give me a fighting chance to make this right.*

CHAPTER 32

Tessa regained consciousness. For a split second, she wasn't sure if she was dead or alive. Breathing or suffocating. Dim lights flickered overhead because half the bulbs were blown out. The pungent scent of mildew and piss permeated the air strong enough to make her gag.

No Simon. No Alex. No Colton.

Pushing onto her hands and knees, she whimpered. Holy shit, everything from tongue to toes hurt. Tessa steeled herself and mustered enough courage to look over her shoulder and check out her back in the mirror. Her belly dropped when she saw the dark red stains all over her shredded shirt. The busted mirror reflected four starbursts of shattered glass which disfigured her reflection. Maybe that was a good thing. Tessa had a feeling if she saw her back with nothing impeding the view, she'd pass out.

She pitched forward and dry heaved regardless because even though she couldn't see the wreckage of her body, she sure as shit felt every bit of it. The room spun a little when she tried to sit up, fingers splayed on the floor. She couldn't see out of her right eye. She hated everything and everyone.

Something brushed her fingertips. She glanced over to see a piece of paper on the floor.

What the hell?

Gingerly, Tessa picked it up and turned the blood-stained note over.

I hope you're faster than your brother.

Why was this here? Her thoughts were foggy. She heaved again, nothing but saliva and bile coming up. Breathing in through her nose, out through her mouth, Tessa grappled to put the pieces of all this together. Simon mentioned something earlier about Lucian being able to see what was happening. No video cameras in the room. The mirror wasn't a two-way either. And Simon never once pulled out his phone to record a thing. Neither had Alex, or Colton. So how on earth would Lucian see any of this?

Tessa shook her head and grunted. Okay, no shaking her head again. That hurt way too much. Her hand fell over the note, and she crumpled it in a tight grip. Didn't Simon mention something about Lucian's brother earlier? About him dying because he hadn't found his *alakhai* in time?

Or...

She pressed a palm to her temple. She must be concussed. Holy shit, was any part of her not bruised or bleeding? She hissed at the cuts stinging her face. Lucian wasn't coming. How could he?

Once a vampire sees the reflection of his alakhai, *they're on borrowed time...*

Tessa looked around the room. *All these mirrors.* Simon seemed obsessed with her reflection. He must think Lucian could magically see her through them. She stared at the crumpled piece of paper again. It must have been placed on her back. And her back had been up against the mirror.

She needed to do something. Get out of here. Defend herself better. Provoking Simon and pushing his buttons hadn't ended with her eating a bullet, but quite honestly, she wasn't able to handle any more torture, so fuck trying that dumb shit again. She could always take a sliver of broken mirror and cut her wrists. End this herself. But she wasn't going out that way.

They'd taken the chairs out of the room. All that remained was her and lots of dried blood. *Maybe there's something in the closet I could use to defend myself,* she thought while crawling across the room to the closet door. The amount of strength it took to drag her body across the floor was more than she had left. Twice Tessa stopped and fell on her face, panting. But when she had a goal to reach, she met it. This was just another goal. A series of steps to process, repeat, and perfect. She reached out with her right hand, scooted her left leg forward, dug her knee into the floor annnd repeat. Now left hand out, right leg in, annnd repeat. Left, right, scoot. Right, left, scoot.

She had no clue how long it took her to reach the closet door, but eventually she made it to the finish line. *Fuck you*, she thought to Simon. Reaching up, Tessa grabbed the doorknob. Jesus Christ, her back hurt! One twist and a grunt later, the door pushed open, and Tessa fell in, panting in pain.

Her vision whacked out again. Working through the agony and double vision, she dragged herself up and patted the wall in search of a light switch. Flicking it on, a small fluorescent light crackled and sputtered to life. With the lights flickering, she pawed at the wall, desperate to find something to use. A shelf, a wire, a handy-dandy gun locked and loaded would be fantastic. Shit, she'd take a screwdriver, a blow torch, even a goddamn bottle of nail polish.

But there was nothing.

Sinking down on her ass, Tessa crumpled into sobs. "Lucian," she whispered through her tears. As the lights flickered and made her more nauseous, she glanced around the tiny closet, furious that this was the end for her.

What a waste. What a stupendous waste of—

Something on the wall caught her attention.

Was that writing? Scribbles and drawings? Tessa crawled over to look at the hand-drawn pictures. Perhaps these images would wipe away the ones parading in her darkened mind. Tessa sniffled and leaned forward. Her heart stopped.

Magan was here!
Beth is da bomb!
Kelly and Dani 4ever
Studio 79 rocks!
RIP ballet

Tessa knew where she was. This was Studio 79, an old school of dance that closed about five years ago. Holy shit! Scrambling to get out of the closet and back into her original position before she was caught, Tessa went off the deep end, clawing at the floor. *Please, please, please*, she prayed. *Please let this work*.

Tears spilled down her eyes and splashed onto her hands as she looked down at the mirrored floor. Re-splitting one of the cuts on her forehead, she dipped her finger in it. Trembling as fear and time seemed to eat her courage, Tessa pleaded over and over and over while leaving her mark.

If Simon was right and Lucian was cursed... this was her only option left. As far-fetched as it might be, she clung to it with the belief that if there was a snowball's chance in Hell Lucian could find her, he would.

Please, please, please find me, Lucian. Using her blood, Tessa left him a message on the mirror in the back corner of the room. Then, with what miniscule energy she had left, Tessa crawled back to the shattered section of the mirror in the front of the room, pried a shard off the wall, laid on the floor, and closed her eyes.

With a full listing of every dance studio—in and out of business—in all of Louisiana, Lucian wasn't stopping until he cleared each one and found his mate. If he had to do this to every inch of the planet, so be it.

With a half-assed plan, he was almost able to catch his breath and sucked in a lung full of fuck-yeah-I-can-do-this. But his ribs ached, and throat burned, reminding him that whatever he thought he could do ultimately wasn't up to him to decide. That was fate's prerogative. *Damn blood curse.* He coughed, hacking up blood so hot it scorched his throat and lips when he spit it out. He cupped his mouth with both hands and spat into them.

"There's napkins in my glove box." Victoria said from the driver's seat.

Lucian popped it open and grabbed a few to clean his hands. The compact mirror lay nestled in his lap so he could watch it while they drove to the third dance studio of the day. So far, the first two were a complete bust. Filled with kids and parents and teachers, not that it stopped them from sweeping the place anyway. They made sure to keep their weapons hidden. No reason to freak humans out or scare kids. Vampires were pros at sweet talking, so getting in wasn't an issue and their speed made quick work of checking the first two buildings off their long list.

Victoria hit a pothole. "Shit! Goddamn roads need to be fixed. Assholes." She waved at Xin and Reys when they sped by with a list of studios to hit on the west side. Dorian and Lena cut to the

Northside. Vic and Lucian were headed east.

Lucian had never been more grateful for the House of Death than this very moment. "Thanks for helping," he finally said.

"Yeah, well..." She snapped her gum and gave a one-shoulder shrug. "I like killing things that piss me off, so..."

Lucian wadded the napkins and dropped them to the floor. Picking up the mirror, he shoved his energy into summoning a magical miracle spell that might make Tessa reappear.

Nada.

"You were going to leave us." Vic popped her gum again.

"I didn't think I had a choice."

"Yeah, well, you did. And you didn't choose us." She hooked a sharp left and picked up a little speed. "I can't say I'm not pissed at you, but," her gaze flicked to him, "you've never done something without your whole heart invested. You must have felt pretty fucking strong about this girl."

"I did," he squeezed his eyes shut, realizing his slip. "I *do*," he corrected.

"Maybe that's why," she popped her gum again. "Maybe your urge to do whatever it took to be with her was because she was poised for fate to expose her to you, and you somehow recognized it on some kind of spiritual level." She cut off three cars in a row, weaving in and out of traffic. "Or maybe her pussy was just that wet and tight, and you couldn't live without it."

Lucian almost laughed at that. Leave it to Victoria to be the crass one. Storing all his energy for this fight, he didn't waste much on conversation.

A flicker in his lap made him stiffen. Tessa's reflection appeared again. He perked up, his grip tightening on the compact. "Come on, *prima*. Show me where you are."

His heart thundered in his ears. Tessa's mouth kept moving. Going by the angle and way her hair impacted his view, he figured she was staring down at him.

Please, please, please find me, Lucian.

He shattered, seeing her mouth say his name like a prayer. Begging him. *Please find me, Lucian.* A growl ripped out of his throat. His body engaged, muscles expanding, fangs elongating, instincts roaring to get to her.

Tessa's face smudged away. She was... she was writing

something.

"*Come on, come on, come on,*" he pleaded. The message was sloppy and hard to make out. His vision crapping out on him didn't make things easier. Narrowing his gaze, he laser-focused on her blood writing. *Studio 79.* Lucian felt a line of tension snap in his mind. "Studio 79," he growled in a deeply animalistic tone. "She's at Studio 79."

Victoria glanced over at him. "Where the hell is that?"

"It's just outside the Warehouse District."

Victoria slammed her brakes and busted a U-y, nearly crashing into two vehicles to do it. "Where?"

Lucian gave her the directions, unable to keep the shock from bubbling out of him. He'd looked at Studio 79 only a few months ago. He was debating on surprising Tessa with it. The old place was in bad shape but had good bones. He wanted to fix it up and present her with her very own studio, so she didn't have to work for someone else making half as much. But something felt off about it and he backed away from going through with the paperwork last minute.

To return here felt like fate mocking him.

The irony wasn't lost on him.

They pulled onto the street. Victoria pulled over and parked about fifty yards away from the building. They couldn't drive through the structure like the Kool Aid man on wheels. It would draw too much attention and Tessa might get hurt. There was no way to tell what room she was in.

Victoria made the call to the others and told them where to go. "Your girl's pretty clever." She spat her gum out on the street. Looking upwards, he knew she was making a quick plan of attack and surveying the layout and best angles to launch from. "I'll start high and go low." Which meant she was going to roof hop her way over to the studio and take out anyone standing watch up there.

"You armed enough?" Holy Hell, his voice was so deep it was unrecognizable. As if the closer he got to where Tessa might be, the more intensity he felt.

"I brought a couple new toys I've been wanting to try out." She waved a nasty looking needle-like spear.

With a curt nod, Lucian tucked the compact mirror into his back pocket and pulled out two nasty looking daggers he borrowed from Dorian's stash.

He didn't wait for his friends to show up. He wasn't waiting another goddamn second to get to Tessa. With his head dipped down, Lucian headed straight for his target with the church bells ringing ten chimes behind him.

CHAPTER 33

Tessa laid on the floor gripping the mirror shard. When she heard someone chuckle, the hair on the back of her neck stood on end. Keeping still, she waited for one of them to get close enough for her to attack. This was a bad plan. The dumbest one yet, but she didn't have it in her to lie there and take their beatings any more than she had already.

Holy shit, did she need therapy.

Tessa had gone from fuck you, to fuck this, to fuck that, to let me die, and now that she was close to tapping out of life, she wanted to hold on to it with a fierce grip and fight. She literally couldn't make up her mind.

The floor made weird noises as her captors walked across it. Simon laughed. She was so tempted to open her eyes and see what was so funny. Her fear forced her to keep still though. Tessa tracked every noise and nuance she heard. The thuds of their footsteps. A click. A zipper. Something ripped. A chair screeched obnoxiously across the floor and stopped mere feet away from her.

Finally, someone approached. Tessa's heart rattled in her chest.

"Get up," Simon snarled from above her.

She feigned being roused. Tried to lift her empty hand up to her face and rub her eyes.

"Get. Up!" Simon wrapped his hand around her bicep and jerked upwards. Tessa twisted and stabbed him with the mirror shard. But she missed her target. Of course, she missed it! *DAMNIT!*

The shard plunged into the meat of his neck, not his jugular. To make it worse, it only buried halfway. Three inches deep wasn't going to do shit.

"Bitch!" Simon yanked the glass out.

Suddenly, Tessa's body locked up. Jolts of electricity shot through her when they tased her. She was immobile, stunned. When the shock stopped, she still couldn't move. Simon dragged her across the floor and hauled her ass into a metal folding chair. Her head lolled to the side as Alex bound her hands and tightened the straps behind her back. The back of the metal chair rubbed against her raw wounds, making her stomach roll. Simon bent down and began doing something to her feet. And Colton? Who the hell knew where that piece of shit was.

Tessa felt like she was freezing, on fire, and electrified all at the same time. Tremors wracked through her. She could barely keep her eyes open. Her breaths were shallow and labored. She felt a pinch. Her torso tightened. The room kept spinning. Had they drugged her again? She couldn't even tell.

"You're sure about this?" Alex asked. Or that's what Tessa thought he said. Noises sounded muffled.

"Yeah, and if I'm wrong, the outcome still remains the same. You got eyes on everything? Where's Colton?"

Tessa's heart fluttered in a weird way in her chest. Was it crapping out on her?

"It's all covered. Relax. Besides, it'll be awhile before Lucian figures it out. If at all."

Tessa was both hyperaware and numbed out at the same time. How was that even a thing?

She thought she heard a thud from above. Blinking sluggishly, she noticed Alex and Simon both look up at the same time. Simon said something she couldn't make out. Alex responded too, but it was lost on her.

Why couldn't her brain function right?

Between long blinks and shallow breaths, Tessa tracked their movements. Restraints dug into her wrists and ankles, and her back rubbed against the chair, making her wounds burn even more, which made it hard to focus on anything. The room dimmed. The men kept talking to each other, but all Tessa could make out were two slightly different tones.

Simon tugged her head back by yanking her hair, and snarled something at her. She didn't have a clue what he said then either. When he let go, Tessa's head fell forward. They left the room. Minutes passed before she was able to muster enough energy to raise her head again. But when she did? Her eyes widened at her reflection.

Oh, God no...

Tessa was in the center of a trap.

And she was strapped with dynamite.

Lucian never felt such intensity pulse through him before. No hunt ever generated this much adrenaline. Double fisting his blades, he semi-wished he had a gun with him as well. But that would make things impersonal. He wanted that closeness when he skinned alive the *Savag-Ri* who took his woman.

Creeping around the building in broad daylight was a joke.

Whoever took Tessa knew Lucian would move the earth to find her. That's what the note was about. *I hope you're faster than your brother.* Jesus, had they played this game with Luke too? Lucian blew out a hiss between his teeth, refusing to get inside his rabbit hole of a mind. Scenting the air, he detected nothing. No mildew, no food, no human, no *Savag-Ri*, no chicory coffee from the cafe down the street... nothing. He was completely nose blind. And with everything in gray scale, it fucked with his head. Craning his neck to track Victoria on the rooftop, he noticed a blur leap.

Blur? Shit, even Vic was out of focus. Lucian brought his attention back to the side of the building. Hurrying, he kept his back flat against the building and closed in on the back door of the dance studio. Above him, he heard Victoria laugh and grunt. She was playing with whoever was on the rooftop before she killed him. This was so unlike a *Savag-Ri*. They usually preferred fighting at night to remain a secret disease on society. This broad daylight, out-in-the-open bullshit was strange. It felt like a trap. Most likely was.

For a split second, just as Lucian quietly shoved the backdoor open, he worried this was a decoy. Even the door was left unlocked. How ridiculous was that?

Ducking inside, he caught a whiff of his mate and Lucian's

suspicions and good sense went up in flames. Crouching, he snuck inside, investigating his surroundings, even though everything looked gray and blurry.

The studio was comprised of a back supply room where the furnace and electrical board were housed. Someone rigged it to a generator. The heavy metal back door shut, plunging Lucian into darkness. Fine by him, he enjoyed working in shadows. Creeping into the long hallway, he counted three doors on the right, four on the left. Tessa's scent was like a blood trail to follow. Every step he took closer to her, the more his heart thundered, mouth watered.

Another thud sounded above his head. A gun fired. *Pop! Pop!*

He clenched his jaw. Victoria didn't own a gun. She preferred her claws and teeth when fighting. Had back up arrived or did the enemy shoot her? As bad as he wanted to check on her, his loyalty and soul belonged to Tessa. He couldn't pull back from his mate. She was all that mattered.

Her scent thickened as he crept down the hall, constantly on guard for an attack. He pushed open the first door on his right and cringed at the creak it made. The room was empty. Sweeping it, and the closet, he quickly left and checked out the next three rooms, going from left to right, down the long hallway.

His nose started bleeding. His lungs felt as though he was breathing fire. Lucian shoved his impending death aside and went into the next room. He was so silent; it made everything around him sound louder. A loud crash from the back door made him jolt. Light poured in from the back when Victoria kicked the damned door open and swaggered into the dance studio, eyes bright with her battle high. She held up a severed head. "Got this one two doors down."

Jesus Christ, she was so damn loud. Aaannnddd there went his element of surprise. Vic didn't even give a fuck. She liked when the enemy knew she was coming. Preening, she tossed the head down the hall like a bowling ball and brushed her hands on her pants. "Clipped me in the shoulder, the dickhead."

Something mewled from the last door on the right. Call him crazy, but he swore he just heard his name. Lucian held his breath and concentrated.

"*Lucian,*" a small, fragile voice squeaked.

"Tessa!" He shot off towards her voice. It was the last door on the right.

Of course, it was.

At the same time Lucian twisted the door handle to push his way inside, Tessa yelled something that got distorted when Victoria slammed into him from behind and tackled him to the ground. He twisted and shoved her away. True to form, Vic doubled her efforts to keep him pinned down. Lucian roared in fury. Why was she keeping him from reaching his mate?

"She says it's a trap, you dipshit!"

Fear shot ice into his veins. He pressed his hands to the door, looking at it like it would light up or some shit. "Trapped how?" It took more control than he had left to not kick the door down anyway. To have Tessa this close and not reach her? Insufferable. "Trapped how, Tessa?" Even as he went in for a repeat, his hand tightened on the doorhandle again.

He needed to get in. His body engaged as instincts ripped through him one-by-one. *Rip off the door. Get mate. Run. Protect. Bite. Turn. Feed.* Victoria came at him again, but Lucian's reflexes were quicker this time and kicked her in the gut, sending her flying backwards. Nothing was stopping him from getting Tessa out of here. Trap or not.

His hand froze on the doorknob again. Lucian's nostrils flared and another set of instincts bubbled out of him as hot as lava. He smelled blood, fear, sweat, piss, and honeysuckle. The combo made him freeze in place. *Trap. Danger. Proceed with caution. Mate hurt. Mate scared. Get her.* "Tessa, I'm right at the door."

"Don't open it! The door's rigged!"

Oh. Shit. "Okay, okay." *Fuck. Shit. Fuck. Shit.* He shook with need to reach her. A flimsy door was all that stood in his way. "Tessa, listen to me."

"*Run!*" She started hyperventilating. "Oh my God, you have to run! *Go!*"

"Not until I get you out of there."

"This is what they wanted! You can't come in here! Run, Lucian."

"I'm not leaving without you."

"You can't reach me. I'm... I'm strapped with dynamite."

Oh... God... He squeezed his eyes shut and blew out a long exhale through his nose. *Dynamite.* The images of the explosion the other day—the limbs and pieces strewn everywhere—were a great reminder of how this would end if he wasn't extremely cautious here. Not that he needed the fucking reminder.

Damned if he was going to let Tessa suffer a fate like that.

But getting her out of here without causing her body further physical damage was going to require a miracle. As far as vampires are concerned, they weren't a religious bunch of creatures. But he prayed on the other side of the door, regardless. Prayed to everything and anything that might listen and lend a divine hand. *Spare her*, he thought. *No matter what else happens, spare Tessa. Please.*

That prayer was the last thing he did as a creature with humanity. Inhaling her mixed and pungent scent of fear and blood, he blew out another exhale through his clenched teeth and then.... *Click*. Lucian turned off everything that made him a decent vampire. His feelings. His instincts. His pride and power. Even his voice was void of emotion when he said, "Tessa, listen to me."

"I'm dead already, Lucian. Run! Get out!"

Her cracking voice threated to shred his heart to ribbons. He shoved that feeling away too. "I'm not leaving without you."

Victoria ran her fingers along the trim of the door. "There could be a clock or something. Strings tied to the door. If you open it—"

The trap would set off and they'd all die.

He was too close to having and losing everything. It's why he had to shove his humanity away and become a machine. It was the only way to survive whatever outcome this had. "I'm not leaving her here, Vic."

"Figured as much." Victoria pursed her lips and looked up. "Let me see if I can get in from the ceiling."

It was a solid idea. She was narrower than Lucian. Maybe she could fit in the venting system? His hands remained flattened on the door. Cheeks tingling, lungs aching, he ignored the scent of burning flesh and didn't allow himself to feel the pain of his skin scorching inside his nostrils. He didn't even bother wiping off the boiling hot blood pouring out of his nose as he said, "Tessa. Focus on my voice."

She didn't respond, only whimpered.

Jesus fucking Christ, this was torment on a new shit-tastic level. To have his mate in danger on the other side of a flimsy wooden door and not be able to tear it from the hinges to reach her? Unacceptable.

"Can you see any wires or string?"

"Yes."

"How many?"

She took a little too long to answer. "Seven, I think." A choked-up sob left her, making Lucian wonder how badly she was injured. If he asked, he'd never be able to stay on this side of the door. Ignorance was bliss in moments like this. But... "What color are you?"

It was the only thing he could think to ask that would give him a clue without the whole picture of what she was like on the other side of the door.

She sniffled and exhaled a shaky breath. "Yellow."

He ground his molars together. *Yellow.* Going by her smell and the shakiness of her tone, he'd say she was teetering on red. "It's going to be okay. We're gonna get you out of there." The words came out far more confident than he felt. Suddenly, Dorian, Lena, Reys, and Xin were with him, which made the hallway feel crowded as Hell.

"Okay," Dorian said behind him. "What are we dealing with?"

"The room is booby trapped, and she's strapped with dynamite. Vic's going in through the ceiling."

"It's no use," Tessa said groggily. "Get out while you can, Lucian. *Please.*"

"I'm not leaving you."

"I can't go to my grave with your death on my hands too. This will have all been for nothing if you don't leave now."

His skin prickled. *All have been for nothing?* What was she talking about?

"I shouldn't have put the studio name on the mirror," she cried. "I... I didn't think it was real. I didn't think you'd actually see it and come. Even if I wished it, I didn't think it would happen."

In her darkest moment, when all hope faded, she'd wished for Lucian. Nothing could give a male more strength than that. "Well, here I am." He almost smiled. "And I'm not going anywhere, prima."

"Please," she cried again. "I can't bear this. Run. If you love me, Lucian, *run*."

His head dropped to his chest with her pleas. He smelled her tears from here. Each Tessa-scented breath he took shredded more of his soul to ribbons. "Get out," he ordered everyone. "Victoria! Get down!"

"No way, motherfucker. We're in it to win it," Xin argued.

"If this goes wrong, which it most likely will, Malachi can't lose the rest of his best fighters. If we all die, Malachi's left too vulnerable." This wasn't about sparing his friends for the sake of caring. It was about the House of Death, King Malachi, and the rest of the vampire population in Louisiana. "We can't all be killed or injured."

It finally dawned on him. This was nothing but a ploy to get Lucian and all his men in one space at one time.

"I chipped a nail," Vic said from down the hall. "This place is more concrete than I thought. The drop ceiling is too brittle and narrow and above it is solid concrete. I can't fit."

"Leave," Lucian ordered again.

Trying to be heroes was what the *Savag-Ri* were banking on. This wasn't just about Lucian. It was about the whole vampire race. The more they killed in one shot, the better for them. Lucian looked over at Dorian, "Get your mate out of here, Reaper. Take the rest with you. Clear the block in case we don't make it out." Lucian didn't want to take his friends, or innocents, to their graves if this didn't end well.

Dorian's eyes hardened. That look said all the things Lucian needed to know. Through clenched teeth, the Reaper growled, "I'll see you soon."

Lucian swallowed the lump in his throat and kept his shit together as each of his friends tapped or squeezed his shoulder, saying their *See-you-soons* and not *Goodbyes*, while his hands remained on the door and boots nailed to the floor.

Once it was just him and Tessa, it took every ounce of control he possessed to pull his hands off the door. "Tessa?"

No answer.

"Tessa, can you hear me?" He heard her wheezing as she tried to breathe. There was also the sound of something dripping. Piss? Blood? A leaky pipe? Taking one step back, he ran a hand down his face. Blood coated his palm.

Okay, okay. I've got this. Think!

Lucian took a couple more steps back and looked down the hall to his right, then towards the open lobby at the front of the building on his left. The room Tessa was in, he knew from the reflections, had four mirrored walls. Could he punch his way through the concrete hallway to reach the inside of her room?

No. He wasn't the incredible hulk, for fuck's sake.

And if Victoria couldn't tunnel her way through the ceiling, then no one could.

Think, think, think...

He started making his way back down the hall. If there was a *Savag-Ri* waiting in the shadows somewhere, one of the others would have taken them out. Vic brought one down already. Lucian had no clue how many were in on this job. Could be one. Could be ten.

But they wouldn't stay long enough to watch Lucian blow himself up. And they made sure there was no way to reach Tessa without doing so.

I hope you're faster than your brother.

Was that in reference to finding his mate, or rescuing her in time? Could the dynamite be hooked up to a timer? Lucian headed into the room next to Tessa's. He checked the perimeter of the room when lightning struck in his chest. He coughed and blood shot out of his mouth and splattered on the floor...

The *hardwood* floor.

But Tessa's room had a mirrored floor, right? They'd deliberately modified it.

Lucian searched for cameras, a weak spot, a chink in the armor, something to give him a break. His gaze landed on a closet door. With one eyebrow cocked, he thought, *What are the chances?* He looked to his right again. *Mirror.* He closed his eyes and tried like hell to summon the blueprints of this place. He'd barely looked at them before inspecting this studio months ago. But he vaguely remembered *boxes.* Shared space.

This once was a small warehouse divided in three long, concrete columns. But the rooms themselves were put up afterwards to make the studio have six dance classrooms, a hallway, a lobby, and a utility room and bathroom. The shared spaces were closets.

Lucian dashed over to the closet in the far-left corner of the room and chose to ignore that his speed was slowing. His curse wouldn't relent, and his deterioration could cost him and Tessa everything. Checking things over, as best he could, he saw nothing tied to it as a trigger. Slowly, he opened the door and spread his fingers on the wall separating him from Tessa. Writing was scribbled all over it. Drawings and notes and dates. An old performance poster hung by yellowing scotch tape. *Studio 79 presents the Nutcracker. December 3, 1986.*

He splayed his hands on the wall over the poster and yanked it off. Driving his fist straight through the drywall, it crumbled. Holy shit, it worked! Wasting no time, he slammed his fist over and over and over, breaking the wall between the two rooms. Again, his movements slowed down. Frustration and desperation forced him to kick the wall with his boots until he broke off more chunks of debris and made a hole big enough to crawl through. Scrambling like an animal, he made it into her room.

As bad as he wanted to fling the closet door open, he couldn't trust it was safe. Now he was plunged into the dark and couldn't see a damned thing in *her* closet. The scents he picked up from Tessa were fucking with his protective instincts big time. Every molecule in his body demanded he run to her right now and damn the consequences.

He might have risked it had she been a vampire. But her human body wouldn't survive the injuries she might suffer if he moved too fast. She was hurt enough as it was.

I'm coming, he said silently, unable to bring himself to say the words out loud. Either she could hear he'd made it this far in the room or she'd passed out. He wasn't sure which option to hope for.

Lucian felt his way along the door. No strings or wires. Good. Cautiously, he cracked the door open and held his breath because if the front door to this room was rigged, the closet door could be too from the other side.

Please, please, please. He wasn't sure who he was talking to this time. God? Some other divine entity? Himself? His ancestors? His brother? The air? The dark? *Please, please, please.* He cracked open the door a little more and peered out.

Tessa sat in the middle of the room, in bright technicolor glory. The rest of the space remained gray. His heart seized. Blood pooled around her chair. She was tied down with her hands behind her back. Wires were attached to her from all angles, making her look like a broken marionette.

None of them, however, lead to the closet door.

Lucian slid into the room, his heart shattering more with each step he took towards his mate. *What have they done to you?*

Wrath surged through him. His tendons snapped as his body locked with fury. Eyes blazing, he closed the space between them in seconds. *Sweet mother of all the unholy....* Tessa was passed out cold. Even in the dim light he noticed that her face was bruised and swollen. Dried blood caked her hair, and she'd soiled herself. The drip, drip, drip he heard was from a puncture wound in her neck. They'd beat her, tied her, broke her, and slowly bled her out. Desperate, he licked her wound, praying his saliva would clot the blood and seal it. She was losing too much blood.

Lucian felt sick with guilt.

His girl was beyond hurt, and instead of asking for help when it arrived, what had she done? Tried to save him. Told him to leave her to die and run to save himself.

He didn't deserve her. But he'd be damned if he was going to let her die *or* let her go. Not today. Not ever.

"It's okay," he said softly. She probably couldn't hear him. He wasn't saying it for her benefit though. It was for his. Lucian's hands shook as he tried to follow each of the wires to see where they led to. He scanned the room for cameras and a detonator. Something. Anything!

She had enough dynamite strapped to her chest to take out a lot more than this one building. He followed the first wire and found it was a dummy. Awesome. The second and third were dummies as well—all taped to the mirrors around her. The fourth was tied to the door and most definitely a trigger. The fifth went up towards the ceiling in the center. Sixth and seventh were on opposite sides and led to parts of the ceiling as well.

Okay. Okay. Stay cool. Be calm. Lucian popped one of the tiles in the water-stained drop ceiling and squinted to look around. In the far corner was the detonation device.

According to the timer, he had twenty-two minutes left to diffuse it.

CHAPTER 34

"How do I diffuse a bomb?" Lucian pinched his cell between his ear and shoulder while using both hands to push the ceiling tile closest to the detonator up and away. Balanced on a chair he snagged from the utility room, he grew impatient for the answer. He hadn't been able to focus on Tessa at all because he couldn't help her until he diffused this damned thing first.

"Ohhh what kind is it?" Xin's excitement wasn't surprising. He loved this shit.

"I don't know. It's on a timer."

"How many wires?"

"Two."

"Two?" Xin repeated. "Psht, cut the red one."

Lucian froze. Shit. He couldn't tell which one was red. "I'm uhhh. I'm colorblind right now."

"Ugh," Xin hung up on him.

Less than a minute later, he heard Xin's steps in the hall. "How do I get in?" he hollered.

"Through the closet in the room next door!"

Tessa remained eerily silent. Jesus, was she dead? He couldn't bring himself to look at her. He'd likely drop everything and just blow up while he held her close and whispered all the things he should have said and never had.

Xin slipped into the room through the closet. "I can't believe we hadn't thought of that." He tensed when he saw Tessa and took in her state. "Holy fuck, man," he whispered.

Lucian couldn't even go there right now. "Which one?" he kept his focus on the timer.

Xin pulled a small blade out of his pocket and jerked his head. "Move it or lose it, big boy." Lucian hopped off the chair. Xin climbed up, cussed about small imaginations, and cut the wire. "There," he hopped back down. "All better."

Lucian couldn't believe it had been that easy. He blew out a breath he'd been holding for far too long and finally turned his attention to Tessa.

"Damn, man." Xin's voice sounded as painful as Tessa's face looked. "I... shit, Lucian. She's—"

"Only I touch her," he growled at his friend. It was stupid, he knew that, but his instincts and curse would have it no other way. Xin backed off, completely understanding.

Grinding his teeth, Lucian made fast work of cutting the wires and unstrapping the dynamite from his mate. He handled the explosive vest with care and passed it to Xin.

"Jesus fucking Christ, were they planning on taking out the entire block?" Xin hissed. "I'll dispose of this safely and get the others up to speed. Meet you outside."

Lucian didn't say a word. Too focused on handling Tessa with great care, he got her completely untied while his heart fell out of his ass. Her eyes were closed, mouth slackened. Her injuries and blood loss were substantial. Holy Hell, how she'd managed to stay conscious this long was beyond him. His woman was so strong it was humbling.

Once free, Tessa slumped forward into Lucian's chest. Catching her, he cooed, "I've got you." His boots slid on the blood pooling on the floor. She was pale and clammy. Cold to the touch. "You're safe, prima."

There wasn't a way to hold her without hitting a wound and making her pain worse. He could only hope she stayed passed out, so she didn't feel his arm slide across her swollen, torn back. He hooked his other arm behind her knees and scooped her up. Tessa's head flopped back. Her eyes opened into slits but she didn't make a peep.

It was like carrying a corpse. Even as deadweight, she was light as a feather. Holding Tessa close to his chest, he carried her out of the room and made it into the hallway. The front glass door was right ahead. The sun shone bright. The street was empty. The exit mere feet away. *The light at the end of the tunnel*, he thought.

Tessa's leg jerked like something tugged at her foot. *What the —*

With her so close, Lucian was able to see everything in color again. *NO!* He noticed, too late, that he'd missed the clear, hair-thin fishing line tied to her ankle.

A high-pitched whining revved up from behind them and he ran towards the glass doors as fast as his slowed-down, cursed form could go. Shielding Tessa with his body, he took most of the hit from the explosion set off by the trigger around her ankle, and they both blasted through the glass doors and slammed onto the street.

Huge hunks of concrete and debris fell around them. Lucian buckled under the weight of something smashing into his back. Tessa lay pinned beneath him.

Pain so horrendous he was stunned and immobilized, blazed through his body and shot out of his mouth. He screamed.

Then he fucking *shattered*.

Can't... breathe. Can't... BREATHE! Lucian wheezed, struggling to find air. Nothing. There was nothing. With Tessa's cold, still body under him, Lucian collapsed and burned.

———⋈———

Tessa awoke in a floaty-dreamy-drunk way. Everything hurt. She tried to speak. Didn't work. She wasn't even sure she had a mouth anymore.

Lucian. Was he here with her? Was all this some kind of warped dream? She cracked her eyes open and vaguely recognized the four-poster bed she laid in. Lucian's bed. *Was... where... shit.* She closed her eyes again.

The next time she opened them, she was still in the bed. But the room was darker. Was it nighttime? She passed out again.

Tessa struggled to move. Lost in sensations of being held down and suffocated, she gasped and jerked awake. Someone loomed above her. "No! No! No!" She fought the assailant until pain robbed her of breath. Her eyes blew wide with agony, and she sucked in a ragged breath to scream with.

Something clenched her chin with a vise grip.

Lucian's face came into view.

He looked like he'd just been to war. Black and blue bruising mottled his features. He had a huge cut on the side of his head. Dried blood and black soot covered most of his golden skin and his usually perfect hair was a wreck. She could smell something burning. Hair and... bacon?

Tessa's eyes crossed as a wave a nausea swept over her. Lucian jostled her again. His mouth moved a mile a minute as he yelled something at her.

She... she couldn't hear it. Why couldn't she hear it? Tessa broke out in a sweat as panic replaced fear. She was deaf. No sound penetrated her ears. Not even a high-pitched tone of panic. Nothing!

Lucian's mouth kept moving, his brow digging down, making him look more intense. He jiggled her head a little, concern blazing in his eyes. She wrapped her hands around his forearms and said, "I can't hear you."

Oh God. The sensation of saying it and not hearing it was awful. Lucian frowned with confusion. He held her chin with one large hand and brought the other to his lips, tapping them.

She almost couldn't see him through the blurriness of her tears. "I can't hear you," she rasped. "I can't hear you, I-can't-hear-you, *I can't hear you*!" Her panic revved into fifth gear, making everything feel tingly. She couldn't tell if he could hear her. Unable to determine the volume of her voice, Tessa pushed her words out with all the air she had left in her lungs. "*I can't hear you!*"

The room started spinning.

Her body hurt so badly... she wanted to die.

Lucian gripped her face and said something again. God damnit! Why wouldn't he listen? She couldn't hear him! *Stop talking if I can't hear you!* As Tessa shook her head violently, he doubled down on his grip to stop her from crawling away. He tapped his mouth again. Conjuring some calmness into her mind, Tessa inhaled... exhaled... inhaled... exhaled...

Her gaze latched onto his lips. She watched them move, trying her best to pick out the words he was slowly saying.

Do you trust me?

Her brow pinched. "Do I trust you?"

Lucian nodded.

"Yes." She didn't even need to think about it.

He tapped his neck next. Tessa's hand rose to hers simultaneously.

This was insane. She couldn't cope. The past few days were riddled with black holes. She couldn't string together a single thought that made sense.

Lucian grabbed her hand and brought it to his mouth. He gently held her middle finger and brought it to his lips, closer to his very sharp, very pointy *fangs*. Tessa was so confused she didn't have the sense to shirk away. He pricked her finger with one of his massive canines. The sting didn't hit her radar at all.

He jostled her chin again, signaling for her to look up at him. They locked gazes as he started sucking on her pricked finger. She was floating. Tessa couldn't pull away from Lucian at all. Not that she wanted to. Enthralled, she felt like she was sinking into something warm and safe. The sensation lasted only a few seconds, but when the spell broke, she realized nothing was different. She still couldn't hear anything.

Why did she think him doing that would fix her? How much brain damage had she incurred?

Lucian held his hand up again, this time making a "wait a minute" gesture. She held her breath, waiting for something to happen. Calmly, Lucian brought his wrist to his mouth and bit down. She imagined it made a crunching noise. Her stomach rolled when he pulled away with blood coating his full-bottom lip. With an encouraging nod, he held his arm up to her mouth.

"Drink," he mouthed.

Tessa shook her head, unable to understand this. What... what the...

Vampire. Alakhai. *Curse...* The memory of Simon's voice rattled her and the vague recollection of what she'd just been through started piecing itself back together.

"Do you trust me?" Lucian mouthed.

Tessa swallowed. Her mouth suddenly too dry.

"Do you love me?" He tensed, waiting for her response.

Do I love him? Of course. She'd gone through Hell to protect him. If that wasn't love, then she didn't know the meaning of the word. "I love you." She should have told him from the start. Maybe if she hadn't waited so long, fearing he'd leave her, all of this could have been avoided.

"Be with me." He leaned in, and his eyes turned glassy with tears as he cupped her cheek. "Be with me, forever, Tessa."

"Forever isn't long enough."

His brow pinched and eyes closed shut, as if her confession just knocked the wind out of him.

Opening his eyes again, she felt like she could dive into his ocean blue gaze and float away. Or drown.

He twisted his wrist in front of her again, enticing her to take it. Blood dripped down from his wrist, soaking his sheets. "Trust me," he said.

"I do." *This is madness. Why am I doing it if it's crazy?*

Because love made you do crazy things…

Tessa wrapped her hands around his blistered, burnt forearm and latched onto his wrist. His blood filled her mouth.

And she swallowed.

Tessa's pupils blew wide as Lucian held her steady so she could pull from his vein. He'd taken so little of her in with that finger prick, he could only pray it was enough to make this work. She'd lost an unimaginable amount of blood, and he wasn't about to make things worse for her. Staring at the extent of her injuries, it was a miracle she was alive. The fact that she was conscious and talking at all had the entire House amazed.

Many of her wounds had been treated by the House physician, but Tessa was still knocking on death's door, thanks to brain swelling, internal bleeding, and the drugs in her system. She'd lost consciousness for the better part of two days already.

As much as he wanted to take her to a human hospital, he couldn't because it required a fair amount of memory wiping later and he didn't want to do that to a surgeon, cops, or anyone else. Instead, Lucian held onto the hope that what Lena said earlier was right. *"No way would fate bring you all this way just to fuck you over."* Running a hand through his hair, he ignored how much of it had burnt off in the back. He was lucky he'd survived too.

That bomb nearly killed them both. By some miracle, a slab of metal had ricocheted off the roof and landed on Lucian, shielding them both from falling debris. But Lucian suffered third and fourth degree burns on his back from the molten metal. Add his blood curse to the mix? Lucian was a barrel of hot coals, lava, and gunpowder.

As soon as they got back to the mansion, Lucian and Tessa were separated. Every vampire in the House fed Lucian, one-after-another-after-another, until he was able to heal enough to no longer stand at death's door. He'd nearly destroyed the treatment room getting out of there to reach his mate. Being separated from her after all they'd been through was a big fat hell no.

There'd been no need to tell him where she was. He'd followed her scent through the mansion like a shark on a blood trail. His curse pulsed, burning him with searing-hot violence. The burn would only cool down once Tessa became his forever.

God, she was a miraculous creature. So damn strong. His heart swelled just looking at her. And as she drank from him, looking ten kinds of broken, confused, and scared, he took tremendous pride in how she was putting her trust in him right now. Trusting him to help her. To do the right thing for her.

The right thing...

He hoped she didn't get mad about this. He should have gotten her consent before taking the steps to change her. But explaining the whole vamp thing when she was deaf and dying would take time they couldn't afford. So, he settled for short and sweet: *Be with me, forever, Tessa.*

Forever wasn't long enough to love her properly, but he vowed to not waste another second of their precious time together. They'd bonded long ago. Now she would turn. Afterwards, they'd mate. Tessa was the light at the end of his burning tunnel.

When her response was "Forever isn't long enough," he went weak.

He didn't deserve this woman. No one did.

Shrines should be erected in her honor. All men should bow at her feet.

He planned to be the first and only vampire on his knees for her. Now and forever.

Carefully, Lucian slid his hand down her battered cheek until his fingers rested over the pulse point in her neck. Her throat muscles worked hard to swallow him down. Her gaze remained fixed on his, even as they glassed over. Licking his lips, he nodded, encouraging her to keep going a little further. He needed to make sure she was well equipped to start the transition. Then he allowed her a little extra because he wanted to enjoy this a moment longer.

She tracked his every move, no matter how small. His breathing. His facial expressions. She took her cues from him like she always had in the bedroom. *Stop.* He let his eyes do the talking to see how well she could understand him now. Tessa pulled off and wiped the corners of her mouth with her thumb. Then the vixen sucked her thumb clean as if she didn't want to waste a drop.

Hot damn, she was everything he could have ever asked for. Vibrating with needs, Lucian licked his puncture wound closed and allowed her to watch it heal right before her eyes.

Clenching his jaw, he waited with bated breath while her breathing evened out. She closed her eyes and laid back on his pillow. Tessa had been badly hurt. It was going to take a prayer and a bucket of blood to heal her properly.

Fucking *Savag-Ri.*

Lucian hoped they'd only beaten her. How horrible was it to put *"I hope they only beat her"* on his wish list? Fucking awful. But this was the world he lived in and the one he was escorting Tessa into. What if they touched her? What if they —

His lips peeled back as a nasty hiss ripped out from between his clenched teeth. If a *Savag-Ri*, or anyone, raped her, he was going to burn this city to the ground. But by the look of her outfit, they hadn't bothered to undress her. It was the only thing keeping him calm at the moment.

Her jeans, or what was left of them, had been cut away once she was safe at the House of Death, so her injuries could be tended to. Her back was the worst. Those lashes, deep and angry, crisscrossed her sweet skin and made Lucian murderous. Some required stitches. The bruising on her face and neck made him want to burn New Orleans off the map. And three out of the four gashes in her forehead had to be glued shut. That made him want to upend the entire world.

All that would be healed soon, he reminded himself. But her mind? This trauma wasn't going to be fixed with blood. That would take time, trust, and someone to be there for her when she needed to talk about it. Lucian was first in line to be her go-to person. Whether it took days for her to face this trauma, or years, he'd be there for her.

"I'm so sorry for everything," he whispered. His heart clenched, because… could she hear him yet? Would she hear him ever again? What if the explosion made her loss of hearing irreparable? Was his blood strong and pure enough to fix it?

Lucian closed his eyes and kept talking to her, his voice cracking like his resolve. "I should have told you everything from the start." He stroked her cheek. "I'll make this right. I swear it."

What if she came out of this and never wanted to see him again? What if she couldn't hear music for the rest of her life?

His chest burned and tightened with the weight of what had been done. *Fuck… Tessa.* What a pair they made. Both a train wreck of mangled limbs and smoking body parts entangled with each other.

"I love you," he said in every language he knew. He ran his fingers through her hair, ignoring the singed, crunchy ends. She'd been cleaned, glued, and stitched up, and was now naked in his bed with all his blankets on to keep her warm and comfortable. "You're so strong, prima. You're so damned amazing, it takes my breath away."

Tessa's arm flinched in her sleep. Then she groaned. Lucian pitched forward, holding his breath, enthralled as her vampire side started to bloom.

The change was different for everyone. Some went through an ungodly amount of pain. Others slept right through it. Some turned violent. Others became punch drunk. The insane ones were usually created by Rogues, which wasn't the case here so no worries about that.

Whatever Tessa was already, in the core of her soul, would now be enhanced. Lucian's blood curse would lift from him, and any qualities he possessed that she needed, would filter into her through their blood exchange. This was part of the mating bond.

Here's hoping what he offered would be enough to save them both.

CHAPTER 35

"Dance, you filthy vampire whore."

Tessa rolled her shoulders back and deadpanned the empty space talking to her. "No."

"Do it, or you die."

Tilting her head a fraction to the left, she arched her brow defiantly. "I said no."

Either a thousand fire ants were chewing on her, or someone had doused her with ice water. Either way, she didn't care enough to investigate. All Tessa knew was her skin felt prickly and alive.

She also knew this was a dream. She'd been able to manipulate her dreams on some level for the better part of two years. Weird, right? But it was a fancy trick she nearly abused on her loneliest nights.

Simon wasn't living rent-free in her dreams. She'd deal with the aftermath of that asshole once she was awake. For now, she craved music. Her mouth quirked upwards as she called forth her lover.

"Lucian," her voice register lowered as she said his name two more times, "Lucian... Lucian." Tessa summoned him out of smoke. Dressed in a black tuxedo, black shirt, and black vest, he was a shadow dressed in sin. Sharp lines flaunted his physique. His mass of wavy blond hair was slicked back by his hand. Without looking down, Tessa knew his pants would be sculpted around his perfect ass and thick thighs.

She always summoned him in black. Delighted that in this realm, she could dress him however she wanted... just like he would send her gowns to wear when they met out in the real world. But this wasn't the real world. It was hers and hers alone.

He stepped forward like a predator out of the shadows. The smoky air dissipated around him, as if curling back to give him room. Here, Lucian could bend nature. Here, Tessa could be the woman-who-never-was.

"What are you doing?" Her mother's disembodied, curt tone hissed in her ear. "That's not what I taught you."

"I know," Tessa beamed as she took Lucian's hand.

"Stop it, Tessa. I didn't waste my life on you just so you could—"

Tessa cut her mother's next words off with a snap of her fingers. Lucian approached, smiling like a predator who wanted to gobble her up. She noticed a red handkerchief tucked into his jacket. She fixated on the bold color for a moment until he tipped her head with his forefinger. "Shall we dance, darling?"

He called her darling. Not Tessa. Not prima. Darling. It made her heart skip a beat. His tone was soft, but still hungry for her. The R in darling had softened too, like he had a slight accent. Boy, she must be making up for trauma issues with this dream, because she was pulling out all the stops. Tessa giggled at the idea. "I'd love to."

She slipped her hand in his. It was warm and strong. He slid his other hand along her waist and held her close. They were a solid pair. A comfortable pair. A playful pair.

Perfecting her stance, Tessa angled her body and elongated her neck. She pulsed in every part of her body—her throat, her wrists, her thighs and even her clit. Without a countdown or beat of music, they kicked off at the same time and waltzed around the empty space. It was perfectly timed and graceful.

Boring.

Lucian's gaze never wavered from hers, and Tessa didn't falter when they transitioned from a waltz into a tango. An eager smile curled her lips. This was more their style. Sophisticated and passionate. Lucian led her around the emptiness, controlled as always.

Tessa lost the imaginary beat for a half-second. Lucian kept going. His speed picked up. The tango steps were lost in a whirl of shadows and smoke. She twirled around, dressed in her simple black leotard, and felt cold and naked.

Alone.

Lucian disappeared. And... and she couldn't seem to find her footing anymore. Tessa stumbled, her heart slamming into her ribcage. The music that played so often in her head faded to silence. The quietness of her dream felt like abandonment.

"Lucian," she tried summoning him again.

"Dance, you filthy vampire whore." Simon came back to haunt her.

Tessa raised both her hands and flipped his disembodied voice a double middle finger. Fuck him. Fuck the silence. Fuck abandonment. With a wave of her hand, she changed her outfit from a black leotard to... nothing. Stripped naked, with not even shoes on her feet, Tessa set herself free.

No outfit. No rules. No inhibitions. No music.

In dead silence, Tessa danced through the empty void like an entire symphony was at the mercy of her movements. No restrictions. No boundaries. She moved like she wanted when she felt the need. She leapt, dipped, twirled, and slammed her hands down on the foggy flooring whenever she pleased. Craning, arching, stretching, crawling, rolling, flipping, she was a slave to the beat of nothing but her soul.

It was violent. It was graceful. It was fluid and intense. Tessa danced for herself and no one else. She wasn't a disappointment. She wasn't toxic. She wasn't a whore. She wasn't a failure. She wasn't a teacher, a daughter, a friend, or a lover. She was just a wild string of notes with no structure or tethers to rules.

The freedom felt divine.

Out of nowhere, an emotion so vicious it became a torrent of electricity, ripped out of her and she arched backwards, nearly bending in half. She didn't call out or fight it. Tessa embraced the heat and bite.

Suddenly, Lucian was with her again. Supporting her backbend with one hand on her arched spine, he didn't hold her up — only poised to support her should she lose balance and fall. Tessa eased out of the pose, breathless and on fire. His gaze heated her from the inside out. Yes. Please. I want more of this. I want all of this. I want you, Lucian. Tessa slid her hands up his arms and tore off his jacket. Next, she unbuttoned his vest and pulled that off, then tossed it to the ground. His grin widened with every layer of clothing she stripped from him.

Off went his shirt. Off came his belt. Down went his slacks. Next went his shoes. She could have snapped her fingers to make this faster, but she liked feeling his muscles under her hands. Enjoyed how solidly he was built. All the dips and hills of his abs, the curve of his ass, the thickness of his thighs. This man was built for fighting. Protecting. Loving.

And he belonged to her.

They picked up where they left off, dancing and twirling in a tango that bordered on violent. Their passion ignited the dancefloor. Everlasting flames caressed them, melting their fates together. Moving with their bodies pressed flush against each other, eye-to-eye, heart-to-heart, they were undefeatable. They were perfection.

I'm home. For the first time in her life, Tessa felt like she belonged somewhere. Not even in the dance studio, continuing her constant training, had she felt so at peace, like she did in Lucian's embrace.

"You're so strong," he said against her ear. "You're incredible, darling."

"Keep me?" She held the nape of his neck, squeezing it as if to hold on so she didn't fly away. "Keep me with you." Of their own accord, her hands pushed his head down to her neck. "Keep me," she whispered as they danced. "And I'll keep you."

Lucian grunted. The small noise sent a shiver down Tessa's spine. "Please," she begged, coaxing his mouth closer to her neck.

His lips brushed the sensitive skin of her throat. "Do you trust me?"

"Always."

"Then dance with me." His breath tickled her collarbone as he bent lower and kissed the dip in her throat. Suddenly, Lucian's movements sped up to a dizzying pace. Only in her dreams would she be able to move like this and keep up with him. They were a tornado across the hidden dancefloor. Her grip on him tightened as his mouth sealed on her neck. She felt a pinch a second before a surge of liquid heat flowed over her from head to toes. They kept dancing.

He drank. She heard him swallow. His arms tightened around her waist, and they both started rising up, up into the air, beyond the dancefloor, beyond reason, beyond the rules of any realm.

They danced on air.

Lucian pulled back and licked his bottom lip. Heat bloomed between her clenched thighs.

"You're the only music I hear," he purred. He set her loose and instead of gravity pulling her down, Tessa remained on his level. Only now she was in a red dress that fit like a second skin. It had a split up her right thigh. She was still barefoot, but ribbons were tied up her calves. She ran her fingers through her thick mass of heavy hair and let it fall down her back. Lucian jerked her into his chest playfully and dipped her backwards to kiss her throat column. Then he reached into the endless sky and pulled down another red ribbon.

"Take it," he encouraged.

Tessa wrapped the silk around her arm. It was thick and soft, cool against her hot skin. Then Lucian let her go again and she floated away, still clutching the red ribbon. Up, up, up, up, up and away...

CHAPTER 36

Enraptured, Lucian pulled Tessa up and out of her dream. With one hand splayed at the small of her back to support her, he kept his other hand wrapped around the nape of her neck. She rode him with abandon. While she transitioned, locked in a dream, his mate moved like he'd never seen her before. It was as though her bones turned to rubber. She arched and rolled, dancing with something more potent than magic possessing her.

This was his Tessa. His darling dancer.

"Keep me," she said in her sleep as she climbed onto his lap. "Keep me and I'll keep you." Her eyes remained closed, but she moved as if she could see him. She wasn't alert, she was aware. The difference was beguiling.

She impaled herself on his cock and rode him in a slow, steady rhythm that had every muscle Lucian owned tightening. "Take it," he encouraged. And she took exactly what she wanted from him.

Tessa was off her chain. It was fucking glorious.

No more seeking perfection. No more limits. Tessa finally found her true self. His goddamn heart exploded with relief.

His curse broke.

She was his. She was free.

She was vampire.

And they were bound together for all eternity.

He hadn't healed like her because he'd not fed enough yet. There was time for that later. Too hellbent on getting to Tessa earlier had left him vulnerable now. She must have sensed it on some level. Their connection was strong, most likely because it had been forged for over two years of learning each other's body languages. But she sensed exactly what he needed and offered it. While lost in her dream, during her transition, Tessa coaxed his mouth to her neck. He could feel her wild pulse under his tongue and grunted with the temptation to bite. Fuck, she smelled so good. Felt so good. And tasted so. Damned. Spectacular.

Unable to keep away a second longer, Lucian bit down. Tessa cried out as her body clamped down on his cock. He fed and fucked her. She fed and fucked him. Hyperaware of everything, he marveled as her body refined under his touch. He threaded his hand through her hair, reveling at the sensation of it thickening between his fingers. Her skin tightened. The jagged cuts and welts smoothed over. Her muscles toned further. Her body temp regulated and rose a fraction. Her spastic heartbeat evened out and pumped strong and fierce.

She was a stunner when human. Tessa, he had no doubt, was going to be a knockout as a vampire. He pulled off her vein, his body repairing itself the rest of the way on its own. Gripping her hips, Lucian guided her as she rocked her way to more pleasure.

Holy fucking fuuuuuuck. This woman was going to ruin his control. He wanted to flip her over and take her in every position he could bend her in. But that could wait. This was her moment. He wasn't stealing it.

"Take it," he urged again. *Take it… Take your new-found freedom. Take my soul while you're at it. Take everything I have to offer. Take your new life and make of it what you will.* "Take it." *Take it. Take it. Take my body. Take my mind and make music with it. Take the air I breathe. Take my vein.*

He held his breath, watching her detonate with another shuddering orgasm. Her labored breathing was from pleasure, not pain. A sheen of sweat graced her sweet face. He held her steady while she rocked against him, harder, faster.

He ground his molars together, about to come.

"Lucian," her tone was pure seduction. "Lucian… *Lucian.*" Her nails dug into his shoulders. Tessa's head dropped back in ecstasy as she continued riding him. He suckled one of her breasts, flicking his tongue against her hardened nipple. He pulled her entire tit into his mouth. Damn, he loved how tight and small her breasts were. He released it to go after the other, this time grazing his fangs across her sensitive flesh.

She cradled his head, holding him there. "Lucian," Tessa's voice cracked. Her eyes popped open as she swerved her hips in fast, short bursts. Immediately, she detonated again, crying out and clamping down on him. "Oh God, I can't stop."

He smiled against her chest. "Then don't."

Tessa lost her rhythm. "Everything feels like it's on fire."

Lucian ran both his hands through her hair, swiping the runaway strands from her face. "I've got you," he flipped her over and took her slowly. Holy mother of God, her body was so tight it destroyed his self-control.

He rode Tessa up the bed until she bumped her head. Pulling out, he flipped her over, spanking her ass hard enough to make his ears pop and Tessa squeal with delight. Placing her hands on the headboard and squeezing her fingers, he ordered her to, "Hold on tight." Then he ran his hands greedily down her body, kissing and biting the back of her shoulder.

"Let go," she said over her shoulder. "Give me exactly who and what you are, Lucian. No more scenes. No more pretending. No more holding back from me."

He stilled.

Tessa cocked an eyebrow at him. "Feed me what you are."

Fuuuuuuck. He nearly came before he had a chance to slide back inside her.

Lucian pressed the head of his cock against her swollen pussy and slammed inside, bottoming out in one thrust. With a flick of his wrists, he lowered the lights and lit all his candles. Tempting as it was to turn on music, he wasn't willing to give up the silence yet. He wanted the beat to be their skin slapping against one another, accompanied by the melody of her moans and the tempo of his thrusts to fill his ears instead.

Lucian gave her everything he had. And then he gave her more. They destroyed his bed, put dents in his walls, cracked the dresser, and even ripped the carpet. They were diabolical together. A dark symphony of desire, passion, and eternal fire.

"Look at me," he gripped a handful of her hair and pulled it as he deepened his thrusts. They were on the floor now, drenched in sweat. Tessa's gaze deadlocked with his. "Who do you belong to?"

"You," she scratched down his arms, drawing blood.

Fuck. Yes.

His thrusts slowed and deepened. Lucian rode his wave of pleasure, taking careful measures to get her on board as well, and they came at the same time.

It was a goddamn out-of-body experience.

Fire and ice coursed through his veins. His cock pulsed as he filled her with cum. Pitching forward, Lucian crushed her mouth with his, just to eat her screams. Even their tongues knew how to dance together.

He never knew a mate meant... *this*. To feel this wild, this complete, this grounded, this strong, this unleashed. With wild abandonment, she tightened her thighs around his waist and rolled him over with her newfound strength.

"Who do you belong to?" she collared his throat with one hand and used her free one to pinch her own nipple.

"You're killing me," he half-laughed, half-groaned.

"Who do you belong to, Lucian?" Her hold tightened on his neck.

He was about to come again, balls drawing up and thighs tensing. "You, Tessa. Always you."

Her head dropped back, and her hold on him loosened. "I need," she groaned, swirling her hips and grinding against him for all the friction she could get.

Lucian propped up on his elbows just to watch his cock slip in and out of her sweet pussy. She came again, but it wasn't enough. He could tell by how her inner walls fluttered instead of pulsed. He pulled her off, picked her up, and brought her back to the bed.

Turning Tessa upside down, they got into a sixty-nine position, with Lucian on top. "Tap my thigh if I fuck your mouth too hard."

Tessa's response? A guttural groan of pure *want*.

When she allowed him to hold her pinned in place like this—his body hovered over hers, trapping her beneath him with little room to move—it was a magnificent gift. One he savored.

Lucian slid his cock between her lips, hissing when her new fangs scraped his shaft. Then he grinned like the Cheshire cat because she moaned so loud, with her mouth full of his cock, and it lit him up. With one hand, she held his thigh, stroking him, coaxing him further down her throat. The other she used to play with his balls as she sucked him off. At this angle, he could push past her gag reflex and she'd take him all with little issue.

This wasn't their first time in this position. And he knew she loved it as much as he did. Maybe even more so.

Lucian dipped down and ate her pussy like a starved man at a banquet. He was merciless with her clit. Sliding two fingers into her cunt, he hooked his digits and gave her g-spot all the attention it needed. Her hips bucked into his face. She bit down on his dick. He froze, letting her ride out the rest of her much needed, bigger orgasm, then he thrust into her mouth and pumped his release down her throat.

Popping off, he spun around and climbed on top of her to kiss her fully, greedily. He wanted their mouths to taste the same. A little him, a little her. "You're unbelievable," he said against her lips.

Tessa lay on her back, half-dazed, with her mouth hanging open as she caught her breath. Okay, breathing was overrated. He came down on her again and kissed her voraciously. Then lifted her off the bed and carried her into the bathroom.

Tessa clung to him with her brow furrowed. "Is it over so soon?"

He chuckled and nipped her shoulder. "Oh, darling, that was only foreplay. I'm far from finished with you."

CHAPTER 37

They pleasured each other for hours until Tessa's energy was completely spent. Once convinced she was sated enough for a break, Lucian drew them a bath and carried her into it. He was still panting from their rigorous cardio workout. And yet, she knew damn well if she asked him for more, he would give it to her. It made her next words give her guilt. "I'm hungry."

He must have expected it. As they spooned in his giant bathtub, with bubbles everywhere, he encouraged her to turn and face him so she could have his neck again. "I don't think I can move anymore," she admitted. She was sore and weighted down with fatigue.

"It's okay." He kissed the back of her shoulder before bringing his arm up and biting down on his wrist. She sat between his thighs, leaning back into his chest, and held his arm to her mouth. Even while drawing from his vein, Tessa still couldn't fully process what happened to her.

Vampire. Blood curse. Alakhai.

She wasn't a changed woman; she was something... *else*. As if she'd shed her skin and became a different creature entirely. Tessa might look human, but she felt all animal.

Her skin felt taut across her bones. Her nipples remained hard, the points aching for his touch and tongue again. Her pussy was swollen with need and she kept scissoring her legs. Her limber joints and the quiet of her mind caused her to sink into his hold and relax against him, even though her bottom squirmed for more pleasure.

More. She needed more. More blood. More sex. More Lucian. More everything.

She'd taken his vein so many times already, it was a wonder he had blood any left. His taste was addicting. He became a drug. Her only fix. She needed him more than she needed anything in her life—including music and dancing.

Red flags waved in her brain. Big ones.

She unlatched from his wrist.

"Lick it," he said quietly.

She obeyed, dragging her tongue along the puncture wounds, and watched them close and vanish.

This was real. "Vampire," her throat felt thick saying the word.

"Yes," he whispered against her neck.

In the candlelit bathroom, in the clawfoot tub, Tessa and Lucian stilled. "I can hear you," she said out loud. She just now realized her hearing was back.

"Yes."

Tessa looked down at her wrists, expecting to see raw skin. Nothing. And her legs weren't bruised... shouldn't they be messed up somehow? Stuck in a sudden brain fog, Tessa pulled her feet up and looked at the bottoms. All good. Shouldn't they be... bloody? Something? Tessa was so confused. All the dots she connected shot off in different directions. She leaned back into Lucian's chest and then realized there was no pain in her back from the lashes that Simon—

As the dots reconnected, recent events hit her like bullets. *Boom! Boom! Boom! Boom!* Tessa lunged forward in panic. Water sloshed over the rim of the tub.

"Hey," Lucian kept his voice soft. "It's okay. I've got you."

Nope. Nuh uh. Her nerves fired in rapid succession. Everything closed in on her. "Shit," she heard Lucian say. The water sloshed, making waves rock her body as she clung to the sides of the tub. Suddenly, Lucian was out of the water and next to her. Crouched on the floor, he put his face in her line of sight. "Look at me, Tessa. You're okay."

She... she needed to get out. She needed to get out!

Bolting from the opposite side of the tub as fast as lightning, she slipped and slammed her knees on the tiled floor.

"Tessa!" he hollered.

"No, no, no, no." She was trapped. Panicked. Confused.

Nothing felt right. No, nothing felt *the same*.

Simon's snarling voice catapulted her into a dark place. *"Dance, you filthy vampire whore."*

She cringed and whimpered. Tessa couldn't tell what was real. If this was a dream, she couldn't manipulate it at all. "Lucian, Lucian, Lucian." She called him like he was Beetlejuice.

"Tessa," he said in a terse voice. "Fucking hell."

"No, no, no." She squeezed her eyes shut to make it all go away and Simon's face came into view. Tessa lashed out and clawed at him, desperate to take his eyes out. The next thing she knew, the room flipped over, and she was on her back. The cold tile bit her skin. She was rendered immobile.

She was blind.

Another surge of panic tore through her.

"It's okay," said a soft, familiar voice. "I've got you."

She shook her head violently, tears spilling down her temples. *Out! Get out! Run!*

"You're safe, Tessa." That voice was angelic. Where was she? Was she dead? "Breathe deep with me, okay? In through the nose, out through the mouth. In…. out…. Good, that's real good. Keep going for me, darling. In through the nose, out through the mouth. In, good, and out, that's my girl. You're doing great."

She followed her instructor's orders. Her nostrils filled with Lucian's scent, and she came careening back into her skin. *Lucian*. Good God, how could a man smell so good? Did he spritz sex all over him? Some kind of pheromone enhancement? Was that even a thing? Regardless of what magic elixir he doused himself in, Tessa homed in on it and used it for a lifeline. She clung to his scent and realized he was the one talking to her. His voice soothed her soul. "Lucian."

"I'm right here, darling. Not going anywhere. Just breathe for me, okay? Inhale. Exhale."

She obeyed. The pressure in her lungs eased. The fight-or-flight response faded. Tessa blinked. Her vision cleared, and she realized Lucian was straddling her, his thighs pressed against her sides, bracketing and pinning her down. He gently cradled her head to keep it from hitting the floor.

Oh God, she was a hot mess. Tessa was certifiably insane. "I'm so sorry," she blurted. "I'm... I don't know what..."

"The transition's almost done," he reassured her. Except it wasn't reassurance. It was a fucking trip wire.

Vampire.

"What are you?" She stared into eyes that were more than just ocean blue. Lucian's irises were the colors of lapis, cerulean, and teal, all swirled together. No human had eyes that color. Not naturally. "What are you, Lucian?" *What am I?*

He tensed for a second. "You know what I am," he said carefully. "And you know what you are now."

She tried to shake her head no, but he wouldn't allow her an inch.

"Breathe for me," he instructed.

She obeyed. Again. It was like her lungs had a mind of their own. "Blood curse," she whimpered. "Y-y-you said you were cursed. You, it, you, it's a blood curse."

Neither of them said another word. Lucan remained eerily still, as if allowing her to get a good look at him for the first time. Her new hella good vision noticed everything from the pulse racing in his throat, to each individual crack of his lips, to the follicles shooting off the top of his forehead in waves of luscious dark blond hair. Lucian was so gorgeous he was hard to look at. And impossible to look away from. Her gaze finally dropped to his mouth.

His mouth was moving, but she didn't hear anything he was saying to her. Frowning, he shook her a little. "Breathe," he mouthed.

She sucked in air.

Hollyyyy shiiiittt. Sounds rushed into her ears. The noises intensified with her next exhale. She could hear the bubbles popping in the tub like a riotous audience clapping. The snaps of wicks as candles burned. The slow drip of the faucet. Lucian's heartbeat. Voices in the house. Music in the distance. A car horn blasting down the road.

Tessa sucked in another breath and now she smelled more. The soap, the cleanser for the toilet, the metal from the faucet, and Lucian. Holy Hell... it was too much all at once. She tried to fight again, to jerk away and run. But Lucian wouldn't allow it. Instead, he bent down and pressed his mouth to hers.

Instinctively, she bit his tongue. But punishment morphed into heady pleasure the instant his blood touched her tastebuds. She sucked on his tongue, drawing more of that rich flavor. But the feast ended as fast as it started. He pulled back and said against her lips, "Our saliva heals. Mouth and tongue cuts last only a heartbeat."

She let that sink in.

Unable to speak yet, Tessa forced her mind to lock down. Again, Lucian must have sensed what she was attempting, and he stopped her. "Talk to me," his voice remained soft and calm. Strong and patient. "Tell me what you're thinking."

He wouldn't want to hear what she was thinking. And she didn't want to say it.

Tessa choked back a sob and turned away from him. The weight on her chest lifted and cool air kissed her skin. She was lifted into the air.

As Lucian carried her into his bed, he kept saying, "I'm so sorry. I'm so fucking sorry."

CHAPTER 38

Lucian was a piece of shit. His heart shattered like a broken mirror. All he kept thinking, as he carried his mate back to bed, was that he'd done the wrong thing. Maybe he should have spent the last of his burning days setting Tessa up in a safe place, getting her therapy, and transferring funds into an account for her to live comfortably for the rest of her life.

And then disintegrate to ashes so she could be free of him forever.

Malachi's warning words assaulted his soul once more. *"You must protect her at all costs. Even from you."*

Laying her down gently on his bed, Lucian bit his bottom lip. She was trying to escape. Run. Get away from her reality. But that wasn't going to happen. No way could he let her go now. The damage was done. The change had been made. And as guilt wracked through him, he crumbled on the floor beside the bed and buried his head in his hands. "I'm so sorry."

But no apology would be good enough. It wouldn't change a damned thing.

"I just wanted to keep you," he confessed. "To love you and protect you." All of which he should have done at a safe distance. Anonymously.

"Lucian," Tessa whispered, sucking in another heartbreaking sob. "I... I have things to tell you."

She was going to leave him. Vanish. Split town and never look back. "Please don't," he lifted his head to look at her. Begging was more effective with eye contact. And yeah, he was begging on his knees right now. He'd grovel for the rest of his life if it meant she'd give them a chance and stay with him. "I swear it was the only way. I know I should have asked for consent. And I tried. Fuck, I tried! But you were dying, and I was burning and time was running out for both of us and I—"

She clapped her hand over his mouth, cutting his excuses off. "Stop."

He shut the fuck up immediately.

Tessa's pretty pink tongue dashed out to wet her full, kissable mouth. It made him hard, and that was so unacceptable right now. Lucian brought his gaze to her eyes. No better. Her whole face was a seductive trap. Vampirism looked incredible on her.

The reality of what he'd done to her made him sick. She was stuck like this now. Forever or until death. Holy shit, what had he done?

"I trust you," she said solemnly.

He swallowed the lump in his throat and almost yacked.

"I need you to explain everything to me, Lucian. Before I can deal with what happened with those m-m-men." Her lip quivered. "I need you to explain *yourself* to me."

Okay, okay, he could do this. Yeah, no problem. He'd told this story a dozen times. He could recite it again. Nodding, he felt cold air hit his lips when Tessa removed her hand from his mouth.

"Since the dawn of time, our kind has been hunted." He blew out a shaky breath. "Vampires," he said slowly, "and Lycan."

Tessa's gaze widened as if she hung onto every word. "Go on."

"Our enemy almost had both our species extinct. Then, a vampire and Lycan ended up seducing the same woman. She got pregnant with their children at the same time." He shook his head. "No wait, not the same time, because they didn't know of each other. The vampire came to her during the day, the Lycan at night. But she ended up pregnant with twins from the two of them."

He rocked back on his heels, remaining on the floor next to the bed. "They abandoned her until it was time for her to give birth." He was messing this story all up. Usually, he recited it with finesse and explanations, maybe even used props, but doing so to his mate would only romanticize and excuse a despicable situation.

"She hated them both," he went on to say. "And when the babies came, she cursed her two lovers for it, by cursing their children."

"That's the blood curse?"

He nodded. "We're destined to live in constant longing."

She let out a shaky exhale, her eyes turning glassy with unshed tears. "Go on."

"Vampires see their mates, their *alakhai*, in mirrors."

"Their All Key," she whispered.

The hairs on his neck and arms stood on end. How had she known the translation? "Yes," he said cautiously. "But when we see them for the first time, our curse clicks into destruction mode. We begin to deteriorate and burn. Many of my kind don't live long enough to hunt down their *alakhai* and bond, turn, and mate with them."

"What happens when they don't?"

"We burn to ash."

She gasped as tears spilled down her cheeks. He wiped them away with his thumbs. Tessa's features softened in what he could only assume was sympathy when she asked, "Is that what happened to you?"

"Yes." His voice was deep and gravelly. "Only I hadn't seen your reflection until after the phone call where I tried to tell you about the story of our curse. When I hung up..." he blew out a breath, his nerves doing a damned good job of fucking him up. "When I hung up, I got into a car accident. Lost too much time healing from it. By then, you'd been taken."

He wanted to ask who took her. Did she have names? Could she describe their appearance? Anything would help him and the others find the sonofabitch who did this to her. Victoria had killed one *Savag-Ri* on that rooftop, but Lucian couldn't shake the notion that there were more involved. *Savag-Ri* never worked solo. But he didn't want to push her yet. Now wasn't the time.

"I remember," she said quietly. "I remember you telling me all this in voicemails."

Lucian's brow pinched. Was her trauma deep enough to erase things so fast? He was relieved she hadn't dropped that story into a black hole.

"Tell me more," she urged.

Where should he pick up the tragic story? "So... cursed babies," he cleared his throat. This was not a good narration, damnit. "The vampire was enraged by how much hate the woman had for him. She died giving birth, so there was no fixing it. Then he lost his head a little. On a mission to continue his bloodline, he bore many other children with many other women whom he'd turned into vampires after they had their babies. He became a monster who couldn't bear to look at his own reflection anymore. He banned all mirrors—not knowing it was the one key to helping his children find their mates. His eldest son—the one who started the curse's cycle—had one day seen a reflection of a woman in the bottom of a well and didn't understand what it meant. I guess he thought it was a ghost. So he didn't look for her, but told his brothers what he'd seen in the water, warning them to not go over to that spot anymore. Over the next few weeks, he grew more feral and aggressive. Started killing everyone in the village below theirs. A mob came after him and brought him to the center of town. Tied him up to burn him at the stake when a girl approached. It was the same girl from the well. The villagers didn't get a chance to use their torches. He ignited on the spot. So fixated on her, he didn't make a sound and with his compelling powers, he lured her into the flames and bit her."

Tessa's eyes widened. "Did they both die?"

"I'm not sure," he confessed. "The story always ended there. But I know things went crazy after that. Vampires were hunted by both *Savag-Ri* and humans for centuries. We were outnumbered for a long time."

Tessa bit her lip. He'd give her all the time she needed to process what he said. With a pinched brow, she whispered, "*Savag-Ri* 7 today. All mine. Thank you, Tessa."

He broke out in a sweat. That was a direct passage from one of his diary entries she must have read. "I uhhh, yeah..." Lucian rubbed the back of his neck, sheepishly. "I hunt them on behalf of the King. For the House of Death."

So. Dumb. He sounded like a tool.

"Hunt how?"

"Kill them." No sense in flowery words. His life was brutal and now hers would be too. "I kill them to protect vampires and humans."

"How?"

"Slowly, if possible." Yup, he was going all in. "Savagely, most definitely."

Her pupils blew wide open. Her mouth parted, giving him a great view of the tips of her fangs peeking out. "Tell me about them."

"They look like humans except for the eyes."

"The cross."

Lucian felt like he was walking on a tightrope with the conversation. Was she trying to piece her experience back together or educate herself? Both, most likely. "Yeah. They have a crisscross on their iris. Thanks to contacts, it's hard to find them when they're living among humans. But plenty have nothing to do with humans and so they don't bother hiding that significant genetic trait. Humans can't see it, only vampires, Lycan, and other *Savag-Ri*."

"Can *Savag-Ri* be made from a human?"

"I honestly don't know." Their secrets ran deep. "I mean, they keep coming, no matter how many we kill, but I think they just reproduce and rely on genetics." They were like an incurable disease.

Tessa chewed on her bottom lip for a moment. "What about if they don't have a cross in their eyes?"

His brow arched. "It's not possible." He thought about it. "Not that I'm aware of, anyway. But they've used humans in the past to do some of their dirty work. Sometimes they even bribe or blackmail them. But if a human is working for a *Savag-Ri*, they're just as awful and are shown no mercy by us."

The color drained out of Tessa's face.

What. The. Fuck.

"Tessa," he said in a low tone. "Tell me."

CHAPTER 39

Tell him. Tessa curled into her shell and refused to give him anything. He was going to kill her. If he thought humans being blackmailed by those fuckers were just as bad as *Savag-Ri*, he would go ballistic if he found out she was on that list.

Tell him.

Nope. *Stay out of this, conscience.*

"Tessa," Lucian's eyes darkened with concern. "Tell me." He rose from the floor with his hands at his side. Was he going to attack? She couldn't imagine him laying a threatening hand on her. That didn't mean she couldn't be wrong though. "Tell me what happened before you were taken."

Tessa crab walked to the other side of his massive bed to put some space between them. *Tell him.* Was she ever going to learn her lesson? Everything could have been different had she spoken up to begin with. *Tell him you love him. Tell him you're in trouble. Tell him everything!*

"I might have maybe committed a murder accidentally on purpose."

His jaw slackened. "Okay," he said calmly. "Tell me more."

Why did he have to sound like her old therapist? *Tell me more. Why do you think that? Blah, blah, blah.*

"I've blacked out a few times." She slid off the bed to stand on the other side of it. Then she snatched the sheet and wrapped it around herself. "I don't remember things. And... this one time, I just remember going to Paxton Brown's. I remember knocking on his door. I... I'm not even certain why I went there to begin with now, but all I remember is my next memory being home with lots of blood on me."

Lucian's head tipped to the side as he glowered. "That's the guy who caused the accident."

She nodded.

"What makes you think you murdered him?"

Because she was crazy. "I don't know. He's not on social media and I never drove past his house again." Only fools returned to the scene of the crime. Duh.

"So why did you—"

"They blackmailed me!" she confessed. "They came into my apartment and had all these pictures of me covered in blood and a man lying in a heap on the ground."

"Wait, whoa, whoa." He was at her with lightning speed.

Tessa put her hands up to stop him from touching her. "I gotta finish!"

He didn't get closer, but she could tell it was killing him to hold back.

Tucking her hair behind her ears, she said, "They had pictures of us at the theatre, Lucian. They said they were going to have me arrested for murder if I didn't lure you out." Her throat tightened and she couldn't breathe. "I didn't do it. I swear I didn't do it."

"I know," his gravelly voice vibrated her chest even with three feet of floor space separating them.

But she wasn't sure he believed her or not. "I swear I didn't give them anything. And the more they tried to pry information out of me, the tighter lipped I got. I wasn't giving you up. You said there were worse things out there and those men were it."

"*Men*," he repeated.

"Three of them. Alex and Colton were the ones who blackmailed me. They came in with this other guy right after I hung up with you. His name was Simon." Panic made everything come out in a rush. "They drugged me and brought me to the dance studio." Everything in her intensified. She wanted to run into his arms. She wanted to crawl up the walls. She wanted to jump out of the motherfucking window. "I gave them nothing," she rasped. "And I tried to make them kill me because I'd rather die than betray you."

Lucian pushed past her defenses and cupped her face with his hands. "Tessa." He smashed his mouth to hers. Clinging, scratching, gripping, clawing at him, Tessa couldn't seem to get a grip. He pulled back and pressed his forehead to hers. "I love you. I love your strength and your courage." His gaze flitted around her face. "I love your devotion to what you love."

She bawled her eyes out.

Holding her tightly, he ran his hand through her hair. "Jesus fucking Christ," his voice cracked with emotion. "You even tried to save me at the end, too. Like your life didn't matter as much as mine did to you."

He was absolutely right. "My life's been a waste from the beginning," she sobbed. "You're too good to die."

Lucian made a noise that was all agony. He buried his face in her neck and fell apart with her. They ended up on the floor with her in his lap and his back resting against the wall.

"Please don't kill me," she mumbled into his chest.

"Kill you?" Lucian pushed her back to look at her and if ever there was an expression that said *I can't believe you'd think I'd ever lay a hand on you, much less kill you...* well, Lucian was wearing it now.

"You said humans who worked with them are shown no mercy."

Lucian's jaw clenched and brow furrowed into a severe dip. "You didn't work with them Tessa. You were *kidnapped*."

"But before that…"

He shook his head, dismissing her next words. "That's not what I meant. That's not—" He brought her into a tight hug. "Fucking Hell, Tessa."

She was going to throw up. He didn't get it. Lucian was almost blown up because of her. "I gave them nothing." She said into his chest. "I refused to lure you out. I even left my phone at home when we met at the diner because I was scared they'd put a tracker on it."

He growled like an animal. "Why didn't you tell me any of this?"

"How could I?"

"*Trust*," he shook her a little. "We're supposed to *trust* one another, Tessa. Was all our time together an act?"

"No!" Now she was a little mad. "But it's not like we have

deep conversations, Lucian. I trust you with my life inside a *scene*." She felt him tense up. "We only knew each other that way. And I couldn't even confess that I was in love with you, much less tell you all this other stuff."

He pulled away from her and turned his head. Rubbing his temple, he whispered, "This is all my fault. Every fucking bit of it." He turned to face her again. "I'll spend the rest of my existence making up for all of this."

She didn't want that. It wasn't his fault. It was everyone's fault and no one's.

"I trusted you," she jabbed him in the chest. "I didn't trust *myself*." He didn't get it. That much was clear by the look on his face. "I'm not sure how to explain myself. My head's a mess."

"You don't have to." Lucian cupped her cheeks again. His face might be the picture of serenity, but Tessa could feel his energy bouncing off the walls with aggression. "When you're ready, tell me everything. If you're never ready, that's okay too."

She released her held breath.

"And," he swallowed hard, "if you aren't ready to be with me, I'll understand."

She shirked out of his hold. "Are you second-guessing your actions now that you know all this about me?"

"Absolutely not." Running a hand through his hair, Lucian realized they were both naked, and she'd dropped her sheet at some point. Talk about vulnerability. There was nothing hiding one from the other. This was real talk. Not pretend. Not hypothetical. *Real.* "Are you upset that I turned you?"

He braced for her answer.

"Of course not," she bristled. "You'd be dead if you hadn't."

She was right, but also wrong. He'd have died—and done so willingly—if he knew for sure she didn't want to turn. It had happened to other vampires. Some turned their mates without consent... others refused to do it without permission.

Lucian had blurred the line.

Tessa worried her lip. "Are you regretting it? Me?"

"Hell no." Lucian never wanted her to think that. Ever. "I was going to run off with you," he said with his head cast down. "I'd already told my King I was out. That night when I called and left you all those voicemails? I'd planned to leave everything behind. I didn't know you were my *alakhai* yet. I just knew I couldn't bear to live without you. When you pulled a Rapunzel out of my window, and I saw the wreck you'd left my room, I panicked. I wanted to tell you everything but wanted to protect you from it too. I tried to get the King to make an exception, but he refused. So, I told him I was leaving." He tossed his hands up. "I was hellbent on winning you back and starting life alone with just you."

The air whooshed out of her as if she had no clue what to say to that. He was willing to give up everything to be with her and he'd bet a million dollars some little nagging voice in the back of her head was saying she wasn't worth that kind of sacrifice. But that would be the old Tessa talking. The broken one. She wasn't that person anymore. Lucian hoped she understood that.

"I love you, Tessa. Always have."

She crossed her arms. "You called me toxic."

He cringed. "Bad choice of words."

"It was the most accurate thing I've ever been called." A tear slid down her cheek. "And I know this sounds stupid, but I don't think I am anymore."

What? Like she could suddenly be cured of issues she'd battled her whole life? Damn skippy she could. If only he could convince her of the phenomenon. That wasn't possible though. She had to figure out how to do it herself.

"You gave it up." He leaned in slowly, getting closer to her mouth. "In your transition, you shed what weighed you down in your human life. And parts of you became more enhanced with your new vampire one."

"So, I'm not bullshitting myself?" Her eyes said, *Please say it's true.*

"No, darling." Lucian ran his thumb along her mouth. "You're not bullshitting yourself."

Tessa's brow furrowed as she looked away from him. "I can't remember everything that happened in the studio."

"It's probably best you don't."

"No," she hugged herself tighter. "I want to remember. I *need* to."

"Allow yourself some time, Tessa."

"We don't have time," she argued. "I feel like I'm a bomb about to explode. I feel like something bad is about to happen."

Or, all the bad that already happened was trying to crack through her newly constructed walls. "Do you remember being in the chair?"

"Which time?" Her eyes unfocused as she growled, *"Dance, you filthy vampire whore."*

Lucian's aggression went ape shit at her tone. He kept it together only because she wasn't saying it to herself as a reprimand. She was repeating what someone said to her. Which, yeah, fuck that. Whoever this piece of shit was, would spend a long time in the Kill Box when Lucian found them.

"He cut my feet," she suddenly blurted. "He told me if I stopped dancing, I was dead."

Lucian groaned and peppered her with more kisses. "Damnit, Tessa." He picked her up and carried her over to his broken dresser. "Pull open the top drawer."

The damned thing stuck because the dresser was cracked. They'd fucked too zealously on it earlier. "Weapons." She said while yanking it open, already knowing what was in there.

He kissed her shoulder as he stood behind her, his body pressed flush against her back. "Next one."

"Files." She ripped it open as if to prove how good her memory was. "About a kink club called The Wicked Garden. I assume you're Pain."

"And you'd assume wrong." He wasn't even mad about it. She had no reason to believe he wasn't Pain, who was listed on a few of those files. "Pain is Reys. I'm holding a few of his notes for him."

"Why?"

"Didn't ask. If he needs something done and can't do it himself, any one of us will step in to help. He asked me to keep these, so I have. That's all." He felt her relax in relief. "We'll get back to the other files in there on another day. But just so you're aware, they're *Savag-Ri* cases. Those who've been killed, their family tree, and some who've taken our own men and haven't been caught yet."

Her heart thudded in her throat, matching his heart rate.

"Next one," he said against her cheek.

"Boxers."

"Dig deeper." With trembling hands, she moved the boxers and undershirts out of the way and found a little red box. "Open it," he kissed her neck, loving how her skin rippled with goosebumps.

Holding the box like it was a fragile bubble, Tessa tipped back the lid to reveal a ruby ring.

"It was my grandmother's." He rubbed his thumbs up and down her belly as he held her close. "I've been saving it." Lucian plucked the ring from its cushioned bed. "And I'm not waiting another second to give it to you."

This felt fitting for the two of them. Right now, in a vulnerable space, spilling their secrets by candlelight, with him at her back. Right where he belonged.

Slipping the ring on, he was shocked at how perfectly it fit her slender finger. It was like it had been made for her. "Perfection," he nipped the shell of her ear. "Open the next drawer."

"Candle replacements."

His laugh was dark and seductive. "They're drip candles, darling. For wax play." Oh lord, her jealousy kicked back in with a vengeance. Was it awful that he liked it? Yeah. Probably. But damn, did it feel nice to be reassured how she felt about him. Especially after everything that happened. "Don't worry." He nipped her again. "I use them on myself."

"Why didn't you bring them to me?"

There it was. The moment he'd been waiting for. "Our contract was for me to be your pleasure Dom. To give you what *you* wanted and reward you. Build you up." It said nothing about what he wanted. A slight mistake he longed to correct but never had. "And bringing you pleasure superseded all else for me anyways. I think I craved your releases more than you did."

"Why didn't you amend the contract so we both got things we wanted?" she asked carefully. Plucking a black taper from the collection, she ran her fingers over it.

"I didn't want to spook you," he admitted. "Just as you never told me you loved me. I think we're both guilty of not wanting to ruin what we had."

"And in turn, ruined it anyway."

She wasn't wrong. "Next drawer."

"Rope," she said, bending down and bumping his groin with her ass. She snatched a red bundle. "I was furious when I saw this. I imagined you using it on someone who wasn't me. And then I fixated on the files of Miss Jane and Pain and lost my shit."

"You had every right to be pissed."

"No, I didn't." She spun around and his hard dick poked her in the abs. "I should have never snooped to begin with. And I should have had the courage to ask you questions instead of running off."

"Trust," he reminded her. "Tell me that will never happen again."

"It won't."

"Good." He flashed her a big smile. "And as for the Shibari..." He pulled it out of her grip. "I use this on myself too." He pointed at the eye hooks in the ceiling to show her where he liked to hang.

She arched her brow. "You do a lot with just yourself."

"Yeah, I do." He pulled Tessa towards the closet next. "That's all changing as of tonight."

Her lust kicked into the air and filled his nostrils. Holy Hell, she was intoxicating. "This," he bumped the box of sheet music with his foot. "That's *my* messy head."

"Oh," she giggled nervously, "I got one of those too."

"So, we understand each other. We remember that it's good to get it all out somehow. Music, dance, writing, however it needs to be freed."

She nodded and bit her lip.

"I'm four hundred and two years old." Might as well address the dates on some of that sheet music, right?

"And yet, you don't look a day over a hundred."

He clutched his heart and rocked back on his heels as if she'd struck him. "Oof!"

Really, he looked the same age as Tessa. Vampires remained youthful and in their prime for a long time. So long as they stayed healthy, their image didn't waver much.

"You must have one helluva skincare secret to look so young."

"It's an entire morning and night routine." Lucian ran the back of his hand across his jaw playfully. "Tedious, but worth it. I buy moisturizer in bulk."

She laughed and leaned into him for a kiss.

A knock broke their magical moment. Lucian made sure he was between Tessa and the door. "Yeah?"

"It's Dorian. Can I come in?"

"Hang on a sec." Lucian snatched a shirt off a hanger and handed it to Tessa before grabbing a pair of sweatpants for himself. He usually didn't give a shit who saw him naked, but Tessa might—especially if Dorian had Lena with him. Running his hand through his hair, furious at the interruption, he swung open his door. "This better be good, Reaper."

"We caught Alex."

CHAPTER 40

Tessa hugged herself and looked out one of Lucian's windows. No, she wasn't thinking about climbing out of it and escaping again. She wasn't thinking about anything. Her brain seemed to have shut off.

It's no secret Tessa had horrific coping skills. She was grateful Lucian understood that better than anyone else in her life ever had. As soon as Dorian came in to say they caught Alex, Tessa shut down in a quiet and calm way. She said she didn't want to go with them to see that guy. If she never saw Alex again, it would be too soon.

Unlike Lucian, she wasn't about seeking revenge. Tessa just wanted it over and done with.

Besides, the last time she sought revenge, she blacked out and might have murdered someone. Although, by the looks on Dorian and Lucian's faces, they were going to more than murder Alex.

Good, she thought. Right? That's good? He's a *Savag-Ri*. They're bad. Horrible. Evil. And they go after and kill her kind.

Tessa's belly fluttered. *Her kind*. She was a vampire.

Hand to the man, if Dracula showed up with a pack of wolves, she was going to fangirl hard.

Smooshing her cheeks, Tessa made a fishy face. While staring out the window into the night, she pulled all her hair over her shoulder and looked up at the moon. Wow, it was silky and thicker than usual. Her hair. Not the moon. Keep up, please. Toying with a tendril, Tessa thought about that scene in Interview with a vampire where the little girl Claudia cut her hair and it grew right back. Would that happen to her? Tessa bit her lip and stormed into the bathroom to find out.

She opened all the drawers looking for a pair of scissors. When she couldn't find any in the bathroom, she grabbed a blade from Lucian's top dresser drawer. Marching back into the bathroom, she got a good look at herself in the mirror.

Okay. Wow. She hadn't looked at herself since before, well, *before* everything. But she vaguely remembered what her reflection was like in the mirror of the dance studio. It was as if she'd been beaten with a bat and hit by a truck. But now? Not even three days later, she was perfectly healed. Healthier than she'd ever looked in her life. Her muscles were more toned. Hair thicker. Eyes brighter and bluer, with a tint of purple. Her lips were plumper too. *Wow.* She was hot.

Leaning into the mirror, Tessa opened her mouth. Lord only knows what she thought she was going to see, but fangs weren't it. Maybe whiter, brighter, slightly different teeth. But not this. She had fangs. Sharp, delicately pointed fangs like a viper. Touching one with the tip of her tongue, she squeaked when she accidentally punctured herself.

"You'll get used to it," mused a blonde woman from the doorway. Dressed in a tight purple top and leather pants, she sported stiletto heels and a braided mohawk. "I'm not sure if you remember me, I'm Victoria."

"Tessa." She dropped the blade and her experimental plans to walk over and shake Victoria's hand.

"Lucian thought you'd want some company. Lena should be coming up soon."

"Company, or a babysitter to make sure I don't do another jailbreak?"

Victoria laughed and Tessa gawked at how huge her fangs were. They were way bigger than Tessa's. Just like her tits, hips, and lips. This vampire was a knockout.

"That was impressive," Victoria said. "I don't think anyone's attempted and succeeded at getting away from the Mad House like that before. I wish I'd caught it on camera."

Someone else knocked on the door and another woman peeked inside. "Knock, knock. Can I come in?" A brunette not nearly as vivacious as Victoria came in.

"Lena, Tessa. Tessa, Lena." Victoria smiled. "She's new, like you."

Lena came forward waving, "My mate's Dorian. The Reaper."

Tessa nodded, unsure of what to say. But Dorian was the one who'd come to get Lucian, and she could tell he and Lucian were close friends.

"Whatcha doing with the dagger?" Victoria pushed off the doorjamb and scooped the blade from the counter. Twirling it, she waited for a response.

Tessa's cheeks grew hot. "I was going to cut my hair to see if it grew right back."

"I'll save you the trouble. It does, but not as fast as that girl in the movie with the hotties. It's more like faster than human speed, slower than Hollywood speed. Good news is, if you get a shit haircut or decide to cut your own bangs, the catastrophe only lasts about a week or two instead of months."

Tessa nodded. "Well, then."

They stood in awkward silence.

"Soooo, Lucian..." Lena finally broke the uncomfortable silence. "He's fun." When Victoria snorted, Lena elbowed her. "Shut up, Vic."

"What? He is fun. That's not what I'm laughing at."

"Then what's funny?"

Tessa stayed quiet while Lena and Vic bounced off each other.

"I'm just trying to imagine what Reaper and Lucian are doing right now. Torture makes me smile."

"You got to *torture makes me smile* from Lena saying *Lucian is fun*?" Tessa cringed a little with humor.

"Oh, hell yeah. Same, same. Lucian's an animal. And right now, with Reaper's toys at his disposal? He's probably painting the walls red with that *Savag-Ri's* guts. So romantic."

Lena's gaze narrowed. "You're creepy and unhinged. You know that, right?"

"Aww," Vic purred, clutching her heart. "Thanks!"

A tiny laugh escaped Tessa before they all fell into silence again. Finally, she said, "This is going to be an adjustment."

"Yeah, but it's worth it. Right, Lena?"

"A thousand percent, yes."

"Were you both made?" Tessa leaned against the sink and crossed her arms. "Reaper's your mate," she said, pointing at Lena. Turning to Victoria, she asked, "Who's yours?"

Victoria gasped dramatically. "Eww. Don't even *tempt* the universe with that crazy talk. I have no mate. Thank fuck. I'm a natural born vampire. Lena's made."

"Can you make a vampire anytime you want?"

"Yes, but it doesn't often go well." Victoria sauntered over and checked her lipstick in the mirror. Swiping a thumb over the corner of her mouth, she angled her face this way and that, then blew herself a kiss. "And the King doesn't allow us to turn humans without good reason. Even then, it needs to be sanctioned and carefully done. The responsibility is huge. Not worth it, if you ask me. Most humans die in the process, which is always a disappointment and really counterproductive."

Tessa felt out of her element. "I was just curious. I wasn't thinking about turning anyone."

"Would be cool if we could though. We could just make an army of vamps and annihilate the *Savag-Ri*. Sadly, that's not possible." Victoria stuffed her hands in her back pockets and tilted her head to the side. Giving Tessa a once over, she said, "He was thinking of turning you. The King wouldn't allow it, so Lucian was going to leave us."

It didn't take a genius to pick up the bitterness in her tone.

"He told me how he'd planned to break away." Tessa tied her hair back in a knot. "He didn't say anything about making me a vampire though."

"He would have only done it with your consent." Vic shrugged. "He's huge on permission. Goes against his honor code to do otherwise. The rush to turn you into a vampire earlier without you being one-hundred percent aware and alert, is going to lay on his shoulders for a long fucking time."

"Vic," Lena warned.

"She needs to know," Victoria snapped back. "We can't lose someone like Lucian. And we almost did because of how much he cared for a human. A *human*. You don't get it because you were human once too, Lena. But that's... that's close to treason. Everything Lucian's worked for he was willing to give up for *her*." She stared at Tessa like a hawk would a mouse. "Thank fuck you turned out to be his mate. I've never in my life heard of that happening before."

Tessa's brow furrowed. "Meeting your mate before seeing their reflection is rare?"

"Un. Heard. Of." Victoria swaggered back into the bedroom, leaving Tessa and Lena to follow like ducklings. "And I'm saying all this to you, so you understand what Lucian's going to be like for a while. He's one of the great ones, Tessa. But he's also vicious and intense. He carries tremendous guilt for his brother's death, and now your kidnapping has been added to his list of bitter regrets. He's going to take full responsibility for what's happened to you. It'll eat him alive until he gets over it. Who knows how long that'll take."

"But it's not his fault." Tessa's cheeks grew hot. "He didn't do this. Those men did."

"And he knew the risks when he got involved with you," Vic bit back. "There's a reason we have The Wicked Garden. It's a controlled safe space for us to get our rocks off and humans can stay safe while with us. Their memories are altered and eventually erased, so they can't be used against us later." She scoffed and tacked on, "I knew he was going to do something crazy. I felt it when he brought you home that night and allowed you to perform for all of us."

Tessa wanted to defend herself somehow. Victoria kept prattling on and didn't give her a chance to try.

"I knew what he was doing," Vic sneered. "He was trying to give us a clue. Give us a chance to fall head over heels in love with you, too. Lucian's never done something like that before. Never in all the time he's lived under Malachi's roof has he brought someone here. And then 'poof!' there you were, dancing in our music room on display for the House. He wanted us to see what he saw in you."

"That's not my fault," Tessa growled back. "I didn't ask for any of this. In fact, I tried to run. *Twice.*"

Victoria's face fell. "I didn't say it was your fault. I'm saying I get what Lucian was doing. And I see exactly why fate made you his *alakhai*. I'm just warning you, Lucian's going to be a handful for a while."

Tessa's hackles raised. Who was this woman to Lucian? A former lover, now jealous? Was she madly in love with him too?

"And that's your business how?"

"Lucian, you and every other vampire in this territory is my business. We've worked so hard to get this far, and I fear Lucian is going to derail if he's not given closure and a way to unleash his pent-up energy." She jabbed a finger at Tessa, "You have the responsibility of making sure he gets those things, because you're his mate."

"And you'd rather it was *you*?" Tessa couldn't help but ball her hands into fists.

Vic looked her up and down slowly. "No," she growled. "This is me being a friend and giving you time to prepare."

Lena groaned and pinched the bridge of her nose. "Vic, you have, by far, the worst people skills I've ever seen. And I hang with barbarians who like to break jaws for fun."

Vic tossed her hands up. "What's wrong with how I said any of that?" She plopped down on Lucian's bed and folded her arms behind her head, relaxing. "You're both too sensitive. Shed that human side, ladies. You can kiss me for that great advice later."

Lena rolled her eyes. "She's right, you know. I mean, speaking from my experience, Dorian went bananas when he thought I was getting hurt. I can only imagine how Lucian's reacting to that prisoner in the Kill Box right now."

"Kill Box?"

"It's exactly how it sounds." Lena walked over and looked out the window. Tessa joined her. "You know, being an *alakhai* is really incredible."

Tessa couldn't agree more, but she didn't say it.

"It broke my heart to hear how vampires have been in constant longing for centuries. Can you imagine that kind of ache?"

Tessa shook her head.

"Me neither, really. I mean, I think I do, but it's not the same." Lena stared at the yard and sighed. "It makes them love us so much, they can't control it. There's no taming it. It's just," she made an explosion sound complete with hand-gestures. Then she flicked her gaze to Victoria. "She isn't wrapped too tight, but her love is all-consuming."

"It's not love!" Vic yelled because she could hear everything they were whispering. "It's... I don't know what. But ewww."

Lena laughed at her. "Stepped in some feelings, did you?"

"So gross." Victoria made a gagging sound.

The three of them ended up busting out Lucian's Bluetooth speaker and turning on music while they waited for him to return. It was actually quite fun. Vic was a little rough around the edges, but she seemed to mean well. And Lena was sweet.

Tessa couldn't figure out if she'd made two friends today or not. It had been so long since she allowed herself that kind of joy. But this was a new beginning. So yeah, maybe she had two new friends to start her fresh journey with.

Now if only Lucian came back soon, she might stop feeling like the walls were closing in on her.

CHAPTER 41

Don't kill him too quick.

Lucian repeated that mantra over and over as he made his way to the Kill Box. It was a small building separate from the mansion that remained heavily guarded and always protected. This was Dorian's playground. The execution chamber.

The place where justice was served.

Usually, Dorian did all the work and had all the fun with the prisoners they brought here, but today it was Lucian's turn.

"Hey." Dorian slammed his hand on the door, preventing Lucian from entering just yet.

"Move or I'll break your arm, Reaper."

"That, right there, is what I'm worried about." Dorian shoved his face in Lucian's. "Do not be swift to react."

"Oh, trust me. This fucker will beg for death long before I give it to him."

"You say that now, but look how I reacted with Lena that night on the street. I didn't even hesitate to annihilate the piece of shit. You *think* you're going to be slow on the torture scale, but I assure you, once you see him… once you are face-to-face with your *alakhai's* attacker? You'll have no control over your actions." He shoved his finger in Lucian's chest. "Seriously, stay back for a while and let me take the reins first."

"Fuck. You."

"We're not going in there until you can at least get a grip on your instincts. Treat this like we do any other *Savag-Ri*."

But Alex wasn't an ordinary enemy. He was the bastard who

hurt and nearly killed his fated mate. Lucian ground his molars together. Probably just cracked a tooth. Deep down, he knew Dorian was right. But fuck that. "I'll give him five minutes." Five minutes to say something helpful before Lucian blew the sonofabitch through the roof. "Any longer is too much time spent away from my mate."

Prolonged torture would never happen here. Not today. Lucian wanted hard and fast answers so he could get on with the carnage and get back to Tessa. Killing Alex would save other vampires from the same fate Lucian and Tessa suffered. Torturing him would likely be a wasted effort because those bastards rarely gave over their kind. They knew once they were in the Kill Box that they were only leaving in a coffin.

Time to start the fun. "Everything laid out and ready?"

"Of course." Dorian flashed an evil grin. "And I already primed him for you."

Man, he had great friends. Always going the extra mile. Shoving the door open, Lucian stormed straight into the stone-floored interior of the vampire kingdom's little death arena.

Alex sat tied with barbed wire to a metal chair. Naked. He'd been badly beaten. Not that Lucian wasn't going to do worse to the cocksucker. He whistled as he made his way to the table of toys, but the smells alone told him Alex was leaking spectacularly as it was.

"Xin got him first. I had sloppy seconds." Dorian leaned against the table and crossed his arms. "Got his meat tenderized enough, I hope."

Lucian gritted his teeth, snatched two metal rods, and sauntered over to Alex. Slamming the metal rods into his thighs, Lucian made sure they struck bone. Alex screamed like a stuck pig.

Sissy.

"First thing's, first. You made her piss herself." Lucian turned back and grabbed the cable wires. Pinching the ends of clamps on the rods stuck in Alex's legs, he strolled over to the electrical box and flipped the switch. He felt no amount of satisfaction watching that *Savag-Ri* spit and convulse as volts of electricity buzzed through his system.

Lucian shut it off.

Alex panted, gasping and groaning.

"Shut the fuck up." Lucian snatched two rods next. These

suckers were twelve inches long and thin as knitting needles. "You tased her. Drugged her. Tried to drain her." He shoved the instruments into both sides of Alex's neck and let go. Blood flowed like little fountains from the other ends of the hollowed-out tools.

"You cut her feet and made her dance." Lucian shoved his hand into Alex's mouth when he tried to talk. "Don't interrupt. It's rude."

Alex squeezed his eyes shut, his nostrils flaring as he gasped for air.

"You blackmailed her." Lucian leaned in, bracing his hands on the back of the chair and got so close to Alex, he could smell his cigarette breath. "You terrified her." He signaled Dorian, who handed him another weapon. Lucian held the M48 cyclone knife against Alex's chest. "You destroyed my girl." He shoved it in, aiming for Alex's heart. "Any last words?"

The *Savag-Ri's* eyes fluttered from blood loss.

Lucian slapped him. "Stay awake, asshole." He held his hand out and Dorian immediately handed him something to help with that. Lucian uncapped the needle and shoved it into Alex's chest. The *Savag-Ri's* eyes blew wide.

Adrenaline was so convenient in *Savag-Ri* serving sizes.

"Wakey, wakey, sunshine." Lucian squished Alex's cheeks. "You don't get to pass out and miss the fun."

Alex spat in Lucian's face. "Keep me all you want, but you're just wasting precious time."

Wasn't that the truth.

"Where's Simon?" Lucian gripped Alex by the throat and started squeezing. "Where. The. Fuck. Is Simon?" He let go, walked backwards towards the electric box again, and wrapped his fingers around the switch. "You're irritating me." He pulled the lever.

Alex sputtered and convulsed, screaming as volts of electricity cooked him from the inside out.

Lucian counted to seven. Slowly. Might have added a couple extra numbers into the mix. Tied his boot. Sang a tune. Then he flipped the lever and cut the juice.

Alex was half-cooked and sizzling like a steak. "How's that feel, motherfucker?" Lucian knew the answer. He'd just suffered through his curse and understood the pain of incineration. "Did I move faster than my brother?" He would never forget that goddamn note put on Tessa's back for him. "How'd you know about Tessa being my *alakhai*?"

Alex's tremors made it harder for him to respond. He yacked all over himself. The fumes from all the vomit, piss, and shit were enough to make Lucian's eyes water. "How did you know?"

"Fuck. You."

Lucian shoved the corkscrew blade further into Alex's chest and started twisting it. "Where's Simon?"

The *Savag-Ri* sputtered a laugh. "Fuck you."

Fuck you. Fuck. You. Wasn't that the same thing Tessa said to them as they tortured her? Broke her? Beat her? Strapped her with dynamite and left her for dead?

"Lucian!"

He heard his name, but it didn't register. All he thought about was Tessa and what they put her through. What they did. What they might have done. What they could have done.

"Lucian! Damnit!"

They took his mate. Abused and blackmailed her. Terrified her. Made her dance on cut feet and broken toes. Called her a vampire whore. She was going to suffer for years with PTSD from this, and for what? Why? All because these cockroaches had a vendetta against vampires for shit that was done so long ago, the carbon date alone was impossible to pinpoint. Fuck that. Fuck this. Fuck Alex and anyone else who ever attempted to lay a finger on his mate again.

"*Lucian*!"

Pulse beating wildly, he slowly swiveled his head in Dorian's general direction. "Yeah?"

"It's done." Dorian cautiously crept closer and reached out to pull Lucian's arm back. "It's over, man."

No, it wasn't. It was far from over. Alex had to pay a lot more than a few minutes of tickle time for what he did to Tessa. But then Lucian looked down and saw what happened.

Alex's jaw was missing. His torso had been torn in half and ribcage cracked open like a lobster. *Well shit*. Lucian stepped back to see all of Alex's insides were in a goopy, overcooked, black puddle on the floor.

Guess he got a little carried away…

"Oops."

Lucian got it now. That detached, white-hot, blinding fury that blacked out the world and let you lose control and sense of self. It wasn't as mind-blowing as he assumed. More like a deep sleep and you awake shaking with too much adrenaline pumping in your system. Only this was amplified because he was a vampire. His instincts were to protect his mate at all costs. Not having her with him made Lucian feral in the Kill Box.

Dorian stayed to clean up, and Lucian left hotter than ever. Sweat poured down his back, soaking his clothes and driving him insane.

Tessa. He was obsessed with her. Needed her. Couldn't breathe without her.

Later, he might reflect on his treatment of Alex, but not today. *Tessa.* Tessa was all that mattered. Not revenge or closure or answers or Simon. That *Savag-Ri* would get his soon enough. But not today.

Not. Today.

This was happening too soon. He was torn between duty and desire. As a mate, he was responsible for Tessa. Allowing her attackers to remain upright and breathing wasn't an option. But this bond and transition was still so fresh, leaving her for five minutes felt too long.

How was he going to hunt and protect and be the king's high guard when his instincts demanded he be with Tessa twenty-four-seven? That was a problem for another day. Hell, Dorian handled it. Lucian could too.

But not today.

He barely remembered getting back to the mansion. Didn't recall kicking open the front door. No recollection of racing up the stairs. Hand-to-the-Creator, he wondered if he'd held his breath the entire trip home. But once he saw his girl sitting in the middle of the floor doing leg stretches with Victoria and Lena, he at least remembered how to talk. "Leave."

Lena and Victoria took off like he had rabies and shut the door behind them.

Tessa's eyes rounded as she stood. "Luci—"

He crushed his mouth to hers and ate his name off her pretty mouth. Tearing off the shirt she wore, he made fast work of stripping them both down. Digging his fingers in her ass, he lifted her up and impaled her with his cock.

Holy Hell, if there was a way to crawl inside and be under her skin, he'd do it.

His actions were driven with a fierce need to mark her, claim her. Smother and inhale her. Wear and brand her. Lucian's hips turned to pistons. Slamming her against the wall, he was blinded with pleasure.

She screamed and gasped his name. Fuck. Yes. His pace quickened, and he smiled against her mouth when he felt her inner walls clamp down and milk his cock. He was far from finished. She was coming until there wasn't a drop left in her.

His fangs throbbed. "Need."

His skin pebbled with a chill even as he felt a fever rise in his veins. Instinctively, Tessa leaned to the side, offering her neck. Her nails digging into his shoulders grounded him a little. But it didn't hold him back from striking.

Hot, sweet life poured down his throat when he bit her.

Tessa tensed under him, before detonating with another climax. "*Lucian,*" her tone was dark, the register lower and so seductive it made his toes curl. He felt like a demon only she had the power to summon.

Probably wasn't too far off the mark with that one.

He was possessive. Wicked. Lucian pulled harder from her vein as if the more he took, the safer she'd be because she was inside him.

Absurd, yes. But he didn't see it that way.

Common sense started to kick in. He was a filthy mess from the Kill Box. Gore was thick under nails and dried to his palms. He didn't want any of that touching Tessa. But he also hadn't been able to control himself or hold back from getting inside her just now.

Keeping her impaled on his cock, his mouth still latched onto her throat, he carried her into the shower and kept them connected. Grappling for the faucet, he got things going and took a few more hard pulls from his mate's neck.

"I'm sorry," he said, pulling off her throat and licking his vicious puncture wounds closed. "I shouldn't be so brutal."

"Don't apologize," she panted.

He pulled back to see her face and make sure she wasn't hurt. What he saw made his heart sigh. Tessa's rosy cheeks, tussled hair, big smile, tiny fangs, and bright eyes told him she was anything but hurt. "Like that, did you?"

"I might have to insist you come home to me every night so ferocious." She tossed him a wink.

"Did I hurt you?"

"Do I look hurt?"

"You look good enough to eat." He propped her on the counter, pulled out and dropped down on his knees to lick her pussy. She was stretched from his dick and wetter than his shower. He grazed his teeth along her clit.

She threaded her fingers through his hair and shoved his face against her pussy. "More."

He attacked her bundle of nerve endings with his tongue until she cried out again. Her thighs quivered, and he felt like a God. Licking her cream from his lips, he said, "You're so damn gorgeous when I make you come."

He could do this all day and night.

"You've got gunk all over you."

Shit. Fuck. Damnit. He forgot, that fast, what he was covered in. Turning towards the shower, he slipped inside.

Tessa followed him, in as if lured by his scent.

He bit back his smile and kept his head down. If she was half as obsessed and beguiled with him as he was with her, the music they would make together was going to blow the roof off this place.

CHAPTER 42

Tessa had to give it to Lena. That woman wasn't kidding when she'd said there was no taming a vampire's love. Lucian practically broke down his own door to get to her earlier. Even though he'd looked like something fresh out of a horror movie, there was nothing sexier than a vampire on the verge of unhinging with need for his mate.

And to know Alex was no longer on this earth, and his death was by Lucian's hands, sparked a really scary fire in Tessa's loins.

It's one thing to have a man say he'd die for you. Another to have him say he'd kill for you. To witness the aftermath of a man keeping his word like the only reason he was put on this earth was to protect, honor, cherish, and avenge you? Ladies, Tessa was here to tell you it's the hottest goddamn thing to ever exist.

And when Lucian ravished her against the wall like he couldn't stand another second without being inside her afterwards?

Ohhhh yeah, a girl could get used to this life.

Lucian stood under the spray of the hot shower and blindly reached out for the soap. Doing a hard suds and scrub, he kept his eyes closed and asked, "Enjoying the view?"

"Tremendously."

Lucian was cut, lean, and built with broad shoulders, chiseled abs, and muscular thighs that suggested he did a lot of running and working out. Did she mention his perfectly shaped ass? Tessa ran her hand across it, marveling at how hard it was. From neck down, Lucian was a wet dream. But his face? Lucian's angular bone structure was to die for. Perfect mouth, stunning eyes, and yeah, his jaw line was razor sharp. "Are all vampires as pretty as you?"

He chuckled and turned to face her. Tipping his head back, he rinsed out his hair. Even the scent of his shampoo made her mouth water.

"You'll have to let me know." His smile was big and fangs bigger.

"Do we sleep in coffins?"

That earned her a boisterous laugh from him. "No, darling. But—" he grabbed her by the waist and spun her around so she was under the spray. He had on the regular shower head, not the rain one on the ceiling. Lathering her hair with shampoo, he chuckled. "I actually ordered a custom coffin with a bump out. It's at The Wicked Garden."

Her nipples hardened. Not from lust. From jealousy. "Go there often?"

"Only off hours when no one's there and shipments are delivered." He bent down to clip her nipple with his fangs, playfully. "Damn, you make me hard with that jealousy rolling off you."

She felt a little worried about that. "I'm not usually this way. I don't understand why I'm so possessive."

"Welcome to vampirism, Tessa. Mates do not share."

"Bummer," she teased. Lucian growled like an animal in her ear. Holy shit, her nipples hardened to the point of pain and her pussy swelled hearing it. "Sooo, it works both ways."

"If anyone even so much as looks below your chin, I'll cut their eyes out."

She was only half-convinced he was joking. As he took care of her in the shower, Tessa's mind drifted. "I want to remember everything," she said. "I can't seem to quiet my head."

Lucian turned the water off and grabbed a towel to wrap around her. "I can take us someplace safe for a little while." His tone was softer now. Whatever storm he rode in on ebbed away.

"Where?"

"My mother's."

His mom's? The offer seemed special and rare. "I'd love to meet your family."

"That'll have to wait." He dried her off. "She's in France for a while. My brother's death hit her hard. And my father..." Lucian's brow pinched. "They were married a long time. Now he's with someone else. My mother hasn't dealt well with it."

"Understandable." She didn't need to ask for details. If she was connecting the dots right, his father must have found his fated mate and had no choice but to leave his wife. That had to be devastating. Could Tessa have survived that if she'd been in those shoes? She looked at Lucian and bit her lip. No, she couldn't imagine. Didn't want to imagine. The idea of Lucian not in her life made her nauseous.

"Hey, whoa." He held her hips to keep her knees from buckling. "I'm not going anywhere, Tessa. This..." he waved his hand between them, "This is forever. For real forever. I'll never leave you."

She crumbled anyway. Maybe Victoria was right, and she needed to shed her human side and toughen up a little bit. "I can't bear the idea of you getting hurt, much less going a day without you. How can I be this ridiculously over the top?"

"It'll pass." He kissed her head. "We're new mates. The bond is gripping in the beginning. We'll feel gutted if we're not in the same room together for a while." He rubbed her back and tucked her in tight to his chest. "I swear it won't stay this intense though. Your body and mind have a lot of adjustments to make. And my instincts are all over the place. We just gotta stick together until it eases up."

But what if she didn't want it to ease up?

Having someone this devoted to her, attentive and supportive, and so hungry for her... Shit, Tessa wasn't sure she wanted it to dial back. The reciprocation of feelings made her feel like she had a purpose finally. She loved being Lucian's. Was excited to be his equal. "Will you teach me to hunt?"

Lucian's jaw clenched, and he didn't answer immediately. Probably because he couldn't stand the idea of Tessa throwing herself into a dangerous situation.

Well, tough.

"I'm not ever going to let someone do what Alex, Colton, and Simon did to me ever again. If you teach me to defend myself, I'll feel more empowered."

"Done."

No questions asked. Boy, she was really liking this.

"Come on. We're going to pack, then you're meeting the King, then we're heading to upstate New York for a few days."

Tessa followed his lead, still feeling like some clock out there in the universe was ticking down to a catastrophe.

Lucian didn't hide his pride as he escorted Tessa down the stairs and into the king's quarters. Malachi was sitting in his chair, gaze locked on the mirror like always. But once Lucian and Tessa entered the room, he stood and turned to face them.

That was a first. Malachi rarely stood for anyone, and he *never* broke his gaze from the mirror unless it was serious.

"Tessa," he purred in a deep, animalistic voice.

Lucian felt her tense up, and he rubbed the small of her back to let her know she was safe.

"Come here, girl." The king held his hands out, welcoming her into his embrace. Tessa didn't budge. If Malachi was insulted, he didn't show it. Instead, he came closer, slowly and gently, as if to not spook her any further. "Welcome to the House of Death."

She swallowed. Gawked. Started to sweat.

Lucian playfully nipped her shoulder. "It's okay."

She blew out a shaky exhale and took a step forward. Malachi dipped his head and reached for her hand to kiss it. "I see fate has a sense of mercy after all." His gaze flicked to Lucian. "Your soul was way ahead of you with her."

"Tell me about it."

As far as Lucian knew, no vampire met their mate prior to knowing they were an *alakhai*.

"Perhaps someone is looking out for you lately," the king mused with a smile.

Lucian's heart thudded at what that possibly meant. "Maybe." Far be it for him to discredit a miracle. Or assistance from the afterlife. It could have been Luke. If the dead actually lived in some kind of afterlife. And... only if Luke forgave Lucian for not saving him in time.

Too many ifs there.

Not gonna lie, the thought of Luke intervening to save Lucian from the same fate he suffered was incredible. It gave him peace in a way Lucian didn't realize he still needed over his brother's death.

"Tessa." Malachi turned his dark gaze back on her. "I owe you an apology." He dropped down on his knees. Lucian nearly fainted at the sight. The king never did this. "Lucian came to me about you, and I denied his every request. Had I not done so, you may have not suffered as you did."

"You were only following rules," Tessa responded with a tremble in her voice. "What King breaks rules that he expects his people to follow?"

Malachi swayed backwards as though she'd shot him in the heart with an arrow. "You would have made an incredible queen among my kind." He stayed on his knees. "And I was told you didn't utter a word of Lucian's secrets to our enemy. Even though you were facing certain death."

Lucian saw red. His fangs throbbed. A hiss flew out from between his gritting teeth. Just the mere mention of her torture set him off. It took a few breathing exercises and a struggle to calm the hell down.

"She's a rare gem," Malachi said, ignoring Lucian's outburst. "And a gorgeous addition to our family."

"D-d-does this mean I'm in?"

Lucian died a little at how cute she was about this.

"Do you want in?" the king challenged.

"I want Lucian. So, whatever it takes to have Lucian, I'm all in."

Malachi held his hand out for her to take. "It requires blood."

Lucian yanked her back against his chest and growled. Again, Malachi didn't reprimand him for it. "I fear your mate might tear my throat out. Tell him to stand down."

Tessa looked at Lucian and, yeah, he felt like an out-of-control wild beast. Damn straight he'd tear his king's throat out. No one's lips but Lucian's were touching Tessa's sweet skin. But he knew this was necessary. Hell, he had to hold back how many vampires when they were in this pickle? Hundreds. So, he knew the drill. He knew this was going to happen whether he could stand it or not.

"Do it," he snarled. "Fast. And don't hurt her."

The king slowly lured Tessa out of Lucian's arms. With his gaze locked on Lucian the entire time, Malachi brought Tessa's wrist up to his mouth and bit down. She didn't whimper. Didn't budge. The entire feeding lasted three seconds.

Felt like three goddamn years.

"Welcome to the House of Death, Tessa." Malachi gently guided her back into Lucian's waiting arms.

The instant their bodies made contact, Lucian found his breath again. "I'm taking her to my parent's estate for a few days." He wasn't asking. He was demanding.

Malachi waved them off. "You've earned it and I owe you. Accept the leave as part of my apology for driving you over the edge."

Guiding Tessa out of the room, Lucian didn't know what to say other than, "I'll be back on duty when I'm ready."

CHAPTER 43

Okay, the king was scary and sexy and scary. Wait, that was two scaries. Yeah, accurate. Tessa hadn't been able to make a peep once his hot, huge paws grabbed her and coaxed her into his... space? Atmosphere? The king's aura was big enough to have its own solar system.

Malachi was terrifying and strong. For him to apologize to Lucian showed he was also willing to admit when he was wrong. She could work under someone like that.

Tessa stared at where the king had bitten her wrist. "Can you switch Houses once you're locked in?"

She and Lucian were already heading to upstate New York.

"Yes, but it's rare."

"Seems lots of things are rare in your world."

"*Our* world," he corrected. Grabbing her hand, he kissed her knuckles, one-by-one, and tipped his head towards her. He looked like a cat with a canary. "How do you feel about all this so far?"

Excited. Terrified. Confused. "I can't wrap my head around it." She liked how open their communication was. It made dealing with things feel doable. "How about you?"

"Restless," he grumbled. They were in a private plane and due to land in New York in about an hour.

"What can I do to help you?"

Lucian's hand dropped, along with his jaw. He stared at her with complete adoration. "How did we mess this up so bad in the beginning?" He cringed as soon as the words were out of his mouth. "Wait. Bad choice of words again."

"No, that's pretty accurate," she laughed. "And I think we both saw what we had and didn't want to risk ruining it."

"Stupid contract."

"Necessary contract." She curled into her seat and leaned on him. Instead of sitting across from each other, they were side by side, holding hands and cuddling. "I wouldn't have trusted you otherwise without it."

"You like having an escape clause."

"Pretty much."

"But now you don't have one."

"Don't need one anymore." She sighed and closed her eyes.

"Tessa?"

"Hmm?"

Lucian was quiet for a moment, then, "Did they say anything to you about my brother?"

She wasn't sure how to respond. Tessa wished she had a better answer than, "I'm still piecing it all together. But... I think so. I remember there being something, but I can't grab it yet. I'm so sorry."

"Don't be." He kissed the top of her head. "It'll hit you when it's safe to resurface. I shouldn't have asked."

"But you can't shake the feeling that something's still hanging over your head, can you?"

He exhaled exasperatedly. "No."

"Same."

They landed in New York, where Lucian had a car waiting for them at the airport. Tessa fell asleep as he drove to his parents' estate. It was close to midnight by the time they pulled up to the big place.

"Whoa," she breathed against the glass window of their rental.

"I can't wait for you to meet Sadie." When Tessa's brow pinched with confusion, he added, "She's been in my family for centuries. First as a housekeeper. Then our nanny. Then... well, she's family. My mother couldn't get her to stop cleaning, cooking, and taking care of everyone though, so now Sadie does as she pleases and lives with my pare," he cleared his throat, "my mother."

"I'm glad they have each other to keep company." By the light in Lucian's eyes as he talked about her, Tessa could see Sadie meant the world to him.

He opened the front doors and ushered her inside. "Sadie!" he hollered. When she didn't answer, he went around, flicking all the lights on. After he locked the door, of course. "Sadie! You here?" Not a peep in response. "She probably went on vacation since my mom isn't around. Or maybe she went with mom and Lizzy to Paris. Or went to stay with Lizzy's kids. I don't know if they went with them or not." Lucian started carrying their bags upstairs.

"Are you sure we should be here?" It felt weird.

"It's still my family home. And... actually no, I'm not sure, but I don't care. This is a safe place for us to clear our heads for a few days. And I want you all to myself without humans or vampires around."

Tessa held the mahogany banister and followed him upstairs. Each step made a weight in her chest heavier. "Lucian, I don't feel right."

He dropped the bag at the top of the steps and was at her in one heartbeat.

Yeah, wow, was she going to get used to that level of speed? Could she run that fast now too?

"Come on." Lucian ignored the bags and scooped her in his arms, carrying her back downstairs.

"This place is insanely romantic." She nuzzled his neck, feeling better now that he was holding her. Oh, for the love of Dracula, she needed to get a grip and put her lust on a tighter leash.

"My parents were crazy for each other. My dad spoiled my mother with praise and kisses so much, we didn't know any other way couples could behave." He set her down in the ballroom and flicked his wrist. Music piped through the overhead speakers. "And they danced... *a lot.*"

Lucian jerked her against his chest playfully, and a song began to play.

Following his lead, she hadn't realized she needed this. To dance, safely, without a goal other than to enjoy it.

"Is this okay?" he checked while leading her across the floor.

"Very." Tessa held her breath as he dipped her back, kissing her nipple through her shirt. Good Lord, she was going to love being a vampire. "How many vampires are in New Orleans?"

"About as many as there are humans." He spun her around with quick footing.

Something clawed at the back of her mind. Simon's words... or... something...

Shaking her head, she refused to let Simon disrupt and ruin this moment. She stumbled between two of the steps, but if Lucian noticed, he didn't act like it. They danced like they breathed: Naturally.

"You're good at this," she finally said.

"I practice." He twirled her around and jerked her back into his chest again with a passionate glare. "Gotta keep on my toes with you."

She laughed and kept the rhythm going as the next song started up. It was one Simon had played for her to dance to. Tessa faltered, losing her balance and nearly landed on her ass if Lucian hadn't caught her. "I'm sorry," she said automatically.

With his brow furrowed, he tipped her chin up with his finger. "Hey, no apologies, okay? You can stumble. Hell, you can fall on your ass. It's okay."

But it was never okay before. Not with her mother. Not with her choreographers or directors. Not with herself.

"Allow yourself the gift of grace, prima."

She cringed at him. "Don't call me prima anymore." Her cheeks flushed as she added, "Please."

"Gone." Lucian acted like he'd taken the word from of his mouth and flung it out the window. "Do you prefer darling?"

She felt all warm and squishy inside. "I had a dream you called me that."

"Oh, yeah?" He started moving them back and forth again, slower now, and not at all in time to the music.

"Can we change this song?"

Lucian didn't ask why. He just flicked his hand to summon another song to play.

"Are you going to teach me all these parlor tricks?"

"Eventually," Lucian teased. "When you stop looking so impressed with me every time I do something mundane." He winked and spun her around. "Your wonder is incredible for my ego."

She laughed and spun into his arms. They weren't even dancing to the rhythm anymore. It fucked with her head. Her impulse was to move to the beat, but her instinct said to follow Lucian's pace. So, they danced terribly, like two middle school kids rocking back and forth, not at all in sync with the music playing around them.

"So..." He playfully nipped her earlobe. "What else did I do to you in this dream?"

This side of Lucian was a breath of fresh air. She wished she'd seen this part of him long ago. But he was right about what he'd said earlier. Their meetings were for her. Not him. His pleasure was derived from her getting off. Anything else he did was part of their contract.

"We danced."

"Like this?"

"No. We tangoed in my dream."

"Ohhh, spicy." He flicked his wrist again, and salsa music piped through the speakers. "Still impressed?"

"Extremely."

He pumped his fist in the air, cheering for his talent.

Tessa spun out of his arms and clapped her hands, taking the lead in a tango. He matched her, step for step, cranking up the intensity as they maneuvered around each other. Passion replaced their playful banter.

"I'd like to learn Shibari." She licked up the column of his throat, earning her a groan from him. "Teach me?"

"Hell yes." His hands dug into her hips. She could feel his hard cock against her belly as they continued dancing.

"And the wax," she added. "I'd like to share those candles with you."

Lucian tripped over his own feet. "You're killing me, darling."

She laughed and twirled way out of his reach. Then blew him a kiss.

"Oh, so it's like that, huh?" He shot off, chasing her with a predator's gaze.

Tessa wiggled her ass at him as she flung open the French doors that led to the back gardens. She took off through the night, laughing and squealing. Lucian was so fast, she couldn't get more than a few feet away before he'd be in front of her. He'd kiss her just before setting her free. Smack her ass and vanish. They lured each other deeper into the garden until he finally pinned her against a tree.

"Found you," he said with a predator's grin.

"Keep me," she hitched her thighs up to wrap around his waist.

"Forever." He ravaged her mouth as she worked on the buckle of his pants, eager to get her mouth on his dick again.

A scent hit them at the same time. Lucian pulled away first, going on high alert.

"What is that?" Tessa unhooked her legs and landed on her feet. Is smelled like—

"Kerosene." Lucian frowned. He tracked the scent, keeping Tessa close behind him to shield her.

"Maybe it's the neighbors?" she offered.

"No, there're no neighbors for miles. My family owns the entire ten-mile strip this side of the Hudson." He froze.

She heard the same noise he had. "Is that... someone crying?"

Lucian bolted.

CHAPTER 44

Fuck, fuck, fuck! Lucian tore through the gardens. By the time he reached the source of the scent, he exploded in fury.

The scene was so twisted, his mind refused to take it all in. *Tessa. Where was T—*

She gasped behind him, able to keep up with his speed because she was now inhuman. Lucian's immediate reaction was to shield her from the view. His second move was to... Oh shit! He didn't have enough weapons for this! He was only wearing his usual two blades.

Well, his usual would have to do.

Ahead of him, in the center of his mother's private garden, Sadie was tied up against a fountain. Chained to the statue of Adonis, her eyes swollen and red-rimmed from crying. On the other side was Lucian's father, Basil. Further back, tied against a tree, was Basil's mate, Anna.

Annnnd that wasn't even the worst part.

The kerosene fumes were coming out of the fountain.

"So, you *are* faster than your brother." A big man in fatigues stepped out from behind an oak, lazily making his way closer with a set of matches. "I can't say I'm disappointed in you, Lucian. You're in the House of Death for a reason. Agility and speed are requirements there, aren't they?"

Lucian squared his shoulders and positioned to attack. "You must be Simon." The pungent scent of fear rolling off Tessa was confirmation enough.

Simon toyed with a match in his mouth, like it was a toothpick. He rattled the box in his hands, teasingly. "Right about now, I figure you're trying to choose who matters most. Your father, maybe?" He arched his brow and swung his gaze back to Lucian with a frown. "But you two didn't really get along that well, am I right? A little animosity there?"

Basil's gaze slammed hard on Lucian's. He must be drugged or something to not rip out of his restraints. His father was a strong vampire. Not as fierce as Lucian by a long shot, but he could fuck shit up if he chose to.

"Your housekeeper's a feisty old broad." Simon tossed her a smug look. Sadie jerked against her binds and yelled something over the gag stuffed into her mouth.

Lucian's breath hitched. He couldn't get riled up. He needed to remain calm and clear headed. Simon was too unpredictable, and Lucian couldn't trust that he was alone. Other *Savag-Ri* might be watching, waiting for Simon's signal to ambush him and Tessa.

"There's also your sister and her three children." Simon spat on the ground. "Yeah, you probably have a soft spot for the little ones, huh? They bring nostalgia back to when times were good. Don't worry, I have something special in store for them once I leave here."

Lucian had no idea how long he should let this piece of shit talk. But if Simon kept flapping his gums and meandering around, Lucian could lure him away from everyone else and take him down without any collateral damage.

"I'd hoped your mother was home. Her sudden absence did put a bit of a damper on my careful plans." Simon peered behind Lucian and blew Tessa a kiss. "She'll make a nice replacement though."

Lucian hissed.

Simon pulled the match out of his mouth. "The order of deaths is completely up to you, Lucian. Go ahead and run with those vicious, hot-blooded instincts of yours and choose. Your family or your mate."

Tessa came a little closer. Lucian put his hand by his thigh, signaling her to not move another muscle.

"Luke was a disappointment. Takes after your father in that way." Simon shot Basil dagger eyes. "He couldn't piece the clues together at all. We kept his mate for two months, beating her... defiling her... bleeding her out. We dumped pools of her blood on his car just to see if he'd lick it off. His desperation was very inspiring."

Ignoring Lucian's warnings, Tessa inched her way even closer and calmly grabbed one of the blades from his hand. He let her have it. He'd rather she be armed than not. And he could do plenty of damage to a *Savag-Ri* with just one knife and his teeth.

Still, Lucian was intrigued by Simon. This was out of character for a *Savag-Ri*. Too precise and targeted. "Why are you going through this much trouble with my family?"

"Simon, please!" Anna screamed from her tree, desperately trying to break free from her restraints. "Don't do this! Please!"

Keeping his gaze locked on Lucian, Simon backed up and pulled a gun out, aiming it at Lucian while addressing Anna. "You left me for a sniveling, disgusting *bloodsucker*."

You left me for a —

Lucian pieced it together. "You and Anna were together before my father took her?"

"I want your mother to live with the loss I feel every day," Simon gritted out. His emotions started running higher, making him shake with fury. "I loved her!" he screamed. "I fucking loved her, and she left me for *that*!" He jabbed his gun at Basil.

Tessa moved a little more to Lucian's left.

Stay still! Stay still!

Simon hopped up on the fountain's edge and snarled at Basil. "So, I'm taking away everything of yours, you vile piece of trash. And when your wife and daughter come home, I'm going to fuck them, and then I'm going to tear them apart, just as you've fucked and torn me apart."

Sadie started fighting her bonds again. Simon balanced himself on the edge of the fountain and kicked her in the head. She slumped immediately. But it was enough. He'd turned his back for two seconds, and it was all Lucian needed.

He ran forward, jumped on Simon's back, and tried to slit his throat. He only managed to stab him before they crashed into the kerosene filled fountain, splashing it everywhere. They thrashed and punched, kicked and bit. Lucian ended up losing his blade after plunging it into Simon's torso, and the cocksucker reared back and held his gun to Lucian's face.

Fuck that.

Lucian hit the barrel just as Simon pulled the trigger. They fell ass over elbow out of the fountain and started beating each other across the grass. The gun sank into the kerosene tainted water. Lucian cracked Simon's face over and over with his fists. Slammed his head into the ground. Tore at his throat.

Simon stopped fighting so hard, but he kept laughing.

The psycho.

Lucian was a blur of fists and teeth. "Tessa!" he roared, "Blade!"

She threw the knife. He caught it in mid-air.

"If I die, you all die," Simon cackled. "And I win no matter what you do."

Lucian reared back with his blade, ready to strike, when he heard shouts behind him. A high-pitched scream pierced his ears and made his blood curl.

"Colton!" Tessa screamed. "Lucian!"

He dropped Simon to attack the one going after Tessa. She was unarmed, unprotected, and untrained for this!

Lucian reached him in a millisecond. Slamming his blade between the fucker's eyes, he ripped the *Savag-Ri's* throat clean out with his teeth. For good measure, he tore out the heart and tossed it into the darkness of the garden beyond.

"Lucian, behind you!"

Too late. A gun fired. Lucian froze, his blade raised in the air.

The air whooshed out of him. His heartbeat thudded in his ears. Tessa's eyes widened in horror. He looked down, expecting to see a gaping hole in his chest.

Oh God, oh God, oh…

Nothing. He felt and saw *nothing*.

"Bitch!" Simon snarled from behind him. A gun fired again. Lucian looked up on the terrace and saw his mother with a shotgun. The image looked so out of place, he thought he was hallucinating. But he wasn't and his mother gave him just the edge he needed. Simon crawled forward, away from all of them, blood staining the grass as he dragged himself over to a bush.

Lucian stumble-ran after him and grabbed the back of his neck. Shoving a boot in his back, Lucian gave a twist, pull, and *yank*!

He plucked Simon's head clean off his shoulders. Simon's body dropped, twitching and contaminating the lawn.

"Help me free them!" Tessa yelled from the fountain.

Jumping in with her, Lucian pulled on their chains, unable to break them. The kerosene made their eyes water something fierce. They couldn't breathe.

"Key!" Tessa coughed. "We need a key! Or wire cutters!"

Lucian dashed to the garden shed and returned with a brand-new pair of cutters. He slid them around a set of links and froze. "Whoa! Whoa! Whoa! Don't move!" He removed the cutters and stared at the chains again. His adrenaline made him hyperaware. "The chains are wired to something."

"Shit." Tessa covered her mouth and stared at the grass. Hopping out of the fountain, she crawled around the lawn feeling for a tripwire or something like they'd used on her. "I can't find anything," she said.

He pulled his father's gag off first, keeping his eye on Sadie, who was still knocked out. "Top of the Adonis," Basil said. "I think it's there."

Lucian reached up blindly annnnnd, yup, there was the mechanism rigged to blow the whole place to Timbuktu. With shaky hands, he brought it down gingerly and looked at the contraption. It was exactly like the one on Tessa days ago. Lucian cut the red wire. Exhaled. Looked around suspiciously.

"Stop moving, Tessa." His chest tightened with fear. "There might be a second trap set."

Fool me once and all that jazz…

Esmerelda ran towards them with the rifle still in her hand. "Basil!" she cried out.

"Don't move, Ez!"

She halted where she was, half-way between her house and her family. Lizzy was nowhere in sight.

Lucian decided to pick the locks. Even though cutting them would have been much faster, he didn't trust something not going *KAPOW* if he cut them. Racing back inside the garden shed, he snagged the tools he needed and made quick work of freeing his father and Sadie. Then he cautiously made his way over to Anna.

Once free, Anna started sobbing and hyperventilating. Basil held her tight and tried to calm her down. Tessa went after

Esmerelda, who only stood there and gawked, completely immobilized with shock.

Sadie...

Lucian lifted the housekeeper's head to cradle in his lap. He pulled the gag out of her mouth and yelled, "She needs medical attention! He fractured her skull!" Blood stained his kerosene-soaked pants. "Come on Sadie, don't you leave us now." He started talking to her, as if coaxing her soul to stay in her body.

Tessa and Esmerelda dropped down beside him. Lucian looked at each of them, but he couldn't stop rocking Sadie. She was made of tough stuff though, right? She always seemed like a force of nature to Lucian. But lying unconscious in his lap, with her face a swollen mess, she looked ancient, fragile, and too good for this kind of bad.

"Call for help!" he roared, tears streaming down his face.

Did no one have a cell phone?

No. How would they? Even Lucian's was inside, and Simon would have taken and destroyed everyone else's before doing God knows what to each of them.

Sadie's mouth went slack. Esmeralda leaned down to talk to her, picking up where Lucian left off. "Come on, Sadie. We have plans, remember? Don't crap out on me now, girl." Then she paused and sucked in a breath. "Wait. There's something in her mouth." Esmerelda swept her long, slender finger in Sadie's mouth to dislodge whatever it was and something went, *beep, beep, beeeeep!*

KABOOM!

The house exploded.

Lucian jumped to put himself on top of three women at once. Marble and centuries old furniture rained down in splinters around them. Basil covered Anna. Everyone held their breath as their life exploded around them. Bits of debris and fire fell around them, making Lucian painfully aware of how flammable they all were. "Run!"

Lucian grabbed Sadie, and they took off, putting as much distance as possible between their kerosene drenched bodies and that fucking fire. Esmerelda simply looked back at the home she loved so much and said, "I was thinking of moving anyway."

She was not okay. Nope. Uh-uh.

But Lucian couldn't fixate on that right now. He had a world of shit to clean up and his priority was Tessa. He snatched her close and squeezed her tight. "Holy shit," his voice cracked. "I can't believe this happened again."

"Well, next time, I'll be more prepared. I'm making mental notes as we go."

He appreciated her light-hearted attempt at making this situation not as horrifying as it really was. But it didn't work.

"There's not going to be a next time," he growled. Not if he could help it.

Anna wailed and screeched in Basil's arms. She started spiraling out of control. Basil slapped her across the face to stun her out of it. She melted into a puddle on the lawn, saying how sorry she was. Babbling about Simon being her ex-husband and how she'd left him for Basil and swearing she had no clue he was a *Savag-Ri* or that he'd be capable of doing anything like this. Admitted he was abusive, but only to her. That Basil saved her from a life of cruelty, and she'd never thought any of this was possible.

Then she ran to Simon's lump of a body and started beating and kicking his corpse.

Lucian was sure that had to be therapeutic on some level.

Esmerelda watched Anna fall to pieces. Silently, she picked herself up and walked over to the blubbering woman. With a calm hand, she stopped Anna from hitting the *Savag-Ri* anymore. "Shhhh," she cooed. "It's not your fault."

"I swear I'd never let something happen to any of you. You're my family. I love you!" Anna broke down all over again and clung to Esmerelda. "Basil," Esmerelda called out calmly, "let's get your mate something to drink and have her sit down for a spell. You all need showers and I have spare clothing for each of you."

She was eerily calm about all this. It made the hair on Lucian's neck stand on end. "Mom," Lucian said while cautiously picking Sadie up and cradling her to his chest. "The house is burning down."

"Mmm hmm. Let's gather in the guest house." Esmerelda oh so gracefully escorted Anna to the two-thousand square foot guest house on the far side of the property. Tessa stayed close to Lucian as he carried Sadie.

A bottle of brandy, two pots of tea, several sleeves of store-bought cookies, and several hot showers, plus a wardrobe change later… things were starting to look up.

Sadie healed. Basil fed her his blood, and just like Lucian always believed, that strong ass woman bounced right back. Thank. God.

As it turned out, Lizzy came home early from Paris. She'd missed her kids too much to stay away from them for long. Esmerelda flew home a day later. Basil called and verified Lizzy and the kids were safe and unharmed. The House of Blood was doubling down on security immediately.

It rained during their short vacation. The bone dust had washed away in the process, giving Simon the opportunity to invade their property. The timing had been perfect for mayhem.

What Simon—and Lucian for that matter—hadn't realized was that Esmerelda had moved into the guest house months ago. That's why the big house looked so empty. All the family photos and precious treasures were moved into the smaller home. Everything that had blown up was expendable.

And Simon's unhealthy obsession hadn't been with Lucian… it had been with Anna. Simon tried to strip away those important to her new family. No one blamed her for it. She, as a human, had no idea she'd married a *Savag-Ri*. Basil had helped her escape an abusive home without ever seeing the man who'd laid a hand on his mate.

That was the difference between Lucian and Basil.

Regardless of the past, Lucian wouldn't have rested until all debts were settled. He got that from his mother.

Tessa sipped her tea from a porcelain cup that matched Esmerelda's. She looked relieved, which brought Lucian a flicker of peace in his warrior heart.

"It's lovely to meet you, Tessa." Esmerelda dropped a lump of sugar into her mouth and sucked on it. "Lucian's told us so much about you."

"Uhhh," No, he hadn't.

Esmerelda tipped her chin in his direction and narrowed her gaze. "Golden as the sun, lithe as a willow, graceful as a scorpion?"

He dropped his glass of bourbon on the floor with a clunk.

A memory of him stealing an old book of mating magic from Sadie's hidden stash of romance novels and witchcraft came to him. He wanted a love as fierce and passionate, beguiling and enchanting and as consuming as what his parents had for each other. So scared of the prospect of one day having an *alakhai*, he'd tried to conjure her up instead.

His mother told him it wasn't possible and was furious at him for trying.

"It's not magic," Esmerelda said, just as she had the day she caught him with the stack of bodice ripping novels and witchcraft.

"It's fate," Lucian said at the same time his mother did.

Holy Hell. He looked over at Tessa and felt pride and love swell in his chest. It hurt to breathe. He got up and held his hand out to her. "Dance with me?"

Tessa sat her drink down and slid her slender hand in his. He led her out into the backyard. Music started playing, thanks to Esmerelda's obsession with having it everywhere and always at her disposal.

Enthralled with each other, Lucian and Tessa waltzed through the yard, around the debris, through the smoke, and into the gardens beyond.

She arched a brow at him. "Scorpion, huh?"

"Oh yeah, no swans for me." He held her close as they moved with perfect footing. "I like my girl a little venomous."

Tessa's head tipped back and laughed. "Much better word choice."

Unleashing a ravenous growl, Lucian crushed her with a searing kiss and swept her off her feet.

EPILOGUE

"You're *sure* that pulley system is secure?"

"Yes, asshat. What? You think I'd let our favorite dancer fall to her death?"

Lucian's eyes narrowed on Victoria. "Don't even say it as a joke." It would be tempting fate. Tonight was Tessa's debut in the vampire world and he wanted it *perfect*. "Ready," he gripped his violin. "Set," he steadied his bow. "Go," he whispered, winking at his mate.

Tessa descended on a red satin sash that unfolded in a graceful flutter from the third story ceiling. She hadn't put on a pair of ballet shoes since her first night in the mansion. And she wasn't wearing them tonight. His mate was above her need for pointe shoes and punishments. She'd found her peace with her past and bloomed into an unimaginable combination of seduction, savagery, and sinful temptation.

Lucian dragged his bowstrings across his violin and for a hot second, looked down at his mother watching from the foyer. She was doing well here. No, that was an understatement. She was *thriving*. Esmerelda hadn't been joking about selling the house. She not only rebuilt and sold the damned thing, she'd transferred Houses and was now under the rule of Malachi.

She and Sadie were living in the Garden District, in a home she enjoyed decorating and hosting small parties in. Tessa was loving it, too. They got along better than Lucian could have ever hoped for. The rest of the family was coming to visit next month.

So much to look forward to, right?

His gaze sailed back to his mate as she practically dripped down the length of red satin strung from a pulley system Lucian and Xin had rigged.

"Dayem," Reys said from the balcony. "She moves like water."

That she did. And boy was he thirsty. Lucian's eyes devoured her every arch, bow, stretch, and sway. She twirled and wrapped herself over and over again, flipping and swinging, practically melting with the red satin until her pretty little toes touched the marble floor in the foyer.

Dressed in all black with a gold overlay, the dress Lucian chose for her set Tessa's hair off like sunrays. She was blindingly stunning. Moving effortlessly through the crowd, keeping her rhythm and dancing to the notes Lucian composed just for her, Tessa was fucking mesmerizing.

She had the entire House of Death enthralled by the end of the first song. Lucian transitioned into two more, pushing her limits a little by throwing the tempo off. She never wavered. Didn't trip. No slip, stumble or falling off-beat for her. She danced by her own rules now. No more boundaries whatsoever.

Maybe she had a bit of a lighter foot tonight because Lucian was able to confirm that she had, indeed, *not* committed murder. Paxton Brown was healthy, sober, and living off grid somewhere in Alaska. The day she remembered going to his house? She'd beat the shit out of him, and he'd let her do it without raising a single hand at her, or to shield himself from her attack. That night, she walked him to an AA meeting, left him at the front door of a community center, and went home.

Those pictures used to blackmail her were fake. How much digging it took to make that façade took epic levels of obsession on Simon's part. May he rot in Hell.

As the song came to the final note, Tessa bent herself into a vampire pretzel.

The House erupted with cheers and whistles, hoots and hollers. Lucian placed his violin down, hopped over the two-story balcony, and landed like a cat at her side.

Tessa immediately jumped into his arms. "That's way more badass than using a bunch of tied up bedsheets to make a descent."

He boomed with laughter and twirled her around, kissing her all the way into the dining room. "We're not staying," he growled in her ear. "You have me too hard to think about desserts and drinks and who knows what Victoria's got up her sleeve for tonight."

Tessa laughed and ran her hands through his hair. "Okay, make a plate of all the things I love, and you can feed me upstairs."

Lucian tossed her a devilish look. "My dick's too big for a plate. I'll have to snatch a platter from the kitchen."

"I'll totally let you feed it to me." She pulled on her bottom lip with her teeth.

"Mmph. Your mouth is so damn pretty."

"Lots of me is pretty."

"All of you is pretty."

Tessa kicked and wiggled until and he put her down. Walking backwards, keeping her eyes on him while she sashayed her hips, Tessa lured him right out of the dining room. "If you catch me… you can keep me."

She shot off with lightning speed, leaving the party behind.

Lucian tore after her with a smile so big, his cheeks hurt.

He kicked his bedroom door closed and sauntered over to where she was laying spread eagle on their bed. "Your turn tonight," she said, waggling a bundle of rope at him.

He rocked the massive bed when he pounced on her. Tessa bounced and laughed even harder after she said, "I absolutely love being a vampire."

Lucian beamed down at her, elated. "And I absolutely, unconditionally, irrevocably love you."

For information on this book and other future releases, please visit my website: **www.BrianaMichaels.com**

If you liked this book, please help spread the word by leaving a review on the site you purchased your copy, or on a reader site such as Goodreads.

I'd love to hear from readers too, so feel free to send me an email at: sinsofthesidhe@gmail.com or visit me on Facebook: www.facebook.com/BrianaMichaelsAuthor

Thank you!

ABOUT THE AUTHOR

Briana Michaels grew up and still lives on the East Coast. When taking a break from the crazy adventures in her head, she enjoys running around with her two children. If there is time to spare, she loves to read, cook, hike in the woods, and sit outside by a roaring fire. She does all of this with the love and support of her amazing husband who always has her back, encouraging her to go for her dreams.

Made in United States
North Haven, CT
30 September 2024